THE TEXICANS

ALSO BY THE AUTHOR

The End of Marriage
Between Sisters
Goodbye, Saigon
Maximillian's Garden
Return from Darkness
Scam

THE TEXICANS

NINA VIDA

a novel

For my son Mark

Published by

Soho Press, Inc.
853 Broadway
New York, NY 10003
Library of Congress Cataloging-in-Publication Data

Vida, Nina.
The Texicans : a novel / Nina Vida.
p. cm.
ISBN 978-1-56947-477-8
1. Ranch life—Texas—Fiction.
2. Mexicans—Texas—Fiction. 3. Germans—Texas—Fiction.
4. Fugitive slaves—Fiction. 5. Texas—Fiction.
PS3572.I29T49 2006
813'.54—dc22 2006042387

10 9 8 7 6 5 4 3 2 1

Designed by Natalia Yamrom, Neuwirth & Associates, Inc.

And not by eastern windows only,
When daylight comes, comes in the light,
In front the sun climbs slow, how slowly,
But westward, look! the land is bright.

Arthur Hugh Clough,
"Say Not The Struggle Nought Availeth," 1869

THE

TEXICANS

READER´S GUIDE

1. The epigraph by Arthur Hugh Clough reads:

> "And not by eastern windows only,
> When daylight comes, comes in the light,
> In front the sun climbs slow, how slowly,
> But westward, look! The land is bright."

What does this epigraph mean in relation to *The Texicans*? And are there ways in which the words can be construed to have negative connotations as well as positive ones?

2. At the beginning of the novel, as Aurelia and her family are fleeing the cholera epidemic, they encounter an old woman sitting at the side of the road. Does Aurelia really cure the old woman or does the incident have another meaning? Might it have several meanings?

3. In the book Aurelia is called a witch, a *bruja*. Is she really? What would we call someone like her today?

4. What reasons might the German settlers have had for being opposed to the practice of slave-holding?

5. What are we to make of Joseph´s motives in marrying Katrin? Why does he fight so mightily against his generous impulses?

6. The author depicts the Comanches as both aggressors and victims. She describes the settlers in the same way. Was there any way in which they could have lived in harmony? Or are there just some cultures that cannot compromise, whose participants would rather die in battle than negotiate a peaceful settlement?

7. Is there some point in the novel at which we see Katrin change? Does she alter for the better? What effect does her change have on the trajectory of the novel?

8. If Joseph had left Katrin for Aurelia, how would it have changed the tone of the novel? Would you have thought less of Joseph and Aurelia? Would you have felt pity for Katrin?

9. What would have happened to Katrin if she had remained in Alsace-Lorraine? What would Joseph have become if he had stayed in Missouri? What would Aurelia's life have been like if there had been no cholera epidemic? Do cataclysmic events alter character? Do difficult circumstances change personalities?

10. There are incidents of racial and religious prejudice throughout the novel. What part do these incidents play in the lives and fates of the various characters? And in Katrin´s case, do you think she merely becomes tolerant of Joseph´s Jewishness and makes an exception for him because he´s her husband or does she actually rid herself of that prejudice? Is it possible to rid oneself of prejudice?

ACKNOWLEDGMENTS

Until I met Frances Kallison, I didn't know whether the world needed another book about Texas, but she took me by the hand and told me about her grandparents, who settled in Texas in the 1870's, about her mother, who was one of the first women in Fort Worth to drive a car, and about the western goods store and sprawling cattle ranch her husband's family owned. As co-founder of the Texas Jewish Historical Society, Frances was intrepid booster and devoted historian of her beloved San Antonio, as at home on a horse as she was at a white-glove tea. She died in 2004 at the age of 96.

Of special help in my research on Castroville was Cornelia English Crook, author of "Henry Castro, A Study of Early Colonization in Texas." After her husband's death she bought one of Henry Castro's original buildings in Castroville, restored it and turned it into a museum. During the long afternoon I spent with her in her home in Castroville, Civil War memorabila of her husband's family displayed around her, she answered my questions about the early days of the Texas Hill Country with endless grace and patience.

Meeting these two remarkable women made me see Texas in a new light.

Nina Vida
Huntington Beach, California
2006

I

AURELIA

San Antonio, Texas
1843

OSCAR RUÍZ, BORN in Mexico, came to Texas when he was fourteen. He had once raised cattle and sheep on a ranch in a fertile valley along the Rio Grande, before Texicans began eating up the land and pushing the Mexicans out. Now he, his wife Luz, their six children, two goats and a donkey lived in Laredito, a squalid, dusty Mexican village on the outskirts of San Antonio. Oscar sold wild birds in the main plaza in San Antonio. Golden canaries and red-breasted cardinals that he caught along the river. When birds were scarce, he sold bits of Mexican lace, dolls with heads fashioned of dried apples, carved saints with wax tears on their cheeks. He moved from spot to spot between the produce wagons and stands of fly-specked beef and pens of wild turkeys, a sack of merchandise slung over his back, twittering birds in homemade wicker cages hanging from his arms.

Oscar's wife was from El Paso, an orphan of mixed Mexican and Anglo blood, abandoned by her father's family when her mother died. Her real name was Cynthia, but Oscar called her Luz—"light" in Spanish—because of her light skin. Luz sold medicine she made from roots and herbs and leaves. She would sit near the low whitewashed wall that surrounded the San Fernando church in the main plaza, not far from the shade of the chinaberry trees, her little pots of colored unguents and bitter syrups arranged on a strip of calico beside her. Every Mexican family in the *barrio* had a few jars of Luz's potions, foul-smelling concoctions she boiled up and stored in *ollas* in her yard. Powdered lobelia seed in apple vinegar made a fine salve for rashes. For constipation she'd mix up a brew of mandrake, buckthorn bark and rhubarb root. Lungwort was good for coughs. And the tonics she made of magnolia bark could reduce fever.

Aurelia at fifteen was the oldest of Oscar and Luz's children. Oscar didn't tell Aurelia that she was his favorite, but he let her bathe his feet and bring him his tobacco, and when he lay in his hammock in the yard he didn't mind if she sang to him or told him stories she made up out of her own head.

She's not like my other children, Oscar told Father Rubio. *Her ears hear better and her eyes see farther.*

Luz always said that all her children were the same to her, and she treated them that way. When she spoke to her children, she used a firm voice and called each one of them by both their common name and their saint's name. In the mornings the children stood in a line near the porch of the house and Luz gave each of them a spoonful of laxative made of powdered cassia. Then she checked their hair for lice. In the evening after supper she inspected each child's stools for worms. *Aurelia Agnes,* she would say, *take your brothers and sisters to the river and dig for goldenseal. Aurelia Agnes,* she would say, *help me carry the pots to the marketplace. Aurelia Agnes,* she would say, *grind the corn for the tortillas.* There was no sign that she liked Aurelia better than her other children.

CHOLERA DESCENDED ON the Rio Grande Valley toward the end of summer, when the air was still sticky with heat and the green sweep of hills had not yet turned gold. It hovered in the Texas air like a hungry bird, swooping down and squeezing life away wherever it could. In San

Antonio, and even as far away as El Paso, someone milking a cow or tending a baby or loading a wagon would suddenly sicken. The illness killed so swiftly that people rose healthy at dawn and died before supper.

The newspapers in San Antonio printed recipes for keeping cholera away: *Fumigate your house with gunpowder smoke. Hang a copper amulet around your neck. Take a daily dose of laudanum. Filter drinking water through burnt bread. Purify your blood with one tablespoon of pepper stirred in a glass of equal parts opium and brandy.* The sick died, poisoned and drunk, but they still died.

"I'm not going to sit still and do nothing but wait for the cholera to take me," Oscar told his wife. "We'll go to Chihuahua."

"But no one has died of cholera in Laredito," Luz said. "It's a disease of those *gringo* Texicans, not Mexicans."

"How can death know the difference?" Aurelia asked. She had never been away from Laredito, except on market day when she accompanied Luz and Oscar to the plaza in San Antonio.

"Death can tell," Oscar answered.

The next morning he loaded the wagon with pots and pans and bedding and foodstuffs.

"I hope the sun in Chihuahua is good for growing herbs," Luz said, and filled a sack with green slips from her garden and placed them next to the bolt of blue cloth she had decided to bring as a gift for her sister-in-law in Chihuahua.

Luz and the younger children sat on sacks of corn Oscar had piled in the middle of the wagon, while Aurelia stood against the wooden rails and looked back at the village. Wildflowers had buried the falling-down fences in drifts of speckled lavender, and clumps of spiny cactus grew out of sod roofs that had been dry over the winter but were now thick with the bitter green blades of spring grass.

The first night they camped in a field. While Luz warmed beans and rice in an iron pot over the fire, Aurelia walked down to the river to get fresh water. It was not yet dark, but she could see other wagons pulling onto the field from the road.

She dipped the jug into the cold black water and thought of how little it pained her to leave Laredito. She had never felt that she belonged there. She had always felt as if she had come from somewhere else, that she was merely passing through, waiting for the moment that would reveal the truth of who she was and where she belonged. *Strange thoughts,* Luz called them. *If you think too many strange thoughts, how will you help take care of your brothers and sisters?*

By the time she got back to the wagon, the field was dotted with black plumes of smoke from hundreds of campfires and the air had turned salty with ash.

"The *gringo* Texicans are running away from the cholera, too," Aurelia told her mother.

"They don't believe the remedies in the newspapers," Luz said.

"The road will be clear tomorrow," Oscar remarked. "*Gringos* won't travel as far as Mexico even to save their lives."

They set out again the next morning, and as Oscar had predicted, the road was clear, the Texicans still camped in the field behind them.

"The *gringos* would rather die of cholera than live in Mexico with Mexicans," Oscar said.

The wagon creaked along the road toward Chihuahua, its wooden wheels flinging choking sprays of sand that ground into a fine dust between Oscar's teeth. He had bought two plow horses to pull the long narrow wagon, and they nipped at each other's necks and tried to pull the wagon in two different directions. By the end of the day, with the children now crying at every bump in the road and Luz's pale cheeks flushed in the heat, Aurelia saw an old Mexican woman sprawled out on the side of the road, her legs turned in a strange way beneath her.

"Stop the wagon, *Papá*," Aurelia said.

Oscar wanted to go on, but Aurelia insisted, and so he stopped the wagon and Aurelia climbed down and knelt in the dirt beside the old woman.

"My legs won't work," she said.

"Do they hurt?" Aurelia asked her.

"Yes. Very much."

Aurelia put her hands on the woman's right leg and immediately felt a burst of heat that spread from her fingers up into her arms and didn't stop until it reached the top of her head. She held her hand on the leg until the heat grew too great to bear, and then she pulled her hand away and put it on the woman's left leg, and the same thing happened, except that now Aurelia looked into the woman's eyes and thought she heard the woman's heart beating.

"Aurelia," Oscar called, but Aurelia didn't answer.

"Where are you going?" the woman asked her. She was sitting up now, sipping water from a canteen she took from the package on the ground beside her.

"To Chihuahua to escape the cholera. Can you walk now?"

"It's possible."

"You can come to Chihuahua with us. It doesn't matter if you can walk or not, we have room in the wagon."

"Bless you and thank you, but I have errands to do." Then she rose up, gathered her *rebozo* around her and walked away with surefooted glides and delicate steps that barely left an imprint on the ground. Aurelia looked back at the wagon, at the faces of her brothers and sisters, and strange thoughts began to form in her head. Oscar sometimes said his headaches went away when she spoke to him, and didn't Luz once tell her that her American grandmother could predict the future?

Oscar shouted for her to get back in the wagon, that they had a long way to go, but Aurelia didn't move. Her brothers and sisters had grown thin and sickly in Laredito. They went to bed hungry some nights. There would be no better life in Chihuahua. Life is where you are, she thought, and the thought made her dizzy.

She stood up and walked toward the wagon. "We have to go back to Laredito," she said to Oscar.

"Back?"

"Are you sick?" Luz said.

"No."

"Did you know that woman?" Oscar asked her.

"No. But we have to turn back."

"We can't turn back," Luz said.

"What was wrong with her?" Oscar asked.

"Her legs wouldn't work."

"But she walked away."

"Yes."

"She was just resting," Luz said.

"No. I felt the bones of her legs under my fingers. They were soft and twisted. No one could walk on legs like those. And when I touched her something happened."

"You're not a saint," Luz said. Her lips, usually loose against her teeth, were now puckered, as if she had tasted something sour. "You're blaspheming against God."

"Wait, wait," Oscar said, looking perplexed.

"Maybe people will pay me money to cure them of cholera and then the children won't go to bed hungry," Aurelia said.

And then Oscar smiled. His smile was as broad as his face, his eyes bright and his chin quivering with delight.

"Aurelia is going to make us rich," he told his wife, and he turned the wagon around and headed back to Laredito.

OSCAR STOOD OUT in the main plaza in San Antonio every day and shouted out to every *gringo* who passed that his daughter, Aurelia Agnes Luisa Ruíz de Sanchez y Lopez, could cure cholera. *She has eyes,* he told anyone who stopped to listen, *that can burn your skin down to where the cholera is hiding and tear it out.*

Soon there was a stream of sick *gringos* clogging the road to Laredito to see if what Oscar said was really true. They camped in front of the small adobe house until it was their turn to pay Oscar two silver coins and come into the parlor where Aurelia sat waiting to cure them. They lay half dead in open wagons or stretched out in the dirt of the road while they waited, too weak to fight for a place in the yard close to the steps that led inside. Some of them died near the gate while they waited, some on their horses, lying crossways across their saddles, legs dangling, the sun burning red crescents into the pale skin of their necks. Some made it as far as the rawhide door of the house, even managed to pay their money before they collapsed and died.

"It's your eyes that heal," Oscar told Aurelia, "so make sure you look deep into theirs." He had her wear black so that she would look older than her fifteen years. And he put a Bible in her hands, and told her not to smile so much, but to keep her little white teeth out of sight and to stare purposefully into the sick person's eyes with her own bright ones.

At first nothing happened. Not one person who stumbled sick and feverish into the Ruíz parlor and let Aurelia stare into their eyes danced, clear-eyed and healthy, out of there. No matter how hard she tried, no matter how much she wanted to cool their hot foreheads, stop their running bowels, remove the glaze from their eyes and the foam from their lips, she couldn't. She tried staring at them with her left eye, with her right, then with both.

"She can't cure anyone," Luz said.

"Maybe you're right," Oscar replied.

"I can," Aurelia said. "I know I can. I just have to try harder."

She didn't know that she could, but coins were accumulating in the *olla* near the door, and Aurelia felt something when she touched a sick person's hand. It was as if their need to be cured were traveling up her fingers right to her heart.

And then one day, for no reason she could determine, a young girl told her she felt better after Aurelia had stared at her for a while.

After that people began to say peculiar things when she looked in their eyes. *I'm cured,* they'd say. *Bless Jesus, the cholera has left me,* they'd say. Those who were agitated and feverish when they came into the parlor grew calm when she held their hands in hers, and those who couldn't stop their moaning would grow as quiet as the desert when she gazed into their eyes.

Oscar would bring the sick into the parlor as though he were ushering them into a church.

"She looks so deep inside of people, she touches their soul," Oscar told his wife.

"Aurelia wants to cure them," Luz said, "and she tries so hard that they believe she can. But she's not a saint, Oscar."

"I see her cure people with my own eyes," Oscar replied. "Who but a saint could do that?"

He ignored the fact that most of the sick that Aurelia cured began to stumble and twitch and groan again when they were down the steps and out on the road. Or that even those who looked like they truly were cured, who got up out of the horsehair chair and walked out into the yard and yelled to the others that it was the truth, the greaser really could do it, usually broke down within a mile of Laredito. Just keeled over and died.

Oscar filled four leather saddlebags with coins that summer. He bought a new black hat and thick leather boots for himself, a new dress for his wife and a silk shawl for Aurelia. The rest he gambled away on the faro tables. He had always gambled, keeping his family on the edge of starvation by stealing money from the metal box Luz kept it in. But now he bet stacks of silver, huge piles of silver, and he felt like a king, as if there would always be money to throw away, as if the cholera would go on and on and Aurelia's powers would bring him riches beyond anything he could imagine.

And then the epidemic was over, and the stream of sick became a trickle. Oscar couldn't believe it. Hadn't he heard that people were talking about Aurelia as far away as El Paso? Didn't they tell stories about how the dead rose when she looked at them, how the sick became well at her touch? He knew the stories had sprung out of mad desperation and had spread, like the cholera itself, without reason, but all he had gained was gone on the gambling tables, and he had no heart for catching wild birds, and he thought it beneath him to sell trinkets in the plaza, and when he looked at Aurelia he was consumed with bitterness.

As for Aurelia, she had begun to have a dream in which she could see the future. She dreamed that her brothers and sisters were in Chihuahua growing up without her, that she heard them calling to her to hurry up and come to them, that they forgave her, that they loved her, that she belonged with them, but their faces became so dim in this dream that she couldn't see their features, and finally she couldn't even hear their voices, and then she would wake up, her heart pounding as if she had been running all night. She tried to tell Luz about her dream, but Luz wouldn't listen. She said it was Aurelia's fault that Oscar had lost all their money. *You're not a Mexican, you're not an American, you're not a saint,* Luz said. *No one in Texas wants you. You don't belong here with your strange thoughts and crazy dreams. It was all a trick. You didn't cure anyone.*

Aurelia understood that Luz spoke to her the way she did because she was in pain. And it didn't matter to Aurelia whether Texas wanted her or not, or whether she was a saint or not, or whether the money she made from cholera had been procured by trickery. If she had thought about herself that way, she would have been angry, and she couldn't think when she was angry. She had once thrashed a boy who called her a half-breed, and then brought him home so Luz could clean his wounds. It hadn't solved anything. She was still who she was after the thrashing. The only thing that had changed was that she was sorry she had done it, and she resolved to think more carefully before she acted. Dreams were for her a way of thinking. She spun out problems at night that couldn't be seen in daylight. But the same dream every night presented a special problem. It was as if a message were being sent that she couldn't read. So every night she dreamed the same dream, and during the day she struggled to understand it. She stayed alert for signs, looked carefully at people in the marketplace, tried to anticipate what words meant when they were spoken hurriedly or cautiously or carelessly, as if in that way the meaning of her dream would be revealed. She was a half-breed, a girl with strange thoughts, who dreamed of running away, but instead of running she made herself stop and listen, forced herself to wait and see. Everything happens in moments, she told herself. I will move from moment to moment. I will listen carefully, then make beautiful turns and say wonderful things and everyone will be caught off guard.

2

April, 1844

"I'VE HEARD SAY this girl of yours can cure people just by looking at them," the man said.

"Aurelia cure you just by the blink of her eye," Oscar replied. "All you got do is stand in her way and there it is, whatever hurt you stop right that second."

Aurelia could see the Texan through the door, talking to her father on the wooden porch. He said he was a Ranger, said he was camped with fifty-six other Rangers down by the Nueces River.

"We were watching for Comanches, and chasing a few, too, and just about every time I got off my horse and went to eating, I got a cramping in my stomach, and Captain Hays, he said there was a greaser girl from a family name of Ruíz curing people of all sorts of illness just by looking in their eye. He said he heard she cured some people of the cholera last summer."

The man's homespun trousers and shirt looked clean, cleaner than they ought to be for someone who spent his time chasing Comanches, even if he was camped beside a river and could have washed his clothes in between times.

"*Sí*, my daughter Aurelia can cure you," Oscar said. His English words were soft and slurry, the way he would have pronounced them if he were speaking Spanish. "You got spots on you, she look at you one time and they're gone. Your boils is gone and your fever. Open sores, too."

The red-and-blue bandanna wrapped around the man's neck was clean, too, and the silver spurs on his boots gleamed as bright as sun on water, as if he spent all his spare time, when his stomach wasn't cramping, pulling a cloth across them to get them that way. He had tied his horse to the gate, and even from the house Aurelia could see that the leather saddlebags weren't dirt-spattered.

"Is that the girl I see standing inside, the one with the long black hair?"

"Ten silver pieces and you can see her up close. She can fix your stomach real fast. I saw her first time cure an old lady in Laredo. We were going to Chihuahua, and an old lady, she said what kind of look is in that girl's eye, she just cure me of the pain in my aching bones, got no more pain in my body. And you ask anybody about the cholera, no one got it here, no one. Laredito, not one person died. Aurelia did that. God makes a big space around Aurelia so nothing can happen to her. Business isn't too good now, but you can go in. Five silver pieces and she'll cure your stomach."

Aurelia moved back from the open door until she was nearly out of the man's sight, until all she could see were snatches of red-and-blue bandanna and an occasional glimpse of blond beard. She would let her father take the man's money first. It wasn't too good to let him stare at her before he paid or he'd think she could cure him from inside the house, that he didn't even have to come in. Then he might just ride off on his horse and take his silver coins with him. Her sisters and brothers were playing *cuartillos* in the yard, little skinny faces intent on the game, but she could hear their stomachs growling with hunger all the way across the yard and into the house.

"I just have a cramping in my stomach," the man said.

"That won't take no more than half a look from Aurelia," Oscar said, "so half the price."

"Well, I don't know." The man kept glancing behind him at the dirt road that had led him into this part of San Antonio, the Mexican part, the part they called Laredito. He appeared to be confused, as if he hadn't expected to see windowless adobe houses with sod roofs, or rows of *jacales* made of mud and sticks and thatched with dried cornstalks, or broken-down horses grazing on dry grass right at the doors of the *jacales,* or so many dirty, ragged children and bony-looking dogs chasing each other beneath the shade of the liveoaks, was surprised to see grown men sitting with their backs up against pieces of sagging fence, shoulders wrapped in colored cloth, heads resting so far forward on their knees that the brims of their black hats skimmed the dirt.

"I'm willing to pay the full price. I don't want a cheap job. I want what anyone gets who pays his money. I want to be able to eat meat and potatoes and have it settle in where it belongs and not pain me afterwards."

"Listen to me." Oscar lowered his voice and put the edge of his palm up close to his face, as though to keep his words boxed into the small bit of space it made between him and the man, as if to show him he was his equal, could get as close as he wanted, wasn't afraid the man would shove him away, call him a greaser or tell him he wasn't any better than a nigger or an Indian.

"I'm going to tell you something I never tell anyone, never, ever in my life, just to show I'm honest and you don't have to worry that I try to take your money for nothing. Dumb Mexicans don't know this, what I going to tell you. They too dumb to understand when you tell them things, anyway."

It pained Aurelia to hear Oscar talk about Mexicans that way, as though he didn't belong to them, didn't want any part of them. And she would have walked out onto the porch and told him so, but there was something about the man with the blond beard and polished boots that made her think of plates of beans and stacks of tortillas. She would let Oscar say what he wanted, no matter how sad it made her feel, because she knew he could hear the children's stomachs rumbling as well as she could.

"My wife Luz is descended from Cortés," Oscar said. "Not too many dumb Mexicans can say that. I bet you never heard one lousy Mexican say that in all your life, did you?"

"I can't believe I rode up here from the river," the man said, as if he had just that second realized he was standing there talking to a Mexican with skin as dark as mud. "I don't know what I was thinking of."

"You know who Cortés was, don't you?"

"I heard."

"Aurelia, she no dumb Mexican girl, no greaser, not with Cortés' blood in her. You think someone with blood like that cheat you, lie to you about how she can heal the sick? Look at her yourself. Go on, look, but you better look quick. Aurelia don't like it when she has to wait like that, standing and waiting, and it's so hot."

The man hesitated a moment and then walked closer to the door.

"Go on, go inside. Go see for yourself what Aurelia can do."

Aurelia turned her face slightly, so her eyes looked past him to the left, to the crucifix on the wall.

"I might take one look," the man said and stepped inside.

Aurelia could tell by the way he survyed the rough log floor and the bare windows, stared at the homemade table and chairs, at the beds against the spotted walls, then let his eyes linger on the strings of chili peppers hanging in the open door, even the way he sniffed the air, that he had never been inside a Mexican house before or stood this close to a Mexican girl.

"People say you're a saint, Jesus in a woman's body," the man said to her and put five silver pieces down on the table beside the door.

"The priest says I'm not anything but a poor Mexican girl," Aurelia replied, and she told him he could sit down in a chair next to the table and she would just kneel on the floor, if he didn't mind.

"You cure people, don't you?" He was squinting, adjusting his eyes to the dull shadows of the room.

"Sometimes." Some people got up and left when she told them that. Some just didn't care. They'd say things like, *Well, I'll be the lucky one,* or

Maybe you weren't trying very hard before. She couldn't tell which kind the man was.

"My stomach cramps up on me when I eat. Do you cure people or not?"

"I'm not sure. If people say I cure them, if they believe it, maybe I do."

"I paid money for you to cure my stomach."

"And I will."

"You said you weren't sure."

"My brothers and sisters are hungry, and we need the silver. Can you hear their stomachs making all that noise outside?"

"It's my stomach I came about. I have pains in it when I eat. I heard you aren't a girl at all, but something made up out of clay and brown flour and dropped down out of the sky."

"I don't think so. But I don't know everything."

"You're the strangest girl I've ever seen."

"Is the pain in the top of your stomach or the bottom?"

"In the middle, I think."

He was staring at her the way some men in the marketplace did, his eyes wavering, the lids fluttering just the slightest bit. *You have a look that men like,* Luz said.

"Your blood is too rich," she said. "Your skin looks pink to me, like your blood is too hot. You can hear my brothers' and sisters' stomachs right now, can't you?"

"I don't hear a thing."

"The noise is so loud, I feel like it's inside my chest. Are you sure you can't hear it?"

"Just do what you do and I'll be going."

He was staring at Aurelia's neck now, at the hollow of skin that the shawl didn't cover. She pulled it tighter around her shoulders, felt the silk's fine pull beneath her jaw. He reminded her of the men in the marketplace who grabbed at her and acted as if she didn't know that they thought Mexican girls were to be used once or twice and then tossed away, men who pretended to like Mexican girls, but who would never walk in the street with one or take one for a ride in a carriage, or marry one.

"I paid my money," the man said. "Is it true or not that you can cure me?"

Maybe this man was like the men who took their time before they began to grab, who started out by asking if she knew of a good lodging house or if she could tell them where to find a cobbler to fix their worn-out boots, and ended by telling her there was a pretty place along the river they wanted to show her, men who spoke to her in short sentences the way this man did, men who didn't ask her name or bother to remove their hats, men with open-faced lust and barely hidden lies.

But it didn't matter what kind of man this was. She had feet for running and a mouth for telling stories. *I have Negro blood,* she would say, and as she spooled out the made-up details of her birth on a plantation in Georgia, their eyes would darken. *I have three children and no husband,* she would say and they would back away. *I put a spell on the last man who spoke to me, and he turned into a horse,* she would say and they would run for their lives.

"Well, can you cure me or not?"

Like all the other men there was something about this one that felt dark and hungry.

"Only God knows that. Who am I to say I can't?"

The man's name was Willie Barnett, and he came to the mud house in Laredito every day after that. Not to see Aurelia. He didn't even speak to her, never even told her whether her look had cured his stomach cramps, just tied his horse to the gate, touched the brim of his hat to show he saw her in the doorway, then came up the steps slowly, as if in no particular hurry, and walked around the porch that circled the house, down the back steps and past Aurelia's younger brothers and sisters playing in the dirt alongside the weedy garden where Luz's herbs grew. He trampled the same morning glories and honeysuckles he had trampled the day before, and then kicked open the rickety gate and walked out to where Oscar was swinging in his hammock beneath the liveoak trees.

Aurelia would stand at the rear window and watch the way Willie talked to Oscar and the way Oscar answered him back. She had watched Oscar in the marketplace when he had taken goods to sell. Trading things. That was the way Oscar talked to Willie.

On Willie Barnett's last visit to the house Oscar asked him if he'd like to sit on the porch where it was cooler. Luz brought two chairs out for Oscar and Willie to sit on. One of the babies, the one who had just been weaned, crawled across Willie's feet. Aurelia watched from inside the house as he nudged the baby away with the toe of his boot—a gentle nudge, not a kick like you'd give a dog—and then bent down and wiped his boot with his handkerchief. Oscar offered him some tobacco, and Willie said he had his own and didn't want to smoke right then anyway, and if he had wanted to he wouldn't have smoked Oscar's, that he didn't like the tobacco Mexicans used, it was too full of dirt and weeds to suit him.

"I've been thinking and thinking about Aurelia," Willie said to Oscar after Luz picked the baby up and took it inside. "I don't want to marry her, you see, but I'd like to buy her." Aurelia was sewing near the open door, bending over the material, taking tiny stitches in the quilt she was making for the baby Luz was going to have in the fall. She looked up, waiting for Oscar to turn toward her.

"She can keep my clothes washed, and do some sewing," Willie said.

"What about the wedding?" Oscar said. "We talked about a wedding."

"I changed my mind. I'd like to buy her. Keep her a while."

Aurelia's heart began to beat in quick spurts against her chest. She put down her sewing and came out onto the porch. It wasn't yet evening, but the sun was almost gone, just a thin arc of orange remaining. She had the power to stop Oscar. She had done it before. She had followed him to the gambling hall and stopped him from selling their wagon for a few pieces of silver.

"A wedding with a priest," Oscar said.

Willie was looking at her now. It was a casual look, with no more feeling than if she had been one of the carved *santos* with wax tears that Oscar sold in the plaza.

"I don't sell Aurelia," Oscar said.

Aurelia went down the steps into the yard and sat on the ground beneath the trees. Luz had come out into the yard with the two babies and she sat down on the ground beside Aurelia. Aurelia waited for her to say something that would save her. It needn't have been much. *You don't have to do it,* would have been enough. Or she could have put her arms around Aurelia and told her that she saw her goodness, that she knew her dreams. But she merely wiped one baby's mouth with the hem of her apron and dandled the other baby on her lap.

Willie and Oscar began to argue. Oscar, who always lost his English when he was angry, was spitting long Spanish sentences into the evening air, letting all his hatred of Texicans out on Willie, shouting at him that he owned Texas, he was here first, it was his country. It made Aurelia want to shout for joy. Oscar would save her. He would take Willie by the knot end of his red-and-blue bandanna and drag him out the gate and tell him that Aurelia wasn't for sale.

"Aurelia Agnes, go grind corn for the tortillas," Luz said.

"No," Aurelia replied.

Willie's words were now getting all mixed up with Oscar's Spanish ones. He kept saying he didn't know how Oscar could think he meant to marry Aurelia, it wasn't what he meant, wasn't what he was after. "Marry her?" he exclaimed. How could he marry her?

"Marry her is the only way you can have her," Oscar said.

"I didn't plan on it."

"Then you can't have her."

Willie was quiet now, but he didn't fool Aurelia. He was playing with Oscar, dangling money in front of him, waiting to see whether Oscar would bend, biding his time before he stood up and walked out the gate.

"Marriage is the only way," Oscar said.

"Well, I don't know."

"In the church."

"I'm no Catholic."

"In the church is the only way."

Willie didn't say anything back, and Oscar turned toward Aurelia. He was pleased, she could tell that by the way he kneaded the right side of his face with his finger.

"If you do this, we can live a whole year," he said.

"He doesn't want to," she replied.

"Well, I don't know," Willie said. He hadn't gotten up and walked out the gate yet. Aurelia thought he might even look as if the idea of marrying her wasn't the worst thing he could imagine.

"I'll buy a bigger wagon with the money and haul goods for the Americans," Oscar said. "I'll make the money grow."

"You'll spend it on the faro tables," she said. "You'll buy *aguardiente* and sleep all day and then the money will be gone."

"If you do this, the children can eat."

She thought of all the promises he had ever made and hadn't kept. She had no reason to believe that this would be any different. She didn't want to marry Willie Barnett. She wanted to be the one who stood up and walked out the gate and didn't look back. And if she married Willie Barnett, who would help Luz in the marketplace and watch out for the younger girls, who sometimes stood in the plaza and didn't know what it meant when the Americans told them they were pretty?

"The money will last a long time, Aurelia," Oscar said.

"God blesses those who sacrifice," Luz murmured.

Aurelia looked at the sky, at the way the disappearing sun pulled the light away. A noisy cloud of grackles, bronze bodies gleaming in the lavender sky, were coming to roost in the branches of the trees, and it seemed to her a wondrous thing that creatures so small could thrash the air so violently and screech from the treetops with such passion.

3

May, 1844

WILLIE SHOWED UP at the church, but he looked uneasy standing at the altar, and when the priest blessed him and Aurelia, Willie began coughing, as if he had something huge stuck in his chest, and when he was through coughing he said out loud, so everyone in the church could hear, "I made a mistake. I shouldn't have come here. I shouldn't have married her," and Oscar, who was sitting with Luz and the five younger children in the front pew, came up to the altar and grabbed Willie by his calico scarf and said if Willie hadn't already married his daughter he thought he'd kill him.

The villagers came to the fandango after the wedding, and they said Aurelia looked beautiful in her wedding gown, with her hair parted in the middle and braided with flowers, and they ate plates of chili and tamales and frijoles and enchiladas and drank *aguardiente* and told Oscar he had made as good a bargain for his daughter as they had ever seen.

The fandango went on all night, floors vibrating to the stamping of dancing feet and the walls bending and cracking in time to the music. Willie wouldn't dance with Aurelia, but sat in a corner of the smoky hall and stared out the open door in the direction of San Antonio while she danced, alone in the middle of all the other dancers, flinging her arms and twirling until the flowers fell out of her hair and her braid came undone. She wanted to beckon him to come to her, that she was a girl like all the other girls he had ever seen, but he wouldn't look in her direction.

She kicked off her shoes and danced in her bare feet. Oscar always said the fandango was like a flower. The dancing begins and it's like a little bud, smooth and tight, and everyone looks and holds their breath and waits to see what the bud will be. *I will be a rose,* Aurelia thought, *with petals that open slowly so that all the other dancers will turn toward me and gasp with admiration.* She twined her fingers into the hem of her white cotton skirt and turned her long neck to the right, as if someone waiting there in that spot against the wall had called to her. Then she lifted her chin and shook her hair and stamped her feet as if what he said had made her angry. She did all these things in perfect time to the music, and still managed to reach down and gather up the coins that rolled across the bumpy floor toward her feet.

Her brothers and sisters, stomachs full of the food Aurelia's marriage had bought, made a circle around her and clutched at the hem of her dress as she twirled and pirouetted, and she smiled at them and cursed Willie Barnett for being who he was and acting as if that could buy the whole world.

When they left Laredito, Willie didn't even wait until they reached the Ranger camp, but took her out in the deep grass along the San Antonio River and told her to lie down. Aurelia could see bathers in the water, young boys on log floats in the middle of the river, and she lay still while Willie yanked the lace skirt of her wedding gown up around her breasts. The young boys' voices carried over the water, and she heard their splashing as Willie said, "Spread your legs." He barely had time to squeeze in and out and tell her she was awful tight for a greaser before he rolled off of her and wouldn't touch her again except to say how disgusted he was at the way she raised her hips and arched her back and didn't cry.

"The blood on your cotton drawers doesn't prove anything. I can tell you've had many men before me."

"If I had a knife, I'd push it into your chest and tear out your heart and throw it away."

"I better sleep with one eye open," he said, and laughed.

She washed in the river while Willie waited on the bank. The water was warm on the surface, but cold where the sun's rays hadn't yet penetrated. The boys were gone, the logs they had been jumping from floating free in the river. She had married Willie because she couldn't let her brothers and sisters starve, but she had not thought of a moment beyond the wedding, had devised no plan as to how she would live with him. And now she saw that he would make her suffer, that he enjoyed the sight of her suffering, relished unleashing his meanness on her. *You will be blessed by God for your sacrifice*, Luz said, but Aurelia wasn't sure that God had noted her sacrifice, and if He had, where was her reward?

"I haven't had any other men," she told him when she came out of the water. "You are the first and only one."

"You can tell me whatever you want, but I know what I know," Willie replied.

When they reached the Nueces he left her there at the river's edge and told her she wasn't too far from the Ranger camp, it was due west, not to worry about Indians, there weren't any here, told her to walk the rest of the way, and if she stayed close to the river she couldn't miss it, there wasn't another camp for fifty miles in any direction.

THERE WERE A FEW canvas tents in the Ranger camp, and some grimy bedrolls and saddles scattered here and there on the ground, and the men didn't look as clean as Willie did. Their trousers were dirt-spotted, and even in the night air Aurelia could smell their unwashed bodies. The cook, a Mexican who told Aurelia his name was Tomás, was preparing the Rangers' dinner, stirring two iron pots with a wooden pole, his face a yellowish shine in the firelight. He let Aurelia sit near the fire and gave her a blanket to wrap around her shoulders.

"We don't see Mexican girls here," he said. "Where are you from?"

"San Antonio."

"You married Willie?"

"Yes."

Some of the Rangers were playing cards, others were lounging against their saddles, dreaming. A few came over to the fire and stared at Aurelia. She stared back, ready to kick anyone who touched her.

"Texas Rangers don't marry Mexican girls," Tomás said. "They buy them and keep them like pets, but they don't marry them."

Horses were tethered to the huisache trees. Aurelia wanted to get up onto the back of one of those horses and ride back to Laredito. She could almost feel herself racing across the camp and jumping onto a horse's back.

"See Captain Hays over there near the bank of the river, talking to Willie?" Tomás asked.

Aurelia looked toward the river. Willie was in shadow, but the man standing next to him, head grazing the branch of a tree, seemed to glow in the moonlight, the silver on his spurs and badge sparkling like fireflies.

"Right now I can tell you what the captain is telling Willie," Tomás said. "He's talking about you, telling him how mixing races is no good, that all Mexicans are stupid and Mexican women are dirty and can't be trusted, that Willie better keep you away from the others or the camp will turn into something we'll all be sorry for." He spat into the flames. "*Gríngos* are stupid. When I'm not cooking for them, I sell them horses the Comanches have stolen from them, I cheat them at faro, I trade them diseased sheep for coffee and tobacco. But they can be mean. Especially Captain Hays. He's a *nevero,* made of ice. He has no feelings. Willie shouldn't have brought you here. It's not a good place for a woman to be." He told Aurelia to stir the pot of beans while he poured more salt into the soup. "Maybe you can help me with the cooking. Do you know how to cook?"

"I can cook anything you want me to cook. I can cure you of anything you want me to cure you of. I know about herb medicines. If someone is sick, I know the right potions to give them. Sometimes I just look at someone and I can cure them. Willie came to see me in Laredito because his stomach hurt and now it doesn't."

"He eats fast, that's why his stomach hurts. He doesn't taste his food. He throws it down his throat instead of chewing it. You should have given him poison. No one would have missed him if you had. Are you a *bruja,* a witch?"

"I might be."

"Have you ever cast a spell on anyone?"

"I never tried."

Aurelia stirred the beans and felt the steam run up her arms and warm her body. Just talking Spanish to Tomás so the others couldn't understand what they were saying made her feel better. Just stirring the beans cleared her head. Cooking comforted her, made her think of Luz standing over her pots, babies on the floor at her feet. Aurelia knew what to expect when you put something into a pot and stirred it. If you always used the same ingredients, there was never any mystery as to how it would come out. Maybe the flavor was too strong one time and too weak another, but it was the same dish. There was no one who could tell you you had made beef tamales when you had made tripe stew.

The Rangers had gathered around the fire now, close to where the cooking pots were.

"Come on, do a fandango for us," one of them said.

Captain Hays was still talking to Willie. Willie, sober-faced, nodded his head as he listened.

The men were shouting at her, telling her to show them some dancing, do some tricks with her feet, bounce around a little so they could see her legs. The moon had laid a night blanket of shiny crystals on the river beside the camp, and Aurelia could see fires visible across the valley and hear the faint sounds of violin music, out of tune and whiny, but rhythmic. She had danced the fandango at her wedding. Every girl in Laredito knew the steps and could dance it for two days and two nights without tiring. If she danced the fandango they would leave her alone. She could bemuse them with her dancing, make them believe that if they touched her she would throw curses at them that would toss them into the sky and over the river and pound them so far into the earth they would never touch anyone else again.

She leaned her head back, lifted the hem of her skirt with her right hand, listened for a moment to the loose chords and disjointed melodies that came drifting from someplace across the valley, and began to dance.

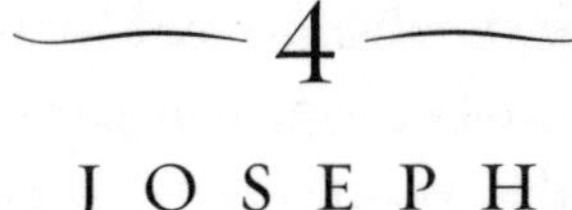

4

JOSEPH

Independence, Missouri
June, 1845

JOSEPH KIMMEL'S LIFE was a simple one. He rose in the morning, ate the breakfast his landlady had set out in the dining room the night before, then saddled his horse and rode the half mile to the Independence Missouri Boys School where he taught Greek, Latin and mathematics to thirteen-year-old boys. In his twenties he had been a mountain man, a fur trapper. He had liked trapping, had only left it because of all the poachers and Missouri farmers swarming over the river in their canoes and keelboats and because beaver hats went out of fashion and the price of pelts dropped. A schoolteacher was what he was now and it seemed to suit him. He had no wife, no children, and, since his brother Isaac's death in Texas the year before, no family obligations. He was as solitary a schoolteacher as he had been a fur trapper. And then on a fine summer morning a few days before the end of the school term he received a letter from Isaac's business partner.

May 20, 1845

Mist. Joseph Kimmel
344 Peech Strete

Independants, Misura

Deer Mist. Kimmel,

Yore leter of Jan'ry 3d recev'd. I disposition'd yore bruther's belongeens like you aks'd. I wil hold boots wach and fob also locket and pitcher found on body. Also tin box. Ther was no Jew preecher so I tole the preest at San Fernando church to berry him. Ther wer litel profit in the stor this last yeer. I wil show you the acc't books wen you arive. If ther be a profit from his shar of the bisines we wil work it out wen you com.

If you want to stay in Texas maybe we can be partners. Jews is smarter than the rest and Im plees'd to be in bisines with them. Wimins hats wil do beter next yeer. The wimin pine for new stiles and with mor peeple commeen to Texas evry yeer we are sure to make mony.

Ther be fine opertunitys in Texas for a yung man. Ther is land to be had. You can farm or raze livestok. Land is seleen cheep 2 dolars an aker. Les if you ain't partiklar whar its at. I heerd of good peeces goeen for one hunerd fifty dolars. Catel are cheep a good cow and caff equl to ten dolars. Yore Brother was taken by the fever but not everbody sickens. Many Peeple prosper. Many grow old. I hav see'd it miself.

But ther be Dangers. You must pay partiklar mind to yore arang-mints. Injuns are vary tuchy they hav 6 senses bout Travlrs, also Mexcans, those greesers wil steel yore shues from yore fete. Breeng bedeen and somtheen to cook in on the trale. You must breeng a good set of blaksmith tules also a good tent aganst the rane and one good pistil 2, if you can aford it.

Yores truely,
Cyril McCorkle

"AREN'T YOU SCARED a wild Indian'll get you?" Mrs. Plummer asked Joseph when he told her he'd be vacating his rooms and leaving for Texas when the school term was over. "I heard they shoot arrows at you, then cut the ears right off your head." Her old eyes gleamed as bright as if she could already see Joseph's wiry body, earless and pocked with arrows, hanging from the coat tree in the immaculately swept hall of the rooming house.

"I think those are just stories," Joseph said.

Joseph's fellow teachers at the Independence Missouri Boys School gave Joseph a pair of suspenders and a calico kerchief as a going-away gift. Then they all crowded into the small lecture hall to hear Joseph's students sing two choruses of "Blow the Man Down."

"Aren't you afraid to travel all the way to Texas with no companions?" Mr. Thurmond asked Joseph when the singing was over. Mr. Thurmond was the headmaster, the one who had hired Joseph two years before.

"I think I'll enjoy the time to myself," Joseph replied.

Mr. Thurmond's wife Grace dished out slices of the cream cake she had baked for the occasion. The cake had the map of Texas traced on the beet-dyed sugar icing.

"Give us a farewell speech, Mr. Kimmel," Mr. Thurmond said when all the cake had been eaten and each of the teachers had come up and shook Joseph's hand.

"I don't know how to make a speech," Joseph said, "and if I tried, I'd probably fail, so I'll just say good-bye." He was about to stop right there, but the boys from his Greek and Latin class were looking at him, waiting.

He had thought he could leave without much fuss. He hadn't made many friends at the school, preferring to be left alone with his books. It wasn't that he disliked people. It was more that with his somber personality, there was no sense inflicting himself on others. He had never snapped at anyone or shouted at any of his students, but he thought there was something inside him that, if aroused, might not be that pleasant for others to see. A short temper is what he thought he had. A temper to be avoided. A mean streak. His brother Isaac, who was the one who knew him best and had seen him at his worst, called it a touch of selfishness, of wanting things his own way. *I've seen no sign of temper in you,* Isaac told him. *You pout sometimes, and think of your own needs before that of others, but I've never seen anything in your nature that I would call disagreeable or describe as temper.* Joseph thought otherwise, even though the whole school had turned out to bid him farewell and were treating his leaving as if they were losing the most beloved teacher they had ever had, the most even-tempered teacher who had ever sat at a desk in front of a classroom and waved a ruler.

"I've been happy as a schoolteacher," Joseph said, "and if my brother hadn't died I would have stayed one, but he did and now I'm heading off to Texas to settle his affairs. I'm thirty years old and I've never been to Texas."

He looked around at the boys. They were listening with the absorption he'd expect if he had told them he was thinking of leaving the planet. He hadn't thought anyone would even notice he was gone, but here they were, students and fellow teachers, headmaster and wife, paying all this attention to him, listening to his words as if they had never heard his voice before. What would they think if he were to say to each and every one of them that when he received Cyril McCorkle's letter he had suddenly realized how tired he was of airless classrooms and spilled ink and boisterous boys, that he had suddenly been filled with the certainty that if he stayed in Independence he would one day die at his desk, a toothless old man who ate pie for breakfast and went to bed before dark?

He picked up the new kerchief and the patterned suspenders and held them out for everyone to see.

"I still don't understand why you're going alone," Mr. Thurmond said. "There are wagon trains heading that way. With more people there's more protection from the Indians. I think it's fine that you want to settle your brother's affairs, but a schoolteacher is hardly the sort of man to cross the plains alone. I don't think you fully appreciate that there will be hazards that you won't be prepared for, not to mention vicious Indians."

"I'm used to traveling alone, and I'm well prepared," Joseph said.

"And I'm not afraid of Indians. I've trapped the Missouri for beaver pelts and camped many times with the Indians. I never saw one sever anyone's scalp or cut off anyone's ears."

"I had thought you a schoolteacher from a tender age."

"And I would have been had my brother Isaac not wanted me to join him in the business of men's suits and hats. I went into the Missouri wilderness to get away from him, and now I'm going into the Texas wilderness because he's dead. He always said I had a streak of contrariness."

"Can you shoot a pistol, Mr. Kimmel?" one of the boys asked, and the others all crowded around to hear Joseph's answer.

"I can shoot a pistol and camp out in the open and set fur traps and have negotiated the distance between the Missouri River and the Mississippi in a canoe. Indians left me as alone as I wanted to be. I believe the stories about vicious Indians are exaggerated."

Then he passed the letter from Cyril McCorkle around for the boys to read. When he got it back, the cream-colored paper with its slanty writing and misspelled words was spotted with sticky red dabs of Texas from Mrs. Thurmond's cake icing.

"Well, I hadn't meant to give you a glimpse of my soul," Joseph said finally, embarrassed that he had said as much as he had. "I've told you more about myself in these last few minutes than I have in the two years I've been here. So mind your new teacher and do your lessons and I'll miss you all and think of you often when I'm in Texas."

Somewhere on the Texas Plains
September, 1845

JOSEPH BROKE CAMP EARLY. He strapped first the tent and then the light bedding to his horse's back and tied on the kettle. Then he put his plate, knife and fork in one saddlebag along with his last tin of dried beef, his canteen, tools, ammunition and gunpowder. In the other he placed cloth-wrapped parcels of sugar, crackers, coffee and salt. He was adept at packing and unpacking his possessions, and could load his horse and look around him and listen for sounds all at the same time.

The night before he had felt the first bite of autumn's cool air. And here along the river beneath the liveoaks, with their shivery green leaves and their limbs draped in lacy Spanish moss, he thought that the worst of the journey must be behind him. He had been warned about the Texas sun, told it would parch him, scald him, crisp his skin. And it had. But no one had told him about the windstorms or the stinging sand that clogged your throat and filled your ears and eyes and nose. Or about the heat vapors that rose up out of the sedge grass like water boiling on a stove and made your tongue dry up and swell in your mouth. Or about hailstones as big as apples and river water that made your bowels run when you drank it.

Or the loneliness. It was strange how he hadn't missed human companionship until now, hadn't thought it of any worth at all. During all those years in the Missouri wilderness with no one to talk to, he hadn't missed human companionship, and here he had been traveling for only two months and he longed for the sound of a human voice. He had seen a plume of smoke on the prairie once midway through his journey, and when he got off his horse and began to prepare his evening meal, he caught himself hoping that the smoke signaled a wagon train that would soon catch up with him, but by the time he had brewed his coffee and was eating his crackers and beef the plume had spread out over the tall grass and spewed up past the timber line into the sky and disappeared.

This morning he thought he saw movement beneath the pecan trees while he was steeping the kettle in the cold water of the river. He had set the kettle down on the bank to allow the sediment to settle, and as he began to fill his canteen his eye happened to pass over a hillock to the east, where larkspur and wild red poppies ran along the moist bank of the river like a bright arrow of color in the golden expanse of flatland. He was sure that he saw the grass flatten in one spot, as though pushed aside by the wind, even though the air was dead still. He had reached for the handle of his single-shot pistol, and then sat staring in rigid concentration at the flattened area.

He had only been able to afford one pistol, not two, as Cyril McCorkle had suggested, and although he had once been able to shoot a rabbit from a hundred yards away, he had somehow gotten away from killing living things and hadn't shot the pistol once on this whole journey. Not at the rabbits that hopped out of the brushwood as he rode past, nor at the high-stepping elk that came in graceful waves across the prairie. Not even at the deer that lifted the earth with their long legs and made the landscape flutter as though a great wind were sweeping through. He still had crackers and flour and beef jerky and didn't miss the taste of fresh meat. He supposed he would kill an animal for food if he got hungry enough.

He studied the grass where he thought he had seen the movement.

"It's nothing but the natural contour of the land," he finally told his horse.

He started off again, but he worried as he rode. He pondered the flattened grass all morning, turning often in the saddle to look back at where he had camped the night before. The thought that a child might have fallen off a wagon on the trail and been left behind, unnoticed and unmissed, gnawed at him. But he hadn't seen a wagon. He hadn't seen anything that even looked like a wagon for the past two months.

At midmorning, he was still unable to dislodge the thought that a child might be lying hurt in the deep grass, and so he swung his horse around and headed back to where he had started that morning. Everything looked just the way he had left it. He walked around the cool ashes of the campfire, kicking dirt clods over with the toe of his boot. He explored the hillock where he thought he had seen the stirring of the grass, but the indentation was gone and the grass there seemed as tall and ripply as the rest of the prairie. He shook his head at his own foolishness, and was glad that there was no one around to see how he had wasted the day. But the idea that grass might move without a wind to move it bothered him. He dropped to his knees and began to crawl through the airless sea of feathery green stalks.

A tall, scrawny man with a face as dark as the earth and eyes the color of sweet cherries lay on his side in the grass, lips trembling in fright.

"I cain't move." He pointed to his bare feet, which were gouged and crusted with blood. "I jumped from the wagon, and when I done fell, I done felt somethin' funny in one of dem ankles."

Joseph sat on his haunches and stared at the man. "I thought maybe a child fell off a wagon. I didn't expect a runaway slave. I could have been bitten by a rattler, or even a centipede crawling around in the grass. I didn't see a wagon. I'd have seen a wagon."

"I done fell off more'n a week past. I could walk some at first, but then it got too bad."

"I thought I saw smoke. I was sure of it."

The man seemed to be taller than Joseph, but he was thin and easy to lift. Joseph carried him back to the cold campfire and wrapped his feet with strips of clean rag. Then he gave him some crackers and beef jerky and sat back and watched while he ate.

"I suppose I could take you to San Antonio with me and collect the bounty. What's your name?"

"Luck, suh."

"I don't believe in slavery, but two hundred dollars is standard for a healthy runaway, and as poor as I am, even fifty dollars for a battered one would be a good thing."

After Luck had eaten his fill and drunk almost all the water in Joseph's canteen, he fell asleep. Joseph poked his shoulder a few times to see if he was dead, he slept so soundly. It had been a shock discovering the man, and Joseph hadn't meant what he said about taking him to San Antonio for the bounty money. Although it was a temptation.

The sun was almost gone when Luck finally woke up.

"One thing I know for sure, you can't stay out here on the prairie," Joseph told him, "so I'll just have to take you with me to San Antonio and figure out what I'm going to do with you once we get there."

He hoisted Luck onto the horse and tied his wrists to the pommel of the saddle with a piece of rope. As he began to lift himself into the saddle, he heard the metal rasp against the sole of his boot and felt the leather slide beneath his fingers.

"Git!"

The sound of Luck's voice, sharp and commanding, startled Joseph. There were only seconds of time and inches of space between Joseph and a firm seat on the horse. But he had stayed on the ground too long, and now he felt himself falling, felt the sharp rocks against his back, heard Luck's "Git!" two more times, and saw him gallop off, his tattered shirt darting like a butterfly in and out of the lacy hangings of the liveoak trees.

5

Hays' Rangers Camp on the Nueces River
September, 1845

SOMETIMES THE RANGERS were gone for a week hunting Indians, sometimes for just a few days. They always left camp in a playful way, laughing and joking, as if going after Comanches were a game they were eager to play. Captain Hays would tell them stories the night before they left camp, stories about the time he was a surveyor out on the plains and got to hunting and killing Indians for the fun of it, without a uniform and without the Republic of Texas paying him for the job. He told them his hearing was so acute he could hear twigs snapping in his sleep, and how one night a band of Indians came crawling up to where he was camped, and before they could pounce on him with their spears and tomahawks he pulled out the three loaded flintlocks he kept at his side and killed two of them, then reloaded and killed three more, and kept reloading until he had killed fourteen, and never even got a scratched elbow. Indian ears make the best souvenirs, he told them. They don't bleed too much and slip neatly into a saddlebag.

Aurelia would sit with Tomás near the cook wagon when Captain Hays told his stories about Indians, and Tomás would whisper to her that Captain Hays always had his men search for Indians in the wrong places, and that was the reason they never encountered any. And he didn't think Captain Hays had ever killed an Indian in battle. Oh, maybe he caught one by mistake a time or two and tied him up and then killed him, but that really didn't count, it wasn't like going into battle with the Indians. If he really wants to kill Indians, Tomás told her, he should ask me, I can tell him where they are.

When Aurelia's stomach began to swell she didn't tell Willie, but waited until he could feel the bulge for himself.

"It isn't my baby," he told her.

"It's yours. You come to me every night."

"It's the others who come to you."

"You're the only one. I know you by the way you groan, by the way you smell. It's yours."

"Anyone who says the child is mine, I'll tell him it isn't," he said.

Aurelia decided she wanted to go home. She wanted to watch her brothers and sisters grow and help Luz gather wild herbs. She wanted to sit in the grass while Oscar dozed in his hammock. She wanted to feel the hot stones of the marketplace beneath her feet as she and Luz carried their bundles of herbs through the streets. She wanted to be rid of Willie.

Are you a bruja? Tomás had asked her. She thought about his question at night when Willie pulled back the horse blanket and climbed on top of her. She thought about it in the morning while she was carrying water from the river. She thought about it when the men called her whore and when Willie kicked her stomach while she was sleeping. It was now almost October and she could feel the baby moving inside her. She decided that wondering whether she was a *bruja* was a waste of time. She had cured people of cholera; she should be able to rid herself of Willie. But she wasn't sure how she would do it. Spells shouldn't take too long to cast. And curses were said to be very effective. She had seen fortune tellers in the marketplace shaking maracas and yelling curses at anyone who didn't pay for their fortune, and there were some who claimed that people fell dead in the street after a fortune teller cursed them. She had no maracas and she didn't know what curses to use, although there were some words the priest said were satanic and blasphemous—magical words that wove webs of mystery and invited disaster, but he never revealed what they were, and Aurelia wasn't sure whether a curse was the same as a spell, and she finally decided that she would get rid of him in her own way.

She gathered a few lobelia flowers from beside the river and sprinkled them onto Willie's head while he slept, and then she leaned over him and whispered in his ear. "You're a cruel man, Willie, and others will make you suffer the way you've made me suffer." And then she laid her hand lightly against his forehead. "Disappear," she said. She didn't specify how she wanted him to disappear. She gave no details.

The next morning Willie and the Rangers marched off to hunt Indians. They looked particularly well turned out that morning, everyone in a different colored shirt and various kinds of vests and trousers. They had cleaned up by the river and trimmed their mustaches and shined their badges, and Captain Hays hardly had to say a thing to them to get them on their horses, they were so eager to go.

"Maybe Captain Hays will find Indians and one of them will kill Willie," Aurelia told Tomás.

"If Willie dies," he replied, "I'll take you home."

Two weeks later Captain Hays returned to camp. Eight Hays' Rangers had died fighting Comanche Indians, he said, and Willie Barnett was one of them.

Aurelia waited for the captain to tell her he knew she had put a spell on Willie and caused his death, but all he said was, "Now you take these things and go on back to where you came from," and gave her Willie's hat and badge and bloody shirt.

Tomás told Captain Hays he thought Aurelia should have Willie's pay for the month. Captain Hays turned red at that remark, the color traveling up from his cheeks all the way into his hairline, and he said he thought Tomás ought to leave, too.

That night Tomás saddled his horse and stole one of the Rangers' horses for Aurelia and before the Rangers were up and looking for their breakfast, Tomás and Aurelia were on their way to San Antonio.

"I WANT TO GET to San Antonio before the Northers come down on us," Tomás said.

"We'll get there before then," Aurelia replied.

It was the second time they had stopped that morning. The first time was when they reached a shallow stream and Aurelia got down from her horse and crept through the shimmery forest of green, foraging for goldenseal to make a skin poultice for her aching legs. They stopped a second time when she saw a patch of dill which she brewed into a potion to ease her nausea. Tomás was impatient to get going again, but she said she thought she'd wade out into the water and search for lichens or algae to spice the rabbit stew he made every evening. The water was cold and she shivered as she ran her hand over the rocks and felt for slime beneath her bare feet. When she came out of the water empty-handed and was putting her shoes on, Tomás said that with her stomach as big as it was she could have slipped and drowned, that from now on she'd best stay out of the water. She merely glanced at him when he said it, but he jumped as if she had screamed at him. And now she sat on the riverbank and watched the river rushing by, wind-whipped wavelets lapping at the rocks and turning the water purple and green with sparks of red. Beyond lay a great deep valley, prairie grass flashing gold in the sun, the horizon like a flat plate in a sea of wheat.

"An able-bodied man on a horse could have covered the thirty miles to San Antonio in a day," Tomás said. "We've been traveling three."

"I'm not an able-bodied man, and the Northers won't come for another month. We'll be in San Antonio long before that."

"I don't know how you figure that."

"There are no clouds."

"There might be tomorrow."

"It will be clear tomorrow."

Aurelia liked sitting here, moss hanging down around her face like lightly knitted strands of silk. Mealy-bugs fed on the sugary leaves of the hackberry trees and the air was misted with mealy-bug dew. She stuck out her tongue to catch the drops. When she was a child, she and her brothers and sisters would catch mealy-bug dew in their hands, then lick their palms. It was sweeter than peach nectar, stickier than candied plums. *Ghost rain,* Luz called it, because it only came when the summer was over and there were no clouds in the sky.

"I'm sorry I ever said I'd take you home," he muttered. "I should have left you with the Rangers and let you find out what they'd end up doing to a Mexican girl with no one to look out for her."

"Maybe you should have."

"I might just leave you and go on ahead."

"I think you should do that if you want to."

"I'm not afraid of you, you know, witch or not. Some people might think you can see into the future, but I don't."

"I didn't say I could."

He shook his head, and then said he was going to see if he could find a quail for supper, he was tired of rabbit.

She watched him walk away with his peculiar loping gait. He said he wasn't afraid of her, but sometimes she caught him watching her out of the corner of his eye as they rode, looking as if he thought at any moment she might turn into a hawk and fly up into the sky. And when he spoke to her, he didn't look at her full in the face, but at a slant, avoiding her eyes.

She hadn't asked him to come with her. She had expected up until the moment he mounted his horse that he'd tell her he had changed his mind. But he *had* come with her. She knew it was because he was waiting for her to do something magical. I'm just a plain, ordinary Mexican girl, she could have told him, but she knew he wouldn't have believed her. She could have told him all sorts of things if she had wanted to. She could have told him that she was in no hurry to get to San Antonio, that she was stretching out the time, making the journey last as long as she could, looking for the spotted dark green tufts of goldenseal and the feathery stalks of dill when she knew it was too early for goldenseal to have sprouted or for the wispy tails of dill to have produced their healing seeds. She could have told him she knew that this time of year the river had tumbled the stones and washed away the lichens and algae. She could have told him that she had had a dream in which Luz was swinging in a hammock instead of Oscar and that the dream had terrified her.

THEY REACHED SAN ANTONIO on the fifth day. Aurelia didn't remember the city as being so big, its broad, flat crescent of land teeming with so many horses and wagons, everyone rushing along, kicking up curtains of dust.

They passed the market, and Aurelia looked for Oscar's figure among the produce wagons, but there was no sign of him. She thought she saw Luz sitting beside the stone wall with her jars of potions laid out on a blue-striped cloth, but it was someone else.

The San Antonio River meandered cold and green here, a lazy serpent sunk deep in its purple bed beneath the cypress trees, only here and there glinting gold where a stray ray of sun broke through the shade. A Mexican girl, her clothes hanging in the low branches of a tree, was bathing downstream, her veil of dark hair floating wet and tangled around her glistening shoulders. Aurelia remembered bathing like that in the river, letting herself drop, unafraid, into the cold green water. She would hold her breath until she floated upward, and when she reached the air she would tilt her head back and lie on the surface and listen to the admiring shouts of her sisters and brothers as they watched her from the safety of the shallows.

They were soon out of the reach of the river's chill and riding through a maze of narrow hardpan streets that seemed stitched together like squares in a crazy quilt. Rows of sturdy adobe houses followed the curve of the road, lush gardens peeking out through iron grilles.

They rode past the crumbling walls and turrets of the Alamo, and then the road became bumpier, the sturdy houses disappeared and the stone sidewalks became dirt paths. There were no lush gardens here, no iron grillework, only a wasteland of cactus and scrubby mesquite on the city's edge, chickens and pigs wandering in dusty yards, children playing *cuartillos* on the porches of tumble-down shacks. Nothing had changed. If anything, Laredito looked dirtier and smaller.

And there was the house. It was the only one in Laredito with a fenced front yard and a gate. *A man with a gate to his house is a man who has something of value inside,* Oscar always said. He never painted the fence, but every spring would put a fresh coat of bright yellow paint on the gate. *If someone wants to know where the Ruíz house is, just tell them it's the house with the gate that looks like a piece of sunlight.*

Tomás waited at the yellow gate while she walked up the steps onto the porch. The mesquite bench, the one the children sat on to put on their shoes, was gone. She hesitated at the door, then turned the handle and went in. Layers of dust lay like a soft cloak over everything and there was the smell in the air of rat droppings and rotting maize. Part of the roof was missing and rain had streaked the rough wood walls Oscar had painted the same bright yellow as the front gate. On the floor where Luz's dish cabinet once stood was a pile of crimson chili peppers. The plants that Luz grew in old pots and kettles and even stuck into glass lanterns and tin ladles were gone, along with the birdcages made of twigs and twisted tin and braided horsehair. There were no beds in the alcove off the main room, merely clumps of quilting laid out on the floor. In the shadowy gloom she thought she saw her youngest brother standing in the doorway. He always stood just in that way, with one foot tucked behind the other. She dropped to the floor, light-headed, and stared at the apparition. He smiled at her and then disappeared. After a while she got slowly to her feet and wandered through the half-empty rooms, then walked out onto the porch and down the steps past the open kitchen to the rear yard.

Luz always kept her pots in rows in the yard, their sides touching, their mouths faced upward so the mixtures inside could catch the full force of the sun. *My baby birds,* Luz would say as she walked along her rows of pots. Now they were scattered across the yard, upended, chipped, cracked, broken, as if they had never held anything of any importance.

There were broken pots near the fence, with traces of Luz's potions still clinging to the shards of fired clay. Aurelia picked up a piece and ran her finger across the white residue, then put her finger to her lips. Yarrow. Bitter and slippery on the tongue, but good for stopping bleeding.

Where were the yarrow plants? The herb garden had been alongside the fence, where the noon sun was the strongest. *Herbs need sun and water and every once in a while a little kiss,* Luz would say. There was no sign of her garden now, only a shed where there had been no shed before, and children sitting in a circle in front of it, stringing red chilis onto heavy twine with metal needles. They were using shards of Luz's pottery to cut the strings. There was an acrid smell in the yard, as if the chilis had spit some of their fire into the air.

A woman yelled through the slats of the shed to the children to tie the chilis tighter, to pull the strings with their feet if they had to.

"They're too loose. How can they dry properly when they're so loose?"

It was Marta, the Oaxacan who sold pots of chili in the main plaza and had nine children and no husband. Luz would always buy a bowl of Marta's chili on market days, and she and Aurelia would share it, each taking small spoonfuls between sips of water. It was so hot and spicy that if you ate it too fast it would burn your tongue and the insides of your cheeks and when you were through your mouth was sore for two days afterwards. Her chili was so fiery that even the hairless Mexican dogs turned away from the leavings.

"Who is it?" Marta squinted in the sun's glare.

"Aurelia."

"Aurelia Ruíz?"

"Yes."

Marta's fingers were stained red from handling chilis, and she had a big square towel hanging from her waist to wipe her eyes. *Chili-stained fingers can make you blind if you rub your eyes with them,* she once told Aurelia.

"You've been gone a long time. What happened to your American husband?"

"Indians killed him."

"Too bad. Was he good to you before the Indians killed him?"

"No.

"You see. I knew it would be no good." She ran her hand across Aurelia's stomach and shook her head. "You should have married a Mexican. Americans don't like Mexicans. He would have left you even if the Indians hadn't killed him."

Marta went into the shed and walked through the strings of chili. She pulled one down and brought it out into the yard and began untwisting the string.

"Where have they gone?" Aurelia asked.

"Who?"

"My family. My brothers and sisters. My mother and father."

"Mexico somewhere. I bought the house from your father and I didn't ask. He sold it to me for ten dollars. There were chickens walking through the rooms when I bought it. And I didn't break your mother's pots. Your father did that. 'My wife died,' he said. Then he went in the yard and threw every pot at the fence."

Aurelia had dreamed this, but she had shoved the dream away, had looked for goldenseal and dill and lichens and algae when she knew there wasn't any, had tried to make time stop so she wouldn't have to hear what she already knew.

"Did you think I just walked in here and took this house? This is my house, and if you're here to claim it, if you've come here to tell me I cheated your family, if you're going to say that the house is worth twenty dollars, even without a roof, and that the chickens belonged to you, and what did I do with them, then you've come here for nothing. No one wanted to buy your father's bird cages. People can make their own bird cages with a few twigs, why should they buy his? And his saints are no good. No one uses saints like those in their houses. You shouldn't have come back. It's not good to go back to where you once lived. If you don't come back, you don't hear bad things. Yellow fever, your father said she died of. Look at you, tears in your eyes, as if you were a good daughter and visited your mother often and worried about her health and brought her good food to eat. You married an American and ran away. You have no right to cry."

Aurelia leaned forward and grasped Marta's chili-stained hands in hers and held them tight.

"What are you doing?" Marta said. She tried to pull her hands away, but couldn't. She began to struggle to free herself, turning this way and that, shouting for Aurelia to let her go. Aurelia didn't feel as if she were holding Marta's hands at all, and Marta's voice seemed far off, her words unintelligible.

Marta's fingers grew swollen, her neck muscles bulged as she yanked and tugged and jerked. She cursed Aurelia, called her a devil, a witch, told her she deserved all the bad things that had happened to her. Her face grew as red as her stained hands.

Then suddenly her ravings stopped. She stood as still as the shards of broken pottery scattered around the yard, her eyes fluttery and her cheeks rolling slightly above her jaw. She looked as if she were awakening from a long sleep.

"*Mi muy amable pobrecita,* my poor sweet child," she murmured, and kissed Aurelia's cheek. "Come and visit me when your child is born. I know that it will be as beautiful as you are."

Tomás, who had heard and seen everything, came into the yard and led Aurelia away.

"I had a sister once," he said as he helped her up onto her horse. "She died of fever and I never had another one. I've been thinking that maybe you're my sister come back from the dead. I've heard of things like that happening. I don't really believe it. You don't look like my sister. And Jesus is the only one who rose out of the grave. But there is something peculiar about you. I've tried and tried to figure out what it is, and I haven't yet. One thing I know for sure, somehow you've muddled my mind, jumbled my head up so my usual way of thinking has turned crooked. And you did something to that woman. I don't know what it was, but if I ran true to my feelings, I'd leave you here and not look back."

And then for the first time he looked straight into her eyes. He thought them the strangest color he had ever seen. Not brown or black or green or blue, but the color of warmed honey, liquid and bright.

6

TOMÁS SAID THAT he would take Aurelia to a place where she could have her baby. A Comanche camp on the Colorado River, he said.

"All the braves and their wives have gone north for the winter buffalo hunt. I used to supply Ten Elk with rifles, and he would give me stolen horses in return. One day he didn't have enough horses, so he gave me his barren sister, Flying Braid. I go there once a year. I can't get rifles anymore, and I can't afford to feed her. She sleeps with anyone who will give her food."

Aurelia had heard stories about the Comanches, how ferocious they were, how they raped white women and cut off the genitals of white men before they drove spears through their hearts. Oscar always told her to be careful when she went to gather firewood along the river, that Comanches sometimes hid among the trees and carried off Mexican girls. *They like the way they smell,* he said. And he told the younger children if they misbehaved he would call the Comanches to come and get them and cook them in a pot. *Comanches like the way little Mexican children taste,* he said.

They traveled through land so dry that Aurelia thought she could hear the grass snapping beneath the horses' hooves. For long stretches there were no mountains, no trees, just brittle shrubs and glimmery sheaths of dry grass rolling out in every direction, with only a bank of clouds hanging over the straight line of horizon to distinguish where the land ended and the sky began. When she thought they would ride forever, when she thought they had come to the end of Texas, Tomás told her that the gray thicket in the distance was the Comanche camp.

The village was on the banks of the Colorado, a grove of hackberry trees to the east of the encampment, the river to the south. Where the circle of tepees ended, the plains stretched out again, flat and empty. The camp was quiet, no fierce warriors with feathers in their hair and scalps on their belts, just children playing in the dirt and old women sitting in groups in front of bison-skin tepees.

Flying Braid was asleep in her grease-stained tepee. When she heard Tomás call her name, she sat up on the soot-stained carpet, her deerskin tunic, laden with bits of tin and iron and beads, tinkling noisily. The inside of her ears were painted red, and a braided horse tail was looped around her neck. A yellow line, as bright as marigolds, was painted from beneath her eyes and across her forehead clear to the edges of her close-cropped hair. She glanced at Aurelia, greeted Tomás in Spanish, and then ignored them both and occupied herself with smoothing her hair where it stuck out from sleeping.

"I have to sit down," Aurelia said to her after awhile. "My legs are numb from riding all day, and I would like something to drink, please."

Flying Braid's mouth quivered. She asked Tomás if this woman was his new wife, and when he said no, she brought Aurelia some curdled doe's milk and invited her to sit on a pile of bison skins.

"I've never brought anyone here before," Tomás told Aurelia, "although I've seen a few white women here now and then. But they don't stay long. The Comanches use them for trade, although I hear one or two of the other bands have white wives. Ten Elk lets me come and go because I bring him things he needs and because he's used to me. I don't know if he thinks I'm the same as a *gringo*, or better or worse, but he trusts me. As far as a Comanche trusts anyone. He says I'm his brother because he shared his wife with me on the buffalo hunt. Still, I think he would take my hair if I ever tried to trick him. Comanches don't think the right way sometimes. They'll loan you their wife to sleep with, but they'll take your hair and your scalp with it if you steal their horse."

"I have never had a baby," Flying Braid said, and she touched Aurelia's stomach and said she thought there was a boy inside.

That night Tomás and Flying Braid slept together on a pile of bison skins in one corner of the tepee and Aurelia slept in another corner. And all night she could hear Tomás grunting atop Flying Braid's body.

Tomás left the village the next morning. Before he rode off he told Aurelia that she would have to leave before Ten Elk and his braves returned.

"If he finds you here, he'll kill you and your baby," he said.

FOOD GREW SHORT in the village, and still the braves had not returned. Flying Braid and the other squaws who had remained in camp scavenged for rats and skunks and insects, which they shared with those who were too weak or too old to scavenge for themselves. Aurelia had never eaten rat before, or lizards or grasshoppers. No matter how hungry she had ever gotten it had never occurred to her to eat such things. Those were the things starving dogs ate in Laredito. People didn't eat them.

"You will die and your baby will die unless you eat what I give you," Flying Braid said.

"I want to eat what you eat, but there is something in my head that keeps me from it," Aurelia replied.

Each day Flying Braid brought Aurelia some of what she had found on the perimeter of the camp, and each day Aurelia refused to eat. Not eating made her dizzy, and sometimes she wandered out toward the river and thought she saw her mother boiling herbs in a pot, and she would call to her, and when her mother didn't answer she thought it might be because she had done something to displease her. Without food, her legs began to shake when she walked and so she lay most of the day on the bison skins in the corner of the tepee. One day she slept all day, not even waking to go outside and pee, and when Flying Braid shook her arm and asked her in a rough voice if she was dead yet, Aurelia replied that she wasn't. But she couldn't remember whether she was in Laredito or in the Ranger camp, and while she was trying to remember, Flying Braid said she thought Aurelia's stomach was shrinking and that the baby would probably die inside her. Then Aurelia remembered where she was and that she hadn't eaten since Tomás left.

"Something keeps me from eating, and I don't know what it is," she said, and Flying Braid told her she could do what she wanted, eat or not eat, it didn't matter to her.

So Aurelia slept the days away. Sometimes she dreamed that Oscar had brought her to the Comanche village to cure the Indians of cholera, and she would get up and crawl out of the tepee and sit in the dirt waiting for sick Indians to come to her, and the sun would beat down on her head so hard she would forget why she was sitting there, and then Flying Braid would pick her up and bring her inside, and she would go to sleep again.

One day Aurelia dreamed she was in Laredito with her brothers and sisters, and they were swimming in cool green water, and she got up and walked toward the river, dropping to her knees in the dirt every few feet to rest, and when she got to the river there was no one there, and she thought if she lay down in the weeds for a while and waited, her sisters and brothers would appear. She waited all day in the hot sun, unable to move, her head turned toward the water, just watching the way the sun licked its surface and made it sparkle. Once in a while an Indian woman would come to the water's edge to fill her water jug, and would jab at Aurelia with a foot or a stick. One woman bent down and shouted in Aurelia's ear. One poured water on Aurelia's head. Aurelia tried to say something to them before they walked away, something about her brothers and sisters and how they liked to swim, especially when the water was this warm and sparkly, but she couldn't make any sounds come out of her mouth. Toward evening Flying Braid came. She picked Aurelia up in both arms, and Aurelia marveled at the easy way she swung her up into the air, with hardly an extra breath, and carried her back to the tepee as rapidly as if she were carrying nothing at all.

That night Aurelia lay in her corner and watched Flying Braid eat. It was a curious sight, the way she ate, filling both hands with parts of rodents and lizards, legs and heads all mixed up together, and then placing them against her mouth and somehow shoving them in, then licking her palms up and down to get every last bit before she picked up some more. Aurelia couldn't see how the food got from her hands into her mouth, and she watched Flying Braid eat with the same interest she had watched the water in the river, and she wanted to ask Flying Braid if she tasted her food before she ate it, or if it just slid down her throat unchewed, but when she tried to speak, no words came out, and it was then that she knew she was dying.

AURELIA ATE THE LIZARD carefully, holding the body between two fingers and delicately gnawing first at its head and then its tail. Flying Braid ate hers greedily, with the body held flat against her face.

"I saw everything starting to die inside me, even the baby," Aurelia said. "I saw its face. It has two blond curls atop its head."

"If you saw its face, that means it is a girl," Flying Braid said, and Aurelia asked if she could have some more lizard to eat, that she could feel the baby inside her crying with happiness.

Flying Braid caught two rats, and she laid them on the stained carpet in front of Aurelia.

"Rats are strong," Flying Braid said, "and when you eat them their strength flows into your body, especially when they are warm from the kill," and she tore off the head and tail and gave Aurelia the choicest bits.

"I thought you were stupid to starve yourself to death when there is food to eat. Stupid people are ruled by their feelings. I once saw a woman die because her husband took another wife. She sat by the river and died. I thought you were going to do the same thing, and I told myself that you were the same as a horse that Tomás left here once and asked me to feed, and I didn't worry about whether the horse ate what I gave it, and so I thought you were the same way, stupid as a horse, stupid as the woman who died because her husband took a second wife. But I see that you're not stupid. No one I have ever seen who was as close to death as you were has ever sat up and decided to live. You must be very strong inside."

Grasshoppers were the most difficult for Aurelia to eat. Their bodies were crisp, but the meat had a stickiness that made her gag. The only way she could swallow them was to imagine they were potatoes, shredded and fried in lard to a dark brown.

But even after eating what Flying Braid gave her, Aurelia remained weak, and Flying Braid told her she might still lose the child. She stayed close to Aurelia's side, and gave her extra portions of what she caught, and brought her medicines that she said would purify her body for the birth, and smeared Aurelia's stomach and breasts with bear grease so that the baby would not struggle too much to be born or work too hard at the breast to draw out the milk. And when Aurelia's legs drew up in pain because of the way the baby lay inside her, Flying Braid made a poultice from the roots of a blue flower and applied it to the twitching muscles until Aurelia's legs were calm and the pain was gone. She grew alarmed when Aurelia began to bleed before the baby was due, and padded Aurelia's vagina with dried moss to keep the baby from coming out and fed her tea made of splinters from a tree that had been struck by lightning. She told her she could not get up now even to pee, and brought a shallow pan and put it between Aurelia's legs.

As the time grew closer for Aurelia to have the child, she told Flying Braid that she felt better and wanted to get up and help gather firewood or scavenge for food, but Flying Braid said that she should save her strength for her first pain.

"The first pain must be fought the way you fight a bear so that the pains that come after that will fear your strength and become timid. You are strong inside, but you have never walked across the plains carrying bison robes on your back and will need to gather your strength and not waste it standing on your feet."

They passed the days telling each other stories. Aurelia's stories were as fanciful as Flying Braid's, and Aurelia thought how alike they were in their differences. But when she tried to kiss Flying Braid for being so kind to her, Flying Braid pushed her away and told her that a hug was all right, but for a woman to wet another woman's cheek with her lips was disgusting.

In the afternoons the old women in the village came into Flying Braid's tepee. They brought their beadwork with them and listened to Aurelia and Flying Braid tell stories. After a while the other women forgot their shyness and joined in the storytelling, and Flying Braid turned their Comanche words into Spanish ones so Aurelia could understand. The stories they told were like beads on a string, each one leading to another and then another, and everyone laughed and cried and forgot how hungry they were.

When the time for the birth came, Flying Braid burned sage outside and then brought the still fuming branch into the tepee and waved it over her head and slapped the bisonskin walls with it until the air was warm and scented. Then she dug a hole in the center of the tepee and lined it with a thick cushion of leaves. She sat at one edge of the pit and stretched her legs across to the other side while Aurelia straddled her outstretched legs, her feet braced against the sides of the pit.

Aurelia's pains had started at dawn and she had pushed against the first one the way Flying Braid showed her, pulling at two sticks Flying Braid had planted in the dirt. She had pulled as hard as she could and waited for the pains to grow timid, but they only grew stronger, and now she shoved her bare feet into the soft dirt of the pit and was dizzy with pain.

Flying Braid called for the midwife, and she came and sat facing the pit and clasped Aurelia around the shoulders and jabbed her knee into Aurelia's back. Flying Braid began to pull at Aurelia's arms and sing to her in a thin papery voice, while the midwife pressed her knee deeper and deeper into Aurelia's back and blew on Aurelia's neck and made groaning sounds, as if she were the one giving birth.

Aurelia began to howl and Flying Braid called for a second midwife, and this one poked at Aurelia's arms and legs with a sharp stick, and soon there were other women in the tepee, and everyone was singing Flying Braid's song, and Aurelia imagined herself standing with the women, and although she didn't know the language of the song, she began to sing, too, and the singing seemed to take her away from the pain so that she barely felt the first midwife prodding her with her knees and blowing on her neck, and couldn't tell if the second midwife was jabbing her with a stick now or pummeling her around the head, or if her arms were at her sides or being yanked out of their sockets. She knew she was in pain, but couldn't find it, and was startled to hear her baby's cry as it landed softly on its leafy bed.

The first midwife showed the child to Aurelia, pointed out the female genitals, and counted all the fingers and toes, but Aurelia already knew the child because when she was dying she had seen its image.

"I call her Yolanda," Aurelia said.

The midwife gave the baby to one of the women to clean and the two midwives took turns kneading Aurelia's stomach until the bloody membrane was expelled. Then they brought an Indian baby into the tepee to suckle at each of Aurelia's breasts to draw off the mucus so Yolanda's first taste of the world would be pure milk.

THE BRAVES CAME home from the hunt with forty bison. They crossed the Colorado and rode into camp, Ten Elk riding ahead, the women laden down with supplies and dragging the butchered bison along behind them until the ground turned bloody and the bison meat was studded with gravel and dirt. Tomás was with them, his hair tied down with a beaded band, a deerskin shirt hanging over his trousers.

When Ten Elk and his braves were in the middle of the camp, swallowed up by women and children, everyone running up to the horses and pulling on the braves' leggings to show how happy they were to see all that buffalo meat, Flying Braid left Aurelia and the baby inside the tepee with the flap closed and started across the clearing. Ten Elk was Flying Braid's younger brother. When they were children she would put a cloth over her head and ghost scare him. But then he began to ride horses. When he was five years old he could ride faster than he could talk. The year he was fifteen he stole eighty-two horses and killed two bears. And since theirs was the largest family in the Colorado band, when he was eighteen he became chief. Now he was thirty-five and a single mean look from him could make Flying Braid's heart jump. She couldn't ghost scare him anymore. She had no husband. She had no voice. She sometimes smeared herself with the juice of juniper berries so that she would have no face. Tomás had brought no tobacco to the camp that summer, so that Ten Elk had had no tobacco to take with him on the hunt. Ten Elk always turned mean when the only thing he had to smoke were dried sumac leaves.

"Where are you going, Flying Braid?" His plucked-out eyebrows and lashless eyes made him look half man, half ghost.

"To greet you," she replied.

Flying Braid couldn't control her shaking now, and the more she shook, the fiercer Ten Elk seemed to her, the sun at his back, the feathers in his hair bristling in the wind. He got down from his horse and walked up close to her.

"Were you hungry while we were gone?"

"No," Flying Braid said. "I dreamed of the afterworld and lost my hunger."

Ten Elk had once danced the beaver dance and had tried to go to the afterworld in his dreams, had tried to see its wonders, but couldn't.

"You still bleed every month," Ten Elk said. "You have no husband. You have no children. Only warriors can dream of the afterworld." She could see by the seriousness of his gaze that he was wondering what medicine she had that let her dream of the afterworld when he had tried and failed.

"I don't bleed any more. For two moons, since you were gone on the buffalo hunt, I haven't bled."

She had never lied to Ten Elk before, but he didn't check the cloths she put between her legs and he was too proud to ask her if she was lying. He would have to speak to her with respect if he thought she no longer bled. She would be the equal of any brave in the band if she was past the bleeding age. Tomás hung back now, out of Ten Elk's sight. If Ten Elk's medicine was strong enough to see through tepee walls, he would know that Tomás had brought Aurelia here and he would kill him. If Ten Elk could see inside Flying Braid's head, he would know that she hadn't gone to the afterworld, and he would kill her. There was no blame for killing an outsider who brought strangers to camp when Comanches were starving. There was no blame for killing a sister who lied.

"You're not old enough to stop bleeding," Ten Elk said.

"I washed myself for the last time when you went to hunt the buffalo." She counted her breaths and waited.

"What kinds of things did you see in the afterworld?" Ten Elk said after a long while.

"I saw blue water and herds of bison and elk and deer. The trees were in leaves, and there were plums and berries to eat. Now that I know how to go to the afterworld, I'll go there often." The air was so fresh on her face it made her smile. Ten Elk was listening and she knew he couldn't see through tepee walls.

"Going to the afterworld is a special thing," she said. "Not everyone can go."

THE BRAVES WERE doing a dance of celebration, and Tomás waited until the dancing was through before he came to where Aurelia and Flying Braid were waiting for him at the edge of the river.

Flying Braid untied the baby from its cradleboard. "She is a very pretty baby," she said, and handed the baby to Aurelia.

"I brought you a present," Tomás said to Flying Braid, and he gave her two sacks of flour and a sack of coffee.

Flying Braid watched them leave. She stood in the short grass and every time Aurelia turned to look back at the village, she saw her standing there.

7

Near the Medina River, Texas
November, 1845

JOSEPH SAT DOWN on the riverbank and took off his boots. There were holes across the soles and a slice of heel was gone. He had once journeyed from the mouth of the Missouri down the Mississippi to New Orleans and hadn't worn out a pair of boots. He had once journeyed three months on a keelboat, skirting the shore and setting traps and looking out for unfriendly Omaha, and then two months of trapping beaver through Crow country all the way to the trading post at the mouth of the Bighorn and hadn't worn out a pair of boots.

He eased his sore feet into the cold water and felt the skin begin to throb and then grow numb. He pulled his feet out of the water, let the air dry them and then put his stockings back on. They were heavy stockings, new when he left Independence. They now had gaping holes from toe to heel.

He looked around him. Nothing seemed familiar. The only thing he knew for certain was that after two months of walking he hadn't run into this particular river before. At least he thought he had been walking for two months. He couldn't remember. His mind had been skipping all day, jumping from one thing to another, and he wondered if not remembering things like time was due to lack of food. It certainly wasn't because he wasn't sleeping. He was sleeping too much, hardly rousing himself when the sun came up before he was stumbling around looking for another place to lie down.

He had a sudden urge to write a letter, to put down on paper how he came to be wandering around the plains, so that when someone found his body they'd know who he was and what he wanted done with the remains. But he had no pencil or paper, and, with Isaac gone, no relatives to notify.

"This way, I say!"

For a moment he wasn't sure he had heard anything.

"Pull harder, he's sinking!"

He yanked on his boots and began to run toward the voices. He could now see wagons lined along the riverbank and men straining to pull a steer out of the bog. The steer was nearly submerged, and the poles the men had slid under its body were bent down into the muck like so many fishing rods.

"If you had a chain, you could attach it to the steer's horns and have your oxen pull him out," Joseph said.

A tall man in a stiff collar standing at the edge of the bog turned and looked in Joseph's direction. "I saw no horse or wagon."

"I have no horse or wagon and no provisions. I am as you see me, my clothes ripped by the rocks of the ravine I fell into yesterday and caked with the dirt of the holes I've slept in at night. Joseph Kimmel is my name. Have I in my wanderings crossed the plains and landed back where I started from?"

"I don't know where you started from, but you are in Texas, and I am Henry Castro of Paris, France. Perhaps you have heard of me."

"I haven't, but then I know of no reason why I should have."

Castro resembled the phantoms Joseph had seen in his wanderings. Long, narrow face, drooping eyelids, and a sag-shouldered body that in the sun's glare seemed larger to Joseph than the leafless tree at the man's back.

"No man walks across the Texas plains," Castro said. "A man rides a horse or sits in a wagon. How have you come here? By what means?"

"I started out on horseback from Independence four months ago. Midway through the journey I was robbed by a runaway slave of everything I owned. For a meal and the loan of a horse I'll try to save your animal."

"I can't spare a horse."

"Then a meal is sufficient. I've eaten little more than grubs and roots for more than two months."

"The meal is yours, but I'm afraid the steer is lost."

"If you have a chain and will choose two of your strongest men to hold me by my feet, I will make an attempt."

Castro, who seemed unperturbed by the animal's braying and shrieking, had one of his men bring Joseph a length of chain.

"Is the length sufficient?" Castro asked.

"It will be long enough to span the distance between the bank and the middle of the bog," Joseph replied.

He slid onto the bog on his stomach, the chain clutched in his hands, two men holding firmly to the heels of his boots. The sand trembled like aspic beneath him and a meaty smell bubbled up from the muck, as though air and fire and beast were boiling deep inside some hidden cauldron.

The steer was silent now, its eyes open in fright, a moist film forming across its nostrils. Joseph wrapped the chain tightly around its head and called for the oxen to pull.

As the oxen pulled, it appeared that the bog was giving way, that the animal would be freed after all. And then Joseph heard a sigh, or perhaps a creak, as of a rotted door closing, and finally a crisp snap as the steer's head separated from its body, and head and rope and chain flew into the air. Joseph studied the sluggish ripples fanning out like smiles from the place where the steer had been just moments before. The animal's frightened gaze seemed not to have disappeared. Joseph was sure of that. There. He could see it hanging a few feet above the bog, its pathetic, sorry gaze outlined in droplets of sand. And then it was gone. Joseph looked around him, as if he had misplaced the animal and by diligent looking would find it again, but there was nothing to find, and the bog was now making sucking noises, the way a person might after a fine meal.

"You did your best," Castro said when Joseph was on firm ground again.

"I had hoped to save it," Joseph replied. His hair was mud-clumped and animal blood dotted his broad forehead. "I thought the chain would bring the animal out. I didn't expect it to tear the beast apart." Joseph extended his gritty palm to the man. "My happiness at finding you is boundless."

There were more than twenty Alsatians in Castro's group. *My colonists,* Castro called them. The way he said it made Joseph think of a king and his subjects. They were from a place called Alsace, Castro explained, a frontier region between Germany and France, and Joseph noted how freely the man talked about his financial arrangements in front of them, the money he had paid for the land, the profit he expected to realize on it when it was all parceled out. Of course, he said, as he and Joseph sat on a log near the campfire, tins of thick black coffee and plates of pork and cornbread balanced on their laps, there were more colonists to come, and he would be going back to France to recruit them as soon as he was able. He had the backing of European bankers, and there was even the possibility that he could settle all of Texas with Europeans, and that he might become president of the republic one day. There certainly was nothing in the Texas Constitution to prohibit a Jew from becoming president, he said.

"We made our way from the ship in Galveston, but had to leave the women and children behind in San Antonio, to be sent for later," he said. "I bought the land and will choose how it's distributed. I'll build a town right here on the banks of this river. I don't expect to become rich, but I certainly don't think I'll find myself poor. Settlers are as plentiful as air in Alsace, yearning for I know not what. Different lives, ease, comfort. I warned the most enthusiastic of them that there would be hardships, but not too strongly, for to dampen their spirit before they left their homes would have served no purpose. But I do reserve credit to myself for luring even the most wary to come with me."

Castro ate slowly and dabbed at his mouth occasionally with a large white handkerchief, which he removed each time from his vest pocket and then replaced. In his well-cut suit with its satin lapels, Castro looked important enough to be president of Texas. And there was hardly a speck of dirt on him. Only the cuffs of his white shirt, sticking out of his coat sleeves, had a few spots on them.

"The crossing was severe," Castro said. "Sickness aboard ship took some lives, and when we landed in malarial Galveston, those who were weakened the most from the long sea voyage grew feverish and died. Whole families. I blame myself. I didn't intend for them to languish there in such a port, where the fog is thick with sickness and death, but they had gone on ahead, and since I was delayed in Paris, I could not warn them to leave for the grant immediately. My responsibility is great, and they complain that I abandoned them to their fate, when the truth is that there were papers to be signed for the land grant, finances to be arranged, colonists to recruit, or there would be no settlement. I left my wife and two sons behind and finally sailed for America, but by the time I arrived, half of those I had sent on ahead were gone. Disappeared. Evaporated. Like kettles of water left on the stove to boil too long. Some dead. Some too frail to travel any further. A few had lost faith that I would arrive at all and headed for Houston or California. Some just wandered away. One man, a butcher from Rheims, drowned in Harrisburg." He sighed. "The difficulties I have faced in bringing even this small group to Texas cannot be appreciated by ordinary men."

A young girl sat on a crate closer to the fire, crocheting a blanket, dipping the bone hook in and out of the line of green yarn. She was the youngest Alsatian in the group, Castro told Joseph. Sixteen years old. An orphan. She was covered in heavy black cloth. Shawl, blouse, long full skirt, hat. All in black. Even her shoes, the toes of which she had burrowed into the mud, were black. Every time Joseph thought he might see the girl's face, she turned her head, and the multi-tiered hat, which resembled nothing so much as a fluttery bouquet of moths' wings, dropped down against her cheek like a veil.

"And what of you?" Castro said. "What brought you to set out for Texas by yourself? Surely, it was more than merely a yearning for adventure."

"My brother Isaac died in San Antonio and I've come to settle his affairs."

"Will it make you a wealthy man, the settling of your brother's affairs?"

"It will be my good fortune if he left no debts for me to pay. My brother was an enthusiastic businessman but not always a prudent one. I have no hope of wealth."

"You are unusual in that. All men have hope of wealth."

"I believe all men have hope of experiencing life to the fullest. It's a dream that some keep tight inside them and never pursue."

"And have you pursued your dreams?"

"I have done what I wanted to do. Trapped beaver in the valleys of Missouri, taught Latin and Greek and mathematics in a boys' school in Independence, and have managed not to let any man tell me I had to be in one place when I longed to be in another. I've trusted no one, have not been one to cultivate friends, have kept my plans close and my possessions closer. I should not have stopped for the slave, but circumstances overcame me. I could easily have survived if the man had left me my pistol, but without game to sustain me, I would certainly have ended up as food for the wolves. And so you find me, without even a horse to get to San Antonio."

"Yours are not the only plans that have been disrupted," Castro said. He glanced at the girl. "Katrin's brother August died of fever in Galveston soon after they arrived. Katrin herself almost died of it.

When my wife and sons arrive from France, she'll live with us. Maybe one of my sons will marry her. There aren't many girls for young men to marry in Texas."

The girl kept crocheting, grimacing slightly as she pushed the bone hook back and forth through tiny loops of yarn.

"It's your good fortune that you encountered no Indians," Castro said.

"Not a one. If there are any, they're as rare as penguins."

"I saw quite a few corpses as we traveled here from Galveston."

"Killed by Indians?"

"Some by sickness, most by Indians."

"I've seen no Indians," Joseph said stubbornly. "I don't doubt that there are a few who are angry enough at the white man's encroachment on their lands to kill—but my opinion is that the settlers spread the stories so as to keep others from coming and taking the land."

Katrin looked up from her crocheting and suddenly Joseph could see her face clearly. Patches of yellow hair, fine as a baby's, curled at her forehead. And what he had thought was a smudge of dirt on her chin was really a little brown freckle. She had a sharp nose and full lips, and the way her round cheeks glowed in the firelight reminded Joseph of polished river pebbles. Separately her features were acceptable. Putting them all together, she wasn't particularly pretty.

"My brother August," she said to him and reached inside the pleated bodice of her black dress and pulled out a locket that hung from a thin gold chain. A dark curl was pressed against the chin of the pale-eyed boy in the portrait inside. "All the hair from August fall out from the fever before he died. Mine, too. It start to come in now, but very thin and ugly, and I think maybe never it will be the way it was. My hair was so thick, and August was always saying it was better to look at than my face. August was good to me. Sometime I cry when I think on him." She snapped the locket shut and let it drop back inside the bodice of her dress and resumed her crocheting. She had the ball of yarn tucked inside the sleeve of her dress and yanked at it every once in a while to free up a strand.

"Do you obey the dietary laws?" Castro asked Joseph. "I note you have left the pork on your plate untouched."

"I don't obey any laws. I just don't eat pork."

"I'll ask Tomás to prepare a fried egg, then. The eggs are fresh, laid by our own chickens this morning."

"I've eaten five biscuits. I'm quite content."

"I promised you a meal," Castro said, and he called for the cook, a short, flat-faced man wearing a beaded strip of leather around his forehead.

"You don't like my stew," the cook said to Joseph.

"I enjoyed the cornbread biscuits," Joseph said, "but I don't eat pork."

"A hungry man eats whatever is cooked for him," the cook said and walked away.

"I hired Tomás in San Antonio," Castro said. "A very good cook, but surly. Is your objection to pork based on health considerations?"

"It's based on habit."

"I have another meaning in mind. Perhaps I am not sufficiently plain spoken."

"I believe you to be very plain spoken."

"Then permit me the indulgence of inquiring further of you—and I don't mean to question you too closely, or cause you embarrassment, but I confessed my Jewishness to you, and I wonder—and of course, only if it does not violate some personal reticence of yours—are you also a Jew?"

"I'm not embarrassed or reticent, and yes, I am a Jew."

"That comforts me."

"I have heard that said before, and the sentiment mystifies me. I find you no different in my eyes since your confession than before."

"The comfort I take is not in any exclusivity, but in a sense of communion. You and I must be the only two Jews on the Texas plains."

"And the others that you have brought with you?"

"Some are Lutherans. But most, like Katrin, are Catholics. One in my position must accept all kinds. Mexicans, Alsatians, Lutherans, Catholics. I try to deal with everyone in the same fashion. My Alsatians are simple, uneducated people, with little understanding of people unlike themselves. I eat pork without hesitation and do not pray or wear a beard, and I try to conform my appearance to theirs, where possible. Have you ever been to Alsace?"

"I was born in Poland, but remember none of it. My brother Isaac said they hate Jews in Poland even more than they do here."

"It is my opinion that it isn't Jews the gentiles object to as much as the peculiarities of Jewish life. Strange dress, strange food, strange rituals. I take it you are not a religious man."

"I never think of religion. My brother Isaac was religious and as a boy I tried to please him in that regard. I don't know exactly what it is that makes me say I'm a Jew. At times I even forget that I am. Pork was served regularly at the boarding house in Independence, and I regularly declined to eat it. I realized that pork was the only thing left to remind me of my Jewishness, and so I suppose I will continue to refuse to eat it. I tried it out of rebellion as a young man. I purposely sat down to a meal of bacon and pork dumplings. I wanted, I suppose, to prove to myself that Isaac didn't have complete control of my behavior. I couldn't eat it. I couldn't get it down."

"Were there many Jews in Independence?"

"I knew very few. I was the only Jew at the Independence Missouri Boys' School. I was well received and respected as a teacher, although I never hid from anyone the fact of my lineage. It was the first thing I revealed. I wanted no whisperings behind my back."

"We had Jews in Alsace," Katrin said. "August sold the jewelry from our dead mother to a Jew for to pay our passage, and he cheat us. He give us too little. August said Jews always do that."

"I remember once in Independence," Joseph said, "I was with Isaac and someone said something about Jews, and I can't even remember what it was, but I remember Isaac saying to me, 'If I were a fighting man I'd fight right now,' and I was younger than Isaac, and stronger, and so I fought the man. I remember the way the man's face looked with the blood running out of his nose."

"She's only sixteen," Castro said when Katrin began to cry. Joseph said she wouldn't be crying if she hadn't said what she did, and he moved away from her and Castro and went and sat by himself near where Tomás was putting the remains of the food into covered tins. Tomás murmured something in Spanish that Joseph didn't understand. Then he put the last tin away and rolled a cigarette.

"I've been a devoted user of tobacco since I was fourteen," Joseph said.

Tomás reached inside the pocket of his overalls and produced a small packet of tobacco and a bit of cigarette paper and handed it to Joseph.

"Castro thinks Mexicans are cattle," Tomás said in English. "When he's through building his little town, he'll let us loose."

Joseph rolled the tobacco into the paper and stuck a twig into the campfire to light it. "I've never known any Mexicans."

After supper one of the Alsatians brought out a fiddle and started to play a catchy tune. Katrin sat on the tongue of one of the carts, bouncing in time to the music, frissons of yellow hair sparking from beneath her bonnet. The blanket-wrapped Mexicans, who had been working on the shelters since early afternoon, cutting reeds and sorting them for size, then standing them up and tying them together, appeared not to need to rest, but worked steadily except for when they stopped to eat, and then they ate sitting in the mud and had a good time laughing at stories that Joseph wished he could understand. Castro passed around a bottle of cognac, letting each of the Alsatians take a sip right from the bottle. He held the bottle out to Joseph and Joseph put it to his lips. When he gave it back to Castro he asked him why he wasn't offering any to the Mexicans.

"Disease," Castro said. "They are an unhealthy lot. Good for laboring, but wherever they are sickness goes with them. It would be best if you reserved your friendship for the Alsatians. I assure you, not all of them think unkindly of Jews. They followed me here. They listen to my instructions and are content in my company. As for Katrin, she's a young girl and doesn't understand. I invite you to stay with us and let us prove our goodness to you."

"I have business in San Antonio."

"I'm sure your business in San Antonio can wait. Your brother is a dead man, after all, and has no pressing needs."

"That may be, but his business partner expects me. And as for staying here, I have no money for land. The forty dollars I brought from Missouri galloped away from me two months ago."

"I'll lend you what you need, just as I have the others."

"I don't take money from anyone."

"It will be a loan. Surely, you have no objection to a loan of a farm of forty acres, plus a lot in town for your house to start you off. Plus the use of oxen and ploughs and seed, and until you're self-sustaining I'll feed you at my expense. All you need do is cultivate the parcel I lease to you and in time buy it from me. A teacher of mathematics will be valuable to me. You can do my accounts and act as my deputy when I'm away. For that I'll give you twelve dollars a month and a horse. What do you say to my proposition?"

"I will have to think about it."

Joseph glanced over at Katrin. Just looking at her gave him an unpleasant feeling. And as for the others, Castro may have lured them to Texas with stories of riches to be had, but he wasn't going to be able to persuade all of them that ownership of a piece of sun-bleached, dried- out, bog-filled land was an improvement over what they had had in Alsace. Already some of them looked uneasy, and Joseph could see the beginnings of disappointment in their faces. It was as if they didn't know where they were or how they got there. Most were speaking German, but some, like Castro, were speaking English, and Joseph could catch snatches of complaint as they huddled around the campfire.

"Have you ever thought of marrying?" Castro asked.

"Never."

"You say that most emphatically."

"I mean it most emphatically. A man with a wife and family is obligated to them. I've been determined to live my life without obligation."

While they were talking a bolt of lightning cracked overhead, and the

Alsatians scrambled beneath the wagons. The Mexicans dropped the reeds they had gathered and covered their heads with their blankets. A glaciate wind howled over the river. Then the rain started. Heavy, torrential and cold. It quickly overflowed the river and turned the campsite into a swamp. Joseph huddled with Castro and Katrin and three other Alsatians under one of the wagons. Castro had the bottle of cognac with him and he kept giving Joseph little sips, and even Katrin took a drink, and when she fell asleep Castro covered her with his own coat, and he and Joseph talked about ancient Greece and Rome, and Castro told Joseph that Alsace had been a part of the Holy Roman Empire for seven hundred years, and then he said he intended to bring more colonists to Texas than Stephen Austin ever dreamed of and that he didn't know how Joseph would get to San Antonio without a horse, and Joseph felt a little drunk by that time, and their voices began to blend into one, as steady as the rain, as even as a thread spooling gently out of its bobbin, and finally Joseph told Castro there was no use arguing about it any longer, that he thought he'd accept his offer and stay a while.

"In the morning I'll send some men to go after the slave who robbed you."

"I don't want anyone going after anything."

"But he has your belongings."

Joseph took another drink of cognac and wiped the rain from his eyes.

"He can have them," he said.

8

Castroville, Texas

JOSEPH LAUGHED OUT loud when Castro told him he was naming the town after himself. Castroville. He didn't laugh because of the name—Henry Castro was arrogant enough to have named all of Texas after himself—but because, with all Castro's regal airs, the town was so miserably common. He thought Castro would have saved his name for something bigger, something on the scale of Galveston or Austin, not on an afterthought of a town on the banks of the Medina River. Why, the town was hardly even a town yet. Castro's stone house had snug walls and a plaited-tule roof and sat right in the middle of the main street across from where the church would go when it was built, but all the other houses were made of rough-hewn logs barely chinked together tightly enough to keep out the rain. And the single path through town was more like a swamp than a road, so that wagons and horses sank and rose like ships on the ocean.

Tomás and the rest of the Mexicans left Castroville when the last log cabin was up and Castro's stone house was finished. Castro said he was happy to see them go, and now when they passed through town, the Alsatians acted as if they had come to rob them. Joseph had even heard some people say the Mexicans were going to join the Indians and take Texas back.

Castro, true to his word, gave Joseph one of the log houses to live in and appointed him the town treasurer. He gave him no money to treasure, merely a set of account books that Joseph kept filled with expenses Castro incurred in his travels from Austin to San Antonio and back to Castroville, recruiting colonists. He hadn't yet returned to Europe to find more Alsatians willing to come to Texas. There was a steady stream of settlers arriving in Texas on their own, and all Castro had to do was travel around the countryside and gather them up.

Joseph thought the job of treasurer a useless one, something that Katrin, as dumb as she appeared to be, could have accomplished, but every time Joseph told Castro he wanted to leave, had to get to San Antonio and see Cyril McCorkle about Isaac's affairs, Castro would persuade him to stay. *My wife is ill in Galveston,* Castro told him in May, *and I have to retrieve her.* He was gone until late June. Joseph was ready to leave for San Antonio when he returned, but now Castro's wife Amelia, who was fat and cheerful and looked to be twenty years younger than her husband, begged him to stay until her sons arrived. They hadn't arrived by July, but it was summer, and Castro said Joseph should wait until the weather cooled some before he headed for San Antonio. In September Joseph told him he was leaving, and Castro asked him to stay until his sons, who had been delayed in Paris, arrived in October. Castro's sons did show up, but in November, and they stayed in Castroville only long enough to pronounce it an uninhabitable place before they headed for Austin. Joseph said he was leaving in December, and that was all there was to it, but Castro departed for San Antonio at the beginning of the month—something about securing financing for another parcel of land—and made Joseph promise he would stay until he returned, which Castro said would be no later than January, and certainly no later than February. Castro returned in March and suggested that Joseph stay until the worst of the cold snap was over. By this time Joseph was beginning to like living in Castroville, and so he said all right, he'd stay until spring.

Spring came, and then it was summer again, and then the hills started to turn color, and Joseph thought it one of the prettiest sights he had ever seen, the way the green clung stubbornly in spots and let itself go to gold in others. He still intended to go to San Antonio to settle Isaac's affairs, and was absolutely certain that one of these days he'd do it. He had been about to go more than once. He had a horse now and money enough to get to San Antonio to take care of things there, and maybe even travel around some before he headed east. And Castro trusted Joseph so completely, he inspected the account books no more than once a month, which gave Joseph plenty of time to figure out why he didn't just leave. Besides the way the hills turned color, there were all kinds of interesting things happening in Castroville. Castro had sold some land down by the river to a man by the name of Monod, who was going to build an inn for travelers. And there were plans being drawn up for a dam across the Medina so a grist mill could be built. Bishop Odin came down from Austin to bless the cornerstone for the Catholic church, which was half finished now, the gray stone front wall already laying its shadow over the swampy main street. A seed store had opened up in April, and there was a harness shop and a bakery. The Alsatian women and children that had been left behind in San Antonio arrived to join their husbands, and the women planted flowers in the front yards of the log houses, and when they weren't milking cows or tending sheep on the gentle dips and sloping honey-colored hills north of town, they organized socials and quilting bees. Just two weeks before Christmas, they staged a living nativity pageant on the banks of the Medina. The weather was unpredictable, with rain coming at odd times, but everyone in town showed up for the pageant and said it was a miracle it didn't rain then with the skies as heavy-looking as they were. The stars were out, and the night was cold enough that everyone bundled up in blankets to watch, and Joseph, who was the only Jew in Castroville when Castro was away, played Jesus. He didn't have to do anything but stand behind the crêche—there was nothing religious in that, he told himself—and stare down at the baby, all swaddled in blankets against the cold. It was agreed afterwards that Joseph was the most authentic Jesus they had ever had.

Everyone in Castroville hunted game for food. There wouldn't be enough to eat if they didn't. The vegetable gardens were in, but the deer foraged in them at night and the rats had gotten into the barn where the corn harvested in June was stored. Castro had brought another butcher from Alsace, the brother of the one who drowned in Harrisburg, a man by the name of Dubuis. He opened up a shop on Jack Rabbit Hill and when there was fresh meat everything was sold before the sun was up, leaving nothing but scraps for the flies to swarm over when it got light.

As for Katrin, he had heard she might marry one of the Castro sons and move to Austin, but he had seen no signs of her leaving. She lived in the Castro house, and was, Amelia Castro said, good company when Henry was away. There now was a path along the main street that was on higher ground and didn't turn to river when it rained, and Joseph sometimes saw Katrin walking along it. She would turn her head away when she saw him, as if he frightened her. He regretted that he had spoken to her the way he had the first time he met her. Amelia once asked him to come to tea in the afternoon, and when he arrived Katrin wouldn't come out of the rear of the house. Joseph and Amelia ate cake and drank tea for a whole hour and Katrin never did appear.

BY MAY OF 1848 Castro's colonists, waiting for grant deeds that didn't materialize, were on the verge of destitution. There were lawsuits pending against Castro for monies collected and not disbursed. Other European impresarios were bringing colonists from Europe, and their towns were prospering while Castroville stagnated. Joseph could have told Castro how to make his enterprise work, but Castro wouldn't listen to suggestions. He refused to admit any defect in his thinking or any lack of attention to detail and adamantly rejected any suggestion that Castroville was not the Eden described in his brochures.

To compound Castro's misery, in March a group of colonists on their way to join the settlement in D'Hanis had been attacked by Comanches and seven people were massacred. In April two wagon trains had come through Castroville, and although no one said anything about seeing any Indians, they did report seeing a man and woman shot through with arrows, with horse tracks all around them, and the woman's shoes and dress missing and the man's hair, including his scalp, gone. A week later Captain Hays reported seeing a trail of fifty Comanches not too far upriver. He advised Castro to post guards around Castroville morning, noon and night, with every man taking his turn at sentry duty.

Joseph liked the solitariness of standing guard on the perimeter of the town with only a musket for company. He didn't have to talk to Castro about accounts or to colonists who thought Castro hadn't sufficiently secured title to the land when Texas was a Republic. These colonists might lose the money they had paid out now that Texas had been admitted to the Union. He didn't have to listen to colonists complain that they hadn't been warned that Comanches had long ago laid claim to the land Castroville sat on.

There were only a few more hours until daylight. Fires burned in the livestock corral, and men stood guard there also. Poised beneath the huisache trees was a Conestoga wagon, hitch and wooden wheels sunk in the tall grass, deer foraging around it, marble eyes glistening. He raised his musket to his shoulder. He had once thought that Comanches weren't too different from the Omahas he had encountered in Missouri. Omahas killed for revenge, but most preferred to steal, and Omahas could be bluffed if you showed your nerve and if your hand was steady. They followed trappers and picked up their leavings and raided their traps, or just waited until the pelts were packed onto the horses and then stole those, and the horses, too, but they didn't have the burning hatred for the white men that the Comanches had. When Joseph thought hard about it, he had to admit that the problem was that the Comanches were here first and it was just white men's laws telling them they had no hereditary right to land they had occupied for a hundred and fifty years. Even Mexicans, who had ceded titles, surveys and documents to the new Texans before statehood, were now dispossessed of their remaining lands without legal recourse. Joseph tried to push such thoughts out of his head and concentrate on the simple fact that the white man was here now and the Comanches would terrorize and murder until they were rid of them.

The deer had skittered away and Joseph sensed movement in the grass to the west. He stood with his back to the wind to mask his scent and leaned into his musket, aiming at a rustling spot in the grass.

"Don't shoot, Joseph. It's Tomás."

"Stand up. Let me see you."

"You're not going to shoot, are you?"

"Closer."

"I'm as close as I'm going to get until you put the musket down."

"It's down. What are you doing here? Castro said you went to Mexico."

"I like Texas."

Tomás was in the clearing now, his body outlined against the fires burning in the livestock corral.

"Do you have a musket or a pistol?" Joseph said.

"No musket, no pistol." He raised his hands, palms facing Joseph. "Nothing." He stepped through the grass toward Joseph.

"What do you want?" Joseph said.

Tomás pointed to Joseph's fur-lined cap. "I'll give you a deer pelt for the hat."

"I don't need a deer pelt."

There were rustling sounds near the wagon.

"How about the boots?" Tomás said. "I could use some new boots. I could get you some Indian moccasins—beaded ones. Real fine ones. Apache work."

"I'll keep my hat and my boots."

"They say Santa Anna buried a treasure in gold somewhere around here. Under an oak tree. Under a branch facing east. You ought to start digging. You'll be a rich man."

Joseph could see the Indians now, crouched down, the bears' teeth on their bison-hide shields glittery circles of light in the darkness. He stood very still as they glided through the thick grass toward him. As they came closer, he saw what looked like beaver pelts artfully pegged along the edges of the bisonhides. They were fringed with shiny strings of horse tails and fluffy rows of feathers.

"Raise your musket so they can see it," Tomás said.

One of the Indians took Joseph's musket, motioned for him to get up onto his horse and pointed in the direction of the rock-strewn mountain to the north of Castroville.

THE CLIMB UP the mountain was steep, the horses' hooves clattering and slipping on the loose rocks. The Indians rode close to Joseph, every once in a while jabbing his horse's flanks with their moccasined feet. It seemed to Joseph that they had been riding for hours, although he knew this couldn't be, because the moon hadn't moved that much in the sky. When they reached the top, the land turned flat and grassy, and the moon, lost in the canopy of trees, was a dull glow overhead. Joseph tried to memorize the way, but there was no trail here, only a soft mashing of dew-covered grass as the horses galloped away from the ridge and deeper into the trees.

The Indian camp was hidden behind a sharp limestone revetment camouflaged by chaparral and shrubby trees. Joseph thought ruefully that Hays' Rangers could have ridden up and down this mountain for ten years looking for it and not found it. Although the smell might have given it away. And the pall of ash that hung like stinging rain in the air.

The camp was quiet, just the neighing of horses and the crackle of twigs burning in open fires. The flap of Ten Elk's tepee was open. Tomás and Joseph entered first and then the six Indians followed. They had shed their bison-hide shields and in the smoky light of the tepee looked pretty ordinary, except for the yellow streaks they had painted across their braids. They sat down on the dirt floor of the tent, slightly behind where Ten Elk was seated on a bison hide eating raw meat from a bowl. Ten Elk said a few words to Tomás, who then motioned for Joseph to sit down on the ground across from Ten Elk.

"Ten Elk says he thinks you're smarter than Castro," Tomás said, "that you'll listen to what Ten Elk has to say and then you'll explain it to Castro."

Ten Elk dipped his hands in the bloody bowl and snared a piece of meat. Then he shoved the bowl toward Joseph.

"It's horse meat," Tomás said. "Ten Elk wants you to eat."

"It doesn't look like something I'd like."

"Comanches like to feed their guests. Otherwise they take their scalps."

Ten Elk didn't look particularly fierce to Joseph, not like someone who'd take his scalp if he didn't eat what was offered to him. If anything, he looked comical. He had painted red circles on his face and plucked out his eyebrows and was wearing a stovepipe hat on his head and a frock coat buttoned backward.

"What is it I'm supposed to tell Castro?" Joseph said. He made no move toward the bowl.

"You better eat," Tomás said. "Or your scalp will go over there in the corner with the other ones."

In the dim light of the tepee Joseph had thought the pile was beaver pelts. Tomás got up and brought one over for him to examine.

"Yellow hair," Tomás said, caressing the fine strands. "Ten Elk likes yellow hair."

There were signs that the hair had once been trimmed in ribbons, a few blue satin strings still adhered to the bloody curls.

"You better eat," Tomás said.

Joseph dipped his right hand into the bowl. Ten Elk had stopped chewing and was watching him. The blood was as warm as fresh milk and clung like a soft cloth to Joseph's fingers. He pulled out a piece of meat, put it in his mouth and tried not to gag.

The pot was back in front of Ten Elk, and he stuffed some more meat into his mouth and wiped the blood off his chin with the back of his hand.

"I told Ten Elk you weren't afraid of Henry Castro," Tomás said, "that you weren't afraid of anything. I told him you walked to Texas from far away."

"I didn't walk to Texas. My horse was stolen."

"You walked to Texas."

"I didn't."

"I told Ten Elk you did. I told him you can make Henry Castro leave Texas."

"Henry Castro won't listen to me or anyone else. He thinks he's a king."

"Ten Elk wants you to tell Castro that all this land belongs to the Comanches, not to Henry Castro. Ten Elk wants you to tell Castro he can keep the land he has if he gives Ten Elk fifty head of cattle, a hundred horses and fifteen saddles. Ten Elk wants you to tell Castro he'll trade two of his squaws for the girl that lives with Castro."

Joseph leaned forward, and the meat rose like a lump of tar out of his throat and onto the dirt.

"The one with the yellow hair," Tomás said.

THE MEDINA RIVER was straight ahead, running fast, freshets of water catching twigs on the bank, knitting them together, then spitting them out. Joseph got off his horse and knelt in the sedge grass, his face in the water, his mouth open. He was sure he could still taste the raw horse meat. It lay on the back of his tongue, sticky and warm. He lifted his head up and let the water run down his face and onto his shirt, and then lay down in the grass, his eyes closed, his face to the sun. If he were smart, he would get on his horse and keep riding until he got to San Antonio. If he were smart. No one would ever know that he hadn't delivered Ten Elk's message to Henry Castro. He'd find Cyril McCorkle, take what money was left from Isaac's share of the business and head back to Missouri. He'd set himself up as a trapper again. He'd go farther into the wilderness this time. He'd head for the Blue Mountains. He'd canoe up rivers and defy rapids and bury himself deep in some forest redoubt. He owed no one anything. He had only stayed on in Castroville because it had pleased him. It no longer pleased him. That Ten Elk wanted Katrin had nothing to do with him.

"THE COMANCHES MEAN to have Katrin," Joseph said.

Castro was at his desk reading documents, shuffling them and signing them and stuffing them into separate piles of folders he had stacked in front of him.

"They mean to have her, Henry."

Katrin was in an adjoining room with Mrs. Castro. Joseph could hear their whisperings.

"I've recruited another fifty settlers from Alsace," Castro said. "You'll come with me to Galveston to get them, and I'll buy you a new suit. Yours is threadbare."

"Ten Elk wants Katrin."

"Hays' Rangers are posted along the Medina and will stop him if he tries."

"It won't matter how many Rangers are posted."

"Fifty colonists, Joseph. Can you imagine how the town has grown in such a short time? I had dreamed it, but had no grasp of its reality. This will be the largest land grant in Texas. My name will never be forgotten. How many men can make that statement?

"You can have my house and farm and if I owe you any money over that I'll pay you back when I've settled my affairs with Cyril McCorkle. My brother is sure to have left some small amount for me. I could have left and not told you. I could have kept riding and not looked back and I thought about it, Henry, I thought about it long and hard, and I finally said to myself, no, I owe it to Henry Castro to tell him and let him handle it."

"The new colonists are all in good health," Castro said. "They shouldn't sicken as readily as some who have come before them. These are young men, newly married. They'll work hard to earn the money to bring their wives. They'll write letters back to Alsace telling of the glories of Texas, of the endless plains, of the freedoms. I've long thought the town could use a woodworker. There is no ornamentation in the buildings. Such as they are, they invite no comparison with the structures in Alsace. I've ordered woodworking tools from France and await notice that the man I interviewed in Paris is yet willing to come to Texas."

"I want no part of this."

"The Rangers will provide protection."

"The Rangers are no match for Ten Elk. And Tomás is no friend of yours."

"I never counted him as one. I am my own friend. I follow my own counsel, and if it is true that Ten Elk has made a proposition of horses and cattle and saddles in exchange for the safety of Castroville, I'm willing to deal with him. I have no fear of savages."

"What of Katrin?"

"I had already thought of marrying her to one of the settlers when they get here next summer. Ten Elk won't dare ask for her once she's married."

"He'll be back before next summer. He intends to have her."

Katrin was in the room now. Castro looked up from his documents.

"There are Indians in the front yard," she said.

Joseph stood on the porch while Castro walked down to the gate.

"You may come inside," Castro said to Tomás, "but the Indians will have to remain in the yard."

"They aren't after your scalp today," Tomás said.

"No Indians in my house."

Tomás came up the steps, glanced at Joseph, but didn't say anything to him or strut the way he did when Castro wasn't around. And when he entered the parlor, he walked slowly, lifting his boots carefully, as if in that way he could keep the mud on them from dropping onto

Amelia Castro's fine rugs. He stopped once to stare at the expensive furniture Castro had brought from France, and then sat down on the red velvet settee while Castro lounged on a pillow in an overstuffed chair, his elbow on the armrest, his chin in his hand. Katrin and Amelia were nowhere in sight.

"Did Joseph tell you what Ten Elk wants?" Tomás asked.

"He told me. He gets no part of Castroville. The land grant is mine. There only remains the documents to finalize it."

"Ten Elk doesn't care about documents. He'll take what he wants."

"He'll take nothing but what I give him."

"He wants saddles and horses and cattle."

"He will have them. I am a generous man. I want no one to think me anything less than fair in my dealings with others, even savages."

"And the girl?"

"He can't have her."

Castro stood up. He was taller than Tomás and had to bend forward to look into his face. It was a trick Joseph had seen him use many times, just that way, standing close to someone, back hunched, eyes half closed, telling them what he wanted, what he would do, what he wouldn't do.

"Ten Elk is vicious," Tomás murmured.

"He can't have her," Castro said.

"Ten Elk wants her," Tomás replied. "Ten Elk will take her."

When Tomás was gone, Katrin came and sat on the needlepoint carpet at Castro's feet. She seemed unperturbed, was even humming as she leaned her head against Castro's knee.

"I do not think the threat of one Indian merits much attention," Castro said.

"I need not have come back," Joseph replied. "And I don't intend to stay. I've done my duty as I see it."

9

Castroville
July, 1848

JOSEPH LOOKED AROUND the room at the solemn-faced Alsatians waiting for the wedding ceremony to begin, the men's hands and faces scrubbed pink, hair patted down with water, the women stiff-backed in crinkled silks that had traveled with them from Alsace across the ocean to Texas. Castro's two sons, Angelo and Lorenzo, had arrived from Austin. Joseph thought fleetingly that if there were any justice in this world one of them ought to be standing where he was.

Katrin had asked Joseph if he would mind if a priest performed the ceremony, and Joseph told her it was all right with him, but he didn't think a priest would marry a Jew to a Catholic, which made her cry. Joseph couldn't figure out if she was crying because he had reminded her that he was a Jew or because a priest wouldn't marry them. It didn't matter, since it turned out the nearest priest was in San Antonio and Castro had to send word to Pastor Kaufman, the Lutheran minister in the German settlement a few miles to the east, that he was needed urgently. Pastor Kaufman, his black suit spotted and his beard powdered with road dust, had arrived on horseback, out of breath, with barely enough time to eat the lunch

Amelia Castro had prepared for him before the wedding guests began to arrive.

"We don't have much time," Joseph said to the clergyman. "We don't need much of a ceremony. I won't mind if there are one or two Jesuses for Katrin's sake, but I'd appreciate it if there isn't any more than that. And we needn't have any more conversation than is necessary about blissfulness and love and eternity. You understand that I'm only marrying Katrin to save her from capture by the Comanches, and I'm grateful you were able to come and perform the ceremony with only three days' notice, but I'd be more grateful if the ceremony is as short as possible because of the Indian problem that I just mentioned to you."

"I understand perfectly," Pastor Kaufman said. "Just this past week I presided at the funeral of a whole family ambushed by Indians on the road up from San Antonio."

"I don't think speeches about Indians are necessary," Castro said.

"I'm Catholic," Katrin said to the clergyman. She was paler than usual in her black gown and winged bonnet. "Will I be married in Christ's eyes?"

"I believe you will be," Pastor Kaufman replied, "and I hope you realize what a good deed Joseph is performing by marrying you." He cleared his throat and began the ceremony.

Joseph stared at the cloth-covered ceiling and tried not to listen to what the pastor was saying. It was incredible, unbelievable, probably the worst thing that could ever have happened to him. He not only didn't want to marry anyone, he particularly didn't want to marry Katrin. His life was over, finished. There was no possibility that he would ever be content with his lot again.

"You are married," Pastor Kaufman said.

Castro poured a mixture of French cognac and water into beer glasses while Amelia served cream cakes on delicate French dishes. Katrin sat on a chair and ate her cake as though she were a guest, and when anyone approached and called her Mrs. Kimmel, she looked at them in bewilderment. Joseph and Castro left the guests inside the house and walked out onto the porch where a dusty breeze was blowing across the yard.

"Last night I dreamed of Indians," Joseph said. "They were getting ready to take my scalp."

"I should have sent her back to Alsace," Castro said.

"All during the ceremony I felt the need to hop on a horse, any horse, and ride away."

"You're a man of great integrity, Joseph."

"I don't think I would have headed for San Antonio. Cities bring nothing but entanglements. Isaac's dead. I don't care about what's left of his business affairs."

"No one can fault you for your thoughts, but what you've done speaks of a great generosity of spirit."

"I think I'd have headed straight for Missouri. I'd have gathered up provisions and made my way to the mouth of the Bighorn and lost myself in the wilderness."

"You can take satisfaction in knowing that you've done a good thing."

"I don't know that I have, but I know that I did it. I've been circumspect all my life. Unencumbered. Solitary. Somehow I've lost sight of that in Texas. I've ruined my life. I'm a fool, an idiot caught by my own conscience and trapped by sympathies I never knew I had and I'm too stubborn to change my mind. That's plain. And don't keep thanking me for it."

"I meant no harm."

"And I apologize, I've been losing my temper a lot lately, just letting it fly and not paying much mind who it lands on. I'm sorry for that, and, despite all, I do thank you for all your courtesies. I've married her. I'm embarrassed to say that I have, but I have, and I'll bide by it and not complain again."

The wedding guests helped load furniture and gifts into the wagon and then everyone gathered in the yard to say good-bye. It had grown cold during the ceremony, and Katrin wrapped two thick shawls around her shoulders and climbed into the back of the wagon with the rest of the household goods. Joseph shook hands with Castro, and Katrin, who for the first time seemed to realize that she was going off somewhere with Joseph, started to cry. Amelia climbed into the wagon with her and tried to explain that brides always cried on their wedding day, that it was a normal thing, that it meant you realized you were leaving your old life behind and starting a new one.

That was when Joseph saw the Rangers riding down the main street in Castroville, heading toward Henry Castro's house. They sat erect in their saddles, their wide-brimmed hats tied beneath their chins, fancy spurs on their high-heeled boots and shiny badges pinned to the fronts of their flannel jackets. Their mustachioed captain, silver fringes on the sides of his goatskin chaps flickering in the sun, was riding a brown-spotted horse. Lying crosswise on the back of another horse was the slave who had stolen Joseph's belongings.

Everyone was stiffly in place. Castro, tall and somber-eyed, on the steps of his house. His sons, taller even than their father, standing protectively beside him. The Rangers majestic on their horses. The Alsatians off in their own tight cluster in the muddy yard. Amelia Castro standing in the wagon, the handkerchief she had been using to dry Katrin's tears trailing from her hand. Katrin, hatless in the morning gloom, crouched on the seat. The black man had been pulled off the horse and now lay in the dirt, hands and feet trussed before him like a pig's.

The head Ranger swung his leg over his horse and landed on his feet with a springy jump.

"Captain Hays, Texas Rangers," he said.

Castro came down the steps. "You missed a fine wedding ceremony," he said. "Had you come earlier, my wife would have had some wedding cake to give you. And what do you have there?

"A nigger," Captain Hays replied. "We found him sleepin' 'neath a tree not too far from here. He had a horse and provisions, and although I found no pistol, he may have hidden it when he heard us comin'. He could have murdered a few of you while you slept if we hadn't caught him."

Joseph felt the air vibrate as Castro turned toward him.

"Joseph?" Castro said.

Everyone assembled in the yard was now looking at Joseph.

"Joseph?" Castro said again.

Joseph looked up at the sky. He felt the weight of the world pulling him down, tying him up, pushing him into a box too small to take a breath in. Moments went by. Castro said his name again, and his voice echoed in the silence, clung to the fence posts, nipped at Joseph's heels.

Joseph strode forward through the mud. "I thought you were lost, Luck," he said. "I looked everywhere for you."

"He didn't say anything about being lost," the captain said. "Where did you lose him?"

"On the way here from Missouri."

"It seems hard to lose a nigger on the plains."

"Well, I did."

"Seems unlikely."

"I told you I did."

"He had a white man's belongeens. What would he be doin' with a white man's belongeens?"

"I gave him some of my things to carry."

Joseph knelt down, his knees nearly touching Luck's shoulder. He felt the man's muscles jerk with cold and fright. "How's your ankle, Luck? Good enough to walk on by now, I'd guess. And speechless at the sight of me, too, as I nearly am at the sight of you." He stood up. "This is my slave, and that's my horse. There's no mistake."

One of the Rangers untied the ropes binding Luck's hands and feet. The skin had burst where the rope had bitten in, and blood dripped steadily onto the dirt.

"He's been with my family since I was a boy," Joseph said. "I thought I'd never see him again."

* * *

THEY TRAVELED NORTH through the prairie, with the Guadalupe Mountains in the distance as their guide, Joseph driving the wagon, Luck sitting beside him with the flintlock in his lap. Katrin was perched on top of the featherbed, tinware banging against wooden table, and copper pots clanging against chairs and bed frame. She had been crying on and off during the day. When she wasn't crying, she was talking, asking Joseph when they were going to get where they were going, what they were going to eat, where they were going to sleep.

"I don't know the answer to any of those questions quite yet," Joseph told her.

"You got a plan?" Luck asked him.

"If I have one, it's to keep going until I can't go any farther and then stop."

"Like where you aim to do it?"

"Somewhere out there," he said and pointed to the endless roll of hill and prairie.

Joseph wanted to ask Luck where he had gone when he rode off on Joseph's horse, and how he came to be captured by the Rangers, but that kind of conversation had a way of getting out of hand, and Joseph didn't want any feelings of pity to prevent him from setting Luck loose when they reached the base of the mountains, where he intended to give him his own good boots and some provisions and tell him to start walking.

"Where are we now, Joseph?" Katrin asked.

"I don't know."

"We grow vegetable in Alsace, a green garden of vegetable," Katrin said. "Will we have vegetables, Joseph?"

"I suppose we will."

"And pork?"

"I suppose we will."

"I like to put pork in a pan and fry. Put in some honey. Pork in porridge, too, with milk, eat with good bread, fresh cheese, or maybe fry in a pan with dried peach. In Alsace in the summer we have fresh peach, in the winter we only have dried. And pork gravy. It make me so hungry to think on pork gravy, Joseph. I put wild honey in the pork juice and cook in the pan. I'm so hungry, Joseph. When will we eat?"

"Soon."

"I'll try to shoot us some birds," Luck said. The prairie was alive with animals. Buff- colored widgeons sleeked their feathers on dust-crusted ponds and jack rabbits hopped to the front and sides of the wagon wheels before bounding away over the dry grass. Meadow larks, doves, bluebirds, and plovers all took turns flying up out of the mottes of timber before skidding together across the sky. When a flock of grouse rose up out of the mesquite grass in front of the wagon, Luck took aim with the flintlock, fired off his shot, and two large birds fell out of the sky ahead of them.

At dusk, Joseph stopped the wagon beside a stream. Luck started a fire and got the birds plucked and ready for roasting.

"We're going our separate ways the first chance we get," Joseph told him. "I married Katrin and promised to take care of her, and that's a promise I intend to keep, but I made no such promise to you."

Katrin sat down on the ground and started to cry again.

"I don't know where we're going, Katrin, or what we're going to do when we get there," Joseph said, "but if you cry all the way, it won't do you any good, other than to make you sick."

"The Rangers will catch me quick out there without a horse," Luck said, and asked Katrin how she liked her meat cooked.

"I like so the skin is crisp and the meat is dry," Katrin said and wiped her eyes.

"You shouldn't mistake my concern for your life for a lifelong commitment to your upkeep," Joseph said to Luck. "You robbed me of my possessions and were gone with them for three years. I thought you were in Mexico, living free."

"I never got that far. I stayed close to San Antonio. I was haulin' firewood to the soldiers down in Laredo. I done tole them I was a freed man, and they never asked to see my papers. I was livin' free until the Rangers catched me. They said I was a slave the minute they laid eyes on me. I tole them I done bought the horse, and they wanted to see the paper for it, and I tole them I didn't have none, and that's how they come to bring me up to Castroville. But I been a freed man since the day I took off with your horse. I don't intend to be nothin' besides free no more."

"Well, you'll be free on your own, then," Joseph said.

No one spoke for a while. Luck busied himself with his cooking, and Katrin watched transfixed as the pale yellow skin of the birds turned brown.

"I cain't head for Mexico without no horse, anyway," Luck said when the birds were done. "And there's a good smell in Texas, like the dirt be good for farmin'."

It was all too much for Joseph. Katrin crying all day as if he had injured her in some way. Luck talking to him as if they were equals. He watched the prairie dogs flick out of their burrows and the cranes and quail and butter-ducks flutter across the tree-shrouded stream. A family of buffalo had gathered to watch them eat, dull eyes gazing stupidly, and suddenly Joseph had had enough.

"I don't intend to keep slaves," he said. "I want no part of it. I want no part of you."

"If you're thinkin' I'm going to Mexico, I ain't," Luck said, and he sliced the birds right there on the blanket beside the fire, and his hand didn't waver as he placed a biscuit and a portion of meat in Katrin's outstretched hands, and then did the same for Joseph.

"We had big garden in Alsace," Katrin said. "What kind vegetable you like to eat, Joseph?" She picked the bones out of the cooked birds with delicate fingers, lay the shredded meat on her lap until she had accumulated a small heap, then ate it all at once.

"If Captain Hays hadn't caught you, someone else would have," Joseph said.

"I like carrot and potato," said Katrin.

"And I wasn't the one who set you free."

"You was the one all right."

"And dumpling," Katrin said. She thought a moment. "And honey."

"And what'll we do if I let you come along?" Joseph said.

"We could trade buffalo hides for seed and git started that way," Luck said. "I know a lot 'bout growin' corn."

LUCK WAS ASLEEP on the ground near the fire, wrapped in a blanket, and Katrin was in the wagon. She was crying again. Joseph couldn't understand it. She had eaten her fill, had talked about vegetable gardens in Alsace, had said good-night, put on her black hat, wrapped her shawl around her, climbed in the wagon and started to cry. Joseph could see clearly now what all the years ahead of him would be.

"August was always saying he will take care of me," Katrin said when Joseph climbed into the wagon and lay down beside her. "And then he die in Galveston and leave me alone."

"People get left alone all the time," Joseph said. "I was left alone when I was a boy. My father brought me and my brother Isaac to New York from Poland. I was six. Isaac was thirteen. My father went back to get my mother. I never saw him again."

"Maybe you leave me, too."

"I won't."

She blew her nose, and Joseph wondered if there was a chance that he could ever grow to love her. Books were shot through with stories of men and women pairing up out of love, and Joseph had always wondered how that felt, if the sensation was akin to craving food or sleep. He certainly didn't feel anything of any particular note for Katrin. When she was quiet, like now, and made no fuss, he found her bearable. And she wasn't truly ugly in the way someone with a deformed jaw or crossed-eyes might be. Her eyes and nose were swollen and red from crying, but they weren't always that way. Sometimes when he looked at her he thought she might even be a little pretty.

He turned on his side and put his arm around her. "I'm not a virgin," he said, "but I carry no diseases that I know of. I often visited a woman in Kansas City. She kept herself very clean, and I never heard of any sickness connected with anyone who visited her. I don't expect you to do things like she did, but if you keep from crying, I'll be satisfied. And if you don't want to do anything, we can just sleep together like brother and sister. I don't suppose you were any more willing to have this marriage than I was, and it won't hurt me in the least if you tell me you'll have none of what men and women do when they're married."

"Oh, Joseph," she said and put her arms around his neck. He didn't have any great urge to touch her or hold her, but she was his wife, and since he was quite sure he wasn't going to have another one, he lowered his trousers down nearly to the tops of his mud-caked boots, then lifted her skirts and slid them along her knees till they reached her thighs.

"I'll just ask you not to talk," he said. "If you don't say anything, it'll be fine."

The opening was small, and he tried not to hurt her, but she was crying again, and he told her that if he could just push a little harder he would get the job done and it would be over. He heard Luck get up and poke at the fire with a stick, and he got to thinking about Luck and the conversation they had had, and he hoped he'd be gone in the morning so there would be no need to tell him good-bye later.

Katrin seemed more relaxed now, almost limp, but then she started to howl, and Joseph thought he'd just quit, since he had begun to feel like he was working too hard at it. It might even have been the hardest job he had ever had. And the moment he thought that, his penis began to grow smaller and smaller. He would have quit for certain then, but Katrin's fingers were biting into his neck and he felt committed to what he had started, as if it were a task he had set himself, and so he closed his eyes tight and conjured up a vision of the whorehouse in Kansas City, of the veranda where the girls sat in their underwear, where no one talked much, where the act between himself and the woman he always chose was quick and made him feel dirty but pleased afterwards, and once the vision was firm in his mind he felt his penis enlarging again, and he slipped inside Katrin, and it was easier now. Then the wagon began to bounce, and all the goods in it were rattling, and he almost forgot where he was it felt so good to be doing what he was doing. And suddenly it was all over, and all Joseph could hear was the spit of the fire, and he waited for her to start crying again. But she didn't. She was very quiet for a few moments, and then she pulled her skirts back down and snuggled against him, her head right in the crook of his arm.

He stared up at the night sky. The stars were out. There'd be no rain tomorrow with the stars so bright in the sky.

"Ten Elk will forget about coming after us when enough time's gone by," he said, "and then we'll go to San Antonio and see what's left of my brother's business interest. I'll buy you something pretty. Maybe a bracelet to match your locket."

He felt warm lying beside her. Comfortable. She wasn't as bad as he thought. He would treat her as if she were one of his students. He would educate her.

She kissed his cheek. "Do you love me, Joseph?"

"And about going back to Missouri, I've been thinking about that, and I don't think I could go back to sitting in a classroom that smells of boys, with no mountains to look at and nothing to dream about and just give the same lessons over and over when there's all this land in Texas."

"Do you, Joseph?" She had put her hand in his and was holding tight to his fingers.

"It doesn't have to be a bracelet," he said. "I could buy you a ring, a little gold one with a stone in it."

He wasn't angry now. He just felt sad. He had missed out on something the books all said was the finest thing a man could experience. He'd never have it now. He'd never know what it was to love a woman the way the books said a man could. No matter how much he tried, he'd never love her that way. He felt it deep inside himself, and the sadness he felt made him want to weep.

"I don't know what love is," he said.

"But I love you, Joseph."

"From what I've read, it takes two people."

She began to whimper.

"I'll try to be a good husband. You're my wife now, and whether I love you or not, we'll both have to make the best of it."

The next morning Luck boiled some coffee and fried a batch of cornmeal for their breakfast, and Joseph thought that maybe it wasn't such a bad idea having someone who could take care of the cooking, especially when Katrin talked a lot about food but didn't seem to know how to go about preparing it.

"Smells good, the coffee," she said, and got out of the wagon. Joseph noticed that she walked with her legs apart and when she went behind a tree at the edge of the clearing she stayed there a long time.

When they started out again, the sky was gray, and the air, warm and windless the day before, had turned frigid. Just before it grew dark, a cluster of chinked-mud shacks appeared on the horizon, their cooking fires striping the sky with purple plumes of ash.

"Look like a camp," Luck said.

"Mexicans," Joseph said. "Indians don't camp out in the open that way. And they put up tepees, not shacks."

"I never been so sleepy before," Katrin said, and she wrapped herself in a blanket and burrowed into the featherbed and went to sleep.

"A man is comin' on horseback," Luck said. "Could be one of them Rangers comin' to get me."

"No, it isn't. It's that damn Tomás."

Joseph clucked to the horses, and the animals picked up their pace. Then he whipped their backs and they began to gallop. The wagon rocked from side to side, and the wooden wheels rattled so hard Joseph thought they were going to fall off.

"Where do we race to, Joseph?" Katrin was sitting up now and sliding from one end of the wagon to the other. "You shake me to pieces and break our furniture. We won't have nothing to start with if you keep up this way."

"Just lie back down and try to hold on," he said.

Tomás caught up with them along about the time the horses began to falter.

"You stole my commission on her," Tomás hollered.

"I married her. She's my wife now."

"You broke your word."

"I never gave it," Joseph said and pulled the horses to a stop.

"My crystal cups!" Katrin said, and she began digging through the boxes until she found the one that held the blue goblets Amelia and Henry Castro had given her and Joseph for a wedding present.

"*Gringos* have no respect for anyone's rights but their own," Tomás said. "They make promises, but don't keep them. The Indians were here first. The Mexicans respect the Indians, honor them and their ways. You *gringos* come with your plows and seed and take away the land."

Katrin was examining each one of the goblets, checking the lips and the sides, running her fingers across the bottoms.

"What have you got in that wagon?" Tomás said, peering over the wooden rails. "Ten Elk will kill you for certain, I can promise you that. He wanted the girl. He has it in his mind, and when a Comanche has something in his mind . . ." Tomás stepped into the wagon and began poking through things, picking up pots, eyeing quilts and bolts of cloth and embroidered pillows. "I told him you can't trust *gringos*, they'll cheat you every time. I should kill you myself for cheating me out of my commission."

"Those is my wedding present," Katrin said. "Joseph, stop him. He's making some ruin out of everything."

Joseph climbed up onto the wagon seat and stared into the tall grass. Did he just see some movement? Were Ten Elk's braves hidden there, waiting for the right moment to show themselves?

"You steal from Ten Elk and he won't forget it," Tomás said. He was going through all the things in the wagon as if they were his. "What's this in the box?"

"Those is my wedding cups," Katrin told him.

"I'm a freed man," Luck said when Tomás glanced up at him, "so don't look at me like you think you done found something to sell, because I'm free."

"I don't deal in slaves," Tomás said and went back to rummaging in the wagon.

Joseph sat back down again, the reins loose in lap. "You've looked in the wagon long enough."

Tomás had hold of the wooden box with the four crystal wine goblets in it.

"I'll take these," he said. "It's the only thing you have that's worth anything. It won't pay me for everything I lost, but I'll be satisfied."

"Those cups is mine," Katrin said, and she snatched the box away from Tomás and tucked it under her shawl.

Joseph thought that if the Indians were going to attack, now was the time they'd do it. He turned his head toward the west where the setting sun had stained the clouds a bright red. He scanned the prairie for painted faces. But he didn't see any, and all he heard was the squeaking of the wagon as Katrin stood up. He looked over at her, and Tomás did, too. Katrin had taken the box with the goblets in it from beneath her shawl. She looked at the box for one long moment, gave a shuddery little sigh, and then handed it to Tomás.

"Do you have any food over in that town there, Tomás?" she asked. She pointed to where the purple plumes of smoke were spiraling into the graying sky. "I'm very hungry."

The Mexican settlement was not like Castroville. It had no gardens, and the houses had barely enough mud on them to keep the twigs standing upright. There was an enclosure for horses, but no cattle grazed nearby. Prairie dogs had dug their burrows into the mud-dried street so that the way was pitted with sinkholes and sand traps and muddy depressions that collapsed when a foot or wheel touched them. Chickens and pigs wandered among the craters, and dark-eyed children stood in the dark doorways of the *jacales* and stared at the wagon as it passed.

Tomás took them to a thatch-roofed cantina at the end of the rutted street.

"This is my little place," Tomás said. "I built it with my own hands, put up every crooked board. Henry Castro doesn't own the prairie and he can't come here and tell me what to do."

The stars shone through the holes in the reed ceiling, but the interior was in hazy darkness, lit only by wax candles that hung on the walls and a fire that blazed in the far corner of the room. Men in big-brimmed hats and blanket coats jostled each other for an inch or two of space at the gaming tables, maybe only room enough for a shoulder, maybe a whole arm, enough space to squeeze out a place to stand, a slice of smoky air big enough to push a few fingers through and throw down a heap of Spanish dollars or a stack of gold pieces on games of Monte. Tired-looking women in tiered skirts, their hair piled high beneath lacy mantillas, danced the fandango, chins tucked into their shoulders, hips thrust forward, high heels pounding narrow holes in the dirt floor, back and forth over the same spot, little bits of dirt shooting out from beneath their feet, while a scruffy-looking band of musicians stood in a row against one wall and scratched out a squeaky accompaniment on their violins.

Tomás cleared a place for them at a long table, and a Mexican woman came and placed steaming plates of beans and flat round cakes in front of them. Tomás said the cakes were called tortillas and he showed Katrin how to fold the beans into them and eat the whole thing together.

"See, Joseph, how good this pancake hold the food, without a drip, too," Katrin said.

"Now that Ten Elk is after you, where will you go?" Tomás asked as he poured rum into spotted glasses.

"Toward the Guadalupe range," Joseph said.

"I will learn to make these little cake, too," Katrin said. She had a brown line of mashed beans across her upper lip.

Tomás poured some liquor into a glass and gave it to Luck. "Where do you come from?" he asked him.

"Virginia," Luck replied. "I was with a family name of Stewart. I might still if I didn't go and take my chance and jump off the wagon when Mr. Stewart wasn't lookin'."

"He isn't going any farther with me than the mountains," Joseph said.

The Mexican woman was back with two more heaping plates of beans and round cakes. Katrin was eating greedily now, scooping up the beans with her fingers and dropping them onto the tortillas, not rolling them the way Tomás showed her, but kind of holding them flat in her hand and nibbling first at the edges and then putting the whole thing into her mouth. Watching her, Joseph realized he was hungry himself, and he picked up one of the round cakes and rolled it around some beans, and didn't even notice that Tomás had disappeared.

AURELIA PINCHED A BIT of cornmeal *masa,* then mashed it into a ball, rolling it in her hands first on one side and then the other until the warmth of her fingers melted the paste enough so that she could feel it begin to move. This little bit was ready now, and she flattened it out between her palms, clapping her hands together until the meal felt as thin as a piece of paper, then gave it a little twirl before she laid it carefully out on the hot stone with the others.

The cooking was done across the garbage ditch from the cantina in a kitchen that was nothing more than an open-air pavilion with a reed roof and open fire pits. The music in the cantina was very loud tonight, and Aurelia couldn't keep her feet still, but would every once in a while make a few taps on the dirt floor with her bare feet. Tomás had given her a pair of leather boots, but she didn't wear them. They had pearl buttons and the leather was finer than any she had ever seen, but they had little red stains on the lining. She asked Tomás if he got the boots from the Comanches, and he told her that all shoes were the same, no matter where they came from, and she told him she'd rather go barefoot than wear a dead woman's shoes.

Yolanda was playing in the dirt at Aurelia's feet, making dirt tortillas on a broken piece of crockery. She was almost three years old. A good child. She didn't move from Aurelia's side in the cantina kitchen. She didn't cry. She didn't even have to sleep until it was time for Aurelia to go into the *jacal* where the other women slept, and then she would lie down in the hammock tucked into Aurelia's *rebozo,* and the two of them would sleep until morning.

Aurelia could smell the smoke that drifted out through the holes in the walls of the cantina and hung like a milky cloud over the ditch where the garbage was thrown. There was always a smell in the kitchen of smoke and garbage, but when the wind was blowing a certain way, like it was tonight, there was also the reek of urine-soaked ground from all those men who didn't walk out into the prairie to relieve themselves, but just stepped out the rear door of the cantina, unbuttoned their trousers and peed.

Two women were tending their iron pots over the open fires, stirring with big wooden-handled spoons, their faces and hair wet and shiny from the steam. A young girl washed dishes in a bucket, lifting the dirty plates in and out of the gray water, then wiping them off with the same rag she used to wipe her face and nose.

Aurelia pulled another piece of *masa* from the big ball that lay on the work table. She woke at dawn every day and soaked the corn until it was soft and then ground it into a stiff paste. She had always made tortillas at home, and she liked the rhythm of it, the way her fingers worked the *masa*, the way it felt against her skin. She knew just how far to stretch the cornmeal paste without tearing it.

The stone was nice and hot. Aurelia slipped a tortilla onto it, then pinched another piece of *masa* and patted it between her hands.

There were eight tortillas nearly done on the hot stone, their centers puffing up. She watched until the puffs rose to half the width of the tortillas, then deftly dropped the raw cake onto the stone, scooped up the puffed-up ones and slipped them into the basket and covered them with a cloth.

Tomás was coming toward the kitchen, walking down the dirt path that paralleled the ditch, then stepping onto the plank that ran across it. He never came to the kitchen in the evening unless it was to tell the women stirring the pots that they had put too much ground chile in the beans.

He was in the kitchen now, his hand in the basket of tortillas. The puffs of air had escaped, and the cakes lay atop one another in flat rounds. She watched him try to peel them apart. One tore, and then another one. When tortillas were hot, sometimes they stuck together and had to be separated carefully. Big, thick fingers like Tomás's only tore them. Slender fingers like Aurelia's could part them without ripping an edge or punching a hole in the middle or tearing them in two. He handed her the basket, and she peeled one out without the slightest tear and handed it to him.

"I've found someone who will take you and Yolanda," he said.

Aurelia stared across the ditch to the cantina. She couldn't see past the veil of smoke hanging in the open doorway.

"A man from Castroville," Tomás said. He was afraid of her and chose his words carefully. "A Jew named Joseph. Ten Elk wanted a blond girl in Castroville, and Joseph married her because the Indian was going to take her. He didn't like her, but he married her, anyway. He has a slave with him he doesn't want either."

Tomás had been afraid of Aurelia since he brought her here and had tried to sell her to a man hauling potatoes from Mexico, a grizzled man with dirt-stained hands and garlic breath. She had stood in the dirt in front of the cantina on that blistery day in June, Yolanda in her arms, and refused to go. "I will plant myself right here, Tomás. I will plant myself and turn into a tree, but I won't go with him," she had said. But Tomás had already put her small bag on the hauler's wagon and put Yolanda on the wagon seat and had the hauler's silver coins in his pocket. "I won't go," Aurelia said, and she pulled Yolanda off the wagon and spit in Tomás' face. It startled him, and he stepped back two steps, stared at her for a moment and then started to laugh.

"You've got spit, but no magic," he had said. "I've been waiting to see some, and you haven't shown me anything yet. Now is the time, Aurelia. Show me your magic." He had laughed again and was about to say something to the hauler when Aurelia began to scream. It was a weak scream at first that made Tomás turn toward her, surprise in his face. She screamed more loudly and the hauler grimaced and Tomás covered his ears. She screamed until the scream felt as if it would tear her body apart. Yolanda began to howl, and the sky turned black and the rain came down in torrents and filled the hauler's wagon with water. Potatoes floated out of the wagon and littered the prairie, and Aurelia and Yolanda screamed so fiercely, so savagely, that the hauler and Tomás bent over in pain. Since then Tomás had been afraid of Aurelia and considered his words carefully before he spoke.

"He's going to farm up near the Guadalupe mountains," Tomás said now. "You can make him take you with him. His wife has a featherbed and dishes and cups. Your life will be better than it is here. Will you go with him?"

"I'll have to see him first," she said.

Tomás led her to a table in the rear of the cantina.

The man, the one Tomás called Joseph, was thin and very tall, with sturdy shoulders beneath his sunburned neck. His wife, her face nearly hidden by a floppy black hat, was sickly looking. The Negro, as dark as the soot-covered walls, seemed isolated in one dark shadowy corner of the table.

"If she decides to go with you, you'll be a fortunate man," Tomás said to Joseph. "She can cook for you and sew. You won't have to pay her. Just feed her and the baby. Neither one of them eats much. Twenty silver dollars and the two of them are yours."

"It doesn't matter what she decides," Joseph said. "I don't want her. I don't know what makes you think I'm in the business of picking up people who have no place to go. I won't take her or the child."

"If she decides to go with you, you can give her and the child to the black man if you want to," Tomás said. "Where you're going, no one will see them together anyway. Look at him, how he's looking at her now." He turned to Luck. "She looks pretty, doesn't she?"

"A man's lucky to have a wife," Luck said. "Mine was sold away from me and sent to Kentucky. I heard she died."

"If it pleases Aurelia, you can have her," Tomás said.

"You've been meddling in my business too long, Tomás," Joseph said.

Tomás was whispering to Aurelia now. He wanted to know her answer, and she told him she wasn't sure, that Joseph looked so angry she could see the anger bubbling under his skin.

"I'm not taking Luck with me anywhere," Joseph said, "and she can't come either."

"What name does this nice little girl have?" Katrin asked.

"Yolanda," Aurelia replied.

"Such a pretty little girl."

Aurelia put her arm around Yolanda and drew her closer.

"We can't take every person we see with us, Katrin," Joseph said.

"She can cook," Tomás said. "She speaks Spanish and English and some Comanche. She can sew. I changed my mind. Ten silver dollars. It's a bargain."

"No."

"Five."

"No.

Tomás sighed. "You are a hard businessman, Joseph. I'll tell you what I'll do. If she decides to go with you, I'll give her to you, because you're my friend. You don't have to pay me anything."

And then he told Joseph about Willie and all the bad things he did to Aurelia, and how he got killed fighting Ten Elk and left Aurelia and Yolanda without anyone.

"This is getting to be too much to listen to," Joseph said.

"She can work hard," Tomás said. "She can carry water and chop wood and plant vegetables. Some people say she cures fevers. I never saw it, but maybe she does. And if you don't take her someone else will."

"I said I won't take her."

Tomás sat down at the table and began drawing a little map on the stained cloth.

"If you follow the Guadalupe River over the pass, there are lots of Comanche up there. And Tonkaway, too." Tomás was making all kinds of little arrows and lines to show Joseph the way. Joseph kept saying he didn't want her and Tomás acted as if Joseph were just a flea on his arm and kept talking.

"The Tonkaway are bitter enemies of the Comanche, but they'll be friendly to you," Tomás said. "They think the white man is going to help them get rid of the Comanches. No one tells the Tonkaway that the Comanche will get rid of the white man first. See these mountains here, you don't want to go too far north. The Comanches sometimes camp on the upper plateaus when they're hunting. Just keep to the southwest, but not so far that you're more than a week's ride from here. I was in Ten Elk's camp a few days ago and saw a white prisoner. Ten Elk's braves captured him after they killed everyone else in his wagon train. The man was as tall as you are, Joseph, but not as thin. They planted him in the dirt like a sapling."

"He tells a lie about the Comanches, Joseph, doesn't he?" Katrin said. She had turned pale while Tomás was talking. He shoved a glass of rum toward her, and she lifted it to her lips, coughing as the liquid struck her throat.

"There was dirt all around him, with nothing sticking up except his head," Tomás said. "They scalped him, then cut off his lips, eyelids, nose and ears. They danced around him for a while, singing songs and enjoying his screaming. Then they left him. The Comanches know how to make dying last for eight days. The cool nights will revive him, and in the daytime the sun will scorch his lidless eyes and the flies will lay their eggs in them. If you're going out into the Staked Plains, you should know these things. I have a Comanche wife, and she told me more than one time how much she enjoys watching torture. Comanche cruelty is in the blood."

"I said I'm not taking her," Joseph said. "People can't be bought and sold, Tomás."

Aurelia could see the Guadalupe Mountains from the door of the cantina on days when the sun had burned the mist away. Velvety smooth green contours touching the clouds. Magical mountains where no one lived, where there were no cantinas, no men to pee in a ditch or stagger drunkenly into the cantina kitchen and hang their arms over her shoulders or try to kiss her or pull up her skirts. Tomás had given her a knife and told her to cut anyone who came into the kitchen that she didn't want in the kitchen. She made a bloody gash on a man's neck, and Tomás said he didn't want her killing his customers and took the knife away. Now she hid behind the sacks of maize when the men staggered in. She held Yolanda tight and put sugar in her mouth to keep her quiet, and didn't move until the men were gone. Yolanda was no longer a baby, and soon sugar wouldn't keep her quiet. And this man, this Joseph, his unwanted wife and slave at his side, sat stubbornly refusing to reveal his goodness.

"Yes," Aurelia said.

Joseph glanced at Tomás. "What did she say?"

"She said she'll go with you."

"I told you, I don't want her."

"The two of them don't eat much," Tomás said.

Joseph shook his head. Tomás had stopped talking. The noise of the cantina seemed to recede into the dark. Aurelia could feel the cool air of the Guadalupes as vividly as if she had reached the top.

She could cast no spell on Joseph, had no herbs that would bewitch him, no curses that would threaten him. Screams would be of no use to her with this man. She looked at the dirt floor and at the gaps in the walls and at the pity in the Negro's eyes and decided to cry. She held her breath and squeezed her eyes shut and blinked, but nothing came. She thought of her brothers and sisters and the empty rooms in the house in Laredito and slowly began to weep. Tears fell down her cheeks and onto her bare feet. A cascade of tears poured onto the table and pooled in the dirty cups. She marveled at the quantity of her tears and trembled at their force. All the tears she had never shed were now a torrent turning the dirt floor to mud. Tears had never come easily to her, but now she couldn't stop them. It was as if she had unleashed a river that would wash the cantina and everything in it away.

"Oh, Joseph," Katrin said.

10

It was a crazy thing to do, letting that girl and her child come along. All morning long, driving the wagon through the prairie, Joseph stewed over it. What made him do it? How could he be so dumb as to take on another two people when he didn't want the two he already had? If he ran into anyone else out on the prairie, he could see now he wouldn't even hesitate or ask them a single question about where they'd been or where they were going. He'd say, *Hop on,* and take them, too.

It was the strangest thing the way he was acting lately, making everyone else's pain his own. Why, in Missouri a boy could stand all day in a corner for not doing his lesson and Joseph wouldn't feel a bit sorry for him, or even look in his direction. Once in a while he'd ask if he wanted a glass of water or needed to relieve himself, but that was about it. He'd known how to keep himself separate in Missouri. And he especially couldn't remember having so much sympathy for someone else's misfortune that he'd say, *Come with me, I'll take care of you.*

And sharing his belongings with people? He couldn't remember that ever happening. Oh, yes, that time he gave five dollars to a man who lived in the same rooming house he did. The man said he needed it for his sick mother in Virginia. And even then Joseph wasn't taken in by the man, and was sure he didn't have a mother, and that if he did she wasn't sick, and since Joseph had an infallible ear for American accents he was more than certain the man wasn't even from Virginia. But he gave him the money, anyway, and told him to keep it, figuring that any man who had to invent a story about a sick mother in order to get five dollars was in pretty sorry shape. But that wasn't anything like this, four strangers riding along with him, waiting for him to make decisions, depending on him, looking at him the way the Alsatians looked at Henry Castro.

So how did it happen? There had to be a reason. In Missouri, with the exception of Sunday dinners at the headmaster's house, he had been pretty good at keeping himself out of entanglements with people. He was always polite when someone invited him to supper, and would send a note telling them he had lessons to prepare or he had a bad cold. He would then tell himself they wouldn't have liked his company, anyway, that it wouldn't have taken two minutes before they saw him for the mean-tempered person he was. There was only so long he could talk to people before they found that out.

Reading was what Joseph had done a lot of in Missouri. No need to have to worry about what living people were saying to you when you could sit in a comfortable chair and read about long-ago dead ones. But then Isaac had gone and died in San Antonio and Cyril McCorkle wrote Joseph that letter.

If he had to make a guess, he'd say it was Texas, is what it was. He didn't seem to be able to say no to anything in Texas. It was as if he had been some kind of empty jug in Missouri just waiting till he got to Texas to get filled up.

Sure, get up on top of the wagon, he'd probably say to anyone else he ran across. *Make yourself comfortable. Sit on the table there in back of Aurelia.* Aurelia. She was in a corner of the wagon to his right, so he didn't have to turn around on the seat to see her. All he needed to do was look out the right side of the wagon, maybe check to see if the clouds meant rain (in a casual way, of course, so not even Luck would know what he was doing) and there she'd be, round face beneath lustrous black hair, and eyebrows that were like two bold streaks of black silk above her honey-colored eyes. "She's a witch," Tomás said when Katrin was helping Aurelia and Yolanda into the wagon. "She can cure you with a look. She knows herb medicine and will fix anything that hurts. You've got to be careful with her, though. She can figure things out and get what she wants with tricks and spells and you won't know she's doing it until it's done. A witch will come in handy when you're dealing with Indians, because you're going to see Indians, Joseph, you can count on it. Aurelia will know what to do. She lived with the Comanches."

Joseph didn't believe in witches or curses or spells, and didn't think that Aurelia crying the way she did was any different from the way Katrin sometimes cried. Of course, it was louder and there seemed to be more tears, and it didn't seem as if they'd ever stop, but it certainly wasn't witchcraft. Katrin felt sorry for her was why he agreed to take her along, that's all it was. But he did wonder if Aurelia could give him some of her herb medicine for the twinges he had been feeling in the pit of his stomach. They started about the time she climbed up onto the wagon. He thought it might be the Mexican food he had eaten in the cantina, or it might possibly be the onset of catarrh, since his throat did feel tight, and he could swear that his forehead was more than a little warm.

They traveled all morning. By noon the limestone rocks strewn over the scrubby ground had grown more numerous and glinted explosively in the sun's glare. As the iron wheels rolled over them, the wagon squealed as if in pain.

When they reached the tree-shaded banks of the Guadalupe River, everyone got down from the wagon and dipped their cups into the blue-tinged water that ran like a transparent sheet over the smooth stones. In some spots branches had dammed it up so it was as green as the sedge grass that grew along the banks. Joseph felt the strongest urge to step into the water and let it carry him downstream. He had once floated a canoe down the Mississippi all the way to Tennessee, not even trapping, doing nothing but enjoying the way it felt to be shoved along by the currents, thinking about nothing but the way the water sparkled, the way it changed colors depending on whether the sun was high or low in the sky. He wished he were on a canoe on the Mississippi now and didn't have four strangers clinging to him

Luck watered the horses and wiped them down. Katrin daydreamed beneath the delicate moss curtain hanging from the branches of the liveoak trees. Joseph settled himself on the bank away from Katrin and stared out into the river as though watching the water birds in flight above the trees. He was actually watching Aurelia. She had stepped barefoot across the black river stones, Yolanda snug against her hip, the water swirling Aurelia's cotton petticoats around her ankles. She dipped Yolanda in the water and ran river water through her hair and washed her feet and hands and tickled her stomach.

She wasn't particularly beautiful. Not beautiful like some of the women in Independence, who had pink cheeks and delicate airs, and wore gowns that showed off their narrow waists. She wore a shapeless chemise and other than the gold-colored flecks in her eyes, there was nothing striking about her. She looked unfinished, almost wild, the way her hair streamed out around her face, and yet he was compelled to look at her every chance he got. He couldn't help comparing her to Katrin. Katrin's hair was limp and lusterless. She had no color in her cheeks. And although she had stopped crying entirely since Aurelia and her child had joined them, she now talked continuously, with hardly a breath in between subjects. He could hear her all morning telling Aurelia about August. *Such a good brother he was. He had the fever on the boat, and I say to him, August, we are here, it is Texas, get up and come with me, and he say to me, Katrin, don't forget me and say your prayers. And I pull him by the arm and I say to him, August, don't go away, but he say to me, I have to because I'm dying, and he did. Right then. And I see a bright light in his eyes like the Holy Spirit is in him already.*

The only thing Joseph heard Aurelia say was, *I've tried to cure people of the cholera. Sometimes they got well and sometimes they died. I always looked into their eyes, and I always saw something there, but I don't think it was the Holy Spirit."*

Yolanda sat on the bank now while Aurelia swam out to the middle of the river where it was the darkest and lay on her back, her eyes closed and her black hair floating around her.

"If it's all right with you, I want her," Luck said.

"I don't know if it's all right."

"Why ain't it?"

"It just isn't."

"You heard what that Tomás said."

"I don't care what Tomás said. It isn't right."

"No one care what I do if they don't see me do it. We gwine be too far from any white folk for them to see."

"Maybe she doesn't want you. Did she say she did?"

"No, but she need someone takin' care of her and her chile. You kin see she ain't gwine make it without she's got someone. Tomás say I can have her if no one want her. Well, I want her."

They started out again, and Joseph could hear Katrin telling Aurelia about the vegetables she was going to plant when they got to the place Joseph was taking them to, about her wedding day, about the cream cake Amelia Castro served the guests.

"It was because of some Comanche Indian we get married," Katrin said. "I will never marry a Jew if I am in Alsace."

"I never met a Jew before," Aurelia said.

"You never know who is Jew and who is not Jew. But Joseph, he is a good one, anyhow."

Aurelia looked about nineteen. Old enough to know what she wanted. And there was no sign that she wanted Luck.

"I was very sick when I come to Texas," Katrin was saying. "But now I eat all the time, and soon I will be very fat and healthy."

Maybe Luck meant he wanted Aurelia to sew his clothes and cook his food. That didn't sound very likely. A slave needing someone to do things for him. There was no question but that he wanted her the way a man wants a wife.

"You asked me if you could have Aurelia," Joseph said to him now.

"I did," Luck said.

"Well, I've always had the idea that words mean different things to different people. When I was teaching in Missouri I used to wonder if I was even speaking the same language as the boys in my class. Boys' minds, after all, are on what they are going to do when the school day's over, what mischief they can get into, what work they can get out of. And here I was trying to push history into their heads, as if they were so many geese in need of fattening up. I used to ask myself sometimes why they needed to know history, anyway. Would they thank me for it when they were grown? Would they even remember where Rome was? Do you mean you want Aurelia like a wife, like I have Katrin? Is that what you mean?"

"That's what I mean," Luck told him.

AURELIA COULDN'T REMEMBER when anyone had paid her as much attention as Katrin did. *Eat some more cornbread,* Katrin said. *Drink some more cider.* She fussed over Yolanda, wanted to kiss her all the time. She gave Aurelia the roomiest corner of the wagon, and when the wind got too cold for a light wool *serape* over bare arms, she wrapped Aurelia in one of her own quilts. It had blue-and-white starbursts all over it, and Katrin said she had crocheted it for Amelia Castro, but kept it when Joseph said he'd marry her.

Aurelia liked her, liked the way she played with Yolanda. She knew Katrin's bones must have ached as bad as her own from all the bouncing they got in the wagon, but she never complained.

"I cry all the time before you came," Katrin told her.

And Luck must have been the happiest person Aurelia had ever seen. He walked around looking as if just breathing was the finest thing he could imagine. And he talked to Yolanda as if she were grown up and understood every word he said. When she grabbed hold of his nose with her pudgy hand, he laughed until he couldn't catch his breath. And he rivaled Katrin in the attention he paid Aurelia. *Are you getting cold back there in the wagon? Do you want to ride up here with me and Joseph? Do you want to stop and rest? Are you hungry? Are you thirsty?*

As for Joseph, she knew he had been watching her from the wagon seat all day, but he hadn't talked to her since they started out. She knew what his looking at her meant. She had known it would happen, but she hadn't planned out in her mind what she would do about it.

They followed the river all day, and in late afternoon Joseph stopped the wagon again.

"This is as good a place to stay the night as anywhere."

Luck said, "We should maybe travel some more before dark."

"We've traveled far enough for one day," Joseph said.

Katrin was out of the wagon first, holding her arms out so Aurelia could hand Yolanda down to her. Joseph usually helped them down from the wagon, but he didn't this time, just grabbed the flintlock, said he was going to see if he could shoot some supper, and left them there. Luck had already unharnessed the horses and was leading them down to the river. He wouldn't have helped Katrin or Aurelia out of the wagon even if he weren't busy with the horses. Aurelia noticed that he talked to her and Katrin, but he wouldn't touch them, not even to take their hands. Katrin tucked her skirts between her legs, hung onto the side rail of the wagon, and as if she were a strong boy jumped down. It made Aurelia smile. When Joseph was around, she would act as helpless as Yolanda. And look now how she was carrying that heavy cooking pot and not even asking Aurelia to take one end of it.

There were a few twigs lying beneath the trees, and while Katrin brought out the dishes and laid them on the ground, Aurelia started the fire. She could see Joseph walking along the river, his flintlock held loosely at his side, his eyes cast down.

"We'll need more wood," she said to Katrin.

Katrin was mixing the batter for the biscuits and didn't look up.

ALTHOUGH THE SUN hadn't completely left the sky, it was almost night on the patch of grass where they sat, the tall grass brushing their faces and only enough light for Aurelia to make out the outlines of Joseph's face.

"You shouldn't be walking without shoes when it's this cold," Joseph said. "If I had any notion we weren't traveling north, the cold nights would tell me different. Didn't Tomás see to it that you had shoes on your feet?"

"The Indians take shoes from the settlers, take them right off their feet after they kill them. I didn't want to wear the shoes he gave me," Aurelia said. "It made me feel like the dead woman's feet were still in them. Did you shoot anything for supper?"

"I wasn't trying."

"There are partridges down along the river. I saw them."

"I just keep going over and over what's happened, trying to make sense out of it. When I was younger, my brother Isaac was always telling me that I'd never be a happy man until I got to know people better. People are what make life interesting, Joseph, he would say to me. I'm not sure I wasn't better off when I kept to myself. It's more complicated being with people than reading about them in books. Everyone liked Isaac. He told stories and jokes and could play the flute. If he were alive, he'd laugh to see what's happened to me. He'd say I've lost my mind, that you don't just jump into being with people like you jump into the river. He'd have called me crazy for taking on four strangers when I don't even know where I'm going or what I'm going to do when I get there."

"Why do you watch me?" she said.

"What?"

"You watch me all the time. I see how you look at me."

"I don't know what you're talking about. I've got a wife."

"When I'm in the wagon, and when I get out of the wagon, when I eat, when I drink, you look at me."

"I look at everyone the same."

"Katrin will see you looking at me."

"Katrin? I sure don't know what Katrin thinks, and as for you, the only reason I brought you along was because you were crying and Katrin couldn't stand it. I'd have had Katrin crying the whole way to the mountains if I hadn't brought you with us."

"You brought me with you because you wanted to."

"You're saying you put a spell on me?" Joseph chuckled and rubbed his chin with his hand. "Well, I'll tell you right now, I don't believe in witches and I only brought you along because Katrin asked me to. So you have to stop talking about me the way you've been talking."

"Soon Katrin will notice the way you look at me, and she'll hate me and Yolanda will suffer."

"Katrin can't hate anyone. She doesn't know how. Everyone and everything is the same to her. And you're mistaken about me. Katrin's my wife and I like her. Before I married her I spent the night walking up and down along the banks of the Medina thinking about miracles, hoping the earth would open up and Katrin would disappear. I don't feel that way now. And you're not making sense. You're thinking something about me that isn't true. People have done that a lot with me in the past, thought I was one thing when I was really another. I don't look at you any way except to see that you don't fall out of the wagon. The truth is I'd prefer to be on my way to Missouri right now. I was thinking about that a few minutes ago. And I might still do it. I might take Katrin and head for St. Louis. She'd be happy in St. Louis. Of course, I still have to get rid of Luck, that's a problem I haven't solved yet. And I don't know what I'd do with you and Yolanda. I don't suppose I could take all three of you to St. Louis. And I don't know what's wrong with me, but I've been feeling strange since we met up with Tomás. I might be getting a fever. My stomach's queasy. I feel irritated. I want to climb a tree and sit in it and not come down."

He took off his coat and covered her feet with it. She could feel his body's warmth in the material. He ran his fingers along the fabric of the sleeve where it rested on her leg and she clutched his hand and held it so tight she could feel the pulse throbbing in his wrist.

"Katrin will hate me, Joseph. You are the one we look to. We need you to tell us what to do."

He yanked his hand away. "I'm not smart enough to tell anyone anything. I've never been a man to care about women very much. I trapped fur and never missed the sound of a woman's voice. I've been living long enough to know what I am and what I think, and I think you're mistaken about me. I'm not looking at you the way you think I am. And maybe you think you know what's going on in my mind, but I don't believe in witches, I have no use for superstition. I saw you in the cantina and I knew that very minute you would be trouble, because anyone Tomás has anything to do with has always been trouble for me. If you keep out of my way, I'll keep out of yours. As a matter of fact, I've been thinking that Luck ought to have you. Yes, I've been thinking that while I was contemplating the river. It will be good all around."

II

THE WAGONS RODE steadily toward them, the wrinkled skin of their canvas tops filling and emptying in the breeze. Pinch-faced, sickly looking children peered dazedly out of the opening of the lead wagon while a man on a bay horse rode alongside screaming curses at the Negro driver and unfurling his whip on the backs of the exhausted oxen. There were four wagons in all, the last one open to the sky and piled precariously with furniture and bedding and ragged Negro children. The load seemed in danger of spilling out onto the prairie at each sinking of the wooden wheels into the pitted ground.

Two white women, eyes nearly closed against the harsh sun, marched weakly alongside the wagons, their faces burned and haggard beneath their sunbonnets. A tattered band of Negroes, gunny-sack clothing spattered with dried mud, stumbled behind, half hidden in the clouds of sand that bloomed around them as the wagons pitched back and forth across the rocky soil.

"How do?" the wagonmaster called out.

"Hello," Joseph called back.

The man was abreast of the wagon now, his gaze flitting from

Luck to Joseph and then to the wagon where Katrin and Aurelia and Yolanda were riding.

"Name's Samuel Henson. Me and my family and my brother Burt and his is travelin' together. Comin' from the Carolinas. My oldest girl and five of the pickininnies died of the fever on the way, and now my best black boy done gone and broke his leg. You got anythin' to do with doctorin'?"

"No."

"I ain't got no more idears on what to do with it. I put a splint on it, but it's beginnin' to smell where the bone poked on through. Where ya headin'?"

"Up the Guadalupe to the hill country."

"We just come from up there. Purty country, but the soil don't seem too good for farmin'. We aim to grow cotton. I heared I could hire niggers right here in Texas from their owners, but we didn't want trouble, so we brought our own. Nine field hands. If we have ter, we can hire the strongest ones out till the cotton's in—or maybe even sell one of 'em. I heared a good healthy buck could bring six hunnerd dollars."

"Seems a little high to me."

"I'd best jes rent 'em out at seven dollars a month. Lord, it cost almost thirty dollar a year just to keep one in feed, and if they ain't no cotton to pick, it don't hardly seem worth it. Been travelin' far?"

"A ways."

"You look like someone. You got that face like I know it from somewhere. Your name John?"

"Joseph. Joseph Kimmel."

"You only got one nigger?"

"Just the one."

"Sure would hate to lose that buck of mine. He's smarter'n all the rest. If the durn leg turns, I'll have to leave him behind. Is that a nigger woman in your wagon?"

"Mexican."

"The other one your wife?"

"Yes."

"I done some doctorin'," Luck said.

"Was that your nigger talkin'?" Henson asked.

"I done fixed a few sores," Luck said.

"This ain't no sore, boy. This a big hole in Nathan's leg."

"I done fixed a few holes. Done cured snakebite with tobacco, done stopped fevers with dandelion juice."

"He's no doctor," Joseph said. "I don't think he understood exactly what you said was wrong with your slave. It sounds like gangrene to me, and I may not know anything about medicine, but one thing I do know is you can't cure gangrene with tobacco and dandelion juice."

"You think it's gangrene?"

"Is the leg black?" Luck asked him.

"'Course it's black. It's a nigger leg."

"Black as night?"

"Blacker'n that."

Henson pointed to a small hill and said that he and his party would be camping there for the night. Joseph had seen nothing all day but monotonous rolling sedge grass and blue sky. And now a bump of a hill had popped out of the flat prairie like a button on a suit.

"I'd be pleased if you and your wife will take supper with us," Henson said.

"MILLIE'S STILL MOURNIN' the girl we lost," Henson said. He passed a pan of beans to Joseph. "It's harder on women than men to lose young uns. Millie was real attached to the girl." Henson's wife had spread a calico cloth out on the ground next to the fire, laid the food out, and now she and her children stood in the shadows watching. Henson's slaves, dusky faces pinched and hungry, leaned against the wagons, waiting for their turn to eat. Joseph could see Aurelia among them, and Luck beside her, Yolanda in his arms.

"Fourteen years she wuz, and purty, too," Henson said. "We buried her in Arkansas."

Burt Henson, who had the same crinkly eyes and crooked teeth as his brother, stared into the darkness while he ate. Joseph hadn't heard him say anything except to ask his sister-in-law to pass him the salt.

"You want some more stew?" Henson asked Joseph.

"I can't eat when everyone's standing around looking so hungry."

"They're used to it. Hardly ever been a time I know of or can remember that they need to eat before night. The mammies make sure the white chillen are fed, and then the black ones, and now we're eatin', and when we're finished it'll be their turn."

Henson waved his fork toward Katrin, who was eating slowly and methodically, lifting her head occasionally to look anxiously over at Aurelia.

"Where'd you find you a German wife, and such a young one, too?"

"I stayed a while in a German town south of here called Castroville."

"I heared that Germans don't keep slaves. That true?"

"That's true."

Henson hadn't said anything more about the slave with the hole in his blacker-than-night leg, but Joseph had caught a glimpse of him being pulled from one of the wagons by Henson and his brother and half carried, half dragged up the hill, then laid out on the ground while they set up a flimsy tent and started a fire. A slender black woman, head wrapped in a towel, two little boys trailing after her, followed them, but Henson and his brother came back alone. All Joseph could see now at the top of the hill was a single column of smoke.

Henson didn't rush through supper. He had another helping of beans and finished the stew and cornbread and pickled radishes. His brother picked his teeth with the point of his knife and watched him.

"I always had me a hearty appetite," Henson said. "I oncet et half a roast pig by myself. Sickened in the night and nearly died, but I owe it to the fact that I et the liver. I never et pig liver before, and some say it'll turn you off pig meat for all time. It didn't do no harm to my appetite for it."

He leaned forward, belched, and then lit his corncob pipe. "Nathan's up that hill yonder," he said between puffs. "Maybe that nigger of yours can cure him, or fix the leg good enough so he can walk on it. Your boy sound pretty sure of hisself the way he talk, like he might know somethin' like he said. So if you don't mind, I'll just let him go and look at ole Nathan."

"WELL, NATHAN, YOU got a right dirty-lookin', smelly ole leg there," Luck said.

Nathan, half conscious, lay on a stained blanket, his leg oozing pus, his bare toes facing the fire. His wife Dilly, her two little boys huddled next to her, sat cross-legged in the dirt and fanned Nathan's face with a piece of muslin.

"I knew a man in Missouri who fell off his horse and broke his leg so badly the bone stuck out at a right angle," Joseph said. "After about a week his leg smelled just like this. The doctor took it off."

"He won't be no use with it off," Henson said, "but it do smell worse than before."

Nathan shrieked. "Not gwine to take my leg. I needs my leg."

"Hush now, Nathan, hush now," Dilly said.

Luck had torn Nathan's trouser leg all the way to the groin. "The smell of this leg is awful bad, Nathan," he said. "Look like somethin' eatin' you alive."

"What I'm goin' do with a one-legged buck?" Henson said.

"If we takes it off, he'll be one-legged but still breathin'. If we waits, you can bury him with his legs and all. We needs a hatchet to do it with, though."

Luck leaned close to Nathan's ear. "You gwine be one-legged, Nathan. Is that all right with you?"

"It ain't all right."

Henson left the tent and came back with a hatchet.

"Which one of you is goin' to do the job?"

"I don't know how to take a man's leg off," Joseph said.

Luck ran his finger over the edge of the blade. "Seem sharp enough. If you got some liquor, he won't feel it as much."

"I ain't got but one bottle."

"Cain't take a man's leg off without whiskey."

Henson pulled on his beard, then left the tent again and came back with a jug of corn liquor.

"I never give any one of my niggers good corn liquor in my life," he said.

"It ain't warm enough for winter," Nathan muttered.

"What we gwine do is gwine hurt some, Nathan."

"Take holt my hand, Nathan," Dilly said. "Come on, take holt."

"He can't think on nothin' but the pain," Luck said when Nathan slapped Dilly's hand away.

"You gonna chop it off like you chop a tree?" Henson asked.

"Like a tree," Luck said.

"Got too much heat in the middle," Nathan said and opened his mouth for the corn liquor.

"He's wastin' it," Henson said. "Look how it's runnin' all down his chin."

"Fire all around it, feel like summer. Got to get to de fields 'fore Mr. Henson get back."

Luck poked a twig into the fire until it began to smolder and glow. Henson had left the tent again. He was outside in the dark now talking to his brother about cotton. Prices being paid for it. The planting of it. The picking of it. The best soil. The worst soil.

"Get holt of him, Joseph," Luck said.

"Mighty warm," Nathan said. "Get that fan up here, Dilly, 'fore I faint from de sun."

Joseph pushed Nathan's thick forearms firmly against the blanket and Luck pressed his fingers into Nathan's groin until he felt the pulse. Joseph watched the arc of the hatchet as it came down on the spot above the knee where the skin was dark and smooth. The blow was sharp, chopping neatly through sinew, bone and muscle.

"Oh, Lawd," Nathan screamed.

"A little more to do, Nathan," Luck said. He pinched the edges of skin with his fingers, then dabbed the open blood vessels with the tip of the hot coal until they were dry and puckery. "You jes hold on, and it be over in no time at all. We got to do it right, or there ain't no use in doin' it at all." He singed the skin around the stump and blisters sizzled up like white blobs of cream on a slice of molasses cake.

"It ain't all right," Nathan hollered.

"Maybe not, but it be over, and cain't go back now," Luck said, and tamped the seeping blood with a clean cloth, then stretched and wrapped the skin to cover the exposed flesh and bone.

"I see you've done this before," Joseph said.

"Oncet or twice," Luck replied.

Nathan screamed all night. When his screaming wore him out, he'd faint, and Luck would lean over him and check to see if he was breathing, and Aurelia would put her ear to his chest to see if his heart was beating and Dilly would pat his face with her hands. He was shrieking now and thrashing around.

"Hush, now, Nathan, you got to hush now before you break the sky open with your hollerin'," Dilly said. "Mr. Henson won't like you screamin' like you is."

"I think maybe he is dying," Katrin said. "August throw himself around like that when he is dying."

"You ain't gwine die, are you, Nathan?" Luck asked him.

"Warm enough, just warm enough," Nathan said and let out a shriek.

"The stump of that leg still smells bad," Joseph said.

"I cleaned it. It's clean as snow. There's no more poison in there."

"Where you put my leg? What you do with my leg?"

Henson stuck his head into the tent. "He's keeping everyone awake."

"There ain't no more corn liquor to give him," Luck said.

"Is you gwine bury it?" Nathan asked. "I got to know where you gwine bury it, so I can find it when I need it. I cain't climb into heaven if'n I ain't got my both legs. Get my leg now, go ahead, get it and tie it on me, I'll be good as new."

"Make him stop that noise," Henson said.

"He's delirious," Joseph said.

"What's that?"

"Feverish, out of his head."

"I don't care if he's dilious or not, but over in the wagons he's keepin' everyone from their rest. And get yourself out of here, Dilly, and take the little ones with you and go back and git in the wagon. This ain't no place for you to be."

JOSEPH MUST HAVE slept. He didn't think he had, but his back felt as if he had been lying on a bed of rocks. The fire had gone out. Nathan was quiet, Luck asleep at his side. Joseph stood up and stretched. Dilly had sneaked back up the hill sometime in the middle of the night and was sleeping with Nathan's head across her legs. Katrin, her black hat mashed against the side of her cheek, lay snoring softly, legs sprawled awkwardly, one arm over her head, one down at her side. Aurelia and Yolanda lay wrapped in a blanket near the dead fire.

Joseph stepped outside and breathed deeply of the fresh air. It was almost dawn and a chalky glove gripped the horizon. He walked down to where Henson's wagons were. Henson's slaves were breaking camp, loading the wagons, harnessing the oxen.

"It be time to leave," Henson said.

"Nathan's not ready to leave yet."

"I ain't talkin' about Nathan leavin'. I'm talkin' about me and my wife and the others leavin'."

"What do you mean?"

"I mean I ain't takin' him. He ain't no use the way he is."

"You're going to just go on and not give him a thought?"

"Oh, I'll give him a thought, but we got to get goin' and he ain't no use to me, so what am I supposed to do about it?"

"Decent people don't run off at a time like this."

"I'm not runnin' off. I'm leavin'. Don't you know the difference? Now, if you want to buy him, that's worth talkin' over. Do you want him? You lookin' so worried about ole Nathan, I suppose you won't leave without him, but I paid four hundred dollars for him, and since he's missin' a leg, I'll take two hundred, if you're fool enough to give it to me."

"He's not my responsibility," Joseph said. "I can't take on another mouth to feed, another person to worry about. I can't do it."

"Then leave him here. He'll be best put out of his misery if you let him just lay and die."

"I can't do that."

"Then take him with you. Twenty dollars will do it. You look like a man who got twenty dollars to put out to keep hisself from worryin'."

"I can't take the man without his family."

"It ain't a family. They's niggers. He don't expect more than what somebody does to him. That's his lot. Dilly will get over it. The little ones don't care. They don't have the same feelin' the way regular chillen do. So what you goin' do?"

"Give me a minute."

"I ain't got long."

Joseph walked back to the tent. Everyone was awake now, Katrin staring groggily into the embers of the fire, Dilly kneeling beside Nathan, Aurelia holding a cup of water to Nathan's lips while Luck wrapped fresh strips of muslin around the bloody stump.

"Lookin' a mite better," Luck said. "Not bleedin' much to speak about."

"They're leaving," Joseph said.

"Nathan," Dilly said. "Mr. Henson ready to leave, Nathan. We got to go. Can you sit up some and we get you in the wagon?"

"I don't know if he know he ain't got but one leg now," Luck said.

"He won't live long riding in a wagon with children and furniture piled on top of him," Aurelia said, "with Dilly having to walk alongside, and no one to give him water or clean the stump of his leg. He'll die for sure."

"Henson doesn't want him, and neither do I," Joseph said, and Dilly sucked in her breath,.

"I got to go with Mr. Henson," Dilly moaned. "I got to go."

"You aren't thinking of leaving Nathan here alone, Joseph, are you?" Aurelia said.

"I had thought about it," Joseph replied.

"But you can't leave him . He'll die if you do."

"I can if I want to."

"You'll never sleep another night through if you do."

"Nathan isn't my business. And he isn't yours either."

People telling him what he ought to do never had sat well with Joseph. He liked to make up his own mind. He wasn't going to leave Nathan behind, he had already decided that, but he didn't need Aurelia telling him what he had to do. Joseph could see he was mistaken about her. She had too many opinions to suit him. He had thought she would be so glad to get away from Tomás she'd spend her time telling Joseph how grateful she was. Instead there was all that talk about his looking at her too much, which he definitely didn't think he did, and now speaking up about Nathan and fussing with Nathan's leg, rubbing a sour-smelling paste onto the stump and murmuring instructions to Luck about how to wrap the wound. Why, she wasn't half the girl Katrin was. Katrin might talk a lot, but she didn't go poking into everyone's affairs like a chicken looking for a place to roost. And Katrin was prettier than Aurelia would ever be. Well, Luck could have her. She had just been Joseph's idea of a girl before, someone mysterious and out of reach, and now he could see that she was all trouble, chiding and pushing and telling him what to do.

"I stay by August until he dies," Katrin said. "I never have in my head one thought I will leave him alone. You must do something, Joseph."

Joseph wiped his face with his kerchief. The morning was cold, but he felt hot, and his temper was beginning to jump, so that it was all he could do to keep from saying something mean to Katrin, when it was Aurelia he wanted to say something mean to. Aurelia was sitting in the dirt now next to Dilly, talking to her in a low voice, telling her Joseph would figure out a way to keep her and Nathan and the boys together, telling her she could see the future all laid out in her mind, telling her how everything was going to turn out all right.

"We got room in the wagon for Nathan," Luck said.

"I started out for San Antonio, not owing anyone anything or needing to be anywhere but where I decided, and now—well, now I find myself tied hand and foot. I can't make a move."

"No one done tie you up but yourself."

Henson was waiting out by the wagons when Joseph climbed down the hill.

"I'll give you twenty dollars for Nathan, and I'd like to buy an ox."

"I'll be needin' every ox."

"I only want one."

"Well, I don't know. Like I say, I need every animal I got."

"I'm taking Nathan off your hands."

"It ain't off my hands. I ain't got him on my hands. You are wantin' to take him, don't put it on me that I'm makin' you to."

"All right, I won't put it on you. How much for one ox?"

"Well, let's see, that's three and four, and the feed and all, and . . ." he was staring up at a tree limb, adding figures in his head. "Twenty-five dollars."

"That's a lot of money."

"Not for the one you're gettin'. He hardly been broke in yet. I been careful to keep him from pullin' too much weight. My wife hardly set in the wagon the whole way here, nor Burt's wife neither. They been walkin' since Missouri."

"Twenty-five dollars is too much."

"A mule cost forty."

"An ox isn't a mule. I'll give you ten dollars."

Henson rubbed his beard with dirty fingers. "Thirty-five dollars for Nathan and the ox, and Nathan's woman and his two pickininnies throwed in for good measure. I'll never get my money out of 'em if I have to feed the little ones till they're growed."

12

THE WAGON WAS MEANT for carrying household goods and maybe one small person or two or three children. It occurred to Joseph that this could have been a geometry problem, so many feet for so many people. If he were in the classroom in Independence he might have written it up on the blackboard and given his students twenty minutes to solve it. But he wasn't in the classroom in Independence and he couldn't even think what the problem was or how to explain it. Nathan had to lie down and Dilly needed room next to him, and Katrin had to have someplace to sit, and then the two boys, they were skinny as wagon slats, but they still took up some room. And, of course, Aurelia and Yolanda.

"You be lucky you got a leg left," Luck said to Nathan, who had been lifted into the wagon first and was stretched out half conscious and mumbling.

"Find what we got when it cold got to warm it up some 'fore it freeze."

"You jes keep makin' noise, Nathan. It mean you alive if you makin' noise."

"You wouldn't know if he was dying," Joseph said. "All you did was chop off his leg. Anyone can chop off a leg with a hatchet. If I had known that was how you were going to do it, I'd have done it myself."

"You didn't, though," Luck said, and jumped off the wagon and harnessed the horses. "I don't know if'n the horses can pull the load when we get everyone on."

"We'll harness the ox."

"The yoke only good for two horses."

"We'll throw some things out, then," Joseph said, and he climbed up in the wagon, picked the table up and heaved it out onto the prairie. Katrin looked about to cry, but instead she pressed her fingers flat against her teeth as if she had a toothache.

"I kin walk alongside," Dilly said. "I'm good at walkin'. I done been walkin' all the way from the Carolinas."

"No one's walking," Joseph said.

"If it too tight in the wagon, I kin stand, don't have to sit."

"We don't need these chairs," Joseph said, and threw two carved-back chairs over the side of the wagon.

"My chairs!" Katrin cried. "You throw everything away that is mine, that I want, that I like, that I need. You don't ask me, you just throw. Maybe you throw me out in the prairie if we have no room."

"Moe and Ben kin stand, they don't mind standin'," Dilly said.

"They can't stand all the way," Joseph told her, and threw the last two chairs out of the wagon.

"Now," he said, and looked around him.

"If we have no chair, what do we sit on in our house, Joseph? If we have no table, what do we eat on in our house?"

"We don't have a house. Go over in the corner next to the pie safe."

"Is too high for me to sit on. I will bounce off."

"Not on top of the pie safe. Next to the pie safe. You sit on the trunk, Dilly."

"And where will Yolanda and I go, Joseph?" Aurelia asked him.

"Who?"

"Yolanda and I. Where will we go?

"Go?"

"Where will we sit, Joseph?"

"She askin' you a question," Luck said.

Joseph nodded his head. "I heard the question. My hearing is good. I may be stupid, but I hear very well." He pointed to a pile of blankets. "There," he said. Then he picked Moe up in one arm and Ben in the other and carried them to the front of the wagon and put them on the seat next to Luck, and they started out.

AURELIA REMEMBERED A WOMAN in Laredito who took every cat she saw into her house until she had more than a hundred cats. She begged on the street in order to feed the cats. Her husband left her, and she cried about it, but that didn't stop her from taking in more cats. She let her cats sleep in her bed and eat out of her plate, and she petted and kissed them and never looked one bit sorry that they had taken over her life. Joseph had collected every single person in the wagon, and was taking them all somewhere with him, and being as careful as he could be that they got there without too much damage, but he didn't look one bit happy about it. He looked angry and sad. Aurelia had heard stories of people who sacrificed themselves to atone for some great sin they had committed. She longed to ask Joseph if that was what he was doing.

IN THE AFTERNOON the wind's gentle blow turned mean. It attacked the wagon in fierce gusts that nearly lifted it up off its wheels. Dirt blew into the air and made the day look like evening. The wagon lurched so violently that Nathan fainted.

By late afternoon the wind had stopped and they found themselves in a broad valley. Wild cattle grazed on the grass hidden beneath the spiny algerita shrubs, and a river, dark and cool, wandered through the grasslands toward the mountains.

"That must be the Guadalupe," Joseph said.

"Look like a fine place to stay," Luck replied.

"PLANTAIN WEED IS GOOD for healing," Aurelia said. She and Dilly were picking herbs to make into a poultice for Nathan's stump. "You see how the leaf is rough against your fingers? You can feel the plant even before you see it."

"Why you lettin' Katrin take care your chile so much?" Dilly said. "She gwine think that chile hers, you let her go on the way she is."

"She knows Yolanda is mine."

Katrin had found a stand of wild plum trees a few yards away and was gathering plums while Yolanda napped in the dark brown leaves beside her. Luck had hiked upriver a ways to chop wood for the fire. Joseph and Dilly's two boys were standing at the river's edge angling for fish with bits of dried pork Joseph had hooked to two liveoak branches.

"And Joseph, he spend too much time lookin' over at you."

The weeds gave easily, as if they had no particular attachment to the earth.

"The roots are no good," Aurelia said, "see how I pull them off? Only the leaves make the poultice strong."

"You best do somethin' about Joseph. It gwine be bad for everyone Katrin find out what's gwine on. We got enough trouble, Nathan and me, without more because Joseph is lookin' at you and Katrin gwine get mad over it she find him starin' at you the way he do, and no tellin' what she do when she get mad, she got a strange look, I don't know how she be if she find out. We gwine farm, we got to have no trouble. That's what I say to you now, do somethin' about Joseph."

Aurelia put the bunch of plantain weeds in her kerchief and sat back on the bank.

"Look at them boys laughin'," Dilly said. "They don't know nothin' yet 'bout this life, 'bout how bad it is. Got to grow more before they know. When I was sole in Alabam—I don't 'member the town—the ole master marry me off to Nathan, and I was makin' babies all the time, and they was takin' 'em from me and sellin' 'em. That was a bad time. I never knowed worse.

"Then we was sole to Master Talbot in Caroline, and when we was sick they didn't make us do no work, so that was some better, but I lost a baby there. O'course when ole Master Talbot passed and we was sole to the Henson man to come on to Texas, Miz Talbot wouldn't hear no ways that Nathan and me would come on to Texas without Moe and Ben, but we didn't have no say in none of it. The way we fixin' now look good for oncet, bein' together and no one gwine say do this, do that, we do for ourself and make somethin' for ourself. And Katrin a strange one, I tole you, she got a look I don't unnerstand, she maybe do us some harm, Joseph keep up lookin' at you, and this whole thing make my stomach poorly, worryin' what gwine happen."

"You go back and boil up the weeds in a little water," Aurelia said, "and when it's thick enough, let it cool and then smear it on Nathan's leg."

"MY BROTHERS WOULD chop wood in the morning," Aurelia said.

"Best time to chop," Luck replied. He swung the axe against the side of the tree, and leaves and wood chips flew into the air. "Just a might more, and we got ourselves some good firewood." He gave the tree another two blows, then stepped back and looked up at the green canopy as it slanted gracefully, held fast to its narrow hinge of wood, then dropped heavily to the ground.

"We didn't use much wood in Laredito," Aurelia said. "It never got too cold." She sat down on the tree stump and watched him work. He attacked the fallen tree with the axe, hacking at it along the rotted seams and then stripping away the leaves with his knife. He knew how to chop legs off, he knew how to chop trees down.

"We went swimming in the San Antonio River in the middle of

October," she said. "I can't swim, but I know how to float on my back. I would look up at the clouds that way. It was very nice."

She didn't feel a single thing for this man. Maybe sympathy, because he had no more power over what happened to him than she had over what happened to her. She would have preferred Joseph, and would like to have said to him, *I'll be your wife along with Katrin. She can sleep on one side of you and I'll sleep on the other,* but she knew that Joseph would never agree to that. She thought if she could touch him while he slept, she could use her power to burrow into his head and make him forget her, but he didn't sleep, he merely dozed near the fire and started at every sound. And she wasn't sure that a spell would work. She wasn't sure she had any power.

"Joseph doesn't realize his own kindness," she said.

"He don't," Luck replied.

"I would make him a better wife than Katrin."

"You would fer sure."

"That isn't possible."

"No, it ain't."

It smelled sweet here beside the river. Fresh-sawn wood and leaves as green as the little apples the Mexican women sold in the plaza in San Antonio. Luck had turned away from the pile of kindling and was tossing wood chips into the water. He didn't just throw them, he pulled his arm back and swiveled on the balls of his feet, and when he let them go he teetered on one leg and watched the arc of the wood as it sailed through the air.

"I'll be a wife to you, but I won't stand for meanness."

He shook his head. "Hope to die."

DO YOU KNOW anything about ranching cattle, Luck?" Joseph sat cross-legged on the ground near the fire, twirling the long string of his leather tobacco pouch around his finger.

"No. Never had nothin' to do with it."

Aurelia was at Luck's side, Yolanda wedged between them. There hadn't been any ceremony, no pastor around to pronounce Aurelia and Luck man and wife, but there it was, the two of them together, knees touching, as plain as plain could be.

"How about you, Nathan?" he said.

"No, never did have." He was holding his leg stump steady while Dilly smeared the last of the paste onto it. "I kin feel the toes itchin'," he said, "like as if I caught a bug bite."

"Those toes is gone," Luck said.

"I feel 'em."

"I don't know anything about cattle either," Joseph said.

Nathan put his hand out in the air where his foot should have been. "Right about there is an awful itch. Those toes is somewhere, else why is they itchin'?"

"The toes is with the foot, Nathan," Dilly said. "I tole you we bury them back where Mr. Henson leave us."

"You musta thought you'd be doin' somethin' comin' up this way," Luck said. "How was you thinkin' on gettin' yourself some food and all?"

"I thought I'd do some farming," Joseph replied.

"You ever farmed?" Nathan asked.

Joseph shook his head.

"Soil's got too many rocks," Luck said. "You heard that man Henson, what he said."

"The cattle appears to be raisin' theirselves right now," Nathan said. "All we got do is hep 'em a li'l. Wood legs work fine. I'll make me one, and then you'll see me go. I see'd a man oncet jump on a horse with a wood leg. It was jes like a spring, it shet him up so fer into the air. Seem like it took fi' minutes for him to come down agin and land hisself in the saddle."

"I see a man with a wood leg in Alsace," Katrin said. "He paint it black and put a shoe on it, but you can still see it is a wood leg."

"Which side of the creek you want, Joseph?" Luck asked. "Ain't no other way we gwine do it 'ceptin' Nathan and me on one side of the creek and you on t'other. Nathan ain't got no leg, but he look strong to me."

"If white settlers find out you're ranching on your own, we'll all pay."

"I'm askin' you which side of the creek does you want."

"They's six of us," Nathan said. "We can hep each other."

"We got to decide which side of the creek you gwine be on and which side we gwine be on," Luck said. "There ain't no other way of doin' it."

"This is a good side, Joseph," Katrin said.

"Is the other side gwine be all right with you, Nathan?"

Nathan looked uneasily at Joseph. "If Joseph say it gwine be all right."

"Aurelia and me, we likes the other side," Luck said.

Katrin leaned toward Joseph. "I like it here, Joseph."

Joseph dropped his eyes to the leather pouch in his hands. He had twisted the string until it broke. A pile of tobacco now lay scattered across his trousers. He looked up at the limestone escarpments in the distance, their white shapes in the moonlight like a flotilla of sailing ships.

"There's nothing says I have to give you anything."

"Nothin' says."

"I could take it all myself."

"You could do."

Joseph had a thought. What if he reached over, picked Aurelia up, carried her to his horse and rode away with her? For a moment the thought felt as real to him as the itch in Nathan's amputated toes.

"Whatever anybody wants is fine with me," he said.

"IT'S GOING TO RAIN," Joseph said. Nathan and his family were inside the wagon, and he and Katrin made a bed for themselves under it. Aurelia and Luck had said they'd find a spot for Yolanda and themselves beneath the trees.

"I ought to go find Luck and Aurelia and tell them to come back before they get wet," Joseph said. "Anyone knows that fever and rain come together. A person can die of fever if he gets wet. My brother Isaac said that must be what happened to our father, that it rained the day he left us, and that he must have gotten wet on his way to the ship, and that was why he never came back, that he probably died on the street of fever because his clothes got wet. Isaac was always worried about me when it rained. Once I fell into a pond and barely pulled myself out again, and Isaac cried when he saw me, and said that I was deliberately trying to kill myself, that didn't I know what could happen, didn't I realize what I meant to him, didn't I—"

"You must leave them alone," Katrin said. "We are together now, Joseph, and you must not look at her anymore. You must not do it."

YOLANDA WAS ASLEEP, wrapped in one of Joseph's coats, with Aurelia's shawl around that and Katrin's starburst blanket over that. Aurelia had one of Katrin's quilts around her. Not one of Katrin's crocheted ones, but a blue patchwork quilt that Katrin said was one of her wedding presents. Luck didn't have a blanket, but had covered himself with leaves. *I slept nearly a whole year with nothin' but plants and leaves covering me,* he told her.

"The air seem like it gwine rain," he said. "The river look low enough so if it rain it won't overflow." There had been a loud rustling of leaves and scraping of branches when he was arranging his covers, and now he was stiffly still. She could see the top leaves glistening damp in the moonlight. Not a leaf moving. Oh, maybe there was one spot where his heart was beating. A single twig fluttering up and down in that spot. Barely noticeable.

"Rivers is good, but they overflows all the time when it rain," he said and came and lay beside her.

Whatever contact he had had with women must have been quick and furtive, because he was inside her and out again and finished before she realized that he was ready.

"You have to take your time," she said, and she showed him where she wanted him to touch her, and he said he had never done that to a woman before, not even his wife, and she said that this was as good a time as any to learn.

13

The Guadalupe River Valley

NATHAN CARVED A WOODEN leg out of mesquite wood. It had a depression for the leg stump and holes on the sides to tie the contraption onto his thigh. At first he could only go a few steps on it before he began to perspire and grimace in pain. But by mid-September he was helping Joseph and Luck chop cypress trees and cut logs for the cabins. He hopped on his wooden leg as though he had been born with it. Sometimes he took the leg off and shoved it into the earth to make post holes, or used it to scoop up dirt and rocks as though it were a shovel.

"I tole you how good a one-legged man could do," he said.

They worked every day from dawn to sunset, with one eye on the sky, for although the days felt as warm as summer, the nights were cold, and they all slept huddled together for warmth beneath the wagon.

Joseph and Katrin's cabin went up first on the west side of the creek. While the men chopped trees, the women and the two boys hauled logs and cleared brush until their faces and arms were criss-crossed with scratches. Since the logs were simply piled one on top of another between the corner posts, the cabin was more rhomboid than square. There was no way to make boards for a floor or to frame a window, and so there was only the dirt for a floor and no windows at all. There was a doorway, but no door.

By the end of November, when Luck and Aurelia's cabin was up on the east side of the creek, and Nathan and Dilly's place was almost finished, a band of Indians in breechclouts and moccasins appeared suddenly, with no sound or warning. They were short and slender, with small heads and tiny hands and feet, and they stood quiet and barely visible in the sheltering screen of the mesquite trees.

"What will they do?" asked Katrin. She had been helping Joseph and Luck hoist a log into place on the cabin wall. The skirt of her black dress was ripped all along the hem and little sprigs of dirt-caked blonde hair sprayed out of the edges of her black hat and spilled over onto her scratched cheeks.

"I don't know," Joseph said.

"Caught us ten trout," shouted Nathan as he came out of the clump of trees into the clearing. He kind of bounced when he walked, planting his wooden leg into the dirt, jerking sideways, holding steady for a split second, then teetering onto his flesh-and-bone leg before sliding the wooden one forward again.

"Where's Aurelia?" Joseph shouted at him.

"With Dilly and the boys down by the creek." Nathan had a tin pail in his hand, and as he hopped water sloshed out of the pail and made big round stains in the dirt.

"They be Injuns behind you, Nathan!" Luck called out.

Nathan looked up. The pail slipped from his hand, and he rammed his leg into the earth as the Indians came toward him from the shadows of the trees.

"Don't give them no cause to harm you," Luck said.

"I ain't movin'."

One of the Indians knelt in the dirt and squeezed Nathan's mesquite leg with his fingers.

"You can have it, you like it so much," Nathan said. "It give me nothin' but problems, that dratted thing, pokin' into me all the time. I's better off crawlin' than wearin' that ole stick."

The Indian took the wooden leg, stuck his fingers into the holes, blew into them, then looked through them, and finally hung the leg around his neck.

Before Joseph and Luck reached Nathan to help him up, the Indians had disappeared across the moist grass.

They came often after that. Sometimes they rode up on their horses, but most times they came on foot. They brought bison hides and bear fat and dried meat to trade for gunpowder and metal pins and bits of colored calico. They called themselves Tonkaways. Unlike the stocky Comanches, they were fleet runners, as swift as the deer that darted along the boggy banks of the Guadalupe.

By the time winter came, with its frigid winds and torrential rains, all three cabins were up. There was no furniture, and the wind came through the uncaulked logs and open doors. They had no beds, but slept between thick layers of bison hides, burrowing deeply into the fur like the Indians did.

For food there were pecans from the trees and wild game from the prairie and fish from the river. The dried meat that the Tonkaways traded them was strong and chewy, and the bear fat not only was good for cooking and easily digested, but it burned more brightly than candles. Coffee and sugar had run out, but they boiled the beans of the mesquite tree in water, stirred in two sticky sweet lumps of wild honey to hide the bitterness, and drank it down quickly.

Nathan made himself another leg. He padded it with pieces of quilting to make it more comfortable, and tied it higher on his thigh so it didn't wiggle as much. And he made it bigger at the bottom than at the top, so that it didn't stick so far into the ground when he put his weight on it. He walked more smoothly on this one, without half the jerks and jumps. Luck told him he ought to thank the Tonkaways for stealing the old leg if this is what came out of it.

The polar winds and rain came often, and sometimes the air was so freezing cold that the rain turned to ice before it hit the ground. At times it rained so long and hard that the creek overflowed and the cabins would be isolated from one another for days at a time. Some weeks the temperature fell so low that ice formed inside the cabins, and there was no way to keep warm except to stay beneath the bison hides. But the cabins didn't wash away in the rains, and eventually the sun came out, the creek went down, and it was warm enough to be up and about again.

And through it all Joseph could feel Aurelia stomping around in his brain, rearranging his thoughts, putting in ideas he knew weren't there a few minutes before, and just generally making him miserable with longing. At night his dreams were full of her. During the day he told himself she had too many opinions, was too outspoken, and wasn't even pretty, but he couldn't help walking along the riverbank hoping for a glimpse of her. She did the same. It wasn't noticeable to anyone, he was sure of that, because she was clever, but when she saw him she would stop and smile, and sometimes he thought he saw her hold out her hand to him, although he couldn't be sure because she only stopped for a moment and then walked away, hips swaying, long black hair ruffling in the breeze.

Katrin knew. There was nothing Joseph could keep from her. She seemed not so much smart as observant, remarking if he ate too little or tossed in his sleep or turned silent at the mention of Aurelia's name.

He resolved to banish Aurelia from his heart. He would be stern with himself and allow no backsliding or excuse-making. He would start out by not crossing the creek when she was gathering pecans. And he wouldn't fish the river in the mornings because that was the time she was hunting wild herbs. And in the afternoons if he saw her walking along the riverbank, he would turn away. He knew that his feelings, as tender as they were, would resist purging, that they would have to be gradually weakened. He likened the process to adding water to a salty stew until it was no longer salty. Ridding himself of her couldn't be done in a day or a week or a month, but he knew if he didn't he would go mad, and if he went mad, they'd never make it through another winter.

JOSEPH AND LUCK set out with the wagon at dawn. They rode north through wet, sharp-smelling grass, clouds like a silver nimbus overhead. A moose, long-legged and slack-jawed, had been following them from the cedar grove, keeping pace, then falling back. He was up ahead now, head hanging low on his bony shoulders as he searched out scarce bits of grass on the barren slope.

By mid-afternoon they reached an island of budding trees. The incline grew steeper. A sparrow hawk warbled a throaty *killy-killy* overhead. It was colder here and juniper trees sprouted from cracks in the limestone and hung over the trail, purple berries dangling in limp clusters at the ends of needled branches. The grass wasn't the gray-green of the grass down below, but a purple-green, with stalks like narrow swords that lay down glistening streaks beneath the horses' hooves.

The prairie was behind them now, and as they continued the ascent up the rocky trail a brisk wind spiraled up from the east and snapped at their cheeks and bent the brim of their hats clear back to their ears. The clouds lay stacked against the mountains as if waiting for the right moment to let loose, but by this time the wind was blowing right straight at their noses and they couldn't mistake the smell.

The sight of naked Indian children at play came into view first, and then the bare-leaved cedar trees thinned out to reveal the twig-and-buffalo-skin huts. The mesquite grass had broken off at the last freeze, and there was no spongy mat to soften the screeching of the wagon wheels and no chance that the Tonkaway would think Joseph and Luck were trying to sneak into their camp and steal what they needed instead of trading for it.

Luck stopped the wagon as slender figures moved toward them. It was a small band, no more than twenty braves, some bare-chested, others in leather tunics with feathers in their hair, many of them with smallpox-scarred cheeks. They pushed Joseph and Luck aside and climbed into the wagon. Coffee tins clattered against crockery as the Indians grabbed stacks of blankets and dragged away sacks of flour. A bolt of cloth fell out onto the dirt. One of the Indians plucked it up and another one tried to knock it out of his hands. Luck fell backwards and Joseph's head slapped smartly against the slats as Tonkaway swarmed over the wagon, and, like a cloud of locusts on a field of cotton, picked it clean.

The Tonkaway ignored Joseph and Luck now that they had nothing more to give them. Squaws gathering berries nearby didn't look at them. An Indian in a black frock coat and feather headdress squatted in the bushes, grunting as he emptied out, then wiped himself with a handful of grass and walked away.

In the afternoon Black Eagle, the tribe's chief, appeared, his deer-skin vest strung with scalps and bear claws and velvety obsidian beads, his buckskin leggings studded with bits of metal and carved bone. He sat down on the ground beside the wagon and one of his braves brought him an assortment of food-filled jars he had taken from the wagon. Black Eagle dipped his hands in the pot of molasses, licked his fingers clean with his tongue. He swallowed the sugared tomatoes without chewing, just ran them past his teeth in noisy gulps, and then opened his mouth and let a whole yam pudding slide down his throat. When he had finished eating, he stood up and motioned for Luck and Joseph to follow him.

They walked through the garbage-strewn camp to Black Eagle's hut. He entered first and sat himself down against a stack of bison hides on a floor littered with graying bones and garbage. A few braves lay indolently around the fire while women in short skin skirts, their bare breasts painted with concentric circles, sat hunched in the corner plaiting horsehair into lassoes and making ornaments for the braves to string in their ears. Black Eagle grunted his appreciation as he accepted the gift of satin ribbon from Joseph. He lifted his deerskin apron and tied a snippet of it around his penis. Then Joseph and Luck sat down across from him and took turns puffing on the chief's foot-and-a-half-long pipe. Although the chief knew a few words of English and Joseph and Luck had learned a little Tonkaway, conversation was as skimpy as though the weight of each word would be counted in the trade.

Black Eagle coughed a few times. Smoke swirled in front of his face and he began leaning forward, as though he were going to fall asleep. A slow toppling movement, his thin eyelids nearly closed, his nostrils beginning to twitch. Joseph leaned forward, too, until his head almost touched Black Eagle's greased hair.

"We want to learn to catch those mustangs like you do," Joseph said, and Black Eagle sat upright.

"He don't understand," Luck said.

"Horses," Joseph said, and made galloping signs on the packed dirt with his fingers.

"That don't look like no horses to me," Luck said, but Black Eagle pointed to the horses that were visible through the open door of the hut and nodded his head.

"We can't herd cattle without horses," Joseph said. He had never thought about horses much when he was a trapper. They had just been the means to get from one place to another. And in Independence he rode a horse from the boarding house to the school and paid it no attention as long as it didn't buck or gallop when there were women crossing the street in front of him.

"We catched us some," Luck said, "but we'd sure like to know how to catch more. We see you out on the prairie with your braves and it seems you catch 'em easy. We wants to know how you does it."

"We'll pay you to teach us how," Joseph said.

"We won't take no horses belong to you," Luck said.

"Maybe there's something we can give you in trade for teaching us."

Black Eagle leaned forward and pointed his finger at Luck and then said the Tonkaway word for Comanche.

"Why is he talking about Comanches when we're here to talk about horses?" Joseph said.

Black Eagle was now waving his fingers around in a circle, hitting his arms with his fists, making signs in the air.

"He sure is tryin' to tell us somethin'."

Finally Black Eagle took an arrow from a quiver that lay on the ground near the fire, placed it to his head and said Comanche again. Then he flapped his arms and with his finger made ten straight lines in the dirt.

"There are either ten Comanches nearby or there are Comanches ten miles away, or ten birds have been shot by Comanches," Joseph said. "Or the Comanche camp is ten miles away as the crow flies."

"I think he wants we should kill him ten Comanche."

"We better go on home," Joseph said.

"He want some blankets, too."

"We have none to spare. His braves already stripped our wagon of everything we had to trade. A half sack of flour more for a few horse-catching lessons, and if that doesn't suit him, then we'll go home."

Black Eagle put two fingers flat against his chest.

"He agrees," Joseph said.

"I guess," Luck answered.

Before they left, one of Black Eagle's wives brought a bowl of cured meat into the hut and laid it in the dirt.

Joseph put a piece of meat in his mouth.

"Tastes a little stringy."

"Hmm," Luck said. He took one bite and then sat staring fixedly at the bones in the corner of the hut, near where the women were weaving the horsehair into rope.

* * *

A SHORT WAYS from the Tonkaway camp, Luck jumped down from the wagon, bent over and retched into the grass.

"We done et Comanche meat. We done et it, no question about it. It were a human bone, a thigh bone, right there in a pile. Comanche meat is what we done et."

"They were animal bones," Joseph said.

"No, it were human meat."

Joseph's eyes began to water, and he felt a tickling sensation in the back of his throat, and then he leaned over the side of the wagon and retched into the grass.

All the way home the taste lingered in Joseph's mouth. He kept spitting into the grass trying to get rid of it.

"It's no use spittin'," Luck said, "we et human meat, you and me, we done it, and we ain't no better than Tonkaways now, so you can pretend we didn't, and you can tell folks we didn't, but we done et it, and you can spit all you wants to, but it ain't gwine change it none."

14

KATRIN

February, 1849

DILLY SIPPED THE COLTSFOOT tonic Aurelia held to her lips while Katrin, who had already changed Dilly's nightgown and swept the floor, busied herself stirring the pot of venison stew and watching that the sparks that occasionally climbed up the unfinished walls of the chimney into the open air didn't land on Dilly's bedclothes and set the bed on fire. Isaac and Moe, still weak from dysentery, lay beside their mother, the whites of their eyes a waxy yellow in the cabin light. Yolanda sat quietly on the cold ground, a rag doll in her lap.

Dilly's boys had gotten sick first, and then Dilly. Nathan had tried nursing all of them, but Luck said he needed him to gather stones for the smokehouse, or it would never be built by spring. Aurelia said she knew all about fevers, she'd take care of Dilly and the boys. Katrin knew that bread and plum pies were better for Dilly than anything Aurelia could dig out of the ground, and she couldn't help glancing at the basket of food she had brought over early that morning. She wanted Dilly to at least taste the bread, although she didn't dare tell her that, since Katrin was of the opinion that once a present was given, the one who gave it no longer had any claim on how it was received or what was done with it.

"Nobody done fer me like this before," Dilly said. Her fever-mantled cheeks were as shriveled as dried plums. "They is some masters on some of those plantations would jes let us die. Can't 'member if there was a time when anyone done fer me like this, it been so bitter all the way."

The last few words trailed off into a cough, the sounds of unexpelled mucus rattling in her chest like marbles in a box.

Katrin had never seen a Negro before she came to Texas. She thought Dilly was beautiful, with her long neck and graceful arms and legs. Next to Dilly, she felt as ordinary as a boiled potato.

"You'll feel better soon, Dilly," Aurelia said.

Katrin had visited Dilly many times, but had been in Aurelia and Luck's cabin only once. On a table in front of the fireplace there had been an assortment of jars and spoons and candle wax and measuring cups for the potions Aurelia was always brewing up out of the weeds she picked alongside the creek. Katrin thought a person could go blind looking at such a jumble of objects, such a cluttery mess all in one place. And although she wouldn't tell anyone this, she was sure that she would be a better mother to Yolanda than Aurelia was. If Yolanda were Katrin's daughter, she would feed her and feed her until her cheeks were big and fat and her arms had dimples in the elbows and she waddled when she walked.

"This medicine is something my mother discovered herself, and it never fails," Aurelia said now. "I saw it cure a woman who was sicker than you are. A Mexican woman. Blanca Maria Espinosa Ramirez Almeda Salcedo Hernandez de Giron y Gutierrez was the woman's name."

Dilly started laughing. Katrin didn't think the name was funny just because it was long, and it probably wasn't the sick woman's real name, anyway, but just something Aurelia made up, and even if she didn't, it certainly wasn't funny enough to laugh yourself into a coughing fit over, but Dilly was bent forward now, and the straw mattress hissed and whispered with her coughing and laughing. Dilly and Aurelia talked together the way sisters would, telling each other bits of their lives. Even now, with Dilly so sick, they were laughing together. Katrin wanted to laugh with them, but she didn't know how. If she hadn't felt so stupid, she would have told Dilly about the village of Riquewihr in Alsace, about how in the fall the leafless grape vines threw gnarled shadows up the whitewashed walls of the steepled houses. She would have told her how much August hated Riquewihr, and that every night of the five years it took him to save passage money to America for Katrin and himself, he would read the contents of Henry Castro's leaflet aloud (Katrin couldn't read) and marvel at its contents. Every colonist, it said, will receive a log cabin 32 feet long and 167 feet wide, two oxen with yokes included, two milk cows and their calves, twelve chickens and one rooster, a plow and a Mexican wagon (it said hardly a word about Indians and absolutely nothing about having to marry Joseph). And although Dilly's story was sad—Katrin didn't deny that it was—she would have asked her, if she dared, what could be sadder than August finally saving 183 Gulden for passage to America, and then dying on the ship without stepping foot onto Texas soil?

"Well, I go home now," she said.

Aurelia followed her to the door. "When you have the baby I'll help you," she said.

Nathan had hung rawhide there to keep out the rain, but light came in at the edges and the square of skin flapped a little in the breeze and let the chill of outdoors dart inside.

"I help myself," Katrin said.

IT HAD BEEN almost as cold inside the cabin as it was out of it, but the awful smell of sickness that clung to Dilly and her children like a shroud was gone, washed away in the frosty air. A light sprinkling of snow had fallen earlier, and trees and chapparal and rocks sparkled in their crystal capes. Katrin's feet slapped firmly into the snowy ground, the Indian moccasins that she wore grasping and clinging to each footfall, chilling her toes till they tingled. She had given her shoes to a Tonkaway woman who had taught her to tan hides with the bark of the liveoak tree. Shoes made in Germany, with good leather, and a heel. She had given Aurelia her only other pair, and although she truly believed that once a thing was given it was no longer yours, she didn't think that was true about shoes. Shoes were special. When you wore them they stretched in some places and shrank in others; they were like your feet when you took them off. The shoes she gave the Indian woman had worn spots in the soles, but the shoes she gave Aurelia were perfect, every button attached, no scratches on the toes, and the only reason she had given them to Aurelia was so that Joseph would see the little pieces of deerskin Katrin now wore on her feet and feel sorry for her.

She stared into the water of the creek. Sometimes it was covered in ice and was thick and sluggish, but today it was a ripply blue torrent running swiftly over the rocky bottom.

Where was the spot Joseph always stood to stare at Aurelia? Was it here? Or was it near the grove of trees? Nathan saw him there. So did Dilly before she got sick. He didn't try to hide himself anymore, but let himself be seen. Katrin sometimes found him there. *What do you see when you look at her?* she once asked him. *Why don't you look at me that way? Is there something you want me to do that I haven't done? Just tell me and I will do it.* Joseph shook his head and said there was nothing she could do.

Maybe it was just a small sickness that Joseph had, this wanting Aurelia. A small disease that would always be part of him, like his brown eyes and curly hair. *Oh, you know Joseph, he looks at Aurelia,* people will say, and then they'll laugh and talk about something else.

But he was so good. He never told her he was sorry he married her or that he wanted to be rid of her. And now that the baby was coming, he treated her with such kindness that sometimes she thought she was mistaken about his wanting Aurelia.

Don't you carry that milk pail, he would say, surprising her in the cowpen, and then he would kiss her cheek and take the pail from her hands. And he had made a window for their cabin, with shutters to let in the light and keep out the rain. And put in a new door and placed a tin bucket filled with water beside it, with a dipper for drinking and a tin basin for washing up. And he made a mesquite table and chairs with buckskin stretched tight across the seats, and promised, if he ever got to San Antonio, to buy her a horsehair sofa with rosettes carved into its wooden frame. Surely those were all signs that he liked her and wasn't going to leave her.

She skirted the edge of the creek, staying in the open, away from the trees, as Joseph had instructed her to do. It was a short walk, barely took any time at all to circle the creek and come out on the other side.

There was a family ranching about ten miles to the east, and Joseph bought two pigs and a cow from them. Joseph said they had a clavichord and the wife knew how to read and write, and Katrin asked if they couldn't please go visit sometime, and Joseph said no, the man had said something about niggers. There's no point in taking chances on anyone finding out about Luck and Nathan, Joseph said. It's best if I'm the only one they see.

She stopped at the *Schweinepenne*, the pigpen where Luck and Nathan kept their hogs, the ones Joseph had bought from the rancher. When he brought them home in the wagon and unloaded them, he washed the wagon boards down with ashes and lye and when he was through he said, *No pork in this house, please, Katrin. You can eat it anywhere else you want, but not in this house, not where I can smell it or see it.*

She pressed her face against the log fence and watched the pigs rooting around in the mud. How ugly you are, how disgusting, and how sweet you taste when fried in a pan or baked in your own juices. She licked at the icicle that hung down from the fence, imagining the deliciousness she had conjured up, but pulled away quickly as the tasteless frozen water nipped at her warm tongue.

It was the slickest near the pigpen, and as she placed her feet to turn, they slipped and she sailed along the ice, her shawl caught beneath her hips, her back as rigid as a sled. There was nothing she could do to stop, and as the momentum increased and the glide grew smoother, she closed her eyes and thought of Alsace, how August made a sled of cherry wood and took it to the highest hill and let her slide down it by herself the first time. August was never selfish with his things. She felt like a little girl in Alsace now, sledding down a hill with her brother watching from the top, and she cheeped with pleasure as she slid.

She didn't remember stopping, and lay dazed, eyes open to the sky. One of her moccasins had been knocked off and as the bruising cold hit her stockinged toes, she suddenly sat up and pressed her hands to her stomach, feeling, listening. But there was no pain, no sensation of harm having been done to the creature growing inside her. She rubbed the soreness in the small of her back where the rocks and stones had stabbed her, and then pulled the moccasin onto her wet foot and stood up. Ice had drenched her shawl and was seeping through her thin dress. She took a step forward and then stopped and looked across the frozen field into the trees. Indians, red paint on their faces, buffalo horns on their heads, sat quietly on their horses watching her.

She started to run. She slipped and fell, then picked herself up again. Her breath was tight in her chest as she ran. The chimes of the Indians jingled as they came out of the white fastness of the trees and swept across the dry wash toward her. One of them reached for her, his horse hovering above her, hooves flailing, pebbles flying up as sharp as bees' bites. He lifted her up and she saw his lashless eyes, his wiry black braids wrapped in fur at the sides of his face. She tried to wriggle free, but he held her fast. She screamed but could hear no sound except for the whish of the wind as the horse skated over the icy banks and through clouds of moss that hung like velvet cloaks from the arms of the liveoak trees.

* * *

LUCK WAS THE ONE who spotted the herd of mustangs idling beneath the mesquite trees.

"Look to me like we got us some good ones," he said as Joseph rode up beside him.

"A little thin," Joseph replied.

"By summertime all the rest the herd gwine be so fat from good eatin', all we got do is stand in one spot and lasso them when they go walkin' by."

The mustangs were rooting for clumps of grass in the ice patches beneath the trees, curling their lips and rubbing their muzzles in dirt and rocks and swallowing whatever came up.

Luck dismounted, moved slowly toward the mustang closest to him and tossed a piece of cloth over its eyes. It snorted once, then turned suddenly docile, its ears quivering slightly beneath the blind. Luck whipped the blind away and forced a bit into the animal's mouth, and as he hopped onto its back, it spun in a circle and then bolted across the field in a crazed gallop with Luck clinging to it like a scab. The mustang bucked and reared, and the harder it bucked and reared, the tighter Luck stuck. When it had finally worn itself out, Luck looped the rope around its neck and tied it to a tree.

Black Eagle himself had gone out on the prairie with Joseph and Luck and shown them how to follow mustangs to where the main herd was grazing. He would wait until their bellies were full and hung like sacks of flour beneath their ribs and then would chase them until they got dried out, headed for water and drank so much they could hardly run. Then he would chase them into a ravine and lasso as many as he could. When he found a stray mustang, he would shoot it in the shoulder and catch it that way. Shooting a mustang in the shoulder might not feel any worse to the animal than a bee sting, but Luck thought it didn't give the animal any chance at all and Joseph thought it was just plain stupid.

It didn't matter what Black Eagle said, anyway. Joseph had discovered that there were as many ways to catch a mustang as there were mustangs to be caught. These had dug up everything green that was to be had beneath the trees and were looking around for something else to eat.

"Go do it, Joseph," Luck shouted.

Joseph picked out a mustang and ran toward it. It seemed as if there were no purpose to his running, as if he were intoxicated by the motion of his legs, caught up in their rhythmic churning, that he would keep running, past the horse and into the prairie. But as he neared the horse, he suddenly veered, his feet rose higher, reached upward in a floating arc, and then he landed lightly on the animal's back. It screamed in rage and surprise. It rose up to shake Joseph off. It snorted and bucked. It dashed across the field in one direction and then another. It chased its tail. It screeched with meanness and terror. Joseph held fast, the horsehair hackamore as tight as a bandage beneath the horse's jaw. He felt as if he didn't need the horse at all, that he was floating above it on a plane of air, that he was a cork, weightless, bouncing, sailing, drifting.

Joseph pressed his head against the mustang's neck, the contours of his body disappearing into the animal's, the two of them sleek and giving the wind no resistance. Then suddenly the mustang stopped, just quit. It snorted a few times, then hung its mane and shivered as Joseph slid off its back.

"He sure know you mean it," Luck said with a laugh.

"It's been a good day," Joseph said. He liked the way he felt after a long day of riding, when his legs were as stiff as two blocks of wood and his arms felt ten feet long and he knew he had earned his supper.

There was only one way out of the grove, through a ravine that branched out from the Guadalupe. The rest of the mustangs were loping ahead. The plan was to circle them through the ravine until they were exhausted, lasso as many more as they could, then wait for Nathan to bring the mare and lead them all back to the corral.

The mustangs were in the ravine, and Luck and Joseph were coming up behind them when Joseph heard his name. It echoed in the canyon and the mustangs turned crazy at the sound and started whirling around and around.

"Joseph, oh, Joseph." Katrin's voice shrilled like a tinny bell in the moist air. Luck's horse reared up, and Joseph turned in the saddle.

"Joseph, Joseph, Joseph," she cried, and Joseph watched in amazement as a horse with an Indian and Katrin on its back galloped past.

BLACK EAGLE AND his seventy braves, paint-smeared faces jutting like stovepipes out of their buffalo robes, rode slowly ahead of Joseph and Luck. Although it had been six hours and the trail had begun to grow cold, Black Eagle found it and held fast, following it over rocky tracts and flooded creeks, pondering the ground and the leaves of the trees for any indication that horses and men had recently passed through. He occasionally leaned far over the side of his horse to spy out horse droppings, pointing them out to his braves with a long stick. As they climbed higher in the Staked Plains, he got down and walked through the frosted brush more often, kneeling to stare more closely at the ground, to examine a broken branch, to test the freshness of hoofprints by the absence of insect tracks. They had seen pecan shells and scooped-out pomegranates along the river when they first set out, but it led only to an abandoned camp. There was no way to know how long it had been abandoned. Comanche camps were all alike. They could move camp in a few hours, and the new one would look exactly the same as the old one.

"It was my fault for not watching her close enough," Joseph said. "My mind was on other things. I never asked myself whether it was dangerous for her to be walking along the creek alone every day to take care of Dilly, never said, Wait for me, and I'll see that you get safely, there and back."

"You cain't watch her every minute," Luck said.

"I should have chased after them."

"They was ridin' too fast to catch," Luck said. "Comanches is garbage-eaters and kin hardly walk, but no one kin catch 'em when they's on horseback."

That evening they found the half-eaten carcass of a horse. Black Eagle examined the remains, flicking aside the tail and plunging his hands into the entrails to feel for warmth. Then he spit into the ashes of the fire and touched his fingers to the charred stones. Not far away, near a clump of trees, he found the trail again in the soft indentations of unshod horses.

"Comanches," he said.

By nightfall of the following day they could smell the stench and see the fires of the Comanche camp. The Tonkaways spread out along the perimeter while Black Eagle, squatting beside his horse, watched from the darkness of the trees. There were sounds now coming from the camp, dogs barking, shouts and stirrings in the tepees, whinnying and movement in the horse pen.

"They know we're here," Joseph said.

The Comanches rode out from the horse corral and massed in the center of the camp while the Tonkaways and Joseph and Luck waited at the timber line. They could all see each other now, and for one long moment they were as still as a painting in a book. Then Black Eagle yelled and his braves charged forward on their horses, muskets blasting a blind fusillade through the darkness as Ten Elk's braves flew across the encampment to meet them.

"I'm goin', Joseph," Luck said, and he kicked his horse and shot ahead. Joseph watched him go, saw the straight back and mat of black hair lose itself in a sea of colliding horses. He looked down at the revolver in his hand and then up again. For a moment his thoughts were as twisted as a ball of yarn, but as he saw the bodies begin to fall and heard the screams, he held his six-shooter out in front of him, lowered his head and charged.

The Comanches criss-crossed the field, their bodies low across their horses' manes.

"Watch out for that one," Luck shouted.

Joseph turned and fired. He couldn't tell whether it was his bullet or a Tonkaway bullet, but the Comanche lifted straight up off the back of his horse, seemed to sit in the air a moment and then fell to the ground.

There were too many places to look at once. Ahead of him, behind him, watching for arrows, dodging bullets. He couldn't see what Luck was doing, couldn't see much of anything through the smoke of gunpowder, couldn't hear much over the noise the Comanches and Tonkaways were making, whooping and shouting, and the sharp pinging of bullets and steady humming of arrows flitting through the choking haze.

The Comanches rode their horses in a way he had never seen before, as if they were part of the beasts. They sometimes ran past their targets they were so fast, but the steady Tonkaways, ungainly looking on their horses, took their time and aimed square, and it was as if the Comanches were birds flying across the sky the way the Tonkaways brought them down.

Joseph rode in among the galloping horses, shooting his revolver as he rode, and when that was empty he began swinging it at the Comanches as they passed by him, catching some in the neck, some in the back, knocking some so hard they fell off their horses.

He became very conscious of his own body, felt the slice of a spear against his thigh and the nick of an arrow across the tip of his ear, but it was a dreamlike awareness, as if his mind and body were separate. He didn't really feel in danger of being killed. The Comanches were no more than a swarm of wasps stinging him as he swatted them here and slapped them away there.

He tried counting how many he knocked off their horses, but there were so many coming at him, breezing by as if they had somewhere else to go, that he lost count. The Tonkaways were winning, but none of the Comanches looked at all afraid. They looked like they were having a good time.

Joseph had never been in battle before. The only time he had fought another man face to face was over an insult to his Jewishness when he was a young man in Independence, Missouri. He had always remembered the look of fear on the other man's face when he hit him, had always held inside him the knowledge that somewhere in his nature there was this cruelty waiting.

By dawn the battle was over. Smoke drifted over a field soaked in blood and covered with the bodies of dead Comanches and Tonkaways. Ten Elk, the Comanche chief, had been taken prisoner late in the battle, and now sat on the ground outside his tepee, his hands tied to his feet. The rest of the Comanche warriors had fled on their horses, leaving the women to cross the clearing with their deerskin travois and haul the bodies away.

"I KIN GO in first, if you want me to," Luck said.

"No," Joseph replied. "I'll go."

It was dark inside the tepee, just the outline of someone crouching against the deerskin wall.

"Joseph?"

"I'm here, Katrin."

She was naked, her white skin speckled with red paint, her nose slit at its tip, the blood from the wound congealing into a crusty mustache on her upper lip.

"I knew you would be soon here, Joseph. I told those Indians, my Joseph he will be soon here."

His knees felt weak, and he sank down onto the dirt beside her. She had never undressed in front of him, had always pulled her nightgown over her underclothes, and then slipped them off. He had not seen how swollen her stomach was. She had wet the dirt beneath her, a puddle of urine beneath her crotch. The arrow of damp straggly hair between her legs was the same yellow color as the hair on her head. And her breasts. He had never seen them before. They had been little lumps beneath her clothes that even in the dark he didn't care to touch. They were criss-crossed with what appeared to be knife marks, and blood was oozing from the wounds. Her nipples were blue, nearly as blue as her eyes, with slender blue veins running through the flesh.

"I waited for you and waited." She didn't put her hands across her breasts or try to hide the damp crotch. She simply sat there as if she had clothes on.

"I've been looking for you as hard as I could," he said, and took off his coat and put it around her.

"I told those Indians, my Joseph he will be soon coming."

THE GREASY WALLS of Black Eagle's tepee reflected the fire that glowed in the stone ring. Ten Elk lay trussed up with horsehair rope in a corner of the tepee. Black Eagle had dragged him behind his horse all the way back to the Tonkaway camp, and the Comanche's legs now trickled blood onto the dirt where he lay. Each brush of his skinless back against the sooty tent wall left a thick red smear. Black Eagle had sliced Ten Elk's stiff braids off close to his scalp, and his hair now fanned out from his head as thick and black as a bristle brush.

Katrin, wrapped in buffalo robes, sat on the ground next to Joseph. The Tonkaway shaman had daubed the slits on her nostrils with white clay and blown on the two seams that ran like pink threads down the sides of her nose until they were dry. *Comanches always slit a woman's nose when she is unfaithful,* Black Eagle said.

The shaman was singing to the captured Comanche in a high, trembly falsetto and jerking his head wildly from side to side. Then he suddenly stopped and crawled away. Black Eagle took his knife from the sheath around his waist, and without a word sliced a slab of flesh from Ten Elk's thigh.

"This is the worst!" Luck exclaimed.

Katrin stared at Black Eagle's knife, at the flesh hanging on its tip.

"I think we'll go home now," Joseph said.

Katrin put her hand on his arm. "No," she said.

Ten Elk, who had given only a mild yelp as the knife sliced through his thigh, was now making clicking noises deep in his throat as Black Eagle put the square of bloody flesh onto the fire to cook.

"You cut a piece from him, Joseph," Katrin said.

Joseph shook his head. "I can't do that."

"This is the worse thing I ever done seen," Luck said.

The smell of burning flesh was as sickeningly sweet as a heap of rotted flowers. Black Eagle plucked the meat out of the fire and tore it into narrow strips, which he shared with his braves. He handed a morsel to Katrin.

"Put it down, Katrin," Joseph said.

She held the strip of flesh in the palm of her hand. "That Indian said he will keep me. I told him, my Joseph he will be soon coming. Look how shiny it is, Joseph, like pork," she said and tossed it into the fire.

Black Eagle reached toward Ten Elk again, this time carving out a thick slice from his hip. Ten Elk gave a little squeak of pain as blood spurted onto the ground, then leaned his head back and breathed rapidly through his mouth, sucking his lip, nodding his head.

They sat there all night while Black Eagle and his braves ate away at Ten Elk's body, relishing every bite and complimenting the Comanche on the excellent quality of his flesh. By morning, he lay in a cradle of blood, singing a song of dying, his wobbly voice high and resonant in the smoky tent.

A small breeze came up with the daylight. It fluttered the flap of the tent, and Joseph opened his mouth to breathe it in. It was his fault, all of it. If he hadn't been thinking about Aurelia, this would not have happened. He looked at Katrin now, at the way she sat carefully watching Ten Elk die, without a tear or a word or a bit of sympathy. Joseph didn't want to know exactly what Ten Elk had done to her. That was too painful to contemplate. He touched her stomach and the baby, his baby, the baby he had hardly given a thought to before now, kicked and bumped beneath his fingers. Katrin didn't react to Joseph's touch. She didn't turn toward him or take his hand or say anything. Her eyes never wavered from Ten Elk's face and the sight gave Joseph a pain so deep and sharp inside him that it took his breath away.

Ten Elk was sighing now, his voice a blend of bubbles and gasps.

"It be all over now," Luck said.

15

March, 1849

JOSEPH WAS FINISHING his supper when the Rangers came. There were seven of them. Only one, a man in a raggedy pair of trousers and a threadbare jacket, came into the house. The new puncheon floor was sticky with resin, and his boots made snapping noises as he followed Katrin from the cold parlor through the covered walkway into the outside kitchen.

"I'm Captain Dawson, Texas Rangers," the man said. He had a red bandanna twisted around his neck, and the badge on his fraying lapel looked as if it had been stamped on by a horse, it was so crooked and bent.

"Please sit," Katrin said. The kitchen was warmed by the stove and full of the yeasty smell of fresh-baked bread. The mesquite chair scraped across the floor as the Ranger sat down.

Joseph could see the rest of Captain Dawson's men through the window, still on their horses. He had seen Rangers camping farther west along the river, but none of them looked the way these men did, scrawny and filthy, and none of them had ever stopped here and come into his house looking as if they had something serious to say.

"I've brought some of my men up from the Nueces," the Ranger said. "Good men. Real plainsmen, used to the wet and the cold and finding their own food. But I can tell you they'd appreciate something good to eat. If you can spare it. Pies is their favorite."

"Cheese and bread I give you," Katrin said, and she pushed the crock of cheese close to Captain Dawson's hand and laid two fat slices of bread beside it.

"They surely do like bread, ma'am," the Ranger said.

"Katrin will bring some out to them," Joseph said.

"They can wait." The Ranger dipped two dirty fingers into the soft cheese and took a bite of bread. "A drover by the name of Haines says you were out at the Bandera pass and sold him some cattle to take to New Orleans." As he moved his mouth, bits of cheese and sharp crumbs fell from his sparse mustache onto his red bandanna.

Joseph remembered the sale. Nathan and Luck had been with him, Nathan riding one-legged on his sorrel, Luck on the mustang he called Pepper, Joseph riding the mustang they had just broken.

"That was about two weeks ago," Joseph said. "We rounded up longhorns in February at the tail end of a blizzard, a hundred head, and took them up to Bandera to sell."

"That's what he said."

"He paid me two dollars each, with no argument. I told him we hadn't sold cattle before, didn't know that much about it, and we settled on a price I thought was fair, considering the work we put in catching them, and then the breaking in of the mustangs to catch them with. If he's complaining about the price now . . ."

"He's not complainin' about the price."

"The cattle were healthy," Joseph said.

"Mr. Haines isn't complainin' about the price or the cattle, and it won't do any good your gettin' angry before you know what I'm here for."

"Well, I certainly remember Mr. Haines, and I'm not angry yet and won't be, if you're not here for something I should get angry about. I sure do remember him. Mr. Haines. I sure do. A tall man, if I remember right, with whiskers. Long ones. And no upper teeth. I remember wondering how he ate with no teeth to chew with. He said he was going to take the cattle to Louisiana, and we had some conversation about whether he'd sell them for meat or tallow. He seemed content with the sale. He didn't say anything was wrong with it to my face."

Captain Dawson had finished the cheese and bread. Katrin poured him a glass of buttermilk.

"I had a ranch in Nacogdoches," Captain Dawson said. "I gave it up. I thought I'd get rich, but I found out I could catch all the cattle I wanted, but they weren't worth much after I caught 'em."

Captain Dawson drained the glass and wiped his mouth with his sleeve. "Mr. Haines told me you were in the company of two niggers, and that he thought one of them was a runaway. Mr. Haines said he was lookin' in his eyes too hard, too haughty, for there not to be a reason for it."

I'll drive them up myself, Joseph said.

No one man kin handle a hundred head of cattle, Luck replied.

The drover hadn't paid that much attention to Luck and Nathan, except to say he'd never seen a one-legged man ride a horse as well as Nathan did. Joseph tried to remember the man's face, what it really looked like behind the whiskers and the missing teeth. Kind-looking. That's what Joseph remembered. He had even shared a campfire with them that night. Told them some stories about Comanches, how one time he was herding cattle on the Edwards Plateau, and when he turned around the Comanches had made off with twenty head. Said he once saw a Comanche steal four horses from a corral in Goliad, with sentries on guard, and no one even heard them. The drover had a banjo and played some old songs that Nathan said he remembered hearing when he was in Virginia.

"You must mean Luck and Nathan," Joseph said, now on guard. "They're freedmen. I never thought to tell Mr. Haines that. It didn't seem anything he needed to know. We've all been ranching here the past year."

"Can you show me papers provin' they're free?"

"I never owned them. I don't have any papers." Joseph felt weary, as though he could see some long road in front of him, had already been running down that road half his life and had another half to go.

"Have you had trouble with Comanches?" The Ranger was looking at Katrin's face now, at the scars on her nose.

"We had some problems, but we took care of them," Joseph said. "We take care of things ourselves. We have no call for anyone coming here and doing things for us. So you've come and told me what you think of Luck and Nathan, and I've given you my answer. I guess there isn't anything more you need to say to me. Katrin will be glad to fix a basket up for your men. We have plenty of food, and you're welcome to it, and I hope you didn't ride too far out of your way to come here today."

Joseph could feel his throat tightening and knew he was sounding angry, even though he was trying not to.

"Savages," the Ranger said.

"What?"

"You know. Savages. Comanches."

"What about them?"

"What about them? Why, look at what they did to your poor wife, that's what about them." He leaned back in his chair as if he intended to stay a while. "We didn't have to worry about Comanches in Tennessee. That's where I'm from, Tennessee. You ever been to Nashville?"

"I never have," Joseph replied. There were all kinds of thoughts going through his head now. Maybe the man would leave once he finished talking. Some men just needed to linger, even when they were ready to go and there was nothing more for them to do. Isaac was like that. Joseph used to tell him that he'd get a lot more sewing done if he wouldn't talk so much to his customers. You can fit them for their suits and talk to them at the same time, Joseph would tell him, but why do you have to keep talking when they're ready to leave and you can see in their eyes that they've got places to go? Why do you have to tell strangers everything you know in the world? Captain Dawson looked at Joseph that way now, as if he were going to plumb his memory all the way back to the day he was born, was going to tell Joseph what the weather was like that day and how many glasses of water his mother drank before she squeezed him out.

"I was born in Nashville," Captain Dawson said. "I was even at the ceremony when Nashville was made the state capital. I was just a boy at the time, but I'll always remember the day, because it rained, and I had forgotten my hat. I've still got a sister and nieces living there, but I haven't seen them in too many years to remember. Where you from, Mr. Kimmel?"

"Missouri," Joseph said. He supposed he could have elaborated a little, been as friendly about where he was from as Captain Dawson had been, maybe tell a like story about Independence, about how they used to raise the flag in the square across from the Courthouse on Independence Day, maybe make some connection with the name of the town and the country's birth, but he could see in the man's eyes that it was too late for that, that he already knew who Joseph was, and that he was priming himself on how he was going to keep him out of the way and do what he meant to do.

Katrin was staring down at the floor, and Joseph wondered if she was going to bend down and wipe up some stain, or if she just didn't know where to look or what to do. The Ranger sat motionless at the table, and Joseph would have thought he'd died sitting there, he was so still, the only sign of life an occasional scrape of his boot beneath the table. He had come here to ask about Nathan and Luck, had brought six Rangers with him. All this talk about Tennessee didn't mean anything, and Joseph wanted to ask him right out what it was he wanted with Nathan and Luck, to hurry it up, get the bad news out, because there was no question in his mind now that the man hadn't stopped in just to be friendly.

"I'll have some water, ma'am, if you please."

Katrin poured some water into the Ranger's glass. He took a long swallow, and then looked at her stomach.

"I'll bet you want a little girl to help you in the house."

Katrin didn't answer him.

"Girls are nice," he said. "Boys help out more on a ranch, though. There's things you can depend on a boy for, especially when the winters are hard like they've been." He wiped his mouth again with his sleeve. "We found two white men shot dead up at Bandera Pass and their horses stole."

So there it was. Two white men shot dead. Joseph got up from the table and stood at the window. The window glass had a few stripes and bubbles in it and wasn't as fine as glass Joseph could have gotten if he had waited till he got to San Antonio, but getting to San Antonio seemed a while off, and a glazier had come by with a wagon load of glass in the spring and Katrin had said she dearly would love to have real window glass in the window. Joseph could see all the way down to the creek. Katrin kept the window spotless, wiped it every morning along with the floor and the table. She had been doing that since Joseph got her back from Ten Elk. She was always scrubbing something, and now Joseph looked through the polished window and wished he could see Luck and Nathan on their horses rushing away, but all he saw was a clutch of mangy-looking men milling around beneath the leafless trees.

"There's a law against harborin' runaways and a law against niggers sellin' cattle," Captain Dawson said.

"We work together here," Joseph said, turning around. "Sharing chores, raising animals. We've each got our place, Nathan and his family across the creek next to Luck and Aurelia, Katrin and I on this side. We help each other. I don't know what we'd have done if we were out here by ourselves. We'd never have gotten a cabin built. And Luck is better at catching mustangs than I am. You were a rancher, you said, so you know that without horses you can't herd cattle. Nathan's only got one leg, but he does more work than a man with two. Neither one of them could kill anybody. I can tell you that right now, for sure and for certain. They aren't the ones you want."

The captain was sipping his water and tapping his fingers on the mesquite table Katrin had worn a smooth gloss on with all her scrubbing. Then he kind of patted the surface and leaned toward Joseph. "Just give us a free hand, Mr. Kimmel. Mind your business, and I won't give you any trouble about it."

Katrin had moved away from the stove and was standing next to Joseph at the window, her hand on his arm, and he could feel the weight of the baby pressing into his side.

"Don't say anything, Joseph," she murmured. Joseph wasn't trying to think of anything to say. He was trying to think if there was a way to warn Nathan and Luck. He was trying to figure out if he could kill six Rangers and their captain and bury their bodies near the pigpen without anyone ever finding out. He was trying to think, and Katrin kept whispering things at him, telling him about the baby, to remember the baby, Joseph, don't say anything that will hurt you, or what will I do about the baby.

"You made a mistake, Mr. Kimmel," Captain Dawson said, "lettin' niggers think they was white men like you did."

IT COULD HAVE been a picnic, thought Joseph, the way the Rangers rounded everyone up, laughing at Nathan when he came out of his cabin without his wooden leg, joking with Moe and Ben about their long legs, how they could probably walk back to Africa with legs like those. In a minute we'll have a log roll, thought Joseph, and then a sack race, and the winner will get to take home a crate of peaches.

The Rangers had brought an open wagon, and they put feverish Dilly, mattress and all, into it, along with her boys. When they brought Luck out of his cabin, he was carrying Yolanda in his arms. Aurelia was beside him. It was cold outside and she had put her shawl around Yolanda.

Captain Dawson chose two cedar trees near the creek where Luck had built a horse barn and had set out a garden fenced with pickets. It was a pretty place, where the winter sun sliced warily through the mist. The Rangers were laughing among themselves, their eyes bright while Captain Dawson supervised the fixing of the ropes to the trees. He was very meticulous in the way he went about it, adjusting and readjusting the length of the ropes, checking the distance needed between the branches he had chosen and the ground. He even stood on his tiptoes next to Luck, who was taller than Nathan, to make sure the branches were high enough. Then he had one of his men test the strength of the branches by swinging first on one and then the other.

The wagon was behind them, dimly visible in the gray light. One of the Rangers lifted Aurelia and Yolanda up into it, and Joseph could hear Dilly's hacking cough and see Moe and Ben, faces broad and open like Nathan's, staring out through the rails.

Captain Dawson hadn't let Joseph out of his sight. He had walked him out into the yard while his Rangers brought Nathan and Luck outside. Now Captain Dawson and one of his men were attaching the ropes to the trees while Nathan and Luck and Joseph stood together watching. Everything was so casual, Joseph thought, as if the two men who were going to be hanged hadn't shown up yet.

"You oughtta get away now and leave us," Luck said.

"I don't believe they'll do it," Joseph said.

"Oh, they'll do it. They like to hang you, too, if you keep standin' where you are."

"If I could get my shotgun some way or other and then run all the way to the creek and start shooting at them from there . . ."

"Why you want to go and start shootin' from the creek?" Nathan said. "You can go climb up on top the roof of your cabin and shoot from there. You can see better from up high."

"You won't be able to shoot them all," Luck said. "It won't do no good to kill two or three or four. You got to kill 'em all."

"We'd be runnin' by then," Nathan said. "Even with my one leg, I can go fast enough to get myself to the horse pen, and then Luck and me, we can start shootin' from there. Comin' from two direction, we can do it."

"Maybe there be some more camped down by the river," Luck said.

"I can only think on one thing at a time," Nathan told him.

"I've been trying to figure out a way," Joseph said, "right up to this second, I'm still trying to figure, and it won't come to my mind. I don't want you to think that I'm one of them, that I'm like they are, because if there was any way in this world that I could get you away from here, I would."

"I know it," said Luck.

"There are things I've done in Texas that I'm ashamed of and that were my fault, but this isn't one of them."

"I know it ain't."

"You can try runnin' to the creek, the way you tole it the first time," Nathan said in a hopeful voice.

Nathan had been in charge of the smokehouse. It had been his idea all the way, how to build it, how to set the stones for the walls, how high the door should be. He had been so particular about putting the door on just right so the smoke wouldn't leak out.

"He cain't run nowhere with them watchin'," Luck said.

"I could run and let the horses out and stampede them, and then you could . . ."

"There be too many of 'em to do it," Luck said. "It be too late now for anythin'."

"Dilly's dyin'," Nathan said. "And what about my boys?"

The ropes were all set now, and Captain Dawson came over to where Joseph was standing with Nathan and Luck. He had a pleased, almost cheery, look on his face.

"We set the ropes nice and tight, so they don't slip."

Nathan had to be helped toward his tree, and Luck walked slowly toward his. Captain Dawson told Joseph to stay back, but he ignored him and walked right up to the trees with Nathan and Luck.

"They couldn't have killed anyone," Joseph said. "I can swear to it that they didn't kill those two men. You can bring them to San Antonio and have a judge decide whether they did or not. You're not giving them their day, you're going too fast on this. It isn't right what you're doing."

"I told you to mind your business."

Joseph felt feverish, cold and hot all at the same time. He thought longingly of the buttermilk in the house, how good it would feel on his parched throat.

"It's the knot that breaks the neck," Captain Dawson said to the Ranger who was slipping the knotted rope around Nathan's neck. Luck's rope was already in place, and looked grimy in the hazy light, as if it had been dragged along a muddy creek bottom.

"We didn't kill nobody, Joseph," Luck said.

"I never thought you did," Joseph said. He was sure he had a fever now with the terrible heat that was boiling up inside him.

Katrin was watching from across the creek, her hand on her hip, her huge belly like a basket of clothes balanced in front of her.

"The black mustang, the one I broke last week, watch his left leg," Luck said. "He got a kick that come when you leas' 'spect it."

Captain Dawson was acting like a teacher, showing the Ranger how the knots should go, twisting the one on Nathan's neck into just the precise position he wanted it.

"Walk away now, Mr. Kimmel," Captain Dawson said.

"Better listen to him, Joseph," Luck said. "Or you be next."

One of the Rangers pushed Joseph out of the way, then brought a crate for Nathan to sit on, since he was trembling so hard he couldn't stand up.

"It ain't your fault, Joseph," Luck said. "Don't go blamin' yourself for this, 'cause you couldn't help any of it."

They hung Nathan first, just yanked him up from where he was sitting. He didn't struggle, but stuck out his stump as though searching for the lost leg. When Luck's turn came, he closed his eyes and swung gracefully upward, and as his feet left the ground, Joseph was overwhelmed by the beauty of the arc they made.

"Move away, Mr. Kimmel!" Captain Dawson yelled as Joseph lunged forward and grabbed Luck's trouser legs.

"Let him go, Mr. Kimmel!"

Joseph had the full weight of Luck's body resting on his shoulders now, and he could tell by the way Luck's legs dangled limply against his chest and his arms hung like suspenders down Joseph's back that he was already dead. Joseph wanted to let go, but he couldn't.

Then everything became quiet. It was a sharp quiet, in which only the unimportant things were heard. The whinnying of the horses out on the plains. The slight whistle of the wind through the canebrake. The creaking sound the ropes made as Nathan's body swayed back and forth from its branch.

The Rangers, their faces now white and joyless, turned away one by one, occupied themselves with their horses, checked their harnesses, adjusted the blankets beneath the saddles.

"Oh Jesus!" Dilly screamed.

The men turned toward the cry, startled, their faces full of fright.

Then Aurelia began to scream, and her voice and Dilly's soared and swooped above the Rangers' heads, past the treetops, through the pale and gloomy sky. They were not like human voices at all. They were like ghostly vibrations from deep inside the earth, like a mountain being ripped from its base, like the Furies erupting from the underworld and screaming their way across the plains.

Joseph fell to his knees, helpless against the sound, and Luck's body flew away from him and floated eerily overhead.

16

TWO HORSES CROSSED the stream toward the wagon, torches fuming and bouncing in the darkness.

"Mr. Williams, good evenin' to you."

"Good evenin' to you, Cap'n Dawson. What you got in that wagon?"

"A load of niggers, Mr. Williams. Found 'em up in the hill country, and I thought right off of Pecan Point, thought maybe you'd want to take 'em off my hands."

"Mr. Holbrook is gettin' rough with me on where I get my niggers from since I bought a young buck and turned out he was stole from a plantation down south."

"Nobody owns these, I'll swear to it, Mr. Williams."

"The last two I bought from you run away the first chancet they got. I'll admit they was good workers till they run away."

"You shoulda chained 'em."

"Can't chain 'em when they're out in the field pickin' cotton. Run clear away out of the cotton field. Set the dogs on 'em, but t'weren't no good. There's people helpin' 'em, I swear, or we'd find 'em."

"I heard tell Mr. Holbrook bought himself one fine horse in New Orleans," Captain Dawson said. "He plannin' on racin' him?"

"He don't confide in me none," Williams said. "I think he jes likes ownin' horses, havin' folk come up here and admire 'em."

"I say if a man can pay for fine horses, makes no difference what he intends doin' with 'em."

"Well, he pays for 'em . The tobacco was not too good last year, but the cotton done all right. Had some worms and some stainin', but we got a hunnerd and three bales cotton lint to the gin by the end of October."

"Sounds like you can use some more hands."

"We can always use good ones. Got forty now, but some of the women is no good. We're ginnin' the last of the crop now and beginnin' plantin' the new one, so if Purnell says they's any decent hands in that oxcart, maybe we can do business, but I got to be careful with the money, or Mr. Holbrook will skin me for sure."

"One thing I know, the weather's turned nice," Captain Dawson remarked.

"We been havin' a good spring all right," Williams replied. "Just a few cold days. Not enough to spoil the sparrigrass beds of Miz Holbrook. Ever tasted sparrigrass, Cap'n Dawson?"

"Can't say as I have."

Williams glanced over at Purnell. "Go see what the cap'n got in the wagon. Go on, Purnell, take the torch and look 'em over real good."

The wagon tilted toward the ground as the man climbed in. Aurelia got glimpses of his dark features in the few thin streaks of torchlight. He knelt down and looked Dilly over, lifted her chin and examined her teeth, then moved over to Moe and Ben and measured their arms and legs with a piece of string. When he got to Aurelia and Yolanda, he looked startled.

"What you got, Purnell?" Mr. Williams called out. "Is it worth my while lookin' in that cart, or are they all half dead?"

"They is some young uns," Purnell said.

"How young?"

"Two boys, looks to be about ten and eleven. And two females and a girl chile. One of the females is sickly."

"What about the other one?"

"She be a greaser. Ain't no nigger blood in her as far as I can see. The girl chile look white as snow."

"The children will grow, Mr. Williams," said Captain Dawson. "Just need some meal and a bit of bacon now and then.

"You got debt papers on the greaser and the girl?"

"No papers, but you show 'em to Mr. Holbrook. They's pretty enough to be in the house."

"How much does that come to, then?"

"Four hunnerd."

"You got a sick one in there."

"Take the sick one off my hands, and I'll take off twenty dollars."

"Take off fifty."

"Cain't do that."

"Twenty dollars and the oxcart throwed in."

"Sold."

Purnell attached his horse to the wagon and pulled it across the stream and then onto the path that ran up through a grove of cypress trees. The horse snorted with the weight of the oxcart, hooves chopping crisply through fallen leaves and broken twigs. Cotton fields stretched in unbroken moonlit rows to the sides of the path, and up ahead on the crest of the hill was a two-story stone house. The path curved steeply upward, and as they passed the house, snatches of piano music floated out into the darkness.

The path grew narrower and soon they were traveling over a bridge, the wheels of the wagon clacking on the wooden boards. The trees were dense here and shut out the moon and stars and left only Purnell's torch to light the way.

Purnell stopped the wagon in front of a row of cabins. He reached in and gave Dilly's bare foot a tug.

"Come on, girl, time to get up."

"Cain't she walk?" Williams asked as he rode up on his horse.

"Don't seem like," Purnell replied.

Dilly moaned and batted her head against the floor of the wagon, as if to rid herself of something that had landed in her hair.

"How sick is she, Purnell? You din't tell me she was dyin'. She doesn't have the cholera, does she?"

"Don't seem like the cholera, Mr. Williams."

"Then what is it?"

"Seem more like worms or quinsy, Mr. Williams."

Purnell climbed up into the wagon. He looked around for Aurelia and Yolanda and the two boys. He rummaged through the ratty quilts that lined the wagon, even looked under the wagon, thinking they might have hidden themselves in the undercarriage or were hanging from the running gear.

"We done lost 'em all," he finally called down to Mr. Williams.

AURELIA COULD HEAR the whinny of horses and men's voices coming closer.

"Dogs can smell a body, livin' or dead, if it's out in the open," Mr. Williams said. "You see somethin' down there? No, not over there, you hear me when I talk to you, I said over there."

Aurelia had dug the hole closest to the river where the dirt was soft, and she and Yolanda lay in it, bodies burrowed into the earth like turnips beneath a loose blanket of ripe loam and rotting leaves.

"Did that grass just move, Purnell? Poke your stick over there."

Yolanda coughed once, a small cough, no louder than a hiccough, and Aurelia put her lips to her mouth and breathed down her throat and rocked her the way she had when she was a baby. "We're playing a hiding game," she whispered. "If no one finds us, we win the game and can go home."

"I din't see no grass move, Mr. Williams. The dogs are gone over to the river, they smellin' somethin' over there."

"Well, call 'em back to smell over there, where I saw the grass movin'."

"I din't see no grass movin', Mr. Williams."

"What use are the dogs, runnin' off in all directions, when the grass is movin' over here? Did you say you thought they was headin' east, or was you just talkin' to hear yourself?"

"I'd say it was likely east, Mr. Williams, and then south they'd go if they was headin' for Mexico. If they go west, they gwine catch themselves some Indians maybe. I say it be clear they done gone east."

"I think there's somethin' over there. Don't you see what I'm talkin' 'bout?"

"The dogs run off to the river, Mr. Williams. They din't smell nothin' here worth their time. Look here, it be nothin' but some rocks."

"You get down and part the prairie grass with your hands, and you beat at the ground till you find somethin', and you poke that stick around till you feel a body, we're not goin' back and tellin' Mr. Holbrook they all got away."

"I say we go over 'cross the river where the dogs is, Mr. Williams. The dogs is leadin' us that way, Mr. Williams. We ought follow the dogs."

NIGHT WAS NEARLY gone, the pink sky swallowing up moon and stars. Aurelia had lost track of time. Had night come and gone once or twice? Had she slept or dreamt that she did? There was no longer any sound of horses or men or howling dogs.

A squirrel, eyes flickering with interest, stopped to stare before it scooted away. A coral snake crawled past. A flock of wild turkeys flew up into the trees. A pack of coyotes, motionless in the rising heat, sniffed the air. One drew close, grass snapping as it approached. It stopped, looked out onto the prairie, and bounded away.

Aurelia uncovered Yolanda's head. Her mouth was full of dirt and leaves.

"*Tengo sed,*" Yolanda said. "I'm thirsty."

Aurelia could hear the tumbling rush of water somewhere, and smell its mossy odor, but she couldn't leave the hole she had dug until dark. Fennel grew wild here. She pulled a few tender stalks loose from the dirt and told Yolanda to chew slowly, that they tasted like licorice water.

"I DIN'T SEE no wagon come by," Williams said.

"I tracked it here," Joseph replied.

"I don't buy stole slaves. Mr. Holbrook skin me for sure I buy stole slaves."

Joseph was sure it was the wagon the Rangers had used. It had traveled approximately eight miles along the Guadalupe, stopped at Dripping Springs, then turned onto the road to Pecan Point. The wheel tracks in the spongy ground were no older than a day. There was no mistake about it.

"No one's been bought nor sold in a month," Williams said. "Ain't seen no greasers neither. You say the Rangers took 'em ?"

"Yesterday."

"Din't see 'em."

"This is where they were brought all right," Joseph said.

"There's no slaves in the fields but what we own. Look for yourself."

Williams waited at the rise while Joseph rode slowly past the cotton fields, his gaze flitting from one stooped figure to another. There was nothing familiar about any of them, just an army of seasoned hands sidling like caterpillars along the furrowed rows.

"I tole you they wasn't here," Williams said when Joseph rode back.

"You're lying. I tracked them here," Joseph said, his anger like a sharp stick between his shoulder blades.

"You got no right callin' me a liar. I could shoot you for that, no one would blame me. So you best keep your mouth closed tight. If there's slaves here don't belong, you show 'em to me, but mind your mouth."

Joseph headed up the path to the slave cabins, five tumble-down shacks that tilted precariously toward the dirt. Joseph went in and out of each one. Except for varying degrees of decay, they were all alike, plank beds near the twig-and-clay chimney, smaller beds made of scantlings near the door, ragged clothes hanging from pegs pounded into the log walls, corn shucks and moss and even wads of cotton shoved into the gaps in the walls, dirt floors hard-packed and as shiny as polished copper.

A young girl with a bandaged leg lay on a plank bed in the last cabin. She sat up, startled at the sight of Joseph.

"Mr. Holbrook own that one," Williams said. "Paid for her, papers and all. If Mr. Holbrook saw me lettin' you run all over this place, I wouldn't have to shoot you, he'd shoot you hisself. But I like to be neighborly, don't want any bad feelin's with you. Might be sometime you want to sell some slaves to me, and we can do business and not be enemies."

Joseph got back on his horse and continued up the winding path, Williams following close behind.

"When did you say they were took?" Williams said.

"Yesterday."

"I'm not sayin' for sure, but come to think on it could be my head boy Purnell bought 'em. Seems I heard he buried one last night that died of quinsy and four other ones run away. I'm sayin' maybe. I'm not for certain. But if Purnell bought 'em and he done promised Mr. Holbrook's good money for a dead nigger and four runaways, Mr. Holbrook will for sure kill him. That don't mean I know anythin' about it, and don't take my meanin' to be that way."

They rode past a forest of mesquite to the cook house, a small stone building with vines creeping between the stones and a portion of the roof lying in moldy pieces beside a bright-green herb garden.

"Mattie, this man lookin' for some people he say Rangers took," Williams said when he and Joseph stepped inside.

"Ain't seen any," Mattie said and wiped her hands on the towel that was tied around her waist. She was a slim Negro woman with light skin and pointed features. A small boy, a piece of cloth tied around his head, knelt on the floor scrubbing pots with the spongy skeleton of a loofah gourd. On a stool near the stove a teenaged girl with darkly freckled cheeks and grass-green eyes sat sewing lace onto the hem of a yellow gown. The room was steamy with the vapors from kettles and frying pans.

"A Mexican girl and her daughter," Joseph said. "And a Negro woman and her two boys."

"Don't know nothin' 'bout it," Mattie said.

"The Negro woman was sick," Joseph said.

"No sick ones here," Mattie said.

"Look around," Williams told Joseph. "Go ahead. You come this far pokin' into our business, you kin go on and finish up."

A narrow door led into the adjoining room. Dampness had crept up through the stone floor and painted a mildewed stripe on the gray walls. Sacks hanging at the windows turned the daylight peach-brown, and the beds were so close together a person could have walked from one end of the room to the other without stepping on the floor.

"Did you say you had papers on the niggers?" Williams asked from the doorway.

Joseph didn't even bother to answer him.

JOSEPH DECIDED TO travel east toward the Pedernales, stopping at small towns along the way.

"Was they carryin' anythin' valuable with 'em?" a drover in New Braunfels asked Joseph. "'Cause they's been lawless Rangers raidin' ranches lookin' for gold. Hit the Sturz place last month, couldn't find nothin', so they took all the curtains off the windows 'fore they set the place on fire."

"Was they a man in the wagon?" a blacksmith in D'Hanis asked

Joseph. "Name of Jack Pearl? I heard Indians scalped him on his way to Twin Sisters to buy hay for his horses."

"Been a Comanche band raidin' cattle up around Quihi Creek," a rancher in Fredericksburg told Joseph. "Kil't a farmer and burned down his place. The Rangers took most of 'em in a fight and was marchin' 'em to Clear Fork when they scattered. Could be I heard about a greaser with 'em."

"I was roundin' up cattle in Palo Duro Canyon," a rancher in Seguin said, "and found myself in the company of an Indian agent by the name of Neighbors. He was takin' a band of starvin' Arapahoes over to the Red River, goin' to put them on the Brazos reservation up there, and he tole me a tale about a white girl could speak Arapahoe. I din't hear about no greasers."

At the mouth of a steep canyon on a tributary of the Guadalupe it began to rain. It rained so hard Joseph couldn't tell where the uneven banks of the river ended and the prairie began. He was soaked through and tired. His whole body ached. His skin hurt. The soles of his feet gave him pain. Even the hair on his head was sore. Straight ahead the river foamed across the swollen prairie toward home. And beyond that lay the city of San Antonio.

17

THERE WAS A ROUGHNESS to San Antonio, an unfinished look, as if everyone had gotten to work making money before the buildings were built and the roads smoothed out. Wagon wheels had carved deep gullies in the unpaved streets and ground the rocks to a fine silt. Where the holes were the deepest, *nopales* and scrubby mesquite had sprung up, and at the far end of the street rabbits ran back and forth across the road.

Stainbach's, a stone building on a narrow street across from the main plaza, proclaimed itself the finest boarding house in San Antonio. At first Joseph couldn't even find the door, which was half hidden by a wagon load of turkeys. And when he got inside, he could barely see his way through the shadowy gloom to the desk against the wall. It was not yet dark, but the fandango in the adjoining building had already begun, and loud music and screams and an occasional fusillade of pistol shots peppered the sky above the open door.

"We got plenty of rooms," the man at the desk said. He was a redhead with a soft ruff of hair girdling his head and chin. "The cheapest ones are near the front door. I take off ten cents because those rooms are the noisiest. It quiets down by dawn, though, I can assure you. You get fed two meals a day and I'll shoe your horse for a dollar a set. With good nails, too, nothing cheap."

"I'll pay the ten cents extra for a room away from the door," Joseph told him, "although I'm tired enough to sleep through a war, if I have to. As for my horse, his shoes are fine. I am hungry, though."

"Beef stew in the dining room till nine o'clock."

The dining room was to the right of the desk. Spilled gravy and hardened lard had stained the muslin cloth on the iron-footed table, and the walls were streaked with soot from the fireplace, which was littered with broken dishes and the skeletal ash of a foot-long log.

Joseph sat down at the table and filled a bowl with watery stew from the stew pot in the center of the table. The stew was salty, the meat in it gray and slimy. There were a few pieces of cornbread strewn across the table with mold growing on their crusts. The other lodgers, probably freighters from the looks of their heavy boots and soiled clothing, ate with abandon, poking each other with their spoons and belching and farting as they reached over one another to snatch morsels of meat out of the stew pot.

Joseph ate just enough to cut his hunger and then headed to his room, which was at the end of a dark corridor studded with heavy oak doors. The room was only big enough for a bed, and the single window had a tattered blind but no glass, so that the ruckus from the street and the produce wagons clattering over the mesquite swept through as if there were no walls. Despite it all, he lay down on the smelly bed, buried his head into the lumpy, sweat-stained pillow and was soon asleep.

In the morning he rose early. Rather than eat what was being served in the big pot in the dining room, he walked out to the main plaza and bought cheese and bread and ate it sitting on a stone wall next to an adobe building with writing on it that said "Cheap Cash Store and Saloon." Through the open door he could see girls in flounced skirts leaning against a gleaming wooden bar. Up ahead vendors had set up tables and were selling songbirds and live chickens. Oxcarts bulging with hay and hides and wood rolled through the plaza, barely missing the barefoot children who ran in and out behind boxes of vegetables and sacks of flour.

When he had finished his breakfast he walked back to Stainbach's and retrieved his horse from the stable and set out. Aurelia had once lived here, Tomás said, and Joseph thought—irrationally and without real hope—that if he rode down every narrow rutted street in the city he would find her.

At four o'clock in the afternoon he found himself in front of the crumbling San Fernando Church on the edge of the plaza. The double doors of the church gaped open, its cracked bell clanging in its stone cupola. He tied his horse to a post and went in.

"Are you Catholic?" the priest asked Joseph.

"Jewish."

"Ah."

"I'm looking for a woman named Aurelia. She once lived in San Antonio. She has a small child with her, a girl."

"There are many Aurelias here. Without her father's and mother's names I can't help you."

Spiraling motes of dust, caught by faint rays of light from the stained glass windows, landed quiveringly on the heads of the saints while the priest waited for Joseph to say something else.

"Would you like to be baptized?" the priest finally asked.

Joseph shook his head, gave the priest a fifty-cent piece, and went out onto the plaza again.

A narrow street veered off to the west. It was hardly a street, merely a cow path with barely enough room for two carts to pass and buildings set so close together their walls cast a dreary shade over the few *carretas* that were loading goods into the side doors of the dingy shops. The shop names, some in German, some in Spanish, were printed across the tops of the buildings or written on signs suspended from ironwork balconies.

And that was when he saw it. A shop with doric columns planted in front of its dirt-streaked windows and a faded, hand-lettered sign propped above the Grecian pediment. McCORKLE & KIMMEL, WOMEN'S MILLINERY. Isaac's store. Just seeing the name Kimmel gave Joseph a little shock. It was as if he had seen Isaac's image on the side of the building.

Through the window Joseph could see a man behind the counter staring at half-empty shelves on the opposite wall. People were passing in the street, but no one went in. Joseph started to turn away, but the man had spotted Joseph and waved for him to come in.

The interior of the store smelled of dried apples and leather. Women's hats were on a table to the left of the door, some of them covered with pieces of paper to keep off the dust. Others were paperless, as if the paper had gotten too dirty and torn and had to be thrown away. The hats hadn't been tried on recently. Even in the dim light of the store Joseph could see the dust that had settled on feathers and veils and brims.

"Are you Cyril McCorkle?"

"I am."

"You're older than I expected."

"How would you know how old I'm expected to be?" His eyes were a bright blue in their dark pouches.

"You wrote me a letter. I tried to figure your age by that."

"Why would I write you a letter when I can hardly write my name?

"It was about my brother."

"Which brother was that?"

"Isaac. Isaac Kimmel."

"Well, you took a good long time in gettin' here, I'd say. We joined the Union and won a war with the Mexicans while I was waitin'. If you've come here lookin' for money, I'd say you're a fool. People ain't buyin' nothin' much. There's been a bad siege of gall-fever and dysentery in town. And the cholera is gettin' bad again."

Joseph had his eye on a hat on the shelf. It had a black veil and a bright green feather. Katrin never wore hats anymore, just tied her blonde hair up in a knot and pinned it to her head.

"How much is that hat?"

Cyril took it off the shelf, blew the dust off and handed it to Joseph. "It was fifty-five cents, but I've had it for a while, so I'll give it to you for fifty."

Joseph counted out the coins.

"When'd I write you that letter?"

"1845. May."

"Four years. Same hats. Haven't sold a one till just now. Haven't bought a one. I'm not in the hat business no more. Sell cloth and shovels and lumber and saddles. "

"You've never changed your sign."

"Don't need to. People know me, know what I sell."

The place wasn't like Isaac at all. There was nothing to remind Joseph of his brother, no neatly stacked bolts of cloth sorted by color and shade and quality, none of Isaac's button boxes—gentlemen's buttons in one box, ladies' in another—none of his imported lace fans displayed on a silver tray. But there were some interesting items scattered here and there. Lanterns in shapes that Joseph had never seen before. Hand-tooled harnesses and saddles that Isaac must have ordered from Europe. They didn't look like American saddles or Mexican ones. The leather was too fine. Isaac sometimes did that, bought expensive things because he liked them, not thinking that he might never get a customer willing to pay the price.

"It's mighty peculiar you waitin' till I don't have a nickel left to give you, and then showin' up like this."

"I hadn't meant to show up at all. I've got a wife waiting at home for me and I promised to be gone no longer than a week. I've been gone almost four and don't intend to stay much longer. I tell you that so you won't think I came here intentionally expecting anything other than the few belongings of my brother that you mentioned in your letter. So I'll just take them now and be on my way."

Cyril went into a back room and came back with a hat box that had French writing on the side.

"You weren't here, so I sold his clothes and his horse. You can see business has turned bad, if you were expectin' any money out of it. Been thinkin' that I might give up business and go into farmin'. If you'd-a come much later the store would-a been shut."

Cyril peered over Joseph's shoulder as Joseph opened the hat box and removed the contents and laid them on the counter. Isaac's watch, solid gold, with Isaac's name engraved on the case. His watch fob. A gold locket containing a watercolor painting of a young girl sitting on a bench in a rose garden. A packet of scented letters tied with pink velvet ribbon. A tin box. Inside the box was a cloth package tied with the same color velvet ribbon as the scented letters. Joseph removed the ribbon and gold coins tumbled out onto the counter.

"Well," Cyril said, "here I was spendin' my money when we were makin' it and he was puttin' his in that box."

Joseph stared at the coins for a few moments, and then counted them out. One thousand four hundred dollars. He hadn't thought Isaac could have saved that much money in his entire life.

"You're mighty quiet for just findin' enough money to buy all of Texas," Cyril said as Joseph put the coins back in the box.

"I'll grant you, it's a lot, but not quite that much," Joseph replied, too stunned to say anything else.

"He never said he had that much," Cyril muttered.

"He never did," Joseph agreed.

Cyril was staring at him now, waiting to see what he would do, and since Joseph hadn't formulated anything yet—in fact, had not yet recovered from the shock of all that wealth laid out on the scratched counter—he proceeded to walk through the store, examining what was on the shelves, poking through boxes and sacks, unrolling bolts of cloth, checking woolens for moth holes, all the while pondering the implications of his sudden windfall.

"Well, what are you going to do with it?" Cyril said.

"I'm thinking," Joseph replied.

There were a few boxes of men's accessories relegated to a spot next to the trash barrel. Neck ties that buckled at the back of the collar, fur-lined mittens with ivory buttons, black elastic arm garters, straight canes with carved animal handles.

Fourteen hundred dollars *was* a lot of money. Even if it couldn't buy all of Texas, it could buy a lot of it, and Joseph thought of how easily it could have been lost to him. He had been so intent on finding Aurelia that he hadn't given a thought to what might have been left of Isaac's business. He could have gone down another street and never seen the store. And even if he had turned down that street and seen the store, he might have decided when he saw Cyril McCorkle through the window that there was no advantage in making the man's acquaintance, that by the meagerness of the goods on the shelves it was obvious there was nothing left of Isaac's investment. And even if Joseph had purposely found the street and the store and gone inside, Cyril McCorkle could have already gone through Isaac's possessions and taken the money for his own. But none of that had happened. Joseph had gone down the right street (mistakenly or not) and had gone into the store and Cyril McCorkle had turned out to be an honest man.

It was then that Joseph decided that the money wasn't entirely his.

He turned toward Cyril. "I'll give you two hundred dollars for everything in the store."

"Now, wait, what sense is that?"

"I'm making you a business offer."

"I ain't got two hundred dollars in goods."

"I know that."

"Seems like you don't. A person would have to be dumb and blind to think there be two hundred dollars' worth of anythin' in this store. Isaac didn't tell me he had a dim-witted brother. He said you were the young one, but he didn't say how you couldn't figure out that this store ain't worth the matches to set it on fire."

Joseph glanced at the shelves again. "I'd say there's no more than fifty dollars' worth here. But I'll give you two hundred dollars, and you pack up what goods you've got and bring them up to the hill country."

"Where is that?"

"North on the Guadalupe River. We could use a store. We'll be partners, just like you and Isaac were. Fifty-fifty."

"There's not enough here to sell."

"I'll buy more. I'm not a shopkeeper. I'll need someone to run it. I'm willing to make you a partner."

"There's Indians in the hill country."

"And ranchers wanting to buy goods. They have to drive over to Fredericksburg now when they need something. There'll be money to be made."

"You just thought of that right this minute?"

"Right this minute."

"Well, I don't know."

"I'm telling you I'm willing to share."

"A few coins throwed my way would be more to my way of thinking. I like to do things my way. You seem like a man wants to tell me how to do it your way."

"I'm easy to get along with. You'll see that I am. I never push anyone to do anything that goes against their nature. It's up to you. I'll give you two hundred dollars if you bring everything in the store up to the hill country. Otherwise you don't get anything. So if you're willing to be partners with me, then we'll be partners. But if you're afraid of Indians, you can stay here without making any money or you can close the doors, like you said."

"Indians don't scare me."

"Then we have a deal?" Joseph said.

"Isaac never told me how fast you talk, you spin my head around so I can't think, comin' in here and wantin' to buy old goods."

"And your services as a shopkeeper. Two hundred dollars for the goods and you."

He was in his fifties, Joseph thought, still young enough to teach the running of a business. The stubborn streak was something Joseph could excuse, or at least get used to.

"It must be lonesome sitting here day after day, the goods getting older and dustier and no one comes in, not even to sit down and talk a while," Joseph said. "I suppose you've thought about all kinds of things you'd rather be doing than this, and if I hadn't come in today and opened up that box and made you an offer, you might be well on your way to somewhere else. It's only natural you'd be suspicious of someone like me coming along and asking you to do something you never thought about doing, but I think we've both found good fortune today, and I take no offense at your calling me dim-witted, since you don't know me, but I'll tell you right now, if you take my offer, my generosity in that regard will stop and I won't expect ever to hear that kind of talk from you again."

"You sure are a prickly sort. I don't know if I want to do business with someone tells me what words I can use. A man can't talk the way he wants ain't a man."

"I'm telling you my conditions."

"Isaac would turn over to see me close these doors."

"Isaac's dead."

"You don't tell me. I saw him. I was there."

"Well, good luck to you," Joseph said and headed for the door.

"Did I say anything yet? Did I say no? Did I say I didn't miss talkin' to people, bein' alone here, Isaac dead and the days each one of them longer than a year? Isaac picked the store out, and said what to put in it, and now he's gone, and you caught me without warnin', talkin' fast and not givin' me a chance. And I didn't call you dim-witted. I said Isaac never did say he had a dim-witted brother, so that's not the same thing, and it's your money to spend any which way you want."

"I've asked you to go into business with me. I'd like an answer."

"Well, if you're fool enough to want to buy a store not worth anythin' and a man set in his ways, then I'm not the one goin' to stop you."

"Good," Joseph said. He gave Cyril twenty gold coins, explained what route to take to the Guadalupe and what landmarks to watch out for, and then he went back to San Fernando Church and asked the priest if he'd ever buried a Jew by the name of Isaac Kimmel.

"I have never buried one personally, but I did send a Jewish body over to Mission San José to be buried. I knew it was a Jewish body because the penis was cut at the tip and I remember how chilled I was to see it."

The priest said the mission was a few miles downriver. On the west bank, he said.

It was quiet as Joseph rode along the river. No wagons, no rutted roads, just a worn path through the sedge grass. The river had changed color. In early morning it had looked purple and without depth or dimension. Now it was a pale green and the branches of the trees, bending in the breeze, laid deep shadows across its surface.

He reached the mission in late afternoon and tethered his horse to a huisache tree not far from the stone wall enclosure and set out on foot across the weedy ground. The mission was a derelict building of crumbling stones, mossy and soot-covered. The portal doors beneath the dome were warped, the doors overlapping at the top and gaping open at the bottom. Part of the roof had fallen in on itself and the sculptured saints of the facade, ravaged by nature and vandals, were broken and chipped, some of the figures gone entirely, some lying in pieces beneath the once majestic arches.

The mission priest, in mud-spattered vestments and a floppy hat, was working in a vegetable garden on a patch of dirt between the chapel and the sacristy. He didn't seem surprised that Joseph had come inquiring about Isaac.

"I remember your brother well. His was only the fourth Jewish body I had ever seen. I said a prayer for him and buried him in the same way I would have buried a Catholic. I was very curious and looked at him carefully. Other than the mark of circumcision, he bore no signs of illness. He appeared to have died suddenly, perhaps in his sleep."

"I'd like to see his grave," Joseph said.

The priest led the way along a shrub-choked path to a gate in a low stone wall, then past marble angels and rusty iron benches and toppled headstones. The cemetery appeared abandoned, although there were signs of freshly dug graves here and there among the weeds and shrubs. Isaac's grave, marked by a plain wooden cross, was at the far end of the cemetery.

"A granary once stood here," the priest said. "The mission needed the ground for burial plots."

"I'm sorry that the burden of his burial fell on strangers. A casket and gravedigger had to be paid for. Isaac would want me to pay all his debts."

"The Moke family and the Epsteins have a burial society that ships Jewish bodies out of Texas for burial. No one came forward to advise what to do with your brother, so they prepared his body and brought it to me. I couldn't promise a Jewish burial, since this is Catholic ground, and they accepted that. The mission paid nothing. I think your brother is at peace here, but if you wish you may take him with you when you leave."

"There's no need to disturb him."

The priest told Joseph to spend as much time at the grave as he liked. Joseph watched him walk back across the cemetery, head down, dark brown robes flapping against the headstones. Joseph suddenly felt foolish. There was no real purpose in seeing Isaac's grave. He knew his brother wasn't in it, that only his bones and a few strands of hair remained. And yet.

"Well, Isaac," he said, "here I am. I'm not sure why I've come. As you always said, a man's actions are more mysterious than the workings of the universe. I'm pretty sure your spirit, if there is such a thing, is somewhere else. You never did like cemeteries."

The cross sagged in the wet ground. Joseph bent over and righted it. He imagined he could see Isaac's shape in the softly curved mound of dirt. His stomach would be right about there, his two legs ending in a clump of weeds.

"If you could sit up and look around you'd see the river running by and birds roosting in the trees, but I think you'd scream pretty loud if you could see this cross sitting on top of you right about where your forehead would be."

It had begun to rain, a moist, humid rain that sat lightly on the branches of the trees.

"Texas is a pretty lawless place. People getting killed for no reason. Yet here I am and don't intend to leave. Besides which, I've gone and done what I said I'd never do. I've taken over your business. I've even taken over your partner, and if I haven't made a mistake, I think he'll make a good one. I don't have the advantage of hearing what you have to say about it. You never wrote much about him, but then you never wrote me about the girl in the locket either. I guess we all have our secrets. At any rate, Cyril doesn't seem to mind being partners with another Jew. At least he made no mention of it. I can tell you, though, that he thought I was deranged at the money I offered. He seems to me to be a man singularly lacking in imagination. He could see nothing but what was on the shelves. He couldn't even see as far as the street outside the door. He let the store fall to dust. You would be sick to see it. But he appears to be an honest man and it will be an adventure to see how our partnership turns out. I'll send the burial society ten dollars to make sure your grave is kept neat and give five dollars to the priest who buried you. He could have refused the commission. I hope you weren't too miserable at the last, that your suffering was brief."

He walked over to the wall, picked a bouquet of bluebonnets and laid them across the grave.

"Thank you for the money, Isaac. My mind is filled with all sorts of possibilities for the use of it."

THE JAIL, A TWO-story building with broken bottles and bits of glass embedded in the plaster of its outer wall, was across from Moke's Store at the other end of the plaza. Vendors wandered through the damp interior of the jail as freely as they did out in the plaza, and overhead, bats as large as crows, their bony bodies nearly as dark as the rafters, clawed at the damp stones. Some of the jail doors were open and whole families were picnicking half in and half out of the cells.

The jailer's office, a windowless room to the right of the main door, was crowded with peace officers waiting their turn to go upstairs where the criminal cases were being heard. Some of them had bought tamales or enchiladas and were eating while they waited, others were sitting on benches along the walls dozing or shouting out the door to passersby, and the air inside was choked by clouds of dust from the street and by flies from the adjacent corral where the jail's work horses were stabled. The commanding officer of the jail, Colonel Weller, had no desk, but sat on a bench along the wall with the rest of the peace officers and was mildly annoyed when someone pointed him out to Joseph.

"I have a complaint," Joseph said.

"About what?" Colonel Weller replied. He was a scruffy-looking man in a tattered uniform, the sleeve of his missing arm pinned up from elbow to shoulder.

"About a group of Rangers who came onto my place up in the hill country without invitation or reason and proceeded to hang two Negroes and kidnap five people. The man leading them said his name was Dawson. Captain Dawson. He said he and his men had been camping on the Nueces."

The colonel walked out into the corridor with Joseph.

"Now, look, that ain't a complaint. A complaint is someone stole your horse or robbed you in the street."

"He said they were Texas Rangers."

"He could have said anythin' he wanted to say. Rangers fought with me in the Army. They followed Zachary Taylor, just as I did as a soldier, and they fought the Mexicans bravely at Monterrey. Finer soldiers you'd never want to see. Things have changed since the war. There are outlaw Rangers roamin' the hill country now, some of them paid a dollar a day by ranchers to kill Indians, some of them chasin' after escaped slaves for the bounty or for the fun of it, all of them dangerous and unpredictable."

"But they killed two men for no reason."

"They must-a had a reason."

"I'm telling you they didn't."

"We just had a war, you know. Men are on their own. Rangers ain't what they were when Austin brought them together and told them to protect the frontier. The frontier's changed. No one knows for sure where it's at any more. Some of the Rangers is now as bad as Indians. I don't claim them for the Army or for Texas, and if you've got complaints, I'm not the one to answer you."

"You're not going to go after them?"

"We have to catch them doin' somethin' wrong first, and I don't know when or where that might be."

When Joseph was outside again he could hardly see, he was so full of rage. Something had come over him while Colonel Weller was talking. He had wanted to reach over and throttle him. And now all he could think of was that he wanted to kill Captain Dawson. He wanted to hang him from the same tree he had hanged Luck from, wanted to shoot him full of holes, wanted to tear his scalp from his head and hang it from his saddlebag.

He rode blindly through the streets, not knowing where he was or where he was heading. He told himself he had to calm down, that no one made him come to Texas, and if this is the way Texas was, he would just have to accept it and swallow his bile or go crazy.

THE AUERBACH WAGON was in the yard when Joseph got home. Herman Auerbach was sitting in the kitchen eating pecan pie while his wife Sophia kneaded bread dough in a wooden mixing bowl.

"You've been away a good long time," Sophia said. "Katrin had a nice baby boy while you were gone." She brushed a curl away from her forehead with two floury fingers. "We got here day before last and there she was, all alone having her baby, and Herman said we couldn't go home and leave her. A big baby she had, too. Doesn't cry much, but he looks healthy enough."

"I heard about the hangin's," Herman said "And when I saw the hogs I sold Luck runnin' loose I knew we better get over here. He wouldn't let the hogs go unless there was somethin' terrible goin' on. I recognized the hogs first thing. Banded neck, black and white."

"I let them go," Joseph said. "I opened the pen and let them out. I let Luck's horses go. And Nathan's, too. And their cattle. None of it was mine to keep."

"There aren't any hogs like that in all of Texas," Herman said. He was wrinkled and gray and looked old enough to be Sophia's father. "I bred them. I knew them right away for the ones I sold Luck. The Rangers must have had their reasons for what they done."

"There were no reasons," Joseph said.

"You'll need help now they're gone. I can let you have Javier. He don't cost much. A few dollars a month and a place to sleep. They must have had their reasons."

"I told you there were no reasons."

"There might have been. We can't know everything."

"Luck and Nathan kept out of everyone's way, and there were no reasons."

"Things happen that we don't know about. I've seen it a hundred times in my life, and I'll probably see it a hundred times more before I die."

Katrin was in bed, the baby wrapped in a quilt lying beside her.

"Did you find them?" she said.

"No," Joseph replied.

He had never felt so tired in his life. He wanted to lie down beside Katrin and go to sleep and never wake up. Instead he picked up the tightly wrapped baby and held him in his arms. He had never held a baby before, had never even studied one up close. A boy. He had corn-silk hair and Katrin's blue eyes and felt no more substantial than a loaf of bread.

When their father disappeared, Isaac took Joseph all the way to New York to look for him. *Maybe he came back from Europe with Mama and they lost their way,* Isaac said. *Maybe Papa forgot where he left us.* Isaac looked for their lost father for years. Whenever he traveled to a new city for business, he would look for him. Joseph always thought such single-mindedness was a sign that Isaac couldn't think logically. *Let him go, Isaac,* he would say. *Who needs a father, anyway, especially one who forgets where he left his own flesh and blood.*

Katrin touched Joseph's arm. "Joseph?"

Sophia had said this was a nice baby. The only thing Joseph knew for certain was that this baby was no different than any other and would grow up in his own way no matter what Joseph had to say about it.

"Joseph?"

He didn't know what to say. But for Katrin's sake, he thought he should say something.

"If you don't mind, I think I'll call him Louie, after my father," he said.

18

The Big K
September, 1851

SIXTY FAMILIES LIVED in about a fifty-mile radius of Joseph's Big K Ranch, most of them sheep farmers, some of them cattle ranchers. None of them had as much land as Joseph did. He owned more than two hundred thousand acres running from Kimmel Creek almost to the foot of the Guadalupe mountains. Except for the sheep ranches east of town and the wheat farmers to the south, everything north of Kimmel Creek and for miles across it to the west belonged to Joseph. The Big K was so big that when Joseph climbed up onto his rooftop lookout, he couldn't see anything but his own land. He didn't think of himself as rich, but the way the silver kept piling up he had to admit he was prosperous. Cattle prices had gone up enough so that it had been worth his while to drive his cattle to Comfort this past month and sell them to a drover to take to New Orleans, so he made money on that. Gold-seekers on their way west had started buying cattle from him, too, and a wool buyer from Shreveport had paid him five dollars a pound in July for the wool from his sheep—Angoras from Turkey with wool as soft as duck down. He had enough money now to hire Mexican *tasinques* to shear the sheep and *pastores* to shepherd them away from the pastures where the cattle grazed (cattle died if all they had to eat was the short grass the sheep left behind) and *vaqueros* to tend to the cattle.

Joseph used every cent he got to buy land, any land, with water or without, land no one wanted anymore, land that had no real value to anyone. Some settlers called it quits and left without trying to sell their land and holdings, and if Joseph had wanted to, he could have just waited a while and then gone up to Fredericksburg and staked a claim without paying any money to those who had given up and were on their way back to where they came from, but he didn't think that was fair when whole families had spent a year or more on their land, had built cabins and put in gardens and lasted through a cold winter. He'd offer sometimes as little as ten cents an acre before the settler left, but he always paid something.

In January Cyril McCorkle had arrived, his horse pulling a wagon full of goods. Cyril said he didn't think he was going to stay, but after he ate a few of Katrin's suppers and got nearly drunk on Joseph's whiskey, he said he thought he'd stay after all. He was sleeping in a tent while the store was being built, but every night he sat himself down at Katrin's kitchen table, drank a glass of whiskey and waited for supper.

Javier was the one who told Joseph that the Hausser place was for sale.

"I rode up there last week looking for strays," Javier said, "and Mr. Hausser told me he was going back to Virginia, that the Comanches stole all his horses and his wife died of consumption during the winter and he owes money to a bank in Louisiana and don't know how he's going to pay. He's got good sheep left and a nice piece of land. The house don't look too good, but it's got a roof."

Joseph had other *vaqueros* working on the Big K, but Javier was the one who worked the hardest and kept closest to Joseph, telling him what was going on with their neighbors in the hill country, who had lost horses to Comanche raids, whose baby had died, whose wife ran away. He was thin and dark and reminded Joseph of a prairie dog, watching from his hiding place in the dirt, every once in a while popping up to tell Joseph everything he saw.

They rode over to the Hausser ranch early in the morning, and Mr. Hausser, a short man with hair growing out of the tip of his nose, was sitting on his front porch smoking a pipe.

"I told your boy here that I was thinking of selling," Mr. Hausser told Joseph.

"That's why we're here," Joseph said.

"You still got those sheep, or did they go and die?" Javier asked.

"I don't do business with no one but Mr. Kimmel. You step over there and wait till we're through."

"I bet you let them die, old man," Javier said, eyes flashing. "You got no business in Texas, you don't know nothing about sheep or land or horses neither. I see your old nags with bones sticking out and I told Joseph it wasn't going to be long before—"

"I tell you what, Javier," Joseph said. "Why don't you go and look at those sheep for me while I talk to Mr. Hausser."

"He's got some temper," Mr. Hausser said as he watched Javier get on his horse and ride out into the sheep pasture. "Mexicans are that way. Most act like a friend to your face, and then knock you down when your back's turned. Your boy's worst than most. He looks right at you and doesn't hide a thing."

"He was attacked by Comanches up at Eagles' Pass and they nearly scalped him," Joseph said. "I guess you can tell that by the way his eyebrows are up higher on his forehead than they ought to be. Getting almost scalped has a way of making a man's disposition turn sour. He doesn't mean anything by the way he talks, and I'm sorry if he said anything he shouldn't have."

Joseph spent lots of time making apologies for Javier, and sometimes wondered if it wouldn't just be easier to get rid of him, and then he'd think of how he could trust him to do things, and even to figure out how to solve a problem when Joseph wasn't around. And he wasn't half bad with the other *vaqueros* when he was in a good mood, and was really pretty generous when someone was sick and needed him to do their work for them.

"Well, what's the difference, I don't care how he looks or what he says. I'm through. I'm leavin'. I just want to get out of Texas."

The man looked as if he hadn't washed in a month. Joseph had seen settlers like him before, who, once they got it in their mind that they were through, stopped doing anything at all to help themselves. Men like Mr. Hausser sometimes just got on a horse and left without looking back, without making a plan or having a destination in mind. A few of them ended up full of Comanche arrows before they got very far.

"Everything's for sale," Mr. Hausser said.

"And the house?"

"The house and what's in it. Make me an offer."

"I don't want to take advantage of you in any way. I know what it's like to have fortunes turn. I watched my brother struggle in business for years, and I didn't always have an easy time of it myself."

"You're pretty prosperous now. I hear they're going to call this part of the hill country Kimmelsburg. That sounds like a prosperous man to me."

"I don't have anything to say about what people call anything."

"Mighty prosperous is what I heard. And here you are come to see what you can take from me."

"I don't want anything from you."

"Then why're you here?"

"I'm here as a neighbor. I'd like to see you stay."

"I've give Texas long enough. It's too damn hard a place to live in."

"Giving up too soon seems the wrong way to go. Sometimes you've got to give a plan a good long time before it succeeds."

"I've tried it for as long as I want. I hate the winters, and the summers aren't any better. And worryin' about Indians stealin' my sheep or maybe killin' me in my bed jitters my nerves so much I cain't hardly think. 'Course, Indians ain't the only things on my mind. Ain't got no more money. And no wife neither. A man cain't live in Texas without he got a woman on the place to help him out. The rain flooded out my house last year and my wife got sick because of the damp, and we could never dry our clothes out, and the walls breathed wet, and I suppose you know she died of consumption. She was a German girl. I hear your wife's German, too. They make good wives when they don't die. But she wasn't used to Texas weather, and now I ain't got the will left to keep gettin' up in the mornin' and lookin' out through that ole broke window and wonderin' where I'm goin' to get the money to keep goin'. I'll just go back to Virginia. I've got family there. If you give me a decent price, I might yet be able to find me another wife in Virginia and get me some good farmland and get rid of this sour taste I got from livin' in Texas."

"I don't know about getting you another wife, but Javier says you owe money to a bank in Louisiana. Maybe I can fix that, loan you money to pay the bank and tide you over, if that will help you some. I loan out at three percent. If you bank with me, I'll give you two. Sometimes people make decisions too quickly and for the wrong reasons and then they're sorry later. I don't want to take advantage of your misfortune."

"I thought you come here to buy me out."

"I'm always willing to buy land, of course, but I don't want you to feel that I'm forcing you to sell. I'd rather lend you money. If you want to give Texas another try, I'll even loan you Javier for a while. If you can stand him. I can tell him how to behave and he'll do it. He does anything I tell him to do. And once he gets to working for you, he'll hold his temper and stick to you like wallpaper. I can certainly spare him for a month or so to catch some horses for you and round up your cattle. Sometimes a job seems too big for one man to do by himself, and just a little help is all a man needs to see his way through a situation."

Joseph could see there wasn't any wood stacked at the side of the house. The man had to be freezing when night came with no wood for a fire.

"Or I can send a few of my cowboys over to get you squared away, if you don't think you can stand having Javier around. I just plain don't want you to think that you have to do anything I say, because this is your place, and I'm only standing here asking you a few questions and trying to see if there's some way I can help you and help myself at the same time. Good neighbors are hard to come by, and I'd sure like you to stay."

"My mind's set. I'm leavin.'"

"All right, then, I'll pay you one hundred fifty dollars for the land and the house."

"Now you say it like I thought you was goin' to. Talkin' so nice and all, I was waitin' to see the Jew in you come out and here it is. You Jews are like vultures, waitin' till a man is so down he can't get up, and then stealin' his goods. Well, I heard Jews can make money out of mud, and I say you're welcome to do it."

Joseph leaned in close to the man and, despite himself, took hold of his shirt at the shoulder. "Why, I take it back about wanting you to stay. I don't want you anywhere around me. I don't want you in the state of Texas, breathing the same air I breathe. That would make me sick. I'm glad to hear what you really think. I'd hate to think I helped someone like you stay in Texas, because you're nothing but a quitter, Mr. Hausser, a coward, afraid of Indians and wet weather, afraid of a little damp inside your house. Your wife probably died just to get away from you. I may be a Jew, but you're the one giving up, running away, not me. I'm just a man who's trying to give you enough money so you don't starve when you get back to Virginia. If you don't want my money, if you think you can do things another way, why, you just tell me right now."

He could see the fright in the man's face, but he wouldn't let go of his shirt, even tightened his fingers on it a little and shoved his face closer.

"Here I've been feeling sorry for you, thinking about your poor dead German wife, a wife like mine who probably cleaned and cooked and baked the way mine does. I was even going to volunteer to tend her grave when you went back to Virginia, but now all I want is to be rid of you, get you clear out of the hill country, pack you up and send you back to where you came from."

Javier had come back and was standing near the steps to the house. Joseph let go of Mr. Hausser's shirt.

"You made me lose my temper, Mr. Hausser," Joseph said. "I try never to do that. I tell Javier that to be mean to someone is the worst thing he can do, and here I went and showed you the worst side of myself, the very worst."

He glanced over at Javier, who was picking his teeth with a twig and smiling.

"It's just what I hear people say," Mr. Hausser said sheepishly. "About Jews that is. They just say those things, and it came out of my mouth without thinking. I don't believe half the things people say."

"Well, I'm sure you're as big a liar as you are a failure, Mr. Hausser. I'll buy your sheep, your house and whatever's in it. I'll have your hundred fifty dollars here for you tomorrow morning, and I want you out of here by afternoon."

JOSEPH COLLECTED THINGS. If something pleased his eye and it was for sale, he'd buy it. Or if he found something out on the prairie that appealed to him, an old arrowhead or a nest with speckled birds' eggs in it, he'd pick it up and take it home with him. An object didn't have to have real value to anyone but him. Sometimes he loaned people money and when they couldn't pay him back, he took goods in exchange. Katrin said she didn't want any of the junk Joseph collected cluttering up her house, especially when she was going to have another baby and needed all the room she could get. So he stored his possessions in Luck's old cabin. There were hand-tooled silver saddles mounted on posts, shotguns standing against the walls. Cowhides, longhorn horns and bear hides were slung over chairs. Buggy whips and ornamental canes leaned in corners. He filled a glass case with bison teeth and arrowheads, ladies' fans, fancy combs, crystal bowls,

Irish lace, Belgian glass, French porcelain. He had a table piled high with books in German and French and even some in English. He grew accustomed to the feel of old porcelain, could tell the quality of lace with a touch of his fingers. He'd pick up an object and hold it in his hands, examine it from every angle, and think about where it had been, who had made it, why it had lasted as long as it had, what stroke of luck had brought it to him, and where it might end up when he was gone.

Lavender-flowered puccoons had grown up around the cedar trees where Nathan and Luck were buried. The creek sometimes overflowed its banks and turned the stones along the old path to their graves an oily gray, and puddles of muddy water would then float in the upturned blossoms of the lacy drifts of verbena. The oxcart was where Nathan had left it, a dead mesquite lying beside it. In the spring lilies sprouted around the rotting bark of the mesquite, and in the summer clumps of top-heavy asters and profusions of morning glories covered it. In the winter pigs ate the yellow blossoms of stinging nettles and cows ate the leaves and when it seemed that the plants were dead to the roots, spring came again and they sprang to life, rain-doused and drinking in the sunshine.

In late afternoons Joseph would sit on the porch of Luck's cabin looking out at the reeds growing like knitting needles in the shallow ponds surrounding the creek. He thought most often of Aurelia on those late afternoons. He sometimes thought he had made her up, that she had never existed at all, but there was evidence all around him that she had once been here. She had left pots of herbs behind (now sere and brown) and dropped her *serape* on the porch as she ran out of the cabin on the day of the lynching (it now lay on a table beside Joseph's chair), and he was sure that he sometimes heard her voice calling to him. He would walk down to the creek thinking she had come back, but would find only scarlet flycatchers on their perches and sparrows feeding on tender grasses, and then he would come back to the cabin and sit silently listening to the shed door banging on its hinges, crushed river rocks falling from its roof like sprays of brown snowflakes, and think about how he could destroy Captain Dawson. He kept a record of the captain's activities in the hill country, a collection of sorts of his depredations, which included all accounts of lynchings of Negroes and Negro sympathizers, as well as indiscriminate slaughter of Mexicans. Joseph also included in his collection of Captain Dawson's rampages any sightings of the captain or information as to his last known whereabouts, which he traced on a map he kept in his cattle inventory. And then he waited for his opportunity.

19

Kimmelsburg
October 1851

KIMMELSBURG WASN'T REALLY a town, just an empty square surrounded by pecan trees and pomegranate bushes. Bishop Smeal came up from San Antonio in October and blessed the cornerstone for the Catholic church, but Comanches were seen riding past the pecan trees right after the bishop left, and although there were piles of stone waiting to be set in place, the church hadn't gotten any further than the cornerstone. The road from Kerrville ended a few miles south of the Big K, and then there was nothing but prairie and hills and Comanches and buffalo. There was no post office, but the mailman—his name was Wilhelm Ludwig—did stop at the Big K on his once-a-week round trip from San Antonio to Fredericksburg and would bring Joseph the *San Antonio Ledger*. Once in a while one of the cowboys got a letter, but that was pretty unusual. Most of them had been wandering over the hill country so long, working at first one ranch and then another, that any relatives or friends they might have had would have given up on them long ago. Joseph never got any letters. No one in Missouri would have written to him. Certainly not Mr. Thurmond, who probably thought Comanches had killed him by now. Joseph would have been more than a little surprised to have gotten a letter from Mr. Thurmond.

Wilhelm had a little buggy that could carry two passengers and two sacks of mail. Joseph always invited him and whatever passengers he had with him into the house, and Katrin would make them all lunch. After lunch, Ludwig would take a nap in the mail buggy, and Joseph would take his passengers across Kimmel Creek and show them his collection. He liked to watch people's reactions when they saw it. Some couldn't take it all in at once, especially the women, who would pronounce themselves faint at the sight and have to go outside and take deep breaths in order to compose themselves. Others, mostly the men, clucked their tongues and shook their heads and said they hadn't seen such a mountain of stuff in one place in all their lives. Joseph, if prompted, would give them a little talk about where he got each piece, and they'd follow him single file through the narrow aisles, and he'd let them pick objects up so they could examine them better. He wasn't afraid they'd break anything, and sometimes he even gave them the thing they were holding if they admired it enough.

"They're just objects," he'd tell them. "Nothing more than curiosities. Certainly nothing to get so excited about that you forget they're just things."

Joseph learned a good bit from Ludwig's stops, how free people were about wanting to know other people's business. If he answered one question, they'd ask two more. Why did he collect the things he collected, why not something else, and what were they all worth, and did he ever try to sell anything, and how did he know where everything was the way objects were piled all over the place, and on and on. He'd stand there and be as polite as he could be, but then he'd begin feeling peculiar, as if he weren't even in the cabin at all, but was outside looking in through the window at what was going on, and he'd stop talking and just stand there until they got the idea that the visit was over.

"JOSEPH ISN'T HERE," Katrin said. "He went to see about buying some more land." She had seen the mail buggy coming when it was still hidden by liveoaks and mesquite and all that was visible were the little puffs of loose sand and dirt and rocks that flew up from the buggy's wheels. Katrin always watched for Joseph that way, stopping what she was doing in the house to come out on the porch and scan the plains for signs of Joseph's horse. Sometimes what she thought was dirt being kicked up by his horse were just dust devils stirred up by the wind.

"It's a mighty cold day," Wilhelm said. He had no passengers with him, and Katrin could see the mail bag sitting inside on the seat, along with the remains of the bread and apples he had eaten on the way up from Kerrville. "My lips are all cracked and raw and I think it's the coldest day I've ever seen."

"It feels like summer to me," Katrin said. She had been out in the yard boiling clothes when she saw Wilhelm's buggy. Lately she could go outside night or day without a shawl, even when she wasn't boiling clothes and standing in the steam, even when the wind was blowing its hardest. Samuel had been born in June, and she had felt hot all the time she was carrying him. He was five months old now and winter was here and she still felt hot. It was probably all the fat that had landed on her before Samuel was born. What did she need with a shawl when she had all this fat on her to keep her warm?

She gave the bubbling water a few more turns with the wooden paddle, and then picked Louie up off the piece of quilt he was sitting on. She could sit Louie down like that when she was working outside and tell him to sit still, and he wouldn't move an inch. Sometimes she let him get up and walk around the yard, but she had trained him not to go past the last row of vegetables and not to put strange things in his mouth and not to dirty his hands.

"You come in and I give you something to eat," she told Wilhelm, "but wipe your feet good before you come inside. And don't make noise, or you wake up the baby."

Wilhelm always brought his buggy around to the new barn behind the house and let his horses feed at the trough beneath the overhang. Then he'd lead them back around the front and tie them to one of the pickets in the fence that Javier had built around the house. There were stepping stones all the way up to the front door, but Wilhelm always managed to track something into the house. Maybe crushed flowers, because Katrin's flower garden was to the left of the path, or maybe even strawberries, when they were in season, because she had fruits and vegetables growing right alongside the hackberry bushes. Hackberry thorns were good for keeping animals away, but they didn't do much for Wilhelm, and he'd sometimes get a torn sleeve or ripped trouser leg on his way to the house. If there weren't any flowers or fruits or vegetables for him to step in, he'd find a nice mud puddle and track dirt into the house that way.

"Last time you come, I scrub the floor two days," Katrin said.

There was a wide flowery smear from Wilhelm's shoes right next to the front door.

"Didn't mean to mash your flowers," Wilhelm said.

"Watch where you step next time," Katrin said and bent down and rubbed it away with her apron. When she was through with that, she got down on her knees and cleaned Wilhelm's boots from the toes to the heels and even made him lift each foot so she could wipe the soles.

"Joseph doesn't appreciate what a good wife he's got," Wilhelm said, when she finally let him sit down at the table in front of the fire. She had made fresh biscuits and she set out a plate of them along with a pot of pickled beets.

When Wilhelm brought passengers with him on his mail run, Katrin noticed that they were more careful about where they stepped than Wilhelm was, but there was still dirt scattered around when they left. Not always from their shoes. Sometimes from mud splatters on their coats. Katrin was crocheting a rag rug, working on it at night, and intended to make it big enough and square enough so people coming into the house could walk on it and never have to put their feet on her bare floors no matter where they stepped.

Joseph had had a man come all the way from Austin to put the floor in the house . The man also built a cellar for storing sacks of flour and sugar and the preserves Katrin put in jars in the summer. Joseph had plans to build a lookout in the attic so he could watch out for Indians, and he was going to make the outdoor kitchen bigger so the pie safe would fit in there instead of taking up room in the parlor. He said when he got through fixing this house Katrin wouldn't remember what the old one looked like. He already had Javier gathering up field stones for a new kitchen and had added a small room for Louie and Samuel to sleep in, although Louie still slept in the bed between Katrin and Joseph. He cried once when Katrin put him to sleep in the room with Samuel. *You're a big boy now,* Katrin told him, but Louie wailed and cried, and Joseph said it was mean to let him cry like that and went and got him.

Katrin didn't want any more improvements to the house, because each one meant more to clean. The new stove Joseph bought had a tin pipe that went out through the kitchen roof, but Katrin had to wipe the soot off the wall every time she baked. Sometimes she started washing soot off the wall and then there'd be a line where she stopped, and she'd end up washing all the walls in the kitchen and then come into the house and wash all the walls in the house. The new floor was shiny when she got through scrubbing it, but if just one person walked across it you could see their footprints. And sometimes there were too many vegetables and fruits in her garden to preserve, and she'd stay up all night for weeks at a time putting them into jars because Joseph said that was what the cellar was for, to store food for the winter. Katrin could hardly keep up with all the cleaning and scouring she had to do and still take care of Louie and Samuel and tend her garden and do all the baking and cooking and sewing and mending and washing and preserving.

"In July it's too hot for passengers," Wilhelm said. "Everyone's waitin' for the rain. I tell them September it'll rain, sure as I am of anything, and then they'll complain because it's rainin'. Now it's so cold no one wants to travel. I always tell people if they wait a few months it'll do whatever you want, and if you go far enough north and east it'll even snow if you wait for it."

"Joseph is always somewhere else," she said.

"All the talk about weather and no one even asks about the Comanches hidin' up near Drippin' Springs waitin' to pounce on you," he said, "and I don't tell 'em, because what good would it do to scare people."

"I tell him stay home a little, Joseph, but he go off all the time." She had Louie on her lap and she kept brushing his lank blond hair back off his forehead. He didn't speak yet, couldn't even say mama or papa. But he understood everything anyone said to him.

"I know all the signs of Comanches, know their habits, I been doin' this long enough," Wilhelm said. He had beet juice rimming his lips. He never used the cloth napkin she put by his plate to wipe his face. Occasionally he blew his nose into it. "But, I'll tell you, it scares me when I come across some unlucky rider who didn't know 'em like I do. In this cold weather, though, even the Comanches stay in their tepees."

"I tell Joseph over and over, stay home. Louie don't talk yet, not one word, and I say Joseph, you stay home, Louie will talk to you. Louie don't like his mama the way he like his papa. He like the way Joseph play with him. Joseph let Louie do anything he want, he let him mess up the floor with bread and jam and he make funny faces so Louie laugh at him. I tell Joseph over and over, stay home, but Joseph smile and don't say nothing. He don't talk to me hardly at all. I can count the words he say to me when he's here."

"Sometimes I wish I could find another line of work," Wilhelm said. "I'd like to get to be twenty-one, and sometimes I think the sun or rain or cold or Comanches will prevent it. But now that Texas is in the United States, I make two dollars more a month on my contract. I think it should be three because of the Comanches and the weather, though."

When he had finished eating, he asked if he could take a look at Samuel again. He had stopped at the Big K with the newspaper the day

Samuel was born and had come into the room with Joseph because Sophia said that the baby looked dead. Joseph rubbed the baby's little arms and legs and breathed into its mouth, and wouldn't leave him alone until he was crying and sniffling and turning pink.

"I never have seen anyone care for a baby the way Joseph did," Sophia had told Katrin. "Herman would have let the little boy die and not thought two minutes about doing anything to prevent it."

"The baby don't look so good," Wilhelm said now, leaning over Samuel's cradle. Louie had been plump when he was born. Samuel looked like one of the dolls Louie carried around. Blue marble eyes, no hair at all, and arms and legs as thin as marsh reeds.

"He ain't growed hardly at all since he was born," Wilhelm said.

"Babies sometimes are weak when they're born," Katrin said and picked the baby up in her arms. "But they grow just fine."

"I almost forgot," Wilhelm said. "Joseph's got a letter."

KATRIN HAD TOLD Wilhelm that Joseph never talked to her, but he did. He said things like *Pass the butter*, or *I think it's going to rain*, or *I hope you slept well last night*. He did lie atop her in the dark, but that was the only time he touched her, and he was quick about it, as if some part of it were distasteful to him. He didn't lie atop her very often, though. Sophia Auerbach told Katrin that Herman could hardly wait till nighttime he was so eager to get her into bed, and he was an old man, nearly sixty, not young like Joseph. Sophia would giggle about the way Herman made love, how he would wear his socks to bed because his feet were always cold.

"Sometimes he wears a jacket, too," she said, "but he's always bare where it matters."

The way Sophia talked it seemed she liked the way Herman was with her, enjoyed what they did together. She said he had pet names for every part of her body and had made love to every one of them. Even under her arms.

"If he doesn't roll me over at least once a night, I worry he's sick," she said.

Well, Joseph wasn't that way. Katrin thought it was because he still thought about Aurelia, although he never talked about her, never even mentioned her name. He never talked about Nathan or Luck either. Sometimes Katrin thought she'd dreamed the whole thing. Except for those two graves with the white wooden crosses Joseph put on top of them, there was no sign that anyone but Joseph Kimmel and his wife and children had ever lived on this land.

Sophia said everyone in the hill country looked up to Joseph, and Katrin told her they wouldn't like him so much if they had to live with him. It wasn't that he was mean to her, she told Sophia; he just didn't notice her. When he came in the house he would sit in a chair and read a book. His favorite one was about how the world started. Every time she saw him reading that one, she wanted to tell him he ought to read the Bible, that all the answers he needed about the beginning of the world were in there. Instead she would say, "Joseph, did you like the pomegranate pie?" and he would raise his head and smile at her.

If he wasn't reading he was doing his accounts. He would dip the pen in the ink and press his lips together, as if the figures wouldn't dare not add up to what he expected. She couldn't understand why he needed to put all those numbers in a book in the first place when he was so good at remembering things. Someone would come to the house to repay a loan, and it seemed like Joseph was just grabbing numbers out of the air the way he could tell them the interest they owed without even figuring it out on a piece of paper.

When he wasn't reading or doing his accounts, he was playing with Louie, reading him stories or just carrying him around on his shoulders. He had even begun to teach Louie to ride, the two of them on Joseph's horse, Louie tied to Joseph's waist with a piece of rope. And Joseph had started bringing Samuel into the bed at night when he cried, so that with the two children between them there was hardly room for Joseph and Katrin. It seemed strange to Katrin that Joseph had so much love for Louie and Samuel and none for her.

"I know what people say about him," she told Sophia, "about how good he is and how fair, but they don't see the way he treats me, how he sits in his chair in the parlor every night without talking. Sometimes I don't think he knows I'm here at all."

"Make him angry," Sophia said. "Whenever Herman hits me, for days afterwards he's as considerate and kind as he can be. He once threw a stool at me and the noise it made when it hit my chest frightened him so much he cried on and off for days afterwards. Anger," Sophia said, "can bring you and Joseph closer together."

Katrin didn't really know how to make Joseph angry, but Sophia was right about so many things that she thought she'd give it a try. It hurt her to do it, but one morning when she was making biscuits, she put three teaspoons of salt into the dough instead of one. And when Joseph sat down for supper she let Louie crawl around on the floor under the table and bang on a tin pot with a spoon. Just those two things ought to have been enough to make anyone angry. But Joseph didn't even make a face when he bit into the biscuits or tell Louie to stop making all that noise, but picked Louie up and made funny faces at him. It seemed to Katrin that Joseph didn't even know he had eaten a biscuit. He could have been on his horse somewhere out in the prairie making faces at Louie for all he noticed anything Katrin did or said. She couldn't think of what else she could do, except maybe not wash the floor one day or let the dirty clothes pile up in a corner or let the windows get so streaked and cloudy he couldn't see out of them. But she couldn't bring herself to go that far. And he probably wouldn't have noticed any of it, anyway.

So when Wilhelm gave Katrin the letter and said it was for Joseph, she put it under her pillow and kept it there. She slept on it at night, and in the morning when she woke up she looked under her pillow to make sure it was still there. She didn't read it. She couldn't read. She didn't know who it was from. All she knew was that she had something of Joseph's, something important, something that he would want to know about, would want to read, and that when she finally gave it to him he would be angry.

THE NEXT TIME Wilhelm came by he was alone and driving a wagon that had a sliding door on the side with lettering that said "U.S. Mail" on it. Joseph went outside to admire it, and Wilhelm asked him how he liked his letter.

"Letter?"

"I thought you'd be surprised, never gettin' any mail, and then gettin' one from Castroville. And from Henry Castro himself. He handed it to me personally, and I told him I didn't think Joseph Kimmel knew anyone outside of Kimmelsburg, and he asked me all about you, and seemed pretty surprised when I told him what an important man you were up in the hill country, and he said he knew you when you just come from Missouri, and I said I've talked to you for over a year and I never even knew you were from Missouri, and he said you were the only other Jew he knew in Texas, and I said I didn't even know you were a Jew, that you must have given it up when you come to Texas. And then I told him you never got a letter from anyone and that you'd probably fall off your chair when you got his."

"When were you going to give it to me?" Joseph said to Katrin. He had the letter open in his hand, was reading it over and over and over.

"I would give it to you. I give it to you now."

He had never talked to her this way. Never. With his face so flushed. And slowly measuring out every word, as if he were trying to keep from shouting.

"You read it, didn't you?"

"How can I read it?"

"Then Sophia read it to you."

"Sophia don't know anything about it, Joseph."

He knew how to shout. She had seen him shout at the cowboys and at Javier when they didn't do what he wanted them to do. She wished he would shout at her now, instead of looking at her with his eyes tight and his mouth set.

"But you knew it was about Aurelia. You knew and you kept it from me."

"Not even a word can Louie speak."

"You knew I would want this letter. You knew it, and you didn't give it to me. You did it on purpose, and I want to know why you did it, what you were thinking about when you did it."

"You never look at me."

"You did it because I don't look at you? Is that what you're telling me you did it for? You kept this letter that you knew I'd want the minute it came just because you think I don't look at you?" He wasn't measuring his words any longer. He was spitting them at her as if he hated her.

"I worry about Samuel all the time. He doesn't grow. I can't see him growing."

"You knew what I'd do when I got it. You deliberately held it."

"Louie don't talk. He would talk to you, but you go away always and leave us. You don't look at me. You don't touch me."

Louie was crying. Katrin picked him up and tried to soothe him.

"I cook for you, Joseph, I keep your house so nice and clean. I do everything for you."

"I'll start out early tomorrow morning."

"Louie don't speak, Joseph. Stay here. He needs you."

She put Louie on the table and wiped his runny nose, and then she buttered a piece of bread and handed it to him.

"Louie is very smart, you know that, Joseph. He understand everything I say to him. I tell him, Louie, run outside and play, and he go to the door. When I call his name, he look up at me. He isn't dumb, Joseph. I can tell he isn't dumb. If you stay home, he will speak. He likes you better than he likes me. He would speak if you stay home. And Samuel doesn't grow. I don't know why he doesn't grow. If you stay home, Louie will speak and Samuel will grow. I don't know why you are the way you are, what makes you like this, that you get a letter and you want to run away. You forgot about her, Joseph. You don't remember her anymore. Stay home."

"Javier can take care of the branding while I'm gone. I'll tell him to stop and check on you every day."

"She don't belong here, Joseph."

"If you need help, Javier can go get Sophia Auerbach. I just won't sleep tonight. I won't waste any more time. Get some food packed for me, and I'll leave right away."

He looked as if he had a fever.

"I don't know why you do this to me, Joseph."

"When I get back I'll clean up Nathan and Dilly's cabin. I haven't looked in that cabin in a long time, but it seems to me I remember a kettle and a brown pitcher and a salt crock. I've got an old pie safe I can put in there, and some forks, and that blue glass decanter I got last month. And the traveling trunk I've got all my Indian arrowheads in. Everyone needs a trunk to store quilts and blankets in. And jelly jars, that wooden chest the Sauers sold me had two dozen jelly jars in it."

The problem was she hadn't held the letter long enough. Wilhelm had told him about it too soon. She had known he would tell him sometime, because Joseph never got letters. She knew Wilhelm would ask how he enjoyed getting one and what it said. If only she had been able to hold it a few more weeks, Joseph might have been angrier. He might have shouted at her. Might even have hit her. But it was too late. Joseph was holding the letter in his hand and talking about going to Castroville to get Aurelia and wasn't even looking at Katrin at all.

20

November, 1851

TWO MONTHS HAD gone by and Joseph had not replied to Castro's letter.

"The letter was written," Castro told Aurelia, "and the mailman has been seen since. There is no question but that the letter has been delivered to Joseph. But I would urge you to reconsider your decision to leave Castroville. Amelia and I have grown very fond of you and your children and would like you to remain with us. Amelia finds the little darkie particularly appealing, and I confess that the familiar way in which you speak of Joseph makes me regret that I had a hand in communicating your whereabouts in my letter to him. I hope his failure to reply is a sign that he sees no connection to your situation. Katrin has had a baby and I pray no harm will yet come to them through my interference."

"Katrin is as dear as a sister to me," Aurelia assured him. Despite Castro's almost violent remonstrances as to the wisdom of a woman traveling across the prairie with two children and no one to protect her, and after stating and restating his hope that her decision to return to Kimmelsburg would not result in any detriment to Joseph and Katrin, he gave Aurelia a wagon and a horse. Amelia prepared a package of corn cakes and pork patties, and Aurelia set out for Kimmelsburg.

The weather was mild and Aurelia expected to be in Kimmelsburg in two days, and in less time if she rode straight through, but by afternoon of the first day Yolanda grew tired of the wagon's bounce and begged Aurelia to stop the wagon for a while.

"Don't go far," Aurelia called out as Yolanda skipped along the riverbank.

Ruben, the baby, had been sleeping, but he now awakened, and Aurelia untied the *rebozo* from around her neck and let him crawl through the thick grass beneath the trees. He was happy to be free, taking fistfuls of leaves and tossing them in the air and laughing out loud. The little doll Amelia Castro made for him out of scraps of cloth was snug in a *rebozo* of its own, a handkerchief that Aurelia had tied across Ruben's chest and hung down his back. He slept with the doll held close to his side, a little boy doll made of brown cotton, with black buttons for eyes.

She watched him as he played. He had Luck's nose and lips and seemed to resemble no part of her. But what child, if not hers, would have ears that had that distinctive whorl at their tips and eyes, set beneath dark brows, a reflection of her own?

Yolanda came running back.

"I saw some Indians, Mamá," she said. "I ran away as fast as I could, but I don't think I ran fast enough."

THEY WERE THREE Comanche Indians. A chief in a horned leather bonnet and two braves. The chief told Aurelia in Spanish that he was called Red Deer and then he motioned for her to hand Ruben to him and to hop up on his horse. Instead she picked Ruben up, took Yolanda by the hand and started for the wagon.

Red Deer removed an arrow from his quiver and told Aurelia again to hand Ruben to him and hop up on his horse.

"No," she said.

He placed the arrow in the string of his willow bow and aimed at Aurelia's head.

Aurelia looked up at the mountains. The clouds were lower than they had been that morning, and the breeze, although still mild, held just the slightest hint of cold.

"We will come with you now," she said, "but tomorrow I will blow my breath into the sky and a Norther will come and the river will overflow and your braves will freeze on their horses."

He merely grunted and pulled her and Ruben up onto his horse and one of the braves took Yolanda onto his while the other brave tied a rope to Aurelia's horse and wagon, and then they headed north. They traveled all day, camping along the river and eating roasted turtle that they scooped out of cracked shells with a horn spoon while Aurelia listened to the hum of Red Deer's thoughts as he pondered what she had said.

That night Red Deer's braves built a tepee made of branches draped with grass. The Comanches took turns sleeping, their bows and arrows beside them, their feet toward the opening of the tepee. Aurelia slept sitting upright, Ruben across her lap, Yolanda by her side, and dreamed about Comanches.

In the morning Aurelia told Red Deer her dream. She told him she had dreamed of a day when settlers would push so far into Comanche hunting grounds that Red Deer would have to move his camp every few days to hunt the few remaining bison, that Those Who Go From Place to Place would wander over the Staked Plains and up into the Guadalupe Mountains, that they would be so hungry they would eat rats and grasshoppers and lizards, so hungry they would pick wood lice from the trunks of trees, not changing horses often enough to cover their tracks, letting themselves be seen out in the open with their wives trailing behind dragging household goods on cedar-pole travois; that soldiers would burn Red Deer's last camp to the ground and leave Red Deer wounded and starving in the sedge grass; that his wives would make a paste of ground roots and hold it to his mouth, and when he vomited it up they would feed him a gruel of wild yam and slippery elm and bayberry bark, a sip every few minutes from their mouths to his; that they would daub his wounds with goldenseal salve and flay their own skin to cover his; that they would walk across the Staked Plains with him on their backs, and at night would dig a bed for him and make a pillow of leaves; that they would carry him east toward the Sabine River through fields of wild asters that spread their pink petals out around them like silken skirts; that the Staked Plains would soon be on fire.

"No," he said, and looked at her with lashless eyes.

They ate pemmican for breakfast and then the two braves rode out into the prairie to hunt for antelope, while Red Deer stayed behind to guard Aurelia and her children.

The sun was like a gold button overhead. There was no breeze. Aurelia lifted her head, pursed her lips and blew a stream of air skyward. She made hardly a sound, but Red Deer, who could hear the jingle of horses' hooves on the crushed rock of a dry wash from half a mile away, turned toward her.

Aurelia blew again, and the sound now clearly resembled the hiss of a snake before it strikes. She blew harder and her breath, now as crackling sharp as lightning, made a sparkly path from her lips past Red Deer's cheek. He stood up and muttered something in Comanche.

Clouds gathered overhead. Aurelia took a deep breath and this time it was as if all the air she had ever inhaled had been waiting to escape—one long smooth whoosh of air that sailed into the sky and dimmed the sun and turned the clouds to thunder.

Red Deer began stomping around and chanting and spitting and shrieking.

A fierce wind began to blow. The sun disappeared. The heavens opened. The river overflowed. Red Deer's braves flew by through the shortgrass, their bodies frozen on their horses. On the small patch of ground beside the river where Aurelia and her children and Red Deer stood, it was as warm as summer.

"You have the spirit of a dead chief inside you," Red Deer said, great drops of sweat falling from his brow.

"I don't think so," Aurelia replied.

"Ghost spirits can hide in a coyote or an elk, in a spring or a rock, sometimes in skeletons or scalped bodies, tiny spirits with bows and arrows, wandering in the world looking for a place to put their power."

"I've never heard of that, but you may be right."

"Sometimes they even hide in a woman."

"That may be true. I won't deny it."

When the weather had returned to the way it was before the Norther came, and the river's overflow slid back into its bed, Red Deer, without a glance back, leaped up onto his horse's bare back, took the reins in one hand and the rope to Aurelia's wagon and horse in the other and rode away.

"Will he come back?" Yolanda said.

"No," Aurelia replied.

When evening came Aurelia gathered sticks for a fire, then covered Yolanda and Ruben with her *rebozo* and lay down beside them. They would sleep tonight and tomorrow they would follow the river. Castro had told her about Irish newcomers escaping hard times, who were settling on a tract of land on the upper banks of the Medina. She would walk until she reached them.

IN THE MORNING the children awoke with the sun, and before Aurelia could head for the river to dig some roots for their breakfast, she saw someone coming on horseback. A young man with long black hair beneath a wide-brimmed hat, his saddle trimmed in silver, his vest and chaps embroidered in blue and gold beads. When he was a few feet away, he dismounted, doffed his hat and swept it across his knees in a graceful bow. She couldn't remember ever seeing anyone do that. She might have once seen the priest in Laredito bow like that before he entered the church, but he may only have been wiping the road dust from his robes.

"I apologize that Red Deer has inconvenienced you," he said in a faintly archaic Spanish. "Red Deer doesn't always know what to steal and who to leave alone. He sometimes forgets that cattle and mules have a more ready market than kidnapped women and children."

"He didn't kidnap me," she said. "He kidnapped my wagon and horse. I brought a Norther down on his braves and froze them on their horses and Red Deer ran away in fright. I would be grateful if you would tell me where I can find my horse and wagon."

"I am sure they are nearby. Where you find Indians and Comancheros there you will always find one or two stolen wagons and one or two stolen horses. I beg of you, what color was your wagon?"

"Blue."

"I see. A blue wagon."

"The horse was brown."

"A good color for a horse."

"You waste your wit on me."

"I have no wit," he said and smiled at her. "I'm plain-spoken and humble."

"Then I will turn you into a plain-spoken and humble stone," she said and smiled back at him.

"I would not like to be a stone, plain-spoken or humble. You say you brought a Norther down on Red Deer and his braves. I saw no Norther. The weather is fine for November."

"I can't explain."

"You say they were frozen?"

"Frozen."

"Since I didn't see it, I have no opinion."

"I require none."

"If I concede that what you say is true, then you are more than a *bruja.* You are a magician. What other tricks can you perform that would entertain me?"

"I don't know what kinds of things entertain you, since I have just met you and cannot read your mind."

"Ah, you can't read minds, but you can change the weather. What else?"

"It's been said that I have cured cholera by looking into the eyes of the sick. I've had some experience in casting spells and performing incantations. I'm familiar with the use of herbs and potions to alleviate physical ailments. I've made one attempt to have someone disappear, and I'm not sure if his subsequent disappearance was a result of my actions or merely coincidence."

"Was that done recently?"

"Not too long ago."

"I have never known Red Deer to run away in fright."

"He threatened my children. I am as unpredictable as the weather when they are threatened."

"I have just come from the trading camp and saw no braves frozen on their horses anywhere in the vicinity."

"They might have melted by now. I have no control over what happens out of my presence."

He laughed out loud and she noticed how white and straight his teeth were.

"Where were you heading before you disturbed Red Deer's spirit and turned his braves to ice?"

"Kimmelsburg. My children are hungry, and if you have something for them to eat in the camp you just spoke about, I would be grateful."

"If you promise not to turn me into a stone, I promise to get you some food. My name is Benito."

"Aurelia," she replied.

THE TRADING CAMP, a temporary village of deer-hide tepees, flimsy lean-tos, Mexican traders and Comanche cattle thieves, was in a valley ringed by stands of purple-fruited junipers and yellow-leafed cottonwood trees. The pungent odor of spilled whiskey and gunpowder clung to the trees and floated in the air like a silty fog. Comanches guarded the entrance to the camp, which was nothing more than a muddy ditch where horses were tethered and stolen cattle corraled. Benito put Ruben and Yolanda on his horse and with Aurelia walking beside him they made their way through narrow lanes crowded with *carretas* tilting with the weight of muskets and pistols and ammunition, past mesquite tables laden with bags of bread, sacks of coffee, bolts of cloth, pots, pans, trinkets, gewgaws. Benito paused now and then to settle a dispute as to the price of a musket or the quality of a pistol, or to inquire after someone's health or congratulate someone on a particularly successful trade, and when he spoke Aurelia noticed that both Mexicans and Comanches listened to him carefully and then nodded their heads and smiled and agreed with everything he had to say, as if he were neither Mexican nor Comanche, but rather some rare form of animal that they had bred among them.

When they reached the slope above the camp a Mexican woman brought them a bowl of beans and a stack of pinole cakes, and they sat on the ground and ate while down below Comanches and Mexicans bet on horse races on a sun-stippled field. Benito hardly spoke, but he watched Aurelia with great curiosity, noting how softly she spoke to her children and how calmly she surveyed her surroundings. Aurelia, for her part, noted everything about Benito. She noted that he ate his food with great delicacy, not tearing at large morsels with his teeth but breaking off pieces with his fingers and then putting them into his mouth, and that he used his neckerchief to wipe his lips instead of the back of his hand, and that he appeared to be contemplating her as intensely as she contemplated him.

"You see that Comanche on his pony and the Mexican trader, the Comanchero, on his mustang?" Benito said when the last tortilla had been eaten and Yolanda and Ruben sat playing cat's cradle with a piece of blanket string. "The Comanchero thinks because he wears clothes sewn with cotton thread that he will race the Comanche and win. He won't win. The Comanche will win. He was here even before the Mexican. He can ride a horse better than anyone has ever ridden a horse. If you stay here a while you will see Comanches betting stolen horses and Mexicans betting wagon-loads of blankets on who is the strongest wrestler, who can ride a horse faster, who can shoot an arrow farther. If you stay here even longer you will see everything there is to see—even sudden death. And in a week it will all be gone . It will be as if this place had never been. We will leave nothing for the Army to find, nothing for the ranchers to chase after. We built this place in ten minutes, we will tear it down in five and leave no trace. Even the garbage will be gone."

"Is everyone in the hill country your enemy?" Aurelia said.

"Not everyone. I have friends in many of the towns. I leave their horses and mules alone and don't kidnap their wives and children. In return they don't chase after me when I steal their neighbors' cattle. They like to tell stories about me. Some of the stories are true and some aren't. They call me *El Jefe* and are proud to tell everyone they meet that they know me. In private they call me a bandit, a savage with fine manners. They wait for news of my death, but don't want me to die. And if I do they'll pretend I'm still alive, because without me there would be no stories. I don't care about their stories. The Comanche will be gone one day, but the Mexican will still be here. That war isn't over. This is Mexican country. If you are a *bruja,* you should be able to see the future. Amuse me. Tell me about the future."

"Specifics?"

"Of course. The future is full of specifics."

"I told Red Deer his future, and it didn't please him. If you have the patience to listen, and if you believe what I tell you to be honestly told and with no intent to deceive, I will tell you what I know of yours. I will keep nothing secret from you, for I see no purpose in not revealing what I know to be true."

"And I trust that everything you will say to me is the truth, and that every word can be relied on, and that if you choose to keep some part secret it will be for good reason, but my future holds no interest for me unless you tell me who you are and how you perform your miracles."

"There is no mystery to who I am. There is nothing miraculous about what I do. And although I know some things, I don't know everything."

"Can you at least tell me where the Army patrols are?"

"I might be able to if I think hard about it."

"Will I die young?"

"No."

"You say that with such certainty that I almost believe you."

"I'm not sure why I know that. It mystifies me that I even said it to you. I speak and at the same time I ask myself where the words come from. Do I make them up? And I tell myself that that must be the answer. And then a Norther comes, and I don't understand anything at all. I'm not even sure that it's the future I see, but merely pieces of a puzzle that I delight in putting together. I store up facts, tiny pieces that no one else notices, no one else cares about. What comes after that is a mystery even to me."

"Do you have a husband in Kimmelsburg?"

"No."

"Then you have no reason to go there."

"I have no reason to go there, although I think I intended to. The future and the present seem to me to be part of each other and as tightly woven as a horsehair rope. I know that I set out across the prairie, against all caution, against all sense, and even as I headed the wagon toward Kimmelsburg I knew I would never get there. And the only real and true thing I know about you is that your life is more than you think it is. Perhaps you will be wounded. Yes, I see a wound. But not death. Not young and not by the Army patrols or the Rangers. In your bed in old age with your family around you."

"So there, you have told my future."

"And you needn't believe anything I say. At this moment my concerns are with the welfare of my children—what is good for them, what is safe for them, what will let them grow up strong and healthy. Other than that, I am as you see me, an ordinary Mexican girl who merely pays attention to the smallest of things."

"That's all?"

She smiled broadly now. "I don't know what else there could be."

21

CASTROVILLE HAD GROWN in the two years Joseph had been away. A limestone church, gray as the day and shaped like a salt box, rose up from a grove of pecan trees near the Medina River. Along one side of the wide, muddy road was a general store, and across the way a blacksmith shop. Just above the spot where the river tumbled and crashed over the limestone rocks, a grist mill, one of its timber walls open to the daylight, hovered like a beetle over the lustrous water. And below, where the dam and raceway turned the river into an obedient pool, was a two-story inn, white plaster thinning to gray on its stone walls.

Joseph got off his horse and looked for signs of occupancy in the inn, but the door was nailed shut, and a cottonmouth snake, as brown as the leaves piled beside the door, was coiled around a stick on the shaded stoop. He swung up onto his horse again. There had been wagons on the muddy street when he left and people working their vegetable plots. There was no sign of anyone now, no horses pulling plows in the fields, and the gardens were brown and dry, just the frothy heads of wild thistle everywhere he looked. A few people looked out their windows at him, but there was no sound, no children's voices, just the papery leaves of the mulberry trees crackling in the breeze.

EVERYTHING IN THE Castro house seemed the same to Joseph. The mahogany tables, the spinet piano, the velvet drapes and French chairs. Even the lace cloths on the arms of the settee. But Castro was thinner and grayer than Joseph remembered, and his head wobbled slightly.

"I have thought of you often and wondered how you were faring," Castro said. "And it was with pleasure that I received the news from Mr. Ludwig of your great success."

Joseph glanced at the doorway to the adjoining room. There had been no sign yet of Aurelia, although he thought he saw a figure in black pass through the short hallway. There were footsteps now and a rustling of petticoats as Amelia Castro entered the room.

"Ah, Joseph," she said, and sat down on the settee next to Castro. "It has been such a long time."

She had lost all her plumpness, and her face beneath her black hat was so thin that her nose stuck up like a bird's beak.

"How is Katrin? I have often worried that her health was too delicate for the rigors of homesteading. She appeared so ill suited for that style of life."

"Katrin is well and I have long ago stopped regarding her as delicate. If anything, I would describe her as robustly healthy. She cleans and cooks and sews and gardens and has borne two children without complaint. And as for our style of life, it is more civilized than you might think. We have neighbors and the beginning of a small town."

"You must be proud of what you have accomplished," Castro said. "To pursue a goal and not fail. To see your work rewarded and not have to live to see what you have built ground back into dust, as I have."

Castro's shoulders seemed narrower than Joseph remembered,

and his height reduced, or was it only the way he held himself now, as if someone had glued his feet to the floor and hung sacks of flour around his neck?

"The drought destroyed last year's crops, and swarms of locusts came after the first rain and ate the tender plants. I would not have my own sons remain here, and so sent them both away to Mexico, as I did the two Negro boys. I thought it best that they leave here. The bounty hunters have been very active in the hill country."

"Lorenzo writes that his two children now speak only Spanish," Amelia said wistfully.

"It was only good fortune that Aurelia and her daughter and the two Negro boys were collected on the prairie by men logging cedar for shingles and that they thought to bring them here. As I wrote you in the letter, Aurelia had a boy child shortly after she arrived. A dark child. Not quite as dark as Luck, but noticeably dark."

It was very quiet in the house. Joseph remembered people always coming in and going out, noisy conversations, Castro's imperious voice louder than all the rest.

"There are no people in the street," Joseph said.

"They keep their misery in their houses," Castro replied. "Whole families devour birds' eggs to stay alive. They eat grass and rattlesnakes. Three families died of eating poisoned herbs. Only coyotes, drawn to the cemetery by the smell, get enough to eat. I have used my wife's money, have mortgaged my interests in the colony to bring more settlers here, and now the money promised me is withheld, the land is in dispute—some say it is owned by the Spanish and some say by the Indians and I am in the middle and nearly penniless. Profit by my fall, Joseph, and guard against rash action, for I am proof that fortunes, even the most bountiful, can change."

"I'm not tied to any fortune, and wouldn't miss it if it left me. Of all people, I wouldn't have thought you would be the one to lecture me about fortunes gained or lost."

"Please forgive Henry," Amelia said. "He has been sorely tested these past four years. I have seen him grieve for his lost hopes as if some part of him had been torn away."

"Texas has treated you so well that you no longer have use for my advice," Castro said.

"I'm no longer willing to be lectured to."

"I merely warn you to take my example. You are content, but contentment can rob you of wariness. I was content, hopeful, joyous, and all of it was based on false promises. Texas has treated me shabbily, lured me here by promises of riches, when all I or my colonists needed was to be defended against the Indians. I was promised safety, protection from assault by Indians, guaranteed water, and then put on lands that no one would venture out to survey, for fear of being killed by savages. I've been abandoned in this venture, Joseph, left to take care of my debts as best I can. There are lawsuits pending, and angry settlers to contend with."

"I'm sorry for your misfortune, but you should have known that promises mean nothing where money is concerned. I've brought no one from Europe. I've promised no one they would grow rich if they joined me in Texas. I have borrowed money from no one to buy land."

"You speak so easily."

"I speak as one who is not bound by money."

"And yet it accrues to you."

"It finds its way."

"You don't covet it?"

"To show you my disdain for it, I am ready to give some of it away to you."

"I have no means to pay it back."

"I don't want it back."

"I can't take it then."

"And so you'll let Castroville die. Your great dream, your grand scheme of a kingdom in Texas. I admit I'm surprised. I see now that if the town survives, it will be in spite of you."

"There would be no one here if not for me."

"And you would abandon them."

"I brought them here. I bankrupted myself to do it."

"No one forced you to do it."

"You've grown hard as well as rich."

"I have grown practical."

Castro coughed into a soiled handkerchief. "And how are Aurelia and her children?"

"I would ask you that."

"Did she not reach Kimmelsburg?"

"You let her go?"

"How could I keep her? She was with us for almost a year, and at the last Amelia's desire to have her stay was no match for Aurelia's eagerness to be gone."

Joseph paled. "You knew I would come for her."

"I didn't know that. The letter was sent two months go. You didn't respond."

"Katrin withheld your letter. I would have been here sooner if she had handed it to me in time. She did it deliberately."

Amelia looked down at her lap and Castro began to pluck at his lips with his fingers.

"I see you've not grown as hard as you would like," Castro finally said.

"How could you have her here in this house with you and let her go?"

Amelia began to cry.

"Calm yourself, Joseph," Castro said.

"I am calm. I'm as calm as I can be. If you want to see my temper, say that to me one more time and you'll see it in full force, you'll see just how angry, just how enraged—"

"She waited for you to come, Joseph. It is clear that something has happened or she would have reached Kimmelsburg by now. My regret is that I did not send her and her children to Mexico as I did the two Negro boys." He put his hand on Joseph's arm. "I'm sorry, Joseph. But

Providence works in mysterious ways. You must forget her. You must think of Katrin. You must not let thoughts of this young woman cloud your mind or you will ruin your life in your way as surely as I in my way have ruined mine."

22

KATRIN OPENED THE DOOR and looked out to see if the Auerbach wagon was in sight yet. Sophia Auerbach always came to visit on Mondays. She brought her four children with her and her quilting. She would come in, kiss Katrin on the cheek, and then, as if she owned the house, look around for something to eat. A chunk of bread or a piece of pie. Anything that happened to be sitting on the table or peeking out from behind the perforated tin front of the pie safe. Although she was fatter than ever, she claimed she never ate at home, that she had too many things to do and no time to eat, that sometimes she went to bed and couldn't remember if she had eaten at all that day.

Katrin didn't hold it against Sophia about the letter. All Sophia had said was that Katrin should make Joseph angry if she wanted him to pay attention to her. She never said anything about a letter.

But what about the letter? she wanted to ask her. I can't read. Why did Joseph say I read it when he knows I can't read? Why did he get angry over something I didn't even do? Holding his letter and not giving it to him was one thing, but I didn't read it. I couldn't. I wouldn't.

There were all kinds of questions she wanted to ask Sophia before Joseph got home. She wanted to ask her whether she should talk to Aurelia when she got here, or if she should pretend she wasn't there, just not speak to her or look at her. And Joseph. Should she heat some water and fill the iron tub for his bath and act as if he hadn't been gone?

"The problem isn't Aurelia," Sophia had said, "it's you. You clean too much. Joseph doesn't care what you do in the kitchen, it's what you do in the bedroom. Look at me and Herman. I don't care about cleaning or housekeeping as long as Herman wants me in his bed. That's the most important thing there is. There isn't anything more important, not dust or dirt or noisy babies. Oh, I do a quilt now and then. I do my best thinking when I'm quilting. And laying on my back. I can think pretty good when I'm on my back and Herman's face is smack up against mine. Aurelia may know more about men than you do, but you're Joseph's wife, and you've got a head start on her."

Katrin looked forward to Sophia's visits, even though she always wondered at how Sophia could just sit at the table putting pieces of cloth together and not even notice that her children were wrecking Katrin's house, running in and out, tracking dirt clods in between their bare toes and dropping them everywhere, jumping on the settee until the seat was mashed down and no amount of plumping up after they were gone could bring the horsehair up to where it was before.

Just the week before, Sophia told Katrin that she had decided that four children were enough, that Herman was getting older and couldn't stand all the noise in the house. "It's harder and harder to get him up in the morning," Sophia had said. "He cracks his toes and scratches his backside and sits on the edge of the bed making noises like he's dying before he's ready to stand up." Sophia had said she knew how to keep from having any more children. Cocoa butter and boric acid. "You mix it up in a box until it looks like fudge," she had said, "and then you shape it into a cone, and when it's hard you—" Katrin hadn't listened to what happened after that.

Sophia spoiled her children. She never hit them, even when they were acting their worst, and she didn't seem to care when they messed up her quilt pieces, but would just sew them together that way, all mixed up, with no design or pattern that anyone could see, so that her quilts were stained, spotted and old-looking even before they were finished. Not pretty to look at at all. Not like the ones Katrin worked when Sophia and her naughty children weren't there. Katrin could make gardens on her quilts. But then she could do a lot of things that Sophia couldn't. Preserve eggs in lime and cream of tartar. Make candles out of lard and keep them from smoking when you lit them. Waterproof shoes with beeswax and suet.

Katrin always had a headache after one of Sophia's visits. It wasn't only that she had to follow each one of the children around, trying to keep them from doing too much damage, but she had to keep an extra careful eye on Louie, too. He always seemed to be standing where he shouldn't be, and more often than not would get knocked over or kicked, and then she'd have to hold him the rest of the day or he wouldn't stop crying.

Aren't you going to come in here and talk to me while I quilt? Sophia would say.

I will in a minute, Katrin would tell her. But it wasn't until afternoon when the little Auerbachs were finished chasing each other and dirtying things up and were so worn out and exhausted that they'd just lie down anywhere they happened to be and go to sleep that Katrin sat Louie down on a chair and talked to Sophia, and it always seemed that she no sooner did that than Herman Auerbach was there with the wagon, waiting to take his family home.

Her eyes went past the vegetable garden now and out into the prairie. No wagon yet. A breeze had come up. She could see the mesquites bending with it and hear the paper-thin leaves whisking against the log walls of the cabin.

Javier had stopped at the cabin early that morning and Katrin gave him a basket of cornbread. He and some of the *vaqueros* were going to take the cattle to the northeast to graze. He hadn't seen the Auerbach wagon either, he said, and then started telling Katrin about how it might have been attacked by Indians, that Mr. Auerbach wasn't always careful about which way he came, that sometimes instead of traveling along the river he'd go wandering out into the prairie right through the Comanche hunting grounds.

When the weather was cold, the way it had been lately, Comanches sometimes attacked people right out in the open. Out of pure meanness. Without wanting anything but the hair on their head.

If we leave the Comanches alone, they'll leave us alone, Joseph always said. *We've got prairie to the south and to the east, and even a little of it to the north. We can let the Comanches have most of the west*. But Joseph hadn't actually told the Comanches how he had parceled out the land, and once in a while they'd show up on someone's farm and take the horses. Javier would get alarmed then, and he and some of the *vaqueros* would camp out near the creek with their rifles, waiting for Comanches to show up. Javier had been half scalped by Comanches and probably knew more about them than anyone, but Joseph told him he was wasting his time watching for Comanches, that they were too smart to be anyplace you expected them to be.

Comanches liked to raid vegetable gardens in the spring, but they hadn't been anywhere near Katrin's. She knew just how high the tops of her carrots grew and how long the rows were, and tied up the green beans with twine herself, and watched them grow from tiny buds into beans and would have known if any were missing or not.

She closed the door again. Louie was still sitting on the floor in front of the fire, eating cornbread. Samuel was asleep in his cradle in the other room. He didn't have any teeth showing and slept too much. Louie was awake twice as much as Samuel was, and was growing at twice the rate.

There was no point in cleaning anything with the Auerbach children due to arrive at any moment. But Katrin couldn't help getting the broom and sweeping the floor a little. She always hoped that Sophia would notice how clean it was when she arrived and how dirty it was when she and her children left. Katrin almost never visited Sophia's house. She didn't like to drink out of Sophia's glasses or eat off her plates. Just sitting in the middle of Sophia's messy parlor surrounded by overturned chairs and yelling children made her feel as if her head was about to come loose.

There was noise coming from the outdoor kitchen, a light banging, as if the curtain had come down again. Javier sometimes opened the window when Katrin had loaves of bread cooling on the rack. She told him and told him that bread needed to sit a while before you ate it, but he never listened.

Of course, maybe Joseph wouldn't bring Aurelia to Kimmelsburg. Maybe when he saw her he'd realized he didn't like her at all, that he liked Katrin better. Maybe Aurelia wasn't even in Castroville when Joseph got there.

She sat down on the settee. She could still feel the hills and valleys the Auerbach children had left in it on their last visit. Well, Joseph couldn't help himself. Something in him forced him to be the way he was. The priest in Riquewihr used to talk about the devil possessing someone's soul. He said that as much as that person tried to fight against the devil, he could never win. *The devil is almost as strong as God*, the priest said.

The noise from the kitchen bothered her. She knew she hadn't left any bread cooling on the rack near the kitchen window. She had given Javier a whole basket of fresh cornbread and watched him ride off with it. He wouldn't have come back this soon looking for more.

She walked out into the side yard and into the kitchen. Standing right inside the door was an Indian. Katrin knew in a second that he was a Comanche by his shiny black hair and the blue breechclout he wore and by the smell of bear grease in his hair.

"Get out of my kitchen," Katrin shouted, and Louie began to cry. "Not you, Louie. Mama isn't talking to you."

The Comanche walked right past her, out into the yard, and then into the house through the front door. Katrin ran after him, picked Louie up, then went into the bedroom and plucked Samuel out of his cradle. When she came back into the parlor the Indian was building a fire in the middle of the floor right next to the settee. He was so busy poking at furniture with the sharp edge of his battle axe that he barely looked up at Katrin. She laid Samuel down on the floor next to the pie safe, sat Louie next to him, and took the musket down.

The Comanche had stopped chopping away at her furniture and gray smoke was now filling the house. He stood up and raised the battle axe over his head. *Comanches can throw an axe and cut a person's head straight off in one throw,* Joseph said. He had found an old axe out on the prairie once. Flint tied onto the wooden handle with leather thongs, the handle pitted and most of the leather rotted away. The axe the Comanche was holding looked as if it hadn't been used too much. The flint was as bright and shiny as the enamel on Katrin's new stove.

"Stop," she said.

The Indian's arm, which had been as straight as a table leg, now wavered slightly and for a moment he looked as if he were going to listen to her the way Louie did and put the axe down and go out the door. But his arm stiffened again, and he and Katrin looked at each other, and she thought she had never been so angry in her whole life. This was her house, her furniture, her children. In the swirling smoke she imagined that Ten Elk was standing in front of her with his two thick braids and a feather in his hair, that he had come back to life just so he could kill her and her children and burn down her house.

Joseph had taught her how to shoot the musket, even how to put the gunpowder in and tamp it down. But it was loaded now, so she didn't have to do any of that. She merely raised it to her shoulder and pulled the trigger.

"The cellar's your safe place," Joseph had told her. "It's where I want you to go if you have nowhere else to run. If something happens and you can't get out of the house, you have the cellar."

He put a hose like the one on her new stove right through the side of the cellar and into the dirt in the back of the cabin. The top of the hose grew up out of the ground like one of Katrin's bean plants. She had even used it to prop some plants up during the summer, and Joseph had warned her again and again not to wrap too many vines around the thing or no air would get into the cellar at all.

The metal door was in the floor behind the pie safe, almost to the wall and hardly noticeable, just a square plate and then a ladder going down to where Katrin kept supplies for the winter. Jars of preserves, sacks filled with flour and coffee and potatoes. She kept extra quilts down there, too, in a trunk, along with the featherbed she had brought from Riquewihr and was too lumpy, Joseph said, to sleep on. There was a barrel of peaches down there, too, and a crate of cured meat. As she lowered herself and the children down the ladder and closed the metal door behind her she tried to remember if she had seen the hose sticking up out of the ground recently, or if she had covered it with dirt when she was digging weeds, or if, despite Joseph's warnings, she had let plants grow into it and close it up and shut off the air.

She put Louie on top of the peach barrel and gave him a cracker from her apron pocket to chew on. She put Samuel down on a stack of bison hides. It was strange how dark it could get, so dark your eyes couldn't tell you where you were and kept flashing images at you of the light you had just left behind. But she knew where everything was in the cellar, just exactly how far one crate was from another, one barrel from another, because she had put them all in there, had stacked the preserves and arranged the sacks, had made sure there was enough room to walk around. Joseph hardly ever went down into the cellar. He had a few kegs of whiskey down here. A half glass of liquor for each of the *vaqueros* once a week. *Just enough to make them happy and warm*, Joseph said. *Just a taste.*

She knew her shot had hit the Comanche. That was certain. A red splotch had opened up on his chest when she pulled the trigger. But she could still hear him up in the cabin over her head right through the floor, jumping around, stamping his feet as if he were doing some kind of war dance. She expected any minute that the metal door would open and she'd see his face again. She was ready for it. She had the musket in her hand, and there was ammunition in the box she was sitting on, and she knew she could sit there wide awake for a week aiming in the direction of the door, ready to shoot him again if she had to. Ready to shoot him a thousand times over if once wasn't enough.

JOSEPH SAW THE SMOKE from a few miles away. He thought it might be Luck's or Nathan's cabin. Or maybe he was mixed up, not looking in the right direction. Maybe he was really looking north to where the Auerbach place was. Or even up on the mesa where the Big K's *vaqueros* bunked. Their cabins were all lined up in a row and had enough wood in them to burn for days, to cook ten steers, to warm half of Kimmelsburg on a winter's night.

It didn't have to be his place that was burning, and he kept hoping he was all wrong about where the smoke was coming from the whole time he was galloping toward it. He kept thinking of all other kinds of reasons why there'd be smoke. Maybe lightning had caught the mesquite trees north of the cabin on fire. But he hadn't heard any thunder or seen any lightning. And the cowboys wouldn't be cooking anything with a fire so big it made the sky turn black.

Maybe it wasn't smoke at all. Maybe it was the tail of a thunder cloud coming south from the Guadalupe mountains and hanging so low over the trees it just looked like it might be smoke. But his heart was beating fast, and he knew none of the things he was hoping for was the answer, but he still couldn't believe it was his house burning until he reached the creek, and then there was no question but that it was his place that was smoking up the sky.

THE HOUSE WAS a fuming skeleton, the frame charred, the glass windows blown out, the path from the creek to the house muddy and littered with empty water buckets. A band of gray-hatted men, faces coated with light gray ash, stood in a helpless knot in the middle of

Katrin's trampled garden. Winter vegetables that when Joseph left had been taller than Louie's head were now mashed down to the ground.

"When we got here your men were working hard to save the house," Herman Auerbach said. "Javier was doin' his best, and I tried helpin', but I could see right away you were goin' to lose the whole thing."

"I told Herman I thought the trees must have caught fire the way the sky looked," Sophia said. She was holding her youngest and the other three were watching wide-eyed from the wagon. "Then we got closer and we saw the house flaming, and I jumped out of the wagon and Herman said, don't go running up there or you'll catch your clothes on fire, so I stayed right here out of the way. It's terrible, Joseph, just the most terrible thing I could think of."

"I got everyone up here soon as I seen the flames," Javier said. He kept pulling at his hat, as if he couldn't make up his mind whether he wanted it on his head or not. "They was runnin' back and forth from the creek, draggin' buckets, but it weren't no use."

"Where's Katrin?"

"I don't know. I looked everywhere for her. I thought maybe she and the little ones got out when the fire first started, or might be the mailman got her and the little ones out before the whole house burned. Then I was thinkin' maybe she run out the house before it caught fire, so I went to the corral and rode out on the prairie almost to the mountains. I didn't see them nowhere. Her horse was in the corral. She couldn't go far on foot. I just seen her this morning, she gave me some cornbread. I tried one time to go inside when it was burning the worst, but it was so hot it burned my cheeks. I could feel my eyebrows going. I wanted to get inside, but I just couldn't."

"I hope you don't keep our money in this place anywhere," Herman Auerbach said, and followed Joseph onto the porch.

The tin bucket on the porch had twisted into a long narrow shape, but the pewter ladle beside it had withstood the heat, hadn't twisted or melted at all, merely turned a silvery color. The floorboards hadn't burned through, but Joseph could feel the heat steaming inside his boots. He pulled the door open and stepped inside. The parlor floor was charred and little heaps of furniture smoldered here and there, delicate plumes of smoke floating up through the burned-out roof, but the worst of the fire was out, just little patches of flame sputtering beneath all the water that had been thrown at it.

"Well, look at that," Javier said.

A dead Comanche was sitting in the fireplace with his head up the chimney.

Herman stepped carefully across the charred floor. "Is that an Indian?"

"Seems like," Javier said.

"Go back outside, Herman," Joseph told him.

"I'm goin' to help look for my money. None of your neighbors goin' to be too happy with you if you kept all our money in here and it got burned up."

"He's got a big hole in his chest," Javier said.

"Katrin!" Joseph hollered.

"If she was in the house I don't see no sign of her," Javier said, and he and Herman followed Joseph through what was left of the house.

"People have patience to wait for their money," Herman said. "If it's burned up, and it's not your fault, I guess we can wait for it. Smart as you are, you'll be making more and be able to pay us what you owe us in time."

Joseph was on his knees now behind the charred remains of the pie safe. "The door was here behind the pie safe."

"The door burned, Joseph," Javier told him. "There's no door left. And no pie safe neither."

"I'm not talking about the pie safe. I'm talking about the cellar."

It was four feet and then a right turn. Joseph had counted it off when he dug the pit and put the door in. He ran his fingers lightly over the rough floor feeling for the bump that would tell him the lid was there. It was hard to see, even without a fire, unless you leaned right up against the wall and turned your head a certain way and the light caught the gleam of the metal hinge. But you could feel it with your foot. Like a ball of sap, although it wasn't sticky. More like a knot in the wood, weak and spongy.

"I can wait for my money," Herman said. "There's no problem there, but you'd better say something pretty quick to the other ones out there. I can't read their minds, but I can sure tell you that if they're anything like me, they'll be wanting to get an answer about their money pretty quick. Where did you put it? Did you have a box, maybe? Did you bury it in the ground outside?"

Joseph felt the pain of the hot metal hinge before he felt the groove where his fingers were supposed to go. Javier was down on his knees, too, now, sticking his knife down into the door to help Joseph pull it up.

THE LIGHT WAS so bright Katrin couldn't see. It looked like a yellow ball climbing down the ladder.

"Joseph?"

"It's me, Katrin."

She couldn't stand up, she had sat so long with her knees bent under her.

"Did I kill him, Joseph?"

"You did."

Herman Auerbach climbed down the ladder.

"Good afternoon, Mrs. Kimmel," he said, and began picking up sacks and looking behind kegs of whiskey, piles of wolfskins, barrels of peaches and crates of cured meats, all the while telling Javier to hold the lantern higher or how in the world was he supposed to see anything.

"Did the Indian burn down my house?" Katrin asked.

"He did," Joseph replied.

"Did you go to Castroville?"

"I did."

"Did you bring Aurelia here?"

"No."

He sat down on a peach barrel and clutched the children to his chest and kissed their cheeks.

"You did just exactly the right thing, Katrin," he said.

"Are you glad to see me?"

"More than glad."

He didn't sound glad and his eyes didn't dance when he looked at her, the way Sophia said they ought to. Nothing had changed. Not even getting almost burned up in her own house made his eyes dance when he looked at her.

"Well, I'm darned," Herman said. He had a money box in his hand and was counting out greenbacks in the lantern light.

23

By May of 1852 a new house, its door and window sashes and eaves the color of spring daisies, rose up out of the charred trees. But glass for the windows hadn't yet arrived from Austin, and Katrin blamed the draftiness of the house for Louie's fever.

"He wouldn't get fever if there are windows," she told Joseph. "The cold air come in and make him sick."

The windows arrived about the time Samuel got sick.

"Too late," Katrin snapped at Joseph.

The house now rocked with the noise of Louie and Samuel coughing. They coughed through June and into July. A velvet sofa arrived from France in mid-August, along with a fancy cabinet from Italy and tables with gilded feet and beveled edges from New York, and still they coughed.

"It's a new kind of fever," Sophia said, and she told Katrin to wrap the children's heads in dampened cloths and drip elixir of magnolia bark down their throats.

By the end of September Louie had stopped coughing, but Samuel lay in his cradle with one fist to his mouth and his eyes shut tight. He was so pale and thin Katrin could see his heart beating in his chest, a small pulse that fluttered beneath the skin like butterfly wings. When she put him to her breast she couldn't feel him sucking, although once in a while she thought she felt him tugging weakly at her nipple. Mostly he lay as still as one of Louie's cloth dolls, his cheeks as wrinkly as old apple skins. She tried prying his lips apart and squeezing milk into his open mouth. He would whimper as milk dropped in delicate sprays onto his wrinkly cheeks, but wouldn't swallow. She tried filling her own mouth with breast milk and, as if Samuel were a baby bird, puckering her lips around his and dribbling milk past her teeth into his mouth. It only made him cry. The doctor rode over to the Big K from Fredericksburg and said he thought Katrin should try milking her breasts, then soaking a rag in the milk and letting Samuel suck on it. But Samuel wouldn't suck.

Louie was well by the beginning of October.

"Samuel is getting better, too," Katrin told Joseph, although Samuel still didn't want the breast and hardly opened his eyes and sometimes turned a dark blue color.

But there were still meals to be cooked and put on the table and pots and pans and dishes to be scoured afterwards. There was ironing to be done. Corn had to be shucked and run through the sheller. Manure in the henhouse needed to be scooped up and scattered onto the vegetable garden. The two cows needed milking every morning and the yard needed to be raked. The grapes were a heavy mass of purple juice on the vines and were ready to be harvested and put into barrels for crushing. Joseph liked the wine Katrin made. If she waited too long, the fruit would rot on the vine. She managed to fill one barrel with grapes and add the sugar and begin the fermentation, but then she noticed that the tomatoes were green and decided she had better pick them in case there was an early frost, and of course there were eggs that needed gathering in the henhouse and vegetables to be pulled from the garden to put in the soup, and pies to bake and biscuit batter to beat. Sophia still brought her quilting and her children over on Mondays, and on Tuesdays the floors always needed scrubbing where the Auerbach children had dropped smeary blobs of rhubarb jam.

All through October two-year-old Louie ran barefoot beneath the pecan trees and Katrin sewed curtains for the windows and Samuel slept. He hardly weighed more than one of the baby rabbits in the hutches behind the house. He barely breathed. He swung heedlessly, mindlessly in the folds of Katrin's apron, eyes closed and cheeks sunken, while Katrin peppered and sliced ham for the smokehouse and filled the washtub with water and stooped in the henhouse and spread green tomatoes in neat rows in the attic to ripen.

No matter how hard Katrin worked, she couldn't catch up. There was never enough time to finish everything she set out to do. She worked frantically, not resting, and only sleeping when she had pushed herself to exhaustion. It made her bitter that Louie had gotten well and Samuel hadn't. She had to hold herself back from pushing Louie away when he tried to climb onto her lap next to Samuel.

Joseph now slept on the new sofa in the parlor. So he wouldn't crush Samuel in his sleep, he said. He rarely smiled. Katrin thought at first that it was because he was worried that Samuel might die, but he said he thought Samuel would be fine, that all he needed was to be held more. Whenever Samuel made a peep Joseph was there to pick him up and walk him around until he quieted down. He told Katrin he thought Samuel was getting better, that he was sure he saw color returning to his cheeks, but she was sure he only said that because he could see that she had already begun to mourn.

Samuel lay dying and Joseph sometimes gazed longingly out the window and Katrin felt as if the ground was slipping from beneath her feet. Rain clouds clung in dark gray shrouds against the Guadalupe mountains while Katrin worked feverishly at her chores and watched Samuel die. It was as if she were trying to outrun the rain that was coming, trying to blow the wind back, trying to beat off the sorrow that was about to carry her away.

"LOOK HOW PEACEFUL Samuel sleeps," Katrin said.

Joseph picked the baby up, put his face next to the wrinkly cheeks, then put him back in his cradle.

"Sophia is coming with the children, and I have to get ready," Katrin said. "She is bringing me flannel to make a nightgown for Samuel. I can feel Samuel's fingers and toes are cold. A nice flannel nightgown will keep him warm. Cotton is good for summer, but flannel is the best for winter."

She went into the kitchen and began to sweep the floor.

SOPHIA LEFT HER children in the wagon. Katrin saw her talking to Joseph in the yard. The light out on the prairie was a delicate gold color, and Katrin thought of the pumpkins she had stored in the cellar. She would make a pumpkin pie. Herman Auerbach raised sorghum cane and Sophia had brought Katrin a bucket of fresh molasses before the children got sick. In return Katrin had given her a basket of pecans that she had beaten down from the pecan trees that grew down by the creek. A dollop of Sophia's molasses on a slice of pumpkin pie and a glass of clabbered milk would make Joseph happy.

Ordinarily Katrin would have gone outside and told Sophia to come in, that there was no reason to stand out in the cold. Instead she went into the bedroom and lifted Samuel out of the cradle and sat down in the chair next to the bed and sang to him in Alsatian. It was a song that her mother used to sing to her. She remembered the words as if she had heard them only yesterday.

Ich weiss, die Mama liebt mich,
Wie sie nur lieben kann;

Sie sagt's, und o, sie tauscht nicht,
Sie hat's noch nie getan.

"I CAN GET a load of French wine," Joseph said.

"Don't know who'd buy French wine," Cyril replied.

Joseph and Cyril were out on the porch with Herman Auerbach. Sophia was in the kitchen. Katrin could hear her banging pots down on the stove.

"How long's it been?" Herman said.

"For the wine?" Cyril asked him.

"Since he died."

"Two days," Joseph said.

"O'course, we could drink it ourselves, or we could tell folks it's beer. Hardly anyone can read anyways nor tell the difference."

It was comfortable in the bedroom. Moonlight settled in pearly pools on the dresser. A small circle of light, scarcely more than a fingernail wide, sat on Samuel's forehead.

Sophia was at the bedroom door.

"My three are eating biscuits and soup. Louie won't eat. He says his foot hurts."

"Louie doesn't talk," Katrin said.

"He talked to me. Aren't you about ready to come out, Katrin? Your husband is worrying you'll sicken next. Are you listening to me?"

"Samuel will be cold if I put him in the ground. I won't put him in the ground. There's no way to keep the frost away when the ground freezes. Even with a hat. I could pull his hat down over his ears, but his nose will freeze."

"You can't hold him like that too much longer," Sophia said, and she laid a quilt across Katrin's knees. It covered Samuel's arms and legs and trailed onto the floor.

"She shouldn't talk about him like he's sleepin'," Cyril said out on the porch. "Ain't natural."

"You ought take him away from her and put him in the ground," Herman remarked.

The Auerbach children were running wild in the parlor. Sophia was in there now trying to quiet them down. Katrin laid Samuel down on the bed and walked to the bedroom door and looked out at the mess. A chair was overturned, sticky fingers had left tiny prints across the walls, and the floor was littered with bread crumbs. Sophia was bent over mopping something up off the floor. She grunted with the effort, and when she stood up again her face was a blotchy red.

"You can go home," Katrin said.

"Does that mean you're going to let go of him?"

"No," Katrin replied, and shut the bedroom door.

KATRIN LOST TRACK of time. She knew that Sophia came every day and turned the kitchen smoky with her burned biscuits, and Cyril and Herman talked out on the porch, and Joseph stood at the bedroom door ashen-faced, but what did any of that matter when it all ended this way, with a baby's flesh turning hard and green?

"She doesn't sleep, just sits in that chair in the bedroom with Samuel on her lap," Katrin heard Joseph tell Sophia. "She won't eat. I don't know what to say or do. She keeps him in the bed with her and doesn't sleep because she's afraid I'll take him away and bury him. I've told her I won't, that it will have to be her own idea. She thinks I don't care, but my heart's broken to think he won't have a chance at life."

Katrin smoothed the blanket around Samuel's little face. He was disappearing, his head shrinking, his lips no bigger than two little grape seeds.

"Katrin?"

Sophia was in the bedroom. As if Katrin had invited her in. As if she could walk anywhere she pleased.

"Did you feed Joseph his supper?" Katrin asked her.

"He says he isn't hungry."

"He always says he isn't hungry, but if you put the food on the table he'll eat it. Did Louie really talk?"

"He did. He said plain as could be, 'My foot hurts.' Would you like to give Samuel to me now?"

"No."

"You must be tired. You should give Samuel to me and then lie down and sleep."

"No."

The room was the same as it had been that morning, a pitcher of water on the dresser, a cold candle in a brass holder, the liniment-soaked rags, but it was suddenly cold, the walls breathing droplets of moisture that ran down onto the rag rug.

"Joseph is very sorry for everything," Sophia said.

"He didn't tell you that. I hear everything you say. I didn't hear him say that."

"He whispered it to me."

"Joseph doesn't whisper."

The candles in the parlor were lit. It was still night, but barely, the moon hanging low over the trees and creeping through the window. On the horizon the first piece of sun had begun to pierce the hazy darkness.

Katrin was six years old and it was summer in Riquewihr, flowers blooming on the hillsides. Mama was in the kitchen rolling out dough for sweet bread with streusel, her fat arms moving up and down on the hardwood slab. Call August and Papa to supper, Mama said, and Katrin ran through the flowers and somersaulted down the hillside, the sun warm on her cotton bonnet and the earth moist beneath her bare feet. Run before the witches catch you, August called out when he saw her.

"Do you think it's too late to plant sweet potato slips?" Katrin said.

"Not too late at all," Sophia replied and took Samuel away.

24

April, 1853

KATRIN DROVE THE FARM buggy into town, taking the same route she took every day—around the creek, then onto the path beneath the pecan trees for a mile, and finally onto the dirt road, Louie beside her holding his silver whirligig tightly in his hand. In the bed of the wagon were the cakes she had baked for sale and the lunch she had prepared for Cyril, along with a pile of quilts—patchworks bought from ranchers' wives in Kerrville, as well as several *colchas bordadas,* brilliantly colored embroidered quilts made by Mexican women living in *jacales* along the Sabinal River.

The town was busier these days, more freighters passing through, more ranchers shopping during the week and doing their banking. It was quiet this morning, hardly any traffic at all, but the street was muddy and she thought as she tied up the horses that she should have stopped the buggy down the road where it was nice and dry.

"Don't put your shoes in the mud, Louie," Katrin said. "Walk by Mama now. Don't run and jump and splash when Mama says be careful your shoes."

It was too late. Louie had mud up over the laces of his shoes and was running ahead into the open door of Kimmel's Store.

There was a wagon in front of the store, the Mexican hauler Katrin bought supplies from, his wife and five children peering out at her from the slats in the wagon. Katrin didn't know the hauler's name. She didn't want to know it, didn't like to be too familiar with someone she did business with. Every time he turned up at the store with goods for sale she behaved as if it were the first time she had ever seen him.

He was hauling kettles today. Katrin could tell by the way they were stacked that he hadn't sold a one yet. Some on top had even begun to rust.

"I pay you three dollars for thirty kettles, no more," Katrin said.

"Viajé mucha distancia," the man said.

"What?"

"Viajé mucha distancia."

"Even if I know what you are telling me, I still offer three dollars."

The man hesitated, then repeated what he had said. Katrin shook her head.

"You will have to be satisfied with three dollars." Cyril had paid nine dollars for a wagon load of Mexican rope last month when she would have given five.

"Matamoros está muy lejos. Necessito seis."

"No, no, you bring the wagon to the back of the store and pile the kettles, don't throw, just pile. I don't want there is kettles everywhere. Go on, go now, you understand me, I can tell you understand me, so take the kettles—the kettles—I don't know the word for kettles—you take them in the wagon in the back and pile them up. No mess. You understand? No mess."

She waited until the man and his wagon and wife and five children had disappeared behind the store, and then she brought the cakes and lunch inside.

Cyril had started a fire in the stove. *He shouldn't put the fire on when it isn't cold outside,* she thought. *He forgets to put it on when there's ice on the ground and puts it on when the sun is shining.* Katrin unwrapped the cakes she had brought and laid them out on the embroidered cloth on the counter, then went back to unload the quilts, which she carried two at a time into the store and stacked neatly on the incoming inventory shelf, after which she took off her hat, sat Louie on a crate next to the bonnet rack and took off his muddy shoes.

Joseph didn't usually come into the store until late afternoon to pick up the day's receipts, but here it was morning and he was talking to Cyril in the aisle next to the shoe display about corn going from fifty cents a bushel to sixty-five, about cotton going from six to eight cents a pound, about hiring men to build the water wheel for the grist mill.

"They've got gas lamps on the streets in San Antonio," Joseph was saying, "and an ice factory with a machine for making ice. We won't have to pay fifty cents a pound to have it brought by ox train from the coast. We can sell it for seventy-five cents a pound."

"When will you mind what I tell you?" she said to Louie. "Now I have to clean the floor, look how your shoes put mud everywhere."

It didn't bother her that she would have to clean the floor. It pleased her to wipe away dirt. She liked the way a well-scrubbed floor smelled. Cyril wouldn't care if there were muddy tracks on the floor. He'd leave them there until next spring if Katrin didn't clean them up.

"I will wash off the muddy shoes when we are home, you don't go outside with your stockings, now listen to Mama."

Louie had already slid off the chair and was climbing the ladder that Cyril kept against the wall.

"You will fall."

"I won't."

Sometimes Katrin thought it was better when Louie didn't talk. He never used to leave her side. Now he hardly listened when she told him not to do something. He was at the top of the ladder now, swinging his legs back and forth, a stubborn look on his face.

Katrin picked out a quilt and carried it to the back door. The kettles were piled into a crooked pyramid near the door and the hauler was relieving himself against the wall. She waited until he was through and then walked over to the wagon and handed the quilt to his wife. The children looked particularly hungry today, so Katrin went back into the store and filled a large basket with fruit pies and cornbread and a jar of honey. Katrin didn't understand a word of what the woman said to her, but she thought she probably liked the quilt by the way she smiled and babbled and tried to grab Katrin's hand through the wagon's slats.

"*Dínero,*" the hauler said and held out his grimy hand.

Katrin gave him the coins and told him to wait. She then went back into the store and brought out a sack of flour, dropped it on the ground at his feet, went back inside, got the broom and began to sweep.

She swept wood shavings into one pile (Cyril had started making wood frames for the pictures he made with his Daguerreotype machine; people liked to be able to hang them on the wall) and broken glass into another pile (Louie had knocked over a set of goblets).

Cyril had bought the Daguerreotype machine from a rancher by the name of Pohl, who had bought it from a freighter in San Antonio, and although he hadn't learned yet how to get it to take a decent likeness (faces tended to be either all gray or all white), he couldn't get enough of playing with it. He must have taken a hundred photographs of Katrin and hadn't gotten it right yet, and the machine kept him so busy he hadn't even noticed that Katrin had put calico pillows on the wooden chairs around the stove and lined up the sacks and tins and barrels so there was room to walk around them, and had put a rainbow of bonnets on a table near the window next to an assortment of Chinese fans—open, of course, so you could see all those pretty scenes of Chinese ladies sipping tea—and that she had painted the door a bright blue, or that she swept the floor every day or that she stood on a ladder twice a week to brush cobwebs from the ceiling or that the store was now as neat as her house.

She didn't know exactly when it was that she had started coming to the store every day, but she remembered that it was a long fuzzy time after Samuel's funeral. She had managed not to think too much when Samuel died. She did remember the open grave banked with bouquets of forget-me-nots, the priest talking about everlasting life, and the awful sensation that she might die of grief. Maybe a month or two after that she had come into the store, looked around at the impenetrable forest of objects, the chaotic mess of muskets and spinning wheels, of wagon spokes and silver-trimmed saddles, watched the way Cyril had to squeeze through the small space between the boxed pistols and Chinese fans to get to the counter, saw how he had to stand on the pile of buffalo hides to oil the battery gun Joseph had gotten from the commander at Fort Lewis in exchange for five hundred pounds of beef, and decided that the store needed her. Besides which, she liked being here. There was a mystery in every dark corner, an unexpected surprise wherever she turned.

"Business been good," Cyril was saying to Joseph. "Katrin been doing . . ."

Katrin stopped sweeping. Cyril had the lowest voice. It irritated her how low his voice could get sometimes. He was talking about her now, whispering almost.

"I say if it makes her happy to run it, then let her," Joseph replied.

That was the first time Katrin had heard Joseph actually say he even noticed that she was running the store. Well, then, it was all right. She didn't have to worry about it any longer. She had been afraid that one of these days Joseph would come into the store and tell her to go home. Cyril never would have, but Joseph was always the one she worried about, what his mood was when he woke up, whether he wanted his breakfast before dawn or at mid-morning, or if he'd say more to her than what he thought about the weather. Well, so it was all right with him if she ran the store. And Cyril certainly didn't mind. He'd be happy if he never had to speak to another customer about gingham or shoes or China dishes ever again. And the customers didn't seem to mind, especially the women, who were always asking Katrin which dress pattern to choose and what size shoe they needed and whether she thought they ought to make their window curtains out of blue cotton or yellow. As for the men who came into the store, as long as she didn't talk too much, they hardly paid attention to the fact that she was behind the counter or that she took their money or that she told them what ammunition to buy for their rifles.

Louie had worn himself out and was now asleep on Joseph's shoulder, his thumb in his mouth. His thumb was always in his mouth when he slept. His teeth had raised a hard red bump right below his thumbnail. Joseph carried him into the back room and laid him on Cyril's bed. She watched how he did it, carefully untangling Louie's arms from his and covering him with Cyril's blanket, then patting his cheek before he went back, and as Katrin swept the pile of wood shavings out the back door and whisked the bits of broken glass onto a piece of tin and emptied them into the trash pail she told herself she would always remember how he did that.

Joseph had gone back to talking to Cyril about the grist mill, how many men Joseph needed to hire to do the job. Katrin put the broom back in the corner and took a piece of flannel and began to dust. She dusted every day. Books, rifles, ammunition, boxes of stationery, bottles of ink, stacks of dishes, pots, platters, hats, valises.

She had brought cold chicken and dumplings for lunch. Cyril liked her pickled beets, but there was also a jar of homemade cheese for Joseph. She would set it out like a picnic on the table Cyril used for making his pictures.

And then she smelled the odor of bear grease. The scent was unmistakable. It was imprinted indelibly on her brain. She turned around and an Indian in buckskin and moccasins, his skin the color of winter berries, came through the rear door. He had a blond boy with him. The two of them walked past where Louie was sleeping on Cyril's bed, past the bonnet rack and the shoe display to where Katrin was standing.

"Well, I'm darned," Cyril said.

The boy was Wally Dorfman. Joseph and Javier and half the men in the hill country had been looking for the nine-year-old since he disappeared right out of his front yard the month before. His name had been posted on the front door of the new church and the bishop had come all the way from Fredericksburg the previous Sunday to conduct a mass for his safe return.

Katrin put her hand out and pulled Wally toward her. Then she reached for the rifle behind the counter.

"Stay by me, Wally, like a good boy," she said.

"Give me the rifle, Katrin," Joseph said.

"It make me so mad to look on that Indian. They took me, they took Wally. Maybe next time they will take Louie."

"He brought Wally home, and you can't shoot him for what he might do in the future. Give me the rifle."

There had hardly ever been a time when Katrin hadn't done what Joseph told her to do. But the way the Indian was walking around the store, the way he was touching the goods, putting his fingers on her silk shawls, picking up quilts and dropping them, putting his mouth on Louie's harmonica, not caring that Katrin had put the rifle to her shoulder and was aiming at his heart made her forget that Joseph was even in the store.

And then Wally began to cry. Great big gulping sobs and giant tears that made his blue eyes turn the color of rainwater.

"Here," she said, and handed Joseph the rifle. Then she wiped Wally's face with her apron and gave him a piece of cake.

"You have a lucky day here today, Wally. You will go home to Mama and Papa."

The Indian had walked over to the corner of the store where the dry foods were kept and pointed to a sack of sugar and a sack of flour. Now he was at the rear of the store pointing to a slab of deer meat that had been brought in that morning.

"He seems to know what he wants," Cyril said.

"We'll give him what he asks for this time," Joseph replied, "but next time if Katrin still wants to shoot him, I won't try and stop her."

"How much flour and sugar should we give him?" Cyril asked Katrin.

"Joseph?" she said. She hated when Cyril asked her questions like that when Joseph was in the store, when Joseph was the one who told everyone what to do.

"Whatever Katrin says," Joseph replied.

"A sack of flour, a sack of sugar, and give all the deer meat," Katrin said.

"Where did they take you?" Joseph asked Wally.

Wally pointed to the north, his tears watering the cake he was holding.

While Joseph was talking to Wally, Cyril helped the Indian load his horse. Katrin stood at the back door watching to make sure he didn't take a crate of peaches or a set of dishes along with the rest of the goods before he left.

The Indian, a Comanche called Red Deer, had been in the store twice before. The first time he came in wanting to buy ammunition for his rifles (Katrin had refused), and she had thought about shooting him then, but she had taken pity on his blanket-wrapped wives trailing behind him and instead gave each of them a yam pudding. The next time he came into the store he had been brazen enough to try to sell her four horses stolen from the stockade at Fort Sill (they were still wearing regulation military headstall, reins and bit), and she might have shot him then, but she had heard that the winter had been especially hard on the tribe, that what was left were mostly the old and sick, and so she traded him two pies and a tierce of coffee for some pelts. Mangy pelts that didn't begin to match Katrin's contribution.

"Don't come back here," she said when the goods were loaded and strapped down with leather strips.

"I got one more thing," Cyril said, and then he went into the store and came out with his Daguerreotype machine

"I told you I don't want no picture of Comanche in the store," Katrin said.

Cyril had tried to take Red Deer's picture the two other times he was in the store, but Red Deer was always moving around and the images wouldn't come out clear enough to tell whether it was an Indian on a horse or a chimney on a house, and now Cyril was fumbling with the Daguerreotype box and tripod and copper plates, muttering about the sun being in the wrong place and there being too much vapor in the air, and he never did get a picture before Red Deer went galloping down the road.

Cyril took the machine back into the store, but Katrin decided to stay outside a while longer to make sure that Red Deer was really and truly gone, that he was still going straight down the road and hadn't come back and hidden himself in the trees across the road.

She had heard that some people were shooting Indians who came into town to sell captive whites. She had even heard that some people were shooing Indians away along with their captives (which Katrin thought a stupid way to retrieve a loved one). But Wally was safe and Joseph hadn't let her shoot Red Deer because he didn't understand about Comanches. Bringing Wally Dorfman back didn't change what they were one bit. Katrin knew them better than anyone. She knew if Red Deer had seen her out on the prairie somewhere he'd probably have carried her off the way Wally had been carried off, the way Katrin herself had been carried off by Ten Elk four years before. She knew if she crossed the creek when the water was low, Comanches could come out of the trees and block her way. She knew if she rode her horse in a canyon, Comanches could be waiting at the top of the next escarpment. She knew she probably would not get another chance to shoot Red Deer, and she was bitterly sorry about it.

"Are you plannin' on settin' out the lunch?" Cyril asked her when she came back into the store.

"Soon," she said.

Joseph was still talking to Wally Dorfman, and Wally was telling Joseph something that Katrin couldn't quite make out. Whatever it was, Joseph's face was turning a somber shade of gray. Katrin was sure it was all because she had aimed that gun at Red Deer. She wasn't sorry she had, only that Joseph had been in the store to see it.

25

August, 1853

JOSEPH NO LONGER came into the store to collect the day's receipts. Katrin brought them home and put the money in the cash box and wrote the numbers in Joseph's account book. She paid the cowboys their wages out of the cash box. She put Louie in the buggy and rode to Castroville and paid for hay for the horses out of the cash box. "And how is Joseph?" Henry Castro asked her. "Joseph is well," she told him. But Joseph wasn't well. He wasn't sick with fever and didn't suffer from any recognizable ailment, but he hadn't left the house since Wally Dorfman told him that he had seen Aurelia in Red Deer's camp up on Edwards Plateau, and that she was there with *El Jefe*, the most famous bandit in the hill country. At first Joseph thought it might not have been Aurelia, but then Wally said she had two children with her, a white girl and a black boy, and that the white girl let Wally ride her pony, and Joseph hadn't been the same since. He had just stopped doing anything but sitting in a chair and reading. The dam and raceway on the Medina was completed, but the grist mill was only half built, the wood slat walls up but the sod roof unfinished, waiting for Joseph to tell the workmen what to do next. The Kimmelsburg Inn was missing a second-floor gallery and white wing doves were roosting in the rafters. He had hired the schoolteacher for the Kimmelsburg School, had bought pencils and slates, but wouldn't tell anyone, not even Katrin, when or if school would start.

In May a troupe of actors stopped at the store and said they had heard there was an inn going up in Kimmelsburg. Cyril told them the inn was only half built, but they could use the meadow in back of the store to put on a play if they wanted. They charged a nickel a family and acted out a play by Shakespeare. Katrin brought Louie and paid a nickel, but barely understood a word. Cyril took Daguerreotype pictures of the actors afterwards, and Katrin invited them back to the house and fed them roast pork, mashed potatoes and cucumbers in cream sauce. Joseph said she shouldn't have invited strangers, no telling what they thought about the world, and he went and sat on the porch by himself the whole time they were there.

Then in June, the German-American Singing Society came to town. Whole families picnicked beneath the trees, the grownups listening to the refrains of old country folk songs that echoed along the banks of the Medina on waves of humid air while babies napped and children skipped shiny white river stones across the water. Katrin baked *pannas* with sausage meat and cornmeal and flour, and when Cyril came to get her and the children in the buggy, he said he could smell the *pannas* a mile away. Joseph stayed home.

When July came Joseph still hadn't ordered desks and chairs for the school, and the teacher, Mr. McAvoy, a fast-talking, rotund Irishman Joseph had hired before Wally Dorfman came back, was boarding with the Ruff family and coming into the store every day to ask Katrin when she thought Joseph would have a school for him to teach in.

Katrin didn't know what to tell him. She could have told him that Joseph spent his days sitting on the porch, smoking and reading. She could even have added that she didn't mind, that she liked to walk out into the garden and look back at the house and see him sitting there, that she liked cooking his meals and washing his feet and cutting his hair and feeling his warmth in their bed. If Mr. McAvoy hadn't been a city man, she could even have described Joseph as being like a bear who had gone into his den for the winter and still hadn't come out.

September, 1853

CYRIL WAS BUSY helping a customer pick out material, a flowery blue cotton, showing her the way the pattern ran one way on the front and another on the back, which Katrin never would have done. She would have laid the bolt of cloth out on the yardage table, then cut a nice flowery piece to put in the woman's hand so she could feel its softness and see the color of the dye up close. She would have told her how the blue in the flowers matched her eyes. She would have told her she had never seen a piece of material that suited anyone as well as that piece suited her. Cyril just didn't plan things out, didn't set his mind on what he wanted to accomplish, didn't see how people needed to be told what to buy.

It wasn't Sophia Auerbach's day to shop—she always came with Herman on Saturday—but there she was with three of her children in the store on a Wednesday. She was looking at parasols, picking one up, unfurling it, spinning it around, then picking up another one.

"I've been waiting to see what kind of cakes you brought," Sophia said. "I hope they're not cinnamon. I've been meaning to tell you, Katrin, your cinnamon cakes are a little too heavy. You should use my receipt for cinnamon cake, it never fails, even in the worst oven."

"Chocolate," Katrin said. "Chocolate today."

Sophia made a face. "I cannot abide chocolate."

There, look at that. Cyril hung the piece of flowery blue material over a bucket as if it were nothing but an old rag and left the woman to ponder it by herself while he disappeared into the back of the store where he kept his Daguerreotype machine.

"I heard that Joseph won't leave the house," Sophia said to Katrin.

"A lie."

"I heard it."

"If he will want to leave the house, he will leave the house. When he don't want to leave the house, why should he leave?"

Cyril was back. "This is the best one yet," he said and held up a copper plate that had a grainy image of Louie sitting on the tongue of a wagon. "Looks more like Louie than if you're starin' right at him."

"Very nice," Katrin said.

Sophia glanced at the Daguerreotype, then spun another parasol. "Say what you want, I wouldn't know him from the picture if you didn't tell me that's who it was. I don't know that there's any use to be made for pictures, anyway, when they don't look like the person."

"You got to look at it in the right light," Cyril said. "You look at it straight you might as well be lookin' in a mirror."

"I looked at it the right way," Sophia said. "It still doesn't look like him."

"I like it," Katrin said. Cyril gave her a pleased smile and walked to the back of the store again, the copper plate balanced gingerly on the palms of his hands.

"Making Daguerreotypes when he should be waiting on customers," Sophia said. "I picked out some dress material, a striped gingham. Cyril cut it, but I didn't pay for it, and I turned around and he was waiting on someone else and now he's gone to do something with his picture machine and left her standing there the way he left me, like he always does, he doesn't even seem to be listening when I talk to him he's in such a rush to get back to that machine. I don't see why Joseph puts up with it. Herman says the store would do better if Cyril would pay more attention to it, especially now that Joseph—"

"He sells the pictures. People like his pictures. Two dollars and twenty-five cents they pay for a picture he makes."

"All I said was that the store would do better. Not that Joseph needs the money. Herman says money sticks to Joseph no matter what he does."

Katrin secretly thought that Cyril shouldn't have to help in the store at all. It didn't suit him and a man shouldn't have to do anything that didn't suit him. She was even thinking of putting a sign in the window, DAGUERREOTYPES BY CYRIL MCCORKLE.

Louie was out in front of the store playing tag with the Auerbach children. At home he was content to play with his peg and ball or his whirligig, but let one of the Auerbach children near him and he turned wild. Little Max Auerbach had lowered Louie into the well one day last summer and left him there until dark, and Katrin told Sophia not to come over anymore.

What was Sophia talking about now? Mr. McAvoy. The teacher Joseph hired. Sophia didn't like him. Katrin could see Cyril over Sophia's shoulder. He had made another picture of Katrin that morning. It shamed her that he was always making pictures of her. He had even put them in a book for everyone to look at. Sometimes when she was done sweeping the floor, she would look through the book. It secretly pleased her that the book had more pictures of her than of anyone else, even if they didn't look like her. Her hair was lighter and she never wore dresses with spots on them. Cyril said the sun dipping in the sky made her hair come out dark and that the spots were only specks of dirt on the Daguerreotype's glass tray.

"I hope that school will be ready soon," Sophia said. "I told Herman I don't think there's going to be a school. It's a puzzle the way Joseph is acting. First he hires Mr. McAvoy, and now not one word about when there'll be a school."

There were crumbs on the counter left over from the yam cakes of the day before. Katrin whisked them into her apron and pushed the front door open, then shook them out onto the dirt.

Sophie followed her out. "Mrs. Ruff says the teacher eats more than three men, and that he has particular tastes and won't eat what she puts on the table. She won't take another turn boarding him, she said, and I told her she ought to go talk to Joseph, that he was the one told the man we'd take turns, that he was the one made all the arrangements without asking us if we would or wouldn't. She said she was afraid to talk to Joseph. I can't understand that, the way people tiptoe around him just because he has money, as if he was about to give them some and would change his mind if they riled him. Well, I say what I think, and I say let Joseph pay for the teacher's board, I don't see why we have to feed him when school hasn't even started yet. Joseph has money to waste. We don't. And since I had no say in the teacher's hiring, I don't see that I have to take a turn boarding him. Mrs. Ruff says he's teaching' her four their ABC's, and that's not fair. If there's a teacher in Kimmelsburg, he should be teaching all. Is Joseph paying him his salary? He ought not until he earns it. You can spoil a man as well as a boy by giving them too much too soon. It's all the same, whether they're in your bed or teaching school. Why won't Joseph come out? I told Herman he ought to go speak to him, find out what's the matter. I don't know why you're keeping it a secret from me. Seems you'd want to tell me what's the matter. Just stewing in your own troubles can make a person sick."

She moved closer to Katrin. "You don't say how Joseph is in the bed anymore. Is he the same as he was, pining over that woman? Seems I've never known him when he wasn't. Maybe you haven't heard, but some ranchers in Seguin killed the Mexican she was with, the one they call *El Jefe.* Put him on his horse, tied a rope around his neck, wound the rope around a tree and let the horse go. The man's head came right off, but they tied it on again and he's been riding around the countryside like that ever since."

"Joseph didn't tell me anything like that."

"You ask Javier, he knows all about it. He told Herman he knew *El Jefe* when they were both living in Matamoros. He says *El Jefe's* father was a priest and his mother a nun. I don't believe any of that, but Javier says it's true, and that the Jesuits took him when he was four years old and educated him for the priesthood, but that he got some idea about Texas belonging to Mexicans."

"No one without a head can ride a horse," Katrin said.

"Well, he isn't exactly headless, Katrin. They tied his head back on."

"Then he has a head."

"I'm telling you he's headless, and he looks like the devil himself, with his *serape* flapping, flames coming out of his nose and his eyes burning like the fiery pits of hell. A rancher in Quihi saw it and said it was the most gruesome sight you'd ever want to see. People as far away as Galveston are talking about the headless horseman."

Peggy and Max Auerbach had climbed up into a tree and were tossing pecans at Minnie and Armand Auerbach. Sophia glanced in their direction, stopped talking for a second, then continued folding and unfolding the parasol that she had taken from the pile of parasols in the store.

"A woman is never too smart that she can't take advice from another woman," Sophia said. "I've had experience with men like Joseph." She dug the point of the parasol into the dirt. "I didn't tell you this, Katrin, but I was married before Herman. He was a freighter carrying goods from Mexico. He fell ill of some mysterious ailment and lay in that bed day and night, he wouldn't get up even to supper, and a candle light would hurt his eyes, so we sat in the dark every night. It was a blessing when he died.

"What I have to say to you now is said with kindness and concern, for I know too well what a sick husband means in a household, but sick or well, people don't understand what is endured, how neighbors look to gossip for entertainment. Listen well, Katrin, when I assure you that no matter your virtuousness, people will speak of Cyril and will say that he is more of a husband to you than Joseph is. You have one thing in the hill country and that's your good name. I've heard over and over how odd it is, that if someone sees you, Cyril isn't far behind. It's only talk, and I know you better than anyone, and I always say, why, Katrin is the most virtuous of women, but I can only do so much. You are the one must explain what your life is, because else people will find ways to explain it for you."

Katrin realized right at that moment that Sophia had just made a speech, that she was always making speeches, and that she made speeches because she liked to hear the sound of her own voice.

"Sophia," Katrin said in the kindest tone she could muster. "You don't know everything."

IT WAS EARLY morning when Katrin walked around the creek to Nathan and Dilly's cabin. She had only been inside once since Nathan was hanged and Dilly and the two boys were taken away. She had thought there might be something she could use, but she already had a bed and a kitchen table and all the quilts she needed. So she had piled the bedding in a corner and swept the floor and threw out the food that was still sitting on the table. Clabbered milk, she remembered, that had turned green. Sophia Auerbach came and took some of the furniture. There had been drifts of dried leaves hugging the log walls. Old harnesses moldered beside rotting barrels and lengths of rope. An oxcart with one wooden wheel missing held bags of moldy seed. She had sat in the oxcart until it grew dark, listening to the tree frogs and katydids and peering at the moon through the cracks in the shed wall. She hadn't been in the shed since.

The latch to the cabin door still worked. It was made of scraps of wood, and the leather slid easily when she gave it a tug. There was the dent in the puncheon floor where Nathan would put on his wooden leg and stamp on the floor to see if the strap was tight enough. The dish cabinet that Nathan made out of the warty branches of a hackberry tree was still here. And the kitchen table, now that she looked more closely at it, was the same one that had held the remains of that long-ago breakfast. She got busy cleaning cobwebs away and sweeping and washing the floor. When she was through she sat at the table and looked around her. Sap had boiled up along the edges of the door hinge, little amber dots that ran lengthwise with the grain of the wood. She counted them, first going up, then down. Seven dots. The wood hadn't cured before it was sawn and planed and made into a door.

Cleaning the old place gave her a chance to think—about Kimmelsburg and the hill country and about how big it was, how people didn't have to know your business if you didn't want them to, and that even if they found out something they might want to gossip about, what did it matter if they did?

She stood up and opened the dish cabinet and looked inside. Spiders had made a nest in some old tin cups. She squashed the spiders with the left hem of her apron, then wiped the cups out with the right hem and put the cups in a neat row on the first shelf.

Everything was clean now. She closed the cabin door and headed back around the creek, swinging her arms as she walked past the pigpen. She had let the pigs out during the summer to forage for themselves, and their pink skin was ripply with fat. There had been a Norther the year before that had ripped all the leaves from the peach trees, but they had come back even stronger in the spring and had fruited so heavily in the summer that the ground was covered with ripe and rotting peaches. She had dried what she hadn't turned into peach pies and tarts and jams and fed the rotten leavings to the pigs.

The pecan trees hadn't been bothered by the dry summer. The nuts were falling early, covering the ground behind the pig enclosure. She would come back later and fill a bucket with pecans. She would make so many pecan pies, Cyril would marvel at the number.

And the mesquite trees, which were nearly leafless now, during the summer had covered the roof of the house with yellow blossoms. Blossoms had fallen down the chimney and when she lit the fire in the hearth and set her stew pot to cook, the scent of mesquite blossoms mixed with the aroma of simmering pork.

As she walked along she wondered whether the grass turning every shade of green on the prairie and the clouds girdling the mountains in a rainbow of color meant the rains would come and the drought would be over. Louie went barefoot in the spring when the grass was green and tender, but not when the summer sun crisped the weeds into barbs and the squirrels tossed green nuts down from the branches of the pecan trees.

The corral was to the north and beyond that the sheep pastures and beyond that the row of sturdy log squares where the cowboys lived. Smoke curled from stout chimneys when it was dark and candles flickered behind rawhide windows, and she couldn't explain how happy she felt. She would plump the dried peaches and bake so many pies there wouldn't be room in the store for all the pies she would bake. She had gone into Nathan and Dilly's cabin expecting to find it cursed, and all she found was dirt and leaves and spiders. There were no ghosts. From now on nothing could frighten her. Not Indians or headless horsemen or anything else.

26

Kimmelsburg
September, 1853

IT WAS BEFORE the sun was full up that Cyril thought he saw men riding alongside the creek. He wouldn't have seen anything at all and wouldn't have had to wonder about it if he hadn't had the urge to pee. He got out of bed, opened the back door of the store, stretched, peed, studied the trees, scratched in a few places, thought he saw the shape of a man on a horse, squinted to get the sleep out of his eyes so he could see better, and by that time whatever or whoever it was had disappeared.

It was only a few steps from where Cyril slept to the small storeroom, past the post that held up the roof, then into the store proper. He stepped over the sacks of coffee, pushed aside the crate of apples, and shoved the tierce of lard and two hogsheads of sugar out of the way so he could get to the stove. *It would suit me if you stop buying goods before we sell what we got,* he told Joseph, who seemed to have recovered from whatever it was that ailed him and was coming into the store pretty regularly now and messing up whatever neatness Katrin made with all the goods he kept buying. Quirts and stirrups and spurs and rope hung from hooks near the ceiling. Saddles and bridles and harnesses and horse collars and riding chaps and saddle blankets and gun holsters and saddlebags, gloves and belts were piled haphazardly on the raw wood floor. On shelves behind the counter stacks of plated ware were squeezed between women's shoes and parasols. *One of these days you'll come in here and I'll be buried to my neck in sacks and crates,* he'd say. And Joseph would just shrug and buy some more.

It was morning, after all, and the trees alongside the creek behind the store sometimes took the shape of animals when the wind was blowing the right way. There wasn't an awful lot of business in the morning, and Cyril had a lot of time to stare at trees and mountains and clouds and could always make something out of nothing if he stared at it long enough. Spider webs caught with morning dew could be a crouching Indian. At night a bush scraping over a pile of rocks could be wild turkeys scrabbling along the smooth branches of a cottonwood tree. And during a rainstorm the sound of rain-whipped trees could easily be mistaken for a herd of stampeding horses.

Anyway, strangers were rare in Kimmelsburg. A dirt road now cut through the mesquite trees and joined up with the road to Fredericksburg. Once in a while a freighter would miss the turn-off and stop at Kimmel's Store for some whiskey or tobacco, and occasionally itinerant peddlers walked into the bank (which was only open for a few hours on Tuesdays and Saturdays) thinking it was an inn and walked out again. Cyril knew just about everyone else. On Saturdays neighboring ranchers came to town to buy provisions. Their wives would buy coffee and salt and sugar and look at the ladies' fashion books and gossip about the neighbors while they picked out dress material and buttons and tried on shoes. Their husbands would buy powder and lead and hammers and nails and lengths of rope and talk about the weather. They'd argue among themselves as to whether it was going to rain or not, and then one of them would ask Cyril what he thought (as if he could read the heavens), and he'd tell them it was going to rain or the wind was going to blow or it was going to be hot, or anything that happened to come into his head.

It might have been Indians. Half the Comanche bands from the hill country all the way up to the Edwards Plateau had died in the 1849 cholera epidemic, and there had been an even worse epidemic of smallpox in 1850, and although there were still plenty of Comanches around raiding outlying ranches, stealing cattle and horses and burning down houses, they weren't that fierce when they came into town, strolling down the street in their paint and feathers. When an Indian came into Kimmel's Store, Cyril would let him roam through the store, feeling the goods on the shelves and sniffing the spices, but he always had his pistol ready beneath the counter. Sometimes they had a few buffalo hides to trade, and would point to what they wanted in exchange. Joseph said to let them have whatever it was they asked for, even if the hides were threadbare, and to give them a bag of sugar when they left. If those were Indians Cyril had seen, they would be riding right out in the open, unless they were of a mind to get shot. It was probably a few mustangs that had pushed their way through the corral fence on the Big K and were taking their time heading for the prairie.

Still, it just might have been Indians.

Cyril looked out the front window. The road was empty. No wagons, no horses, no sign of anything but a few rabbits, noses twitching in the breeze.

It looked like rain, dark clouds settling on the distant mountains, a quicksilver patch of sky changing colors overhead. There'd be few, if any, customers today. The road turned to mud when it rained. Last year a wagon toppled into the creek during a storm. Joseph happened to be riding by and rescued the woman and three children inside before they floated away. It was Saturday and the road was dry so far, but ranchers praying for rain so there'd be hay for the cattle weren't likely to come to town for provisions. That suited Cyril. He liked not having to haul sacks or measure out coffee or talk about the weather.

Well, he'd fry some bacon and eat it with a few slices of Katrin's cinnamon apple cake and drink a pot of coffee, and that would get him almost to lunch time. In the afternoon he'd take a nap, then maybe sweep up a little, then take some pictures of the hackberry trees down by the creek (tree leaves and branches were a lot easier to make pictures of than people), and by then it would be time to ride over to the Big K for supper.

It was probably just trees blowing against Mr. Groff's windows across the street. (What else could it be when there was only one street in town for horses to ride down and Cyril was sure there weren't any riding down it?)

Mr. Groff was the dentist Joseph found in Austin pulling teeth in the back of a wagon and stitching saddles when there were no teeth to pull. He was a big man with a rough way of talking. He not only had small feet, but he had small hands that he told Cyril were good for getting into tight spaces in people's mouths. The day he came into town Cyril was the first one at the door wanting to have an aching tooth pulled. Mr. Groff's dental instruments were still in a small leather carrying case, but he had unpacked the rest of his possessions. A sheet of greased leather, its surface a dimply gray, hung from a roof beam. Bullwhips and quirts, riding chaps and bridles and harnesses, as well as horse collars, belts, holsters and saddlebags lay in neat rows on the floor. While Mr. Groff opened his leather case and took out a green-glass bottle, uncorked it and poured some sour-smelling liquid onto a rag which he pressed to Cyril's nose, Joseph came in and offered Mr. Groff thirty dollars for a hand-tooled saddle Cyril hadn't even noticed. Once the tooth was pulled and Cyril was back in the store, he told Joseph he would have made Mr. Groff an offer for the saddle (a really special one with butterflies and gold bugs worked in it) if his tooth hadn't been hurting so much (which wasn't the whole truth; Cyril had also been thinking about the Daguerreotype he had taken of Katrin that morning).

He lit the stove, poured some water into the pot of day-old coffee and set the pot to boil, then took the slab of bacon that was curing in the open fireplace, hacked a thick hunk out of it and slapped it in the iron skillet. Katrin had baked the cinnamon apple cake for him last night and it sat on the counter now. Cyril had watched her make it while Joseph was in the parlor reading a book, and he couldn't imagine why Joseph would want to be anywhere else but watching Katrin beating cake batter, her round arms encircling the mixing bowl, her skin glowing in the candlelight. The cake looked nothing like it did when Katrin handed it to him. He had nibbled on it before he went to bed and there were big handfuls gouged out of the side and chunks missing from the middle.

Bacon had to be God's gift to man. The smell of it, the taste—crisp, fatty, slightly salty. He bent over the skillet, took in the aroma, then grabbed the sizzling slab with his knife, let it cool for a few seconds and ate it in two bites. He didn't drink when Joseph was anywhere around. But the sky did look like rain, and the store was more than a little cold. A sip of whiskey would do to keep his joints from aching. He took a bottle of whiskey off the shelf and poured some into a glass, then sat down on the pile of rugs next to the stove and thought about Katrin and the smell of cake baking and the way her face flushed as she worked.

On Sundays when the store was closed and Joseph was over in the old cabin counting his collection (or dusting it or rearranging it or just staring at it), Cyril would cut firewood for Katrin or beat rugs or pull weeds out of her vegetable garden. Last Sunday he painted the steps to the front porch (Katrin washed the steps with lye, and paint didn't last but a couple of months before it had to be done over).

He stood up. He was sure now there were men outside. There was no mistaking the noise horses with nailed-on iron shoes made.

JOSEPH RODE AHEAD, Javier and Cyril following, and behind them the twelve vaqueros Javier had awakened from sleep. They didn't go through town. Joseph said surprise was essential and going through town would be the worst thing to do, so they cut across the creek, then through the large stand of pecan trees and traveled parallel to the dirt road so that when the time was right they could just come out from between the trees without being seen.

Cyril had ridden out to the ranch house right as the sun was coming up. He had seen, he said, five men, maybe six, up on the dentist's porch about to hang three men. "Rangers?" Joseph asked him. "Couldn't tell," Cyril replied. "Were they blacks they were hanging?" Joseph asked him. "Mexicans," Cyril replied.

"Sally won't go," Cyril hollered now, struggling to keep his old mare trotting.

"Go on back, then," Joseph said.

Joseph had thought they would be lynching blacks, but he wasn't surprised that it was Mexicans. Rangers had lynched Mexicans who rounded up wild horses, and sometimes lynched Mexicans because they didn't like them and didn't want them in Texas. A family of Mexicans had been slaughtered up near the San Saba the week before and Joseph had heard that fearful Mexicans were living in burrows they dug out of the prairie. Lately it had been all Javier could do to keep the *vaqueros* from heading down to the military garrison at Piedras Negras and fighting the Mexican war all over again.

Or it could have been that bandit *El Jefe*. An Army officer had stopped at the Big K in August to buy horses and told Joseph he wasn't sure *El Jefe* was dead at all, that it might be someone else riding around without a head.

"You know what I think?" he said. "I think *El Jefe* went to Mexico with all the money he made selling stolen horses to the Army."

"Do you know what happened to the woman who was with him?" Joseph asked him.

"I heard she went to Galveston," he replied.

Anyway, *El Jefe* wouldn't be hanging Mexicans, he'd be hanging Americans.

Joseph couldn't think who else it might have been, because he didn't want to get himself all stirred up thinking it might be Captain Dawson. Joseph had tracked him all over the hill country for three years. Every sighting, every rumor, every story, no matter how fanciful, had him tearing over the plains with Javier and the *vaqueros*. The last time was the lynching of a Mexican and a black near the Llano

River, and they had almost caught him then, but the place Dawson had chosen to hang the two men was out in the open and he had seen Joseph and his men coming from a ways off. The bodies of the hanged men were still warm when Joseph reached them.

It had begun to rain now, and the ground, parched for the past six months, was soaked through, the prairie grass flattened and slicked down, the noise of the horses buried in whipping branches and slapping rain. It would be too foolhardy of the man to come back here. It was probably just another band of renegades, one of the many roaming Texas since the war ended.

Javier rode up beside Joseph. "The men are sayin' they want to run at the 'rinches'."

"No one runs at anyone till I tell them."

The roof of the dentist's building was peeking through the trees now. Then Joseph saw the ropes hanging like twists of horse hair from the carved railing of the second floor gallery. It all came into focus slowly, like one of Cyril's Daguerreotypes, blurry around the edges, and then a little sharper, and finally as clear as could be—six men standing partway on the road and partway on the wood planks in front of the store, and three Mexicans lined up on the first floor porch in front of the sign that said MR. GROFF, DENTIST AND SADDLER.

The sun was dipping in and out, sometimes bright, but mostly as dim as lamp light. Joseph and his men were approaching the road, and he could see the Mexicans on the porch plainly now. The first one in line already had a rope around his neck. The second one collapsed while Joseph was looking at him, just suddenly fell over as if someone had given a rotted fence post a shove, and sat down on the steps, legs sprawled out in front of him. The third man, although still standing, looked about to die of fright.

"I can't hold 'em back," Javier said, and the *vaqueros* galloped ahead, horses' hooves splashing through the mud holes, hollering *"muerte a los rinches"* and waving the pistols Joseph had given them to protect themselves against Comanches when they were rounding up strays. Some had already reached the porch and were freeing the three Mexicans. Others were chasing after the ragtag bunch of men who had left their horses behind and were fleeing on foot, *vaqueros* shooting the ones they could and looping *riatas* around the necks of the ones who were a little faster and had gotten a little farther, and then galloping down the street with their trophies dragging in the mud.

One of the men had made it to his horse, and even before he turned around Joseph recognized the slope of his shoulders and the way he wore his hat, the brim drawn up in front and touching his neckerchief in back. And yet when Dawson turned around Joseph felt a sensation akin to astonishment that it was really him. He had always, in his mind, given Dawson the benefit of a certain amount of cunning, thought he knew Joseph was tracking him, thought him at least smart enough to stay away from a place as poisonous to him as Kimmelsburg, where a five-hundred-dollar reward for his capture was posted on the front door of Kimmel's Store.

Dawson was in the saddle now, whipping his horse and spurring its flanks and heading for Joseph's east pasture. Joseph headed right after him.

Dawson veered off to the west, riding blindly, probably not remembering he had been here before or that the two trees where he had hanged Luck and Nathan were still standing not far from the turnip fields where Joseph's sheep foraged. He must have forgotten the shape of the land, couldn't figure out where he was or how far he had ridden. There hadn't been a shepherd's cabin when Dawson hanged Luck and Nathan, or a corral where the *vaqueros* tied calves to snubbing posts and branded fancy K's onto their left hips. Joseph's two-story house with its lookout tower hadn't yet been built, nor was the row of cabins the *vaqueros* lived in situated on the ridge in the middle of the thousands of acres where Joseph's cattle grazed. Captain Dawson probably never did know where the shale was that could trip a horse or where the waterfalls were that suddenly turned up and changed the land to river. Joseph knew all of it, every inch of it, could draw the location of every rut, every hole, every tree stump, every outcropping of rock.

Dawson kept looking back at Joseph, turning in the saddle, hoping, Joseph supposed, that Joseph would get tired and fall back, but Joseph hadn't spent the night rounding up Mexicans to hang. Joseph was wide awake and fresh.

Dawson was past the shepherd's cabin now. Joseph slowed his horse slightly, letting the distance between them widen. He had only to keep back a ways, let Dawson think he had the lead. Then Joseph would push him to where he wanted him to go. Dawson had been busy lynching people for so long he had forgotten (if he ever knew) the basic tactics any rancher would use when herding cattle—angle to the north and the cattles' inborn instinct to run from predators pulls them to the south. Dawson was doing just as Joseph had planned, but to help him along, to keep him going in the right direction, Joseph raised his rifle and aimed at a spot left of the captain's ear, then pulled the trigger and watched Dawson yank his horse sharply to the right and head toward the cliff.

Dawson turned around again, rain beating at his face beneath the turned-up brim of his hat, and stared at Joseph, and it seemed to Joseph that it was the longest, most mournful stare he had ever seen. At that moment Joseph could have shouted to him to watch out—and for a split second he thought about it. But only for a second. And then the rain stopped and Captain Dawson and his horse left the ground. They flew for a few miraculous moments in the clearest sky Joseph had ever seen before they fell into the canyon below.

LOVE

October, 1854

KATRIN SAT IN THE KITCHEN all day mending clothes while Louie marched his tin soldiers up and down the kitchen floor. In late afternoon Louie went outside and brought in a few sticks of firewood and Katrin started a fire in the stove.

Cyril ate his supper and went back to the store. Katrin watched Joseph pick at his food, neither of them talking. When he had finished he went into the parlor to read. What was it he held on his lap and pretended to read so carefully? Lists of cattle prices? Names of ranchers ready to sell him their land and move on? His head moved now. Was that a sigh?

She heated water for his bath, poured it into the tin tub and then warmed the bed with a pan of hot coals.

"You take your bath and go to bed," she said. "I clean the kitchen."

He lay in the warm water listening to the sounds Katrin made in the kitchen. Homely sounds. The scrape of chairs, the creaking of hinges as she opened the kitchen door and scooped water from the bucket into the dishpan, the squeak of hinges as the door closed again. She was scrubbing pots now, the whisk of the loofah sponge harsh and grating, the splash of water needle sharp against the sides of the pan. She opened the kitchen door again, emptied the dishpan, closed the door.

He had enough of soaking, enough of bathing. He stood up and swiped at his skin with the towel she had laid out on the chair beside the tub, then went into the bedroom and got into bed.

She was in the bedroom now, adjusting curtains, straightening the Daguerreotypes into neat rows on the dresser. The bed dipped on her side as she settled in.

"Is too cold," she said.

She got up again and closed the window, then came back and slid into bed.

"Is still too cold," she said.

She was up yet again, pulling another quilt out of the chest at the foot of the bed. She spread it over him and sat down on the edge of the bed.

"Sofia says things about Cyril and me," she said. "It's not true."

"I know it isn't," he replied.

JOSEPH OPENED THE FRONT door and walked out onto the porch. Ice had formed on the eaves of the house and he saw his breath in the night air. Katrin was in the kitchen asking Louie if he wanted more butter on his biscuit. Cyril was already eating.

"Them beef dumplin's is the best," he heard Cyril say. "I ate dumplin's in Mississippi once't were almost as good, but you ask me which ones I'd choose in a contest I'd say yours wins hands down. It's like choosin' between a stallion and a plow horse. When they say beef dumplin's is all alike, I kin tell 'em it ain't so."

Cyril never waited for anyone else to sit down, but would fill a plate and stand by the window and eat, and when his plate was clean Katrin would fill it up again. Louie's voice now, as hushed and whispery as the breeze in the rushes that grew in the still pools along the Medina. Then Katrin's again.

"Joseph."

She called to him in the same voice she used to call Louie in from play.

"Joseph. Supper."

Her industriousness amazed him. She baked bread every day. She made preserves of everything—watermelons and cucumbers and tomatoes and beets. The pie safe was full of pies and cookies and bread and cake. There was always the smell of yeast in the house. She was outside now, a shawl around her shoulders. "The supper will be cold. Come inside."

He hadn't asked her to, but she had fit the house around him. His boots, heel to heel and toe to toe, were next to the fireplace. The book he had been reading was on a small table beside his chair, his heavy coat on a peg on the wall, his socks in a darning basket on the floor next to the sofa. There was no little spot, no corner where Joseph's shadow didn't hover.

"I've just been admiring how the Medina looks with the moon on it," he said.

The store made more money now that she ran it. She treated it the way she treated him, the way she treated Louie and Cyril, dutifully and with great interest in the smallest of things. She counted money in the same careful way she measured flour out for her cakes. She could add and subtract and had learned to write her numbers and had filled account books with records of sales and purchases. She dealt with freighters firmly and didn't waver from the price she was willing to pay. He knew he ought to love her, and in a way he did.

"The moon and the river will be here long after we're gone," he said.

She no longer asked him whether he was going to leave her. She never asked him whether he thought about Aurelia. She had settled into life better than he had. She accepted everything. He relied on that. He relied on her.

He talked to her now. Not in the way he talked to Cyril or Javier, but the way men and women who care about one another talk—about serious things, important things, things that matter. She no longer asked him whether he was going to leave her or whether he was sorry he had married her or whether he still thought about Aurelia. She had settled into life better than he had. She accepted everything on its face. He relied on that. He relied on her. He wasn't sorry he married her. She knew him so well that he didn't even have to tell her that.

"I don't know how long after we're gone anything we've built or bought or planted will be here," he said.

"You can't think on that, Joseph," she said. "You have to think on what we do today and whether we do it right. That's all we can do."

THE FAMILY BALESTERO

DON RAMÓN BALESTERO, his wife, Doña Elena, and their two children arrived in San Antonio in 1855 in a shiny black carriage outfitted with carriage lamps imported from France. They appeared to know no one in the city and spent the first three months in the most expensive suite in the newly constructed Plaza House Hotel, after which they moved into a three-story house on King William Street, which all agreed who saw it (no one was actually invited inside) could not have been duplicated for less than twenty-five thousand dollars.

It was not clear what profession Don Ramón had followed previous to his arrival in San Antonio, but by 1857 he was the owner of a flour mill and a lumber yard and was said to have a major interest in the Bank of New Braunfels on Commerce Street. He was a handsome man with impeccable manners. A deep scar on his right cheek was rumored to have been the result of a duel he had fought with the viceroy of Spain, an argument over a duchy promised to Don Ramón by the Spanish King and usurped by the viceroy.

Doña Elena had black hair that she wore in ringlets around her face. She was never heard to speak, but her gentle manner gave all who witnessed it definite proof of her patrician upbringing, probably as the daughter of a Spanish grandee or possibly even an Indian maharajah.

The two children were most certainly adopted, since the girl, fair and blue-eyed, and the boy, as dark-skinned as a Maya chieftain, resembled neither of their parents. Each morning a servant would deliver the girl to her classes at the Ursuline Academy for Girls and the boy to his at St. Mary's Institute for Boys.

At mid-morning Don Ramón would ride his horse (a chestnut Arabian) to his office in the New Braunfels Bank and Doña Elena would drive her phaeton to a rundown section of the city called Laredito where she delivered food and medicines to needy families. The medicines were in small clay jars like the ones the herb sellers used in the marketplace on Main Plaza. In some circles it was whispered that Doña Elena had supernatural powers and could cure the sick merely by looking at them, whispers which were immediately discounted, since she appeared to be normal in every respect.

By the fifth year of the Balestero family's residency they had blended into the rhythms of the city. Their comings and goings were no longer remarked on, their ancestry no longer of interest, their past no longer a subject for conjecture.